the
BOUNDLESS
Sublime

LILI WILKINSON

Switch Press
a capstone imprint

The Boundless Sublime is published by Switch Press,
a Capstone imprint
1710 Roe Crest Drive
North Mankato, MN 56003
www.mycapstone.com

Library of Congress Cataloging-in-Publication Data
is available on the Library of Congress website.

ISBN: 978-1-63079-100-1 (jacketed hardcover)

Summary: Ruby Jane Galbraith has nothing left. After an
accident tears her family apart, she finds her entire world
obliterated. And it's all her fault. The only thing that makes
sense to her is Fox — a gentle new friend who is wise, soulful,
and clever, yet oddly naive about the ways of the world. Fox
understands her loss. Her pain. And he offers her a way out —
a chance to find peace in a community that seems guided by
love. He asks her to join him at the Institute of the Boundless
Sublime. Ruby knows one thing for sure: her life without Fox
is a life she doesn't want to live, and the Institute is the only
way to keep him. But as she's drawn into the Institute's web,
Ruby begins to learn its sinister secrets.

Designed by Kay Fraser

Image Credits
Shutterstock: ivgroznii, (waves) design element, Picsfive,
(black paint) design element, smileimage9, (water) design
element

Printed in China.
010731S18

For my grandfather Jim, who climbed the bridge.
And for my father, John, who chose his own path.

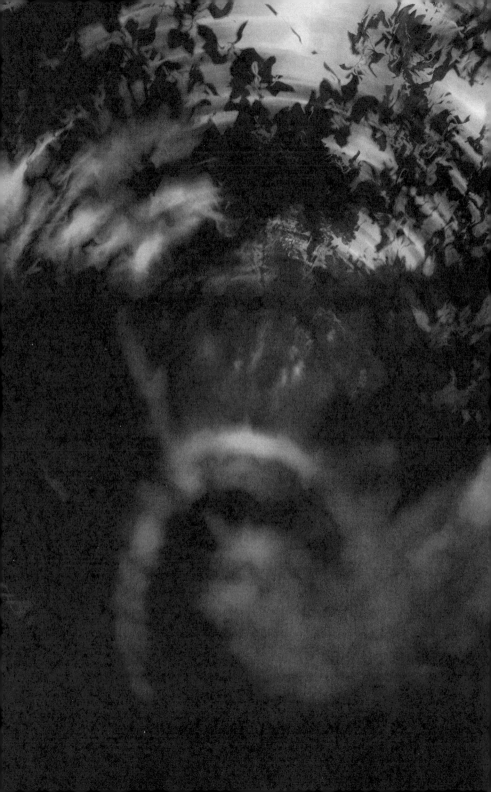

1

My name is Ruby Jane Galbraith, and I'm no messiah.

For a long time, there was grief. It pulled me down into suffocating darkness and kept me anchored there. I went through the motions. I showed up at school. I ate food and watched TV and took algebra tests. But I didn't feel anything. It was easier that way.

Mom wasn't as good at hiding it as me. She stopped going to work and answering the phone, pulling the curtains of her sorrow tightly around herself. She sat all day in the living room, staring at the TV and smoking cigarette after cigarette. Sometimes I'd come home from school and find her vacant-eyed, with a perfect cylinder of ash protruding from pale lips. I'd speak to her, tell her about my day and the outside world, and it would take minutes for the cylinder to tremble and collapse, spilling ash down the front of her nightgown.

We ate frozen meals straight out of the plastic containers. I ordered them online with Mom's credit card, and we pretended not to be home when the delivery man came. Mom ate hers robotically, even when her teriyaki chicken was so hot from the microwave that it was burning her throat. Once I suggested we order pizza or Indian for a change, but Mom shrank visibly before me, folding in on herself. The idea of having to answer the door and interact with a stranger was too much. I didn't suggest it again.

My piano accumulated a thick layer of dust. I didn't even open the lid. Even seeing it there, crouching close-mouthed in the corner of the living room, felt too loud. Music brought feelings, and our house was a feeling-free zone.

I went out a lot, sneaking into nightclubs and losing myself in the thumping repetitiveness of dance, staying long after my friends had left. I arrived home in the small hours of the morning, sweaty and exhausted, to find Mom still slumped on the couch with the home-shopping channel shouting at her. She wouldn't look at me as I staggered to my room and fell onto the bed, still fully clothed. It was the only way I could sleep, with my ears ringing from the club and my mind so numb that nothing could intrude. The blissful darkness would hold me for a few hours, and then I'd wake up and go to school, leaving Mom behind on the couch.

Thanksgiving passed without comment, then Christmas, then my birthday. I couldn't imagine celebrating anything ever again.

We didn't talk about it. Ever.

★ ★ ★

I saw the school counselor a few times. Helena wore voluminous floral caftans and tinkling earrings. She advised me to keep a dream journal and start an herb garden. I did neither. When she asked me how I was feeling, I lied and told her I felt OK. The truth is, I didn't feel anything. She always seemed to believe me, though. She told me I was making amazing progress. She told me I was brave. She told me her door was always open.

"How is your music going, dear?" she asked in our first session after winter break.

"My what?"

"Your music. Mr. Andrews tells me you are a very talented composer and pianist."

When I was little, the word pianist used to make me snigger. I watched the bright wooden parrots swinging from Helena's earlobes.

"Um," I said. "OK."

"You know, music can be healing. A very therapeutic way to express and process grief."

I made obedient understanding noises. I didn't want to express or process my grief. I wanted to be left alone in the deep darkness. Nothing could hurt me down there, because I couldn't feel.

"You should write a song," said Helena, "and dedicate it to Anton."

I felt ripples in the darkness and let it draw me in deeper. There would be no songs. Not now. Not ever. Nothing to fill the void.

"Promise me you'll try?" Helena leaned forward.

"Sure," I lied. "I'll try."

"I have something for you," she said, her eyes bright. "A birthday present." She fished around in her purse and pulled out a little silk bag. I took it, spilling out its contents into my palm. A string of beads, like bubbled orange glass. I blinked. Helena had bought me jewelry?

"They're amber," she said. "They have healing properties."

Was she serious?

"I know it sounds crazy," she said, with a self-deprecating eye roll. "But it's actually scientifically proven. The heat of your skin causes a chemical reaction that releases a certain kind of oil from the crystal."

"Resin," I said.

"I'm sorry?"

"Amber is a resin," I told her. "Not a crystal."

Helena shrugged this off. Scientifically proven, indeed. "Anyway, the oil is absorbed by the skin. Mothers use these beads for teething babies. They can cure eczema and asthma, as well as provide an overall feeling of peace and well-being. I thought you could use some of that."

What a load of bullshit. If amber did secrete some magic oil so powerful that merely holding it against your skin was enough to produce an analgesic effect and cure miscellaneous ailments, then people wouldn't be putting it on tiny babies. Especially not patchouli-scented people like Helena, who probably didn't believe in vaccination or pasteurized milk.

That was what I should have said to her. It's what the old Ruby would have done. I should have told her that there was no way a string of old sap was going to mend my broken heart or pull me up out of the darkness.

But I didn't say it. I thanked her politely.

I didn't want to be healed. I didn't want to come up out of the darkness.

Minah was waiting for me outside Helena's office. She didn't ask me how I was. That was the good thing about my friends. They didn't ever try to get me to talk about my feelings. They understood me. Minah's hands were smeared with red, black, and gold, her black jeans, torn and splattered with flecks of oil paint, hardened to a shiny crust.

"Been in the studio?" I asked.

She nodded. "Still not sure what to do for my final project," she said. "We're supposed to be designing items of furniture, but that sounds so utilitarian. I want to make a monster. I'm really into monsters right now. The grotesque, you know?"

"You could make a couch that eats people," I suggested.

Minah's dark lips curled into an ironic smile. "I'm totally obsessed with this Goya painting of Saturn eating one of his sons. Goya painted it on the wall of his house, over some insipid inspirational thing he'd done earlier. He was all dark and depressed because he was sick and had gone deaf and there was political shit going on in Spain. Saturn is looming up out of the darkness with this wild hair and gaping mouth. He's already eaten the baby's head and one arm, and is taking a bite out of the other arm. Everything is dark and muted except Saturn's bulging white eyes and the bright red blood on the baby. It's awesome."

I nodded and tried not to picture it in my head. "Sounds great," I said, but I couldn't quite keep the wobble out of my voice.

Minah looked away, suddenly uncomfortable. "I need coffee."

When we were younger, we'd mostly hung out at my house. Minah's parents were strict Malaysian Catholic and didn't approve of any of her schemes or projects. When she'd pierced her nose (on her own, with a safety pin), they'd gone ballistic. My parents were a bit more laid-back. But Minah didn't come to my house anymore. I hadn't said anything. Hadn't told her about things at home. But she knew most of it and was a good enough friend to not bring it up. She also knew better than to ask me to visit the abandoned parking lot outside a boarded-up Irish pub, where we used to huddle on milk crates with Ali and Harrison and Flick, blowing out clouds of breath-steam and cigarette smoke in the chilled air. I only saw the others at school now and had the occasional cup of coffee with Minah.

We walked side-by-side down the empty hallway. As we passed a garbage can, I held out my arm and let the amber beads slip through my fingers to mingle with half-eaten sandwiches and banana peels.

★ ★ ★

Auntie Cath flew from Florida to visit us. Her bronzed skin and bright clothes looked out of place in our house, where everything was cold and pale and ashen. She took one look at Mom slumped on the couch in her nightgown and called Uncle Marco to tell him that she would be staying for quite a while and to ask him to send some more clothes.

She bustled Mom into the shower, chattering away as if nothing was wrong. She was relentlessly cheerful and bossy, making Mom wash her hair and put on actual clothes instead of the ash-dusted nightgown, which Auntie Cath insisted on throwing in the trash. Then she sat Mom back down on the couch and herded me into the kitchen.

"Why didn't you call?" she said, her voice low so Mom wouldn't hear. "If I'd known she was like this, I would have come earlier."

Because we're doing fine. Because we don't want you here. Because we like it this way.

"I'm sorry," I said. "I didn't want to worry you."

Auntie Cath's lips pursed in concern, and she put her arms around me — a fluttering, faint hug, like being embraced by a butterfly. "You poor thing," she said. "I know it's been difficult. Well, don't worry. I'm here now. I'll fix everything."

I wanted to believe her. I wanted to hug her back. To bury my face in her shoulder and cry. To let her take care of us.

But I couldn't.

Auntie Cath set to work. She cleaned and scrubbed and disinfected. She went to the supermarket and filled our pantry with Milano cookies and smoked almonds. She made pumpkin soup and brewed pots of tea. She opened the curtains, filling our house with weak winter sun, and bought flowers to freshen the stale air. She threw away Mom's cigarettes.

Mom did as Auntie Cath told her, obedient and passive. But even though she washed her hair and put on moisturizer and a bra, I could tell she was still the same inside. You could change the outside of a person with body lotion and flowers and hair conditioner, but there was nothing you could do to change the inside, especially when the inside of a person was blank, dark, and hollow.

I felt sorry for Auntie Cath. She was trying so hard. I could see the effort it took to be that cheerful all the time. I knew she was hoping some of it would rub off on us. But we'd forgotten how to be cheerful. I knew how it would go. Eventually Auntie Cath would give up. She'd go back to Florida, and Mom would go back to her chair and her cigarettes. The flowers would die. The food in the fridge would rot. And Mom and I would crumble into ash again.

★ ★ ★

"I've got a special treat tonight," Auntie Cath said after dinner one night, tapping one of her gold rings against her wine glass.

She got up and went to the fridge, returning with something pale green, topped with clouds of whipped cream.

I felt the steak I'd just eaten turn hard and cold in the pit of my stomach.

Auntie Cath placed the pie in the center of the table and disappeared into the kitchen to get plates and forks.

"I know it's your favorite, Ruby," she said with a wink as she sat down at the table and sunk a knife into the key lime pie, fracturing the Graham cracker crust.

I felt Mom stiffen next to me as Auntie Cath served her a giant slice.

It wasn't my favorite.

Mom's face had turned the color of bone. She stared down at her plate and fork. Auntie Cath looked from her face to mine and then sagged in understanding.

I didn't need to try it. I could already taste the sweet creaminess and the tang of lime mingling on my tongue. I wanted to throw up.

"Well," said Auntie Cath brightly. "Maybe it's a good thing. We should be celebrating Anton. Enjoying the things he enjoyed, in honor of him." She scooped up a forkful and pushed it into her mouth, closing her eyes in pleasure.

My jaw clenched. I ground my teeth so hard that I imagined them shattering into fragments. The shards would slice open my gums, filling my mouth with the taste of blood instead of oversweet lime. I'd spit them onto the plate, red flecked with sharp white.

"What if we all told a story about Anton?" Auntie Cath suggested. "A happy memory?"

Mom started to rock gently back and forth, her face completely blank.

I pushed my chair back and headed to my room. The walls felt close, pushing in, suffocating me. I texted Minah, but she didn't respond. Probably busy working on her latest art project. I considered texting someone else, anyone, then decided it probably didn't matter. It was better to be alone. I pulled on a jacket and black boots and headed for the front door.

Mom and Auntie Cath were still sitting at the table. Cath was talking to Mom in a low, soothing voice. Mom's face showed no expression.

"Ruby, it's almost eight," called Cath. "Where are you going?"

"Out."

★ ★ ★

The club was exactly how I wanted it to be: loud and anonymous. It was sleazy enough that I could slip in without showing any ID but not so sleazy that I couldn't deter any groping hands with a swift elbow and a dark glare.

I welcomed the dark, frenetic anonymity of the dance floor. Nobody stared at me with sympathetic frowns wrinkling their brows. Nobody offered understanding hugs. Nobody shifted their weight uncomfortably as they tried to figure out what to say. On the dance floor, I wasn't Ruby Jane Galbraith. I was just a body jumping and writhing with all the other bodies. I wasn't anybody at all.

A guy tapped me on the shoulder. "Hey," he said, yelling into my ear to be heard over the music. "Can I buy you a drink?"

I glowered at him, and he backed off. I wasn't there to make new friends. I was there to forget.

I stayed until my clothes were soaked with sweat and I was so exhausted I could barely stand. Then I wearily found a taxi and headed home.

★ ★ ★

"Does your mother know you stay out this late?"

It was after three. Auntie Cath was sitting on the couch, a book open on her lap. *Moving Through Grief: Recognize the Divinity Within.* Ugh. The music from the club was still pounding in my ears. All I wanted was to fall into bed and let the thumping rhythm of it batter me into unconsciousness.

"Sit down for a minute," she said. "Do you want a cup of herbal tea?"

I shook my head and grudgingly perched on the arm of the sofa.

"I'm really worried about you. You and your mom. It's been six months. You can't shut yourselves up in here forever."

Watch me.

"You need to be strong for your mom, Ruby. She needs you now, more than ever."

What did she think I'd been doing for the past six months? Who did she think had done the laundry and ordered the food and gone to the sketchy convenience store for cigarettes? Who did she think was making sure the bills got paid?

"It's natural to grieve when you lose someone, but your mom . . ." Auntie Cath sighed.

When you lose someone.

Lose. People say that a lot, when someone dies. I'm sorry for your loss. It makes it sound careless, as if my brother were a door key or umbrella left behind on the train.

And the worst part is, they're right. I was careless. It was me. My loss. I lost him.

"Have you spoken to your father?"

My muscles tensed. This was an ambush. Auntie Cath had carefully avoided mentioning Dad the whole time she'd been here. She knew that Mom wouldn't cope, wouldn't want to hear about him, so she'd waited for an opportunity to get me alone. I swallowed.

Auntie Cath reached out and touched my hand. "I know it's hard. But no matter what happened, he's still your father. He's grieving too. He needs you."

I couldn't look after Mom and Dad at the same time.

"Don't let this tragedy tear your family apart," said Auntie Cath. She sounded as though she was quoting directly from the horrible book she was reading. "What happened was . . ." She shook her head. "It was just awful. But it wasn't your father's fault."

Was she stupid? I knew that. I knew it wasn't his fault. That was why I hadn't spoken to him. I got up from the couch and walked away.

"You need to let go, Ruby," said Auntie Cath, as I opened my bedroom door. "You need to move on."

That would never happen. I wouldn't let it happen. I was never going to let go. I didn't deserve to let go.

Because it was my fault. All of it. It had all happened because of me.

2

"So did I tell you I've decided on my major project for art?"

I shook my head. Minah was a good friend. She didn't comment on the way I'd choked in third period when Mr. Petrovski had called on me to articulate the major underlying theme of *King Lear*. She didn't ask me what had happened when I'd gone and sat in the library after lunch instead of going to chemistry. She knew I'd wanted to be alone. She respected that.

Minah grinned. "I'm building a bed out of pig bones."

"Really?" I made a face.

Minah looked devilishly pleased with herself. "It's going to be amazing. I got the bones from a slaughterhouse. They've still got bits of meat and gristle clinging to them."

It sounded awful, but I supposed that was the point. Minah delighted in making art that disgusted people. If someone felt queasy when looking at one of her pieces, she knew she'd succeeded. One time a pregnant lady had thrown up when she saw Minah's sculptural recreation of Arcimboldo's *Vertumnus* made entirely with rotten fruit and maggoty vegetables. Minah had bragged about it for weeks.

We reached the intersection across from the park, where Minah and I usually parted ways.

Minah hesitated. "Do you want to come and hang out with the others?"

I hadn't been able to bring myself to go to the Wasteland. The very thought of it made the thick, dark blankness swirl and eddy around me, revealing things I didn't want to see.

But I wasn't ready to go home and face Cath's forced optimism. And there was safety in numbers. In groups, nobody expected me to carry half the load of social interaction. I wasn't responsible for awkward silences.

"Sure," I said.

Minah nodded, trying to disguise her surprise and trepidation. "So Flick thinks she can get us tickets to this underground art-slash-music club that specializes in liturgical deathcore. There's a metal band that performs whole Catholic masses in Latin. Are you interested?"

It sounded awful, but awful in a way that was loud and eliminated the need for conversation.

"Maybe."

The crosswalk signal began to tick. But I didn't move, because I had seen him, and he had taken my breath away.

His face was turned up to the sun, eyes closed. The tilt of his head made his sandy hair fall back from a smooth, pale forehead. His strong brows angled into a thoughtful frown, but there was a smile on his full, soft lips. He was . . . perfect, lit up like an angel in the pale winter sun. His clothes were slightly too large — brown old-man slacks and a tucked-in cream shirt buttoned all the way to the collar. The cuffs fell over his wrists, covering most of his hands. He didn't seem to feel the cold, even though he wasn't wearing a coat. At his feet was an open cardboard box. He was one of those weird people, the ones who handed out free bottled water to raise awareness for . . . Jesus or animal rights or refugees or something. They were always there — on the corner by the newspaper stand. Every day. But I'd never seen this guy before. I'd never seen anything like him before.

It wasn't that he was good looking — although he was. It was something else, something that touched my core and made me certain that I had to speak to him, to know him, that he could change my life.

If only I'd known in that instant *how* he would change my life. Would I have behaved differently?

"Ruby?" Minah was talking to me.

I muttered some generic response. Minah followed my gaze.

"Holy hell," she said. "That guy looks like an angel. Do we know him? Does he go to our school?"

I shook my head. "I don't think so."

I couldn't associate someone like him with anything as mundane as school. I imagined him running through fields of waist-high grass and swimming in crystal-clear waterfalls.

"Of course he doesn't," said Minah. "He's one of those Hare Krishna or whatever guys."

I didn't care what he was. I just wanted to look at him.

"I want to paint him," breathed Minah appreciatively. "There's something about him. Something . . . wild."

There was. Something wild and unknowable, like the distant speck of a bird in the sky. The sun moved behind a cloud, and the boy tipped his head back down, his hair flopping into his eyes. Eyes that immediately met mine, as though he could tell I'd been watching him.

A jolt somewhere inside me made my knees weak. It had been a long time since I'd *felt* anything. For the briefest of moments, a spark flared in the darkness.

The boy's eyes were soft and brown, and full of concern and . . . recognition. I had the oddest feeling that he'd been waiting for me. That we'd been waiting for each other.

"He's looking at you," said Minah. "The hot wild angel boy is looking at you."

I didn't say anything. A corner of the boy's mouth turned upward in a half-smile that was more like a question. He reached up and pushed his hair back from his eyes.

"You should go talk to him," said Minah.

Talk to him. See those eyes up close, gazing at me through the sandy fall of his hair. Talk to him . . . about what? I felt the tiny spark extinguish, and my throat closed over.

I wasn't the sort of girl who talked to boys. Not anymore. "I have to get home." I turned to walk away.

"What about the Wasteland?"

The thought of being around other breathing, living humans made panic rise in my throat. "I can't."

I heard Minah sigh, but she didn't say anything else or try to follow me.

I hurried past store windows and offices, trying to cloak myself in emptiness so nobody would notice me. I hunched my shoulders and jabbed at a crosswalk button.

"Excuse me."

I turned around and stared. It was him. He was even more beautiful close-up.

"I'm sorry if I startled you." His voice was soft and husky and deeper than I'd expected.

"I —" I had to get away from those concerned, gentle eyes

before they saw me for what I really was.

"I think I can help you." He reached out and touched my arm. Even through my jacket and sweater, it made my skin burn.

"You've got the wrong person." I yanked my arm away.

"You think you can hide inside your grief," said the boy. "You let it bind you, hoping it pulls you down deep enough that nobody will be able to make you out. It doesn't work on me. I see you."

I felt my gaze drawn up to meet his, and I saw compassion, understanding, warmth. And something else. Something I recognized.

I saw pain.

"You're hurting," he said. "And people are trying to pretend that everything is normal. They try to cheer you up by doing normal things. Things you used to enjoy. But they don't understand that for you, nothing will ever be normal again. That the person they're trying to cheer up doesn't exist anymore."

What if he really was an angel? I knew I should walk away. But . . . he saw me. This boy *saw* me. I'd been invisible for months, hiding in plain sight. Being *seen* like this made me giddy with exhilaration and terror. I had to know more.

"So what do I do? Am I going to be like this forever?"

The boy smiled. "You can let it keep pulling you down into the darkness. Or you can fly."

He pressed a water bottle into my hand and walked away.

I didn't go dancing that night. I stayed home and helped Auntie Cath make cannelloni and put in a load of laundry. When had I last washed my sheets? I couldn't stop thinking about him.

You can fly.

What would that even look like?

Auntie Cath prattled on happily, obviously convinced that our late-night chat had been responsible for my turnaround in attitude. I put on my good-girl face and made the appropriate responses, but inside everything was in turmoil.

I'd thought I'd never feel like this again.

I wasn't sure I wanted to.

We ate the cannelloni and watched a ridiculous TV show about girls competing to marry an oil tycoon. Auntie Cath ran a constant cheerful commentary, while Mom and I sat silently. As soon as it was over, I went to my room, shutting the door carefully behind me, then dug in my backpack for the bottle of water the boy had given me.

I'd taken them before, the free water bottles. Everyone had. They were great on a hot day when you'd forgotten to pack one of your own and didn't want to fork over two dollars for a new one. But I'd never really looked at the bottle before.

It was a regular plastic bottle, with a sealed lid.

The label was paper and had been glued on slightly crooked. There was a weird symbol on it, white on black. A triangle, with a horizontal line cutting through its center. At the top point of the triangle sat a circle with a smaller circle inside it. Underneath the symbol read:

BOUNDLESS BODY
BOUNDLESS MIND

That was it. No contact details. No website. I'd thought they were advertising something. And maybe they were. Maybe it was some viral marketing campaign.

I twisted the cap to break the seal and brought the bottle to my lips. It tasted like . . . like water. Maybe the faintest hint of something else. A trace of bitterness. But it could have just been the plastic of the bottle.

I lay awake, listening to the strains of chatter and music coming from the television downstairs. It was the same as every other night. Whenever I started to drift off to sleep, Anton's face would flash into my mind. I dug my fingernails into my palms to stop myself from falling asleep. I didn't want to see his face. I couldn't.

How could I fly, knowing that Anton never would?

★ ★ ★

I didn't go to school the next day. I knew nobody would care. One of the very few perks of living through a family tragedy is that teachers get pretty flexible about your attendance. And anyway, what was the worst that would happen? They'd call my mom? She hadn't picked up the phone for six months.

When I emerged from my bedroom sometime after midday, Auntie Cath announced she was taking Mom shopping, and Mom didn't protest. I was invited too, but I declined, complaining of a sore throat. I paced the house, restless and fidgety. Finally, I grabbed my coat and headed out. A walk would do me good.

I didn't know whether I'd see him again — the wild angel boy. But I wanted to. Against all my better judgment, I wanted to see him again. I wanted to be seen.

He was there, on the same street corner as he had been the previous day, a fresh cardboard box of bottled water by his side. As I approached, he offered a bottle to a passerby, saying something I couldn't hear. The person — a middle-aged woman pushing a stroller — screwed up her nose and quickened her pace, as if she couldn't get away from him fast enough. He didn't seem at all bothered.

I approached him from the side, so I could see his face, but he was still slightly turned away from me. I felt my skin ripple in anticipation.

"Um. Hey," I said.

He turned. As he saw me, his face broke out into the most beautiful smile I'd ever seen. I'd made him smile. It felt like the greatest achievement of my life.

"It's you," he said, seeming delighted. "I knew I'd see you again."

I was completely tongue-tied. How was I supposed to talk to someone like him?

"Who . . ." I shook my head. "Who *are* you?"

"My name is Furicius," he said. "But everyone calls me Fox."

Fox. It suited him. He was wild and beautiful like a fox. And maybe dangerous, if you were an unsuspecting hen.

He looked at me expectantly.

"Uh," I said, trying to remember how to be a human being. "Ruby. I'm Ruby."

"Ruby," Fox said it slowly, as if he were trying it out for the first time. Then he reached out and formally shook my hand. "It is a great pleasure to meet you, Ruby."

"Do you want to get a cup of coffee or something?" Check me out. That sounded pretty normal. Maybe a little overconfident, even.

Fox looked at me with a slightly puzzled frown. "I don't drink coffee."

"Oh." *Stupid, stupid. Of course he doesn't want to talk to you. Idiot.*

"But I do drink juice," he said gently, a smile playing around his lips.

"Oh," I said again. "OK."

He reached out and took my hand, and for a moment I forgot how to breathe. The simple act of intimacy almost made me burst into tears. I couldn't remember the last time I'd been touched like that, skin to skin. It was electric. I felt vulnerable and exposed.

"Are you all right?" Fox's fingers tightened on mine in a reassuring squeeze.

I found my breath and nodded. I squeezed back, and suddenly Fox's hand was a life raft, the only thing stopping me from sinking deeper into empty blackness.

"Do you need to take that?" I gestured to the cardboard box.

Fox shook his head. "It'll be here when we get back."

I took him to a café that I knew had a juice bar. Fox looked curiously around as we went in, at the linoleum tables and band posters on the walls. A waitress came over, and I ordered a latté. She looked expectantly at Fox, who smiled up at her.

"Hello," he said. "My name's Fox. It's lovely to meet you."

The waitress looked confused. "Great," she said. "Can I get you anything?"

"What's your name?"

"Josie," said the waitress, glancing at me. "Do you want coffee?"

Fox shook his head. "I don't drink coffee."

The waitress took a deep breath.

"Juice," I said, leaning forward. "He drinks juice."

"OK," said the waitress. "We have orange, apple, ginger, pineapple, carrot, and grapefruit."

Fox looked delighted. "And I get to choose one?"

"One, or a mix. You can have all of them if you want."

"All of them together in one glass?" Fox shook his head with a disbelieving smile. "Who knows what that might do to me. May I have apple juice? Thank you so much, Josie."

The waitress smiled insincerely and disappeared into the kitchen. Fox carefully inspected everything on the table — the laminated menu, a tea-light candle in a glass holder, the salt and pepper shakers, and the little packets of sugar and artificial sweetener.

"What are these?" he asked, holding up a pink packet.

"Splenda," I told him. "It's an artificial sweetener."

"Artificial?"

Had he really never been in a café or restaurant before? "You use it instead of sugar. To make tea or coffee sweet."

"Because sugar is bad for you." Fox nodded. "Right. And this isn't bad for you?" He shook the packet.

"Oh, I'm pretty sure that's bad for you too. But a different kind of bad."

Fox's puzzled frown deepened. "So why use it?"

I shrugged. "People like sweet things."

"People seem to like lots of things that are bad for them."

"Yep."

Fox chewed his bottom lip, thinking. "People are strange," he said finally.

The waitress reappeared with Fox's apple juice and a latté for me. I reached for a packet of sugar but saw Fox's alarmed expression and decided to go without. He then proceeded to tip a good three teaspoons of salt into his juice, stirring it with the straw.

"That's *salt*," I said.

Fox nodded. "Yes."

"It's going to taste disgusting!"

"Salt is a cardinal element."

I made a face. "Do you always put salt in your apple juice?"

"I have salt in everything. Don't you?"

I shook my head. "You know that salt is also bad for you, right? Like sugar?"

Fox laughed. "Don't be silly." He lifted the striped plastic straw from his juice and cocked his head to the side. "What is this?"

"You've never seen a straw before?"

Fox shook his head.

I explained what it was for, and Fox put it back in his salty apple juice and tried an experimental suck. A brilliant smile lit up his face, and he looked just like a little boy.

"That's *wonderful*," he said.

I stared at him. "Are you Amish or something?"

"I don't know what that is," he said. "But I don't think I am."

"Do you go to school?" I asked.

"Schools are full of lies," Fox said, his tone automatic, as if he were reciting something. "I learn from the world. The drizzle of rain on a windowpane. The tickle of wind that heralds a storm. The rise and fall of my breath, and the rhythm of my heart. The voices of birds and trees."

I raised my eyebrows, and Fox laughed at my expression.

"Sorry," he said. "I get carried away sometimes. No, I don't go to school. But I like learning about . . . well, everything."

He raised his arm to gesture at the world, and his oversized shirt-sleeve fell back to his elbow, exposing his wrist and forearm, dusted with golden hair and freckles. I imagined what it would be like to touch his arm, to press my lips against his wrist.

I sipped my coffee and tried to get a grip. "What about your parents?"

"My parents?"

"Don't they worry about you, out here all day instead of in school?"

Fox smiled gently. "Daddy understands that there are more important things in the world than school."

Daddy? What was he, five? "And your mom?"

"I don't have a mother." He said it simply.

"Oh," I said. "I'm really sorry. I didn't mean to pry."

"You weren't prying," said Fox. "Being truly alive means being completely honest with everyone. Including yourself."

I had a million questions and no idea where to start. Fox was like a box of puzzle pieces with no picture on the lid to guide you.

"Are you being completely honest with yourself, Ruby?"

The question caught me off-guard. My mind searched for something to say to distract him, change the flow of conversation, but my mouth betrayed me and told the truth.

"No."

Fox waited, watching me with patient eyes.

I twisted a napkin in my hands. Could I tell him? Could I say the words out loud? Would the world end? Would Fox turn his beautiful face away in disgust?

I glanced around the café. About half the tables were occupied — retirees enjoying an afternoon coffee, a few kids cutting school. A man in a bus driver's uniform. The waitress glanced over at our table. My throat jammed closed. I couldn't.

Fox pushed his chair back and stood, tugging me up with him. "Let's go for a walk," he said. "I know somewhere."

I nodded. He headed for the door. "Wait," I said. "We have to pay."

Fox blinked. "Oh," he said, and his cheeks went pink. "I don't — I didn't think . . ."

"It's OK," I said. "I'll get it."

Fox followed me to the counter, where I pulled out my wallet and handed the waitress a twenty-dollar bill. She counted out the change as Fox watched, fascinated.

"May I?"

I handed him the ten-dollar bill, one-dollar bill, and a few coins. He rubbed them all with his fingers, held them up to the light, smelled them. The waitress glanced at me and made a *That guy is nuts* face. I felt a weird surge of protectiveness and steered Fox out of the café.

"I thought it would be different," he said quietly, staring at the money. "More beautiful. More dangerous. But it's so . . . mundane."

He handed the money back to me.

"Fox," I said. "Was that the first time you've handled money?"

"It's strange," he said, his brow creasing. "That people suffer so much, do such ugly things, all because of something so trivial."

He laced his fingers in mine and led me down the street to the park.

It was a gray, desolate day, and the icy wind was keeping all but the most enthusiastic dog walkers and joggers at home. The trees were bare, and the grass was trampled and muddy underfoot. Fox led me to the pond, an artificial mini-lake populated with straggly reeds and a few ducks. We sat down on a park bench that faced the water.

"Isn't it beautiful?" Fox asked, his eyes shining. "I feel so in love when I come here."

I swallowed. "In love?" I said, trying to sound casual. "Who are you in love with?"

He looked at me, his eyes thoughtful. "It depends," he said, "on what I'm thinking about. Sometimes I come here and I feel totally in love with ducks. Sometimes I feel as if I'm in love with all of humanity. Sometimes I'm in love with a single leaf or flower. But today . . . today, Ruby, I feel like I'm in love with you."

For a moment, the darkness fell away, leaving me pink and exposed. My heart pounded, and my mouth turned dry.

"My little brother died," I blurted out. "And it's my fault."

Fox didn't say anything.

"I was supposed to pick him up from soccer practice. Mom was working, and Dad had been on the night shift. I was supposed to pick Anton up at six. But I didn't. I forgot. I was with my friends. We hung around talking after school, and I lost track of time. There was a guy there I liked — Ali. I was trying to impress him. He offered me a drag of his cigarette, and I took one, even though I never smoke. I almost choked, and he laughed at me. I didn't hear my phone ring." I took a deep breath. "When Anton couldn't get in touch with me, he called Dad. Except Dad wasn't home. He was at the bar with some of the guys from his work. He'd been drinking all day — since he'd clocked off work that morning."

I felt my chest starting to heave and struggled to draw breath.

"Anton went running over when he saw Dad's car pulling up. But Dad was driving too fast. He tried to swerve. . . ."

Fox still didn't say anything. Did he hate me now that he knew the truth?

"They wanted to let Dad out on bail until the trial, but he refused. He said he didn't deserve to be out in the world. He's in jail now. I don't know exactly where. Mom sort of fell apart. It's like she's been sleepwalking ever since. My family is broken, and it's my fault. All because I wanted to show off to some stupid boy."

I took a deep breath and stole a look at Fox. He was staring out across the pond. He certainly didn't *look* revolted.

"What do you see, when you look out here?" he asked at last.

"Um." I looked around. Wasn't Fox going to say anything about what I'd told him? "The pond, I guess. Trees."

"What do you notice about the trees?"

I squirmed. "They have no leaves. It's winter, so everything looks dead."

I turned back to Fox and saw the hint of a smile tweak the corner of his mouth.

"Look again," he said. "Look closer."

I did. And I realized that the trees weren't all bare at all. There were pink and green buds starting to swell on every branch. Winter was almost over. Beneath the trees, green spears were pushing through the soil, spears that would soon become irises and daffodils.

"Oh," I said softly.

"How do you feel?" Fox asked. "Do you feel different now that you've told me?"

"I —" I took another deep breath. "I feel . . . better. Sort of *cleaner*, like I've opened a window to let stale air out."

"See?" said Fox. "Honesty. Honesty will free you from the weights that tether you to your sadness."

"But that doesn't change what I *did*."

"You can't change that. No matter how bad you feel."

"I don't think Mom will ever forgive me," I said, my voice barely more than a whisper.

Fox reached over and brushed my cheek with his fingers, delivering a pulse of electricity. "Then you'll have to forgive yourself instead."

If anyone else had said that, I would have dismissed it as

impossible. But with Fox . . . with Fox, everything seemed possible.

"Come have dinner with us," said Fox. "I want you to meet my family."

Dinner. Making small talk with strangers. Questions. More questions. Being polite and normal and human. Smiling and passing the butter. The thought of it was suffocating. I shook my head, but I couldn't quite bring myself to refuse. To see where Fox lived . . . to puzzle together the pieces of his mysterious life. Could I really turn that chance down?

"Don't worry," said Fox. "You don't have to speak if you don't want to. Nobody will pressure you. We don't work that way."

I hesitated.

"And I'll be there with you the whole time," said Fox. "I won't leave your side. Please."

I swallowed my terror. "OK," I said. "I'll come."

3

"You live here?" I said, looking up at the house.

It was old and huge, built of stately red brick with lacy fringes of white Victorian latticework. High walls surrounded a dense jungle of garden. It looked like a house out of a fairy tale.

"Sometimes," said Fox, leading me up a winding, overgrown path toward the porch.

"I can't believe I've never noticed this place before," I said. It was only a ten-minute walk from my house.

"You can't see much from the sidewalk because of the wall," said Fox. "Welling says we should take it down and put up something more welcoming, but Lib doesn't want to."

Who were Lib and Welling? I'd find out soon enough. My heart was hammering as we climbed the steps to the green front door. It was slightly ajar. Fox pushed it wide open and led me in.

The house was even more beautiful inside. I'd expected it to be posh and opulent, but instead everything seemed simple, clean, and calm. The walls were painted white, and the pale floorboards were lined with rugs made of some natural fiber. White linen curtains fell in front of the windows, and candles glowed on mantelpieces and side tables. It felt like a spa. I half expected to be handed a glass of cucumber water and a terry-cloth bathrobe.

But there was a warmth to it. The house felt *lived in*. This was a home.

I thought of Mom sitting on our sofa, a burning cigarette dangling from her inert fingers. I thought of Auntie Cath, with her jingling bracelets and bright clothes. I thought of my piano, silent under a layer of dust. It all felt a million miles away from this tranquil oasis.

"Come on," said Fox. "I'll introduce you to everyone."

He led me through a serene living room and down a hallway to an enormous, gleaming kitchen, full of afternoon sun glinting on copper bowls.

I counted five people in the kitchen, all adults. They were working at various chores — peeling and chopping vegetables, mixing a dough-like substance, measuring out spoonfuls of something that looked like powdered vegetable stock. Everyone seemed to have a job to do, and everyone looked . . . content. Nobody was stressed or rushing or bossing the others around. It felt very harmonious just to be there. They all wore similar clothes, loose-fitting shirts in neutral shades of cream, gray, and beige and dark pants. I couldn't see any brand names or labels anywhere.

One or two of them looked up as Fox guided me forward. Panic rose in my throat. I'd spent months trying to move unseen, keeping my head down and going unnoticed. If I could slip past everyone, maybe nobody would notice the parts of me that were missing.

"Everyone, this is Ruby," said Fox. "She's staying for dinner." Five pairs of eyes turned to me, and I wanted to burrow down into the ground like a rodent. The black tide couldn't hide me this time. I was exposed.

A gray-haired woman dried her hands on a tea towel and took a step toward us. She was tall and thin and had clearly once been very beautiful. Her face was rumpled into deep lines, her cheeks and eyes slightly sunken. Her brown eyes had lit up when she saw Fox, but her smile faltered when he introduced me. But then she was beaming again, and I wondered if I'd imagined the fleeting look of sadness. She stepped forward and enveloped me in a hug — a real hug, not the weak, chestless embraces I'd gotten from relatives and insecure fellow teens. She smelled faintly of sweat and vegetables and something else — something sweet and natural. I resisted for a moment, but it felt good to be held, and against my will, my body relaxed.

She pulled back, still holding me by the shoulders, and stared down into my face. She held me there for a moment, considering me, her smile still firmly in place. "Welcome," she said at last.

Her name was Lib, and she seemed to be the matriarch of the house. She introduced me to the others. I shook hands with a good-looking brown-skinned man in his thirties named Welling and received another hug from Stan, a wiry old Caucasian guy with white hair in a long ponytail. Maggie was short and Asian and in her early twenties. The way she grinned at me immediately reminded me of Minah. The last was Val, a giant, pale man with a scarred face, who ducked his head when Lib said his name and didn't make eye contact with me.

Stan winked at me. "Ruby, we were discussing the relationship between the mind and the body."

I blinked and looked to Fox for help.

Fox tilted his head. "Well," he said thoughtfully. "The mind has no physical form. You can't see it or weigh it or measure it with a ruler. So what is it? How does it interact with the physical world?"

"Aha! There is no physical world," said Stan, pointing at Fox with his kitchen knife. "Everything we experience is a fabrication of the mind. Who says the things I see and feel and taste are the same things that you see and feel and taste?"

"Of course there's a physical world," said Maggie, rolling her eyes. "It's pretty arrogant to assume that everything exists only for you. That if you stopped breathing, the whole world would just puff out of existence."

"If a tree falls in a forest and there's no one there to hear it," I heard myself say, "does it make a sound?"

Eyes turned toward me, and I felt my cheeks burn red. What a stupid thing to say. The biggest philosophical cliché in the book.

"Ruby," said Fox, frowning, "that's an *amazing* question." His face broke out into a proud grin as he turned to the others. "Isn't it?"

He'd never heard it before. The others nodded and smiled, a little indulgently. The question obviously wasn't new to them, so they weren't all as sheltered as Fox. I looked around at each face. It didn't seem like any of them were related. A little piece of the Fox puzzle clicked into place. It was a commune. Fox lived in a commune. One of those hippie places where everyone meditated and the kids were home-schooled. That explained a lot. I wondered if they were some sort of New-Age Christians.

The conversation flowed to other topics, and I kept my mouth shut, afraid of embarrassing myself further. Lib handed me a knife to chop up celery for a salad. Fox was sent to set the table, and I listened as the others debated big ideas. Stan was talking about atoms and particles and how they behaved in predictable ways.

"They follow rules," he said. "They're probabilistic."

"So?" asked Maggie.

"So if we're made up of atoms, and atoms obey the rules of nature, can we really be said to have free will?"

Welling chuckled. "People are more than atoms and particles."

"Are they?" replied Stan. "What else is there?"

And they all laughed, as if Stan had said something hilarious. I smiled — the laughter was contagious. But I had no idea what had been so funny.

Fox came back in, his eyes going straight to me, his brows quirking a little to check that I was OK. I smiled at him and gave a little nod. Looking over at the others, I saw Lib's eyes dart from Fox to me and back to Fox.

"Dinnertime!" she said, a little too brightly, and I wondered what she thought of me. Did she think I wasn't good enough for Fox? She was probably right. Nobody was good enough for Fox.

We filed into the dining room and sat down around a large wooden table. Candles twinkled over an iron fireplace, and the room felt warm and cheerful. Bowls and platters of vegetables were placed on the table, and Lib gestured for me to take a seat.

Fox walked around the table with a large glass jug, pouring water into everyone's glass. The water looked slightly cloudy. When he got to me, he paused and glanced over at Lib.

"Bottled water for Ruby, I think," she said.

Fox nodded, put the jug down, and left the room, returning with one of the plastic bottles of water they handed out. I looked at him.

"We drink a kind of mineral water," explained Stan.

"Somewhat of an acquired taste. We don't want to scare you off when we've only just met you!"

The meal was wholesome and tasty. Raw spinach and almond croquettes were drizzled with sage-infused oil. There were two kinds of salad topped with nuts and seeds, and artichokes stuffed with avocado puree. Everything tasted a little over-salted. I remembered Fox adding salt to his apple juice at the café and wondered why such seemingly healthy people ate so much salt. Probably a weird commune theory that sodium cured cancer or something.

The conversation stayed philosophical, and I listened intently as they discussed systems of morality, whether it was possible to be truly objective, and the definition of reality. The only people who didn't contribute were me and Val, who spent the meal mechanically shoveling food into his mouth, rarely looking up from his plate. Every now and then, Fox pressed his knee against mine under the table and we'd glance at each other, sharing secret smiles.

"Well, Ruby?" asked Lib, once the meal was over and Welling and Val were clearing away the dishes. "What would you like to know?"

"I'm sorry?" I asked.

Lib smiled. "We're sure you have lots of questions for us."

I hesitated.

"Anything," said Lib. "You'll find nothing but honesty here."

"Are you Christians?" I asked.

Stan and Welling both laughed. Lib shook her head. "No, Ruby," she said. "We're not religious at all."

"Religion is for the weak," said Stan. "We're not interested in make-believe gods floating around on clouds. We believe in science. The science of possibility."

Hippies then, I guessed. They were probably into yoga and homeopathy. I thought of Helena and her healing amber beads. She'd claimed they were validated by science too.

"What about the water bottles?" I asked. "Why do you hand them out?"

"People get thirsty," said Lib. "Water is better than some awful sugary soft drink."

"You're trying to convince people to be healthier?"

Lib nodded.

"Imagine how much better the world would be if everyone wasn't so muddled by the poisons they consume daily," said Stan.

I frowned. "So . . . why isn't there any other information on the label? About your message? Or a link to a website?"

"What's a website?" asked Fox.

I glanced at him to see if he was joking. He wasn't.

"We aren't a charity," said Welling with a shrug. "If people aren't actively searching for the truth, there's no number of websites that will help them."

"But then why hand out the water bottles?"

"People get thirsty."

The whole thing made no sense to me, but I didn't want to be rude. Instead I offered to help clean up, and Maggie and I were sent into the kitchen to wash the dishes. Maggie filled the sink with cold water — no detergent — and swirled plates and bowls around in it, handing them to me once they were clean to be dried and stacked on the counter. I thought of Auntie Cath loading our dishwasher at home, filling the dispensers with detergent. Cold water seemed to have done the job just fine.

"So," said Maggie, giving me an evaluating look that reminded me even more of Minah. "What do you think?"

"Um," I said, trying to figure out a way to be polite.

"Don't worry," she said hastily. "I know how it all looks when you first arrive. I was totally like that too."

"How long have you been here?"

"A few months. I don't know how long I'll stay. I really like the vibe, you know? The food, and the tranquility of it all. But I'm not like them."

"What do you mean?"

"This place is sort of like the entry level," said Maggie, reaching for another bowl. "The really hardcore members are at the Institute. They've all lived these incredibly hard lives — so many of them are abuse victims or ex-addicts."

The Institute. It sounded creepy.

"I'm not like that," Maggie continued. "I mean, I've been messed up, but nothing like that. I'm not in it for the long haul, you know? I'll stay until it gets too weird, and then I'll move on and try something else."

"This isn't the first place like this you've been to?" I wondered how many strange little communes there were, right under everyone's noses.

Maggie cocked her head to the side. "Nothing quite like this," she said thoughtfully. "But I've definitely tried out alternative lifestyles. I was really into yoga for a while. After that I lived with a bunch of anarchists, but they were too angry. I spent some time with the Hare Krishnas, walking around the city and singing. That was fun."

"It sounds like you're very spiritual."

Maggie let out a snort and handed me a wet bowl. "Actually, I think that's my problem. I'm not spiritual enough. I can't surrender all my doubts and thoughts and questions the way you're supposed to. I can't stop *thinking*, you know? My mind never stops turning over and over and over." She made a circular movement with her hand. "Anyway, I hope you stick around. It's an interesting experience. And you don't have to be all gung-ho about it if you don't want to. Everyone's really accepting of whatever you want to be."

"Thanks," I said, feeling genuinely warmed by Maggie's openness.

"So . . . hopefully I'll see you again?"

I nodded. "Definitely."

Once the dishes were done, Fox took me on a tour of the house, showing me a large formal sitting room and a cozier living room where they had what Fox called "family time" every evening. Then he took me upstairs, where a series of bedrooms led off a long hallway. At the end of the hall was Fox's room. We went inside, and I was surprised to see how spartan it was. Just a bed with a tartan blanket, a small chest of drawers, and a picture of a sailboat on the wall — the generic kind you might see in a motel room. No posters or books or knick-knacks. No clothes on the floor.

"It's so . . . clean," I said to Fox. "Where's all your stuff?"

"I only live here some of the time," he replied. "Mostly we live at the Institute, and we're sent here to stay while we give out the water bottles."

"The Institute?" It didn't sound any less creepy when Fox said it.

"It's far away," he said. "It's . . . different there."

"Different how?"

Fox's expression became serious. "It's . . . away from everything else. No distractions."

"Is that a good thing?"

"Yes," said Fox, but there was doubt in his voice. "Daddy says I shouldn't stay out in the real world for too long. I get too sad."

It was so strange to hear the word *daddy* come out of Fox's mouth. It made him sound like a child.

"Sad?"

Fox nodded. "Sad about the world. You've seen how ugly everything can be. How people don't know . . . don't appreciate how beautiful life is. How easily wasted. You understand. I know you do."

I swallowed. I did understand. Fox clenched his hands into fists and stared down at them, his brow crease a little deeper than usual.

"I think if people don't *do* something, humanity will end up as broken mutants, numb from all the artificial chemicals they've put into their bodies. They'll burn everything — the coal, the forests. The rivers and oceans will turn to contaminated sludge, and everything will be mountains of garbage. A race of toxicant mutants, ruling over a kingdom of trash."

His usually quiet voice had deepened, developing a harsh tone, and I saw anger and grief in his expression. For a moment, I was a little frightened by him.

"What can we do?" I asked. "How do we stop it?"

Fox pushed his hair from his eyes, and the anguish faded from his face. "I don't think it's difficult. It's about understanding each other. About living honestly. About treating our bodies as precious vessels instead of garbage disposals." He glanced sideways at me, his expression shy as he took my hand. "And love. It's about love."

4

I went back the next day. And the next. And the day after that. I felt myself uncurl from my cramped crouch in the darkness and stretch. My body felt clear and pure from all the nuts and vegetables. I started to join in the dinner conversations. I stopped fearing the sound of my own voice.

I got to know the other inhabitants of the Red House. Matriarch Lib ruled over everyone with a kind and watchful eye. Welling was always immaculately groomed and friendly, greeting me with a wide grin. Stan regaled me with crazy stories of traveling through India and South America in the 1970s, taking drugs and searching for enlightenment. "I didn't realize," he said, pausing his constant bouncing motion for a moment, "that what I was searching for was inside of me. I had it all along. I should have just stayed home and watched *The Wizard of Oz*."

Maggie was loud and abrasive, continually getting into heated arguments with the others and then being gently chided by Lib. She was a hurricane of thoughts and ideas, whirling around the Red House, unaware of the destruction that her moods could wreak. But everyone was so warm and friendly, the house somehow closed in behind her in the wake of her passage. Within a few minutes, everything would be back to normal. They were accepting like that. It made me feel safe; if they saw the cracks in me, they wouldn't panic.

I saw Maggie in full force one morning (a school day, but I seemed to have forgotten about school), when I'd come over to see if Fox wanted to go to the park. I walked into the kitchen to find Maggie scowling up at the silent mountain that was Val.

Val was the only inhabitant of the Red House whom I hadn't gotten to know. Fox had told me that Val had been around forever, as long as he could remember, and that Val never spoke. He just lumbered around and collected cicada husks from the garden, lining them up on the windowsill in his bedroom like tiny paper lanterns.

"You clumsy idiot!" Maggie was yelling. "What were you thinking?"

Val was staring down at the kitchen floor. As I approached, I saw fragments of an earthenware bowl mixed with shredded kale and strawberries.

"Nothing," Maggie continued. "You were thinking nothing. Because you don't think, do you? You're just a giant useless hunk of toxicant flesh."

Val's expression didn't waver.

"Maggie," I said, stepping forward. "Is everything OK?"

Maggie ignored me. "I don't even know why they let you in. How can someone like you ever be sublime, when all you are is *body*? Just stupid, ugly face and fat and skin."

"I'm sure he didn't mean to break it," I said.

"Shut up!" Maggie yelled, whirling around on me. "What

the hell would you know? You're not one of us. You don't belong here."

I mumbled an apology and slipped out of the room, down the hallway, and out the front door of the Red House, pulling it closed behind me and taking deep breaths.

You don't belong here.

If I didn't belong there, where did I belong? Not at home. Not at school. Not with my friends. Perhaps the only place for me was drowning deep in stifling darkness.

I headed down the front path to the street.

"Wait." Maggie had opened the front door and was following me out. "Don't listen to me," she said, taking a step forward. "Of course you belong here. I'm in a bad mood."

I could feel her hand trembling on my arm. Sweat was beading on her forehead. "Are you sure you're OK?" I asked. "You don't look so great."

Maggie shook her head, like a dog shaking off water. "I'm fine. Feeling a bit . . . you know. It's hard, trying to be a better person. I was really struggling back at the Institute. That's why they let me have a stint here at the Red House. They thought I might find it easier. But . . . I don't know. Sometimes it's harder being closer to all the things you've given up."

I wondered what kinds of things Maggie had given up, but it didn't seem right to ask.

"What's the deal with Val, anyway?" I asked, changing the subject.

Maggie leaned toward me conspiratorially. "Nobody's really sure, but there are rumors. People say he used to be a hit man, working for some bad guys. That he tortured people. But then something happened — his people turned on him and left him for dead. Something inside him broke, and he went all quiet and still. I think he's been at the Institute for ten years or so. He's like a rescued puppy, totally loyal. One hundred percent."

We headed back inside to the kitchen, where Val was still standing, staring down at the broken bowl.

"Don't worry about it, big guy," said Maggie, giving him a playful punch on the arm. "I'll help you clean it up."

In any other family, it would have gone differently. Val would be ostracized for his size and his silence. Maggie would have been punished for her outburst, and seethed with resentment for days. But in the Red House, things fixed themselves. When conversations got heated, they played out logically until everyone agreed with each other. When Maggie's temper got the best of her, everyone waited patiently until she fizzled out and apologized. It felt natural, like the shifting of the winds or the turning of seasons. I came to learn that all storms in the Red House passed quickly, that problems were solved and disagreements were settled amicably. It was a kind of magic, and at the center of the magic was Fox.

They all loved him, and how could they not? Fox was sweet and generous and thoughtful. He was interested in everyone and everything, and his enthusiasm was infectious. He could always defuse Maggie's outbursts. He could always make Welling laugh. Sometimes I saw Lib looking at him, a glow of pride softening the lines on her face.

When we weren't together, thoughts of him filled my mind. I fantasized about kissing him, running my fingers through his sandy hair. I dreamed about his soft lips, his serious eyes, the smattering of freckles across the bridge of his nose. I relived every conversation we'd had over and over, remembering the husky gentleness of his voice, the way his mouth tilted into a wry smile. I scribbled down his words in a journal Helena had given me, trying to re-create the way he spoke, the way he could capture delicate, fleeting thoughts and ideas and express them so simply and beautifully that it was like poetry.

I wanted him. I was consumed by wanting him. I twisted in my bed sheets every night, his name on my lips, my fingers drawing the stories on my body that I longed for him to write. I knew it should feel wrong, this *wanting*. I knew I didn't deserve Fox. I didn't even deserve the fantasy of him. I didn't deserve to want anything as much as I wanted him. But I couldn't stop. Fox was a fire that had lit up my darkness and set me aflame.

Did he feel the same way about me? Fox was very physical. He was constantly touching my hands, my shoulder, my cheek. He laced our fingers tightly together. He stared into my eyes, and I couldn't imagine he felt anything other than the exact mirror of my own desires. But he threw words like *love* around so easily. He was in love with everything about the world — the ducks in the park, spring flowers, drifting clouds, the smell of rain. When he told me he loved me, did he mean he loved me more than those things? He'd never tried to kiss me, but there was something sensual about the way his fingers lingered on my skin, the way his eyes would sometimes travel over my body before he'd turn away, blushing. I didn't believe he was as innocent as he seemed.

We'd spend hours lying in the grass in the park, gazing into each other's eyes, and in those moments I was sure I wasn't imagining it. What I felt was real, and it was like nothing I'd felt before. I knew Fox felt it too. I knew it was only a matter of time before the mental and emotional spilled into the physical, and our daytime intensity would merge with my fevered nighttime fantasies.

I hadn't been to school for over a week. I got up each morning and made polite conversation with Auntie Cath, who would hand me a packed lunch comprised mostly of pre-packaged snacks — mini chocolate bars and individually wrapped crackers and processed cheese dip. When I was a kid, I loved food in little packets. Opening each one was like opening presents on Christmas, special and definitively mine. Now I'd hold them up to read the long strings of preservatives listed on their sides and shudder. Who knew what those chemicals did? Nothing good, that was for sure.

I would head out the front door as if I were going to school, but turn left instead of right at the end of our street and cut across the park and up the hill to the Red House, dumping Auntie Cath's lunch in a trash can on my way. I considered feeding it all to the birds, but I figured the birds didn't need to be pumped full of preservatives either. I was doing them a favor.

Walking through the squeaky iron gate into the dark green jungle beyond the wall was like entering the Secret Garden. I felt special, chosen, privy to secrets that nobody else knew. Occasionally I'd see someone else on the street outside the Red House — a parent pushing a stroller, a postal worker, joggers, and dog-walkers. They wouldn't even see me. Their eyes glazed over the high red brick wall of the Red House as though it wasn't there.

Didn't they notice it? Didn't they wonder what was on the other side?

I knew they didn't, because I hadn't. Before I'd been to the Red House, before I'd met Fox, I'd never looked around. I hadn't wondered what lay behind walls or doors. I hadn't wondered what existed in the minds and hearts of the people I passed each day. I felt as if all my senses were heightened, that I was opening up like a flower, suddenly aware of how much possibility there was in the world.

Fox always met me at the front door, throwing his arms

around me with a face-splitting grin. "You came back," he'd whisper into my hair.

"Of course I did," I'd whisper back, breathing in his Fox-smell and feeling peace and calm and joy wash over me.

★ ★ ★

One morning we found Welling in the dining room surrounded by boxes of bottled water.

"Ruby," he said, smiling. His white teeth stood out against his brown skin. I felt myself blush. He was the only member of the Red House I found a bit intimidating. Even though he was younger than Lib and Stan and Val, somehow he was the one who seemed the most like a grown-up, who made me feel the most like a little kid. But I was curious about him. How did someone like him end up here, instead of being a charismatic lawyer or politician?

"What are you doing?" I asked, approaching the table.

"I was just heading out," he said, lifting one of the cardboard boxes. "It's my turn to hand out water." He considered me. "You should come."

Welling wanted my company?

"Um," I said, glancing at Fox. Did he mean both of us?

"Please," he said. "You'd be doing me a big favor. It can get pretty boring standing on a street corner on my own. I could really use the company and, well, to be honest I'd like to get to know you a little better. You seem interesting. Fox certainly thinks so." He raised his eyebrows at Fox, and I saw Fox's cheeks flush crimson.

"You should go," Fox said. "There are some things I've been meaning to do around here anyway."

Welling's smile was warm and welcoming, and I felt flattered that he wanted to spend time with me. I could always hang out with Fox in the afternoon.

"Sure."

We went to the main shopping strip near the park, where I'd first seen Fox. With a rush of adrenaline, I remembered first seeing him, remembered that first brilliant spark of connection as our eyes met.

Welling pulled out a bottle of water, scanning the surrounding strip for potential recipients.

"Why water?" I asked.

Welling shrugged. "People get thirsty," he said. "And you never know, someone might start a conversation, and that could be the thing that changes their lives. It did for me."

"Do many people stop to talk?" I asked.

Welling's movie-star mouth curled in a regretful smile. "Not many," he said. "Most people don't want to realize that their lives are empty. It's too hard, too big to comprehend. You have to be a special kind of person to accept the kinds of possibilities we offer."

Did Welling think I was a special kind of person? I took one of the water bottles out of the box and examined the label. It was the same as all the others — the weird triangular symbol and the words BOUNDLESS BODY BOUNDLESS MIND printed below. It was clumsily put together, with an ugly sans-serif font and off-center spacing. Minah would have fainted. Would I have stopped to talk to Welling? Probably not. Not until Fox, anyway. If not for Fox, I never would have gone to the Red House. I never would have met them all. I'd still be sleepwalking through life, drowning in the black tide.

"Do you want me to hand some out too?" I asked.

Welling shook his head. "Absolutely not," he said. "I'm not asking you to promote anything you're not sure about. That wouldn't be fair."

I considered him carefully. He didn't look like your average commune-living hippie. He was clean-shaven and well groomed, oozing casual masculinity. Even though he wore the same plain linen pants and shirt as the others, Welling's looked different somehow. Neater. Tailored. Crisp.

"How did you know?" I asked. "When you were sure about all this. What made you decide?"

Welling handed a bottle of water to a passerby and told her to have a nice day, before turning back to me.

"I used to be a broker," he said. "It wasn't quite as crazy as it is in the movies — no private jets or massive orgies. But there was a lot of money. A lot of casinos. A lot of women. I was ruthless, and it paid off. I made my first million dollars by the time I was twenty-five. I partied *hard*. I usually didn't remember much between Friday night and Monday morning. I thought I had it all. When you have money, everyone wants to be near you. But none of it's real. None of it matters. I realized that one day when my boss had a heart attack right in the middle of a meeting. We were sitting in the conference room, a bunch of dudes in suits, talking numbers, and the boss slumped over in his chair. We thought he'd fallen asleep. Nobody was brave enough to try and wake him up. We kept going with the meeting. It wasn't until the very end that we all stood up, and he stayed there, his head on the conference table. Someone eventually reached over to him, and realized what had happened. We called an ambulance, but it was too late. He'd been dead for over an hour, and we didn't care enough to notice."

"How were you supposed to know?" I asked. "It sounds like

you just thought it'd be too embarrassing if you woke him up."

Welling offered another bottle to an elderly man walking a small, fluffy dog. The man shook his head and looked disapproving.

"Have a nice day, sir," Welling called after him. "What does that say, though? That we were so busy worrying about being embarrassed that we let a man die? I realized, then, in the conference room, that money doesn't mean anything. My boss had more money than anyone else I knew, but it didn't make a difference in the end. It didn't stop him from having a heart attack — hell, all the booze and cocaine almost certainly *contributed* to his heart attack. And nobody really cared. I mean, people started fighting about who was going to take over even before the ambulance arrived. But nobody cared that he had died. Nobody missed him. His life had been totally empty. And I didn't want to be like that. I wanted my life to mean something. So I followed the paramedics out the front door of the building, and I never went back."

"You just quit? But how did you know nobody cared? Didn't he have a family?"

Welling acted like he hadn't heard me. "Walking away was the easiest and best thing I've ever done. I felt free for the first time in my life. I gave a bunch of money away and traveled to India and Finland and Turkey and Ghana. I realized how many different kinds of people there are in the world, each person so unique. But eventually my money ran out. I came back here, ready to sign up with another firm and start all over again. The thought of it made me feel physically ill. I didn't want to be a part of the corporate machine. But what choice did I have?"

I knew that feeling. Trapped inside your own life as if there was no way out.

"I was heading to a job interview, and I was shaking all over. My mouth was so dry, I didn't think I'd be able to speak. I started to sweat, and my heart was beating a mile a minute. I couldn't breathe, and I honestly thought I was going to die. I stumbled in the street, and someone caught me. Handed me one of these."

Welling held up a bottle of water.

"And I had an avocation. Like a bolt of lightning. I *knew*. All my fear and panic evaporated. It was Stan that day, with the water. He told me that money was my prison, a prison I'd chosen for myself. But I could make a different choice, if I was strong enough. He invited me to the Red House, and I've never looked back."

I bit my lip, skepticism battling with envy. I wanted to be sure. I wanted to *know*. I didn't feel as though I knew anything. But I wanted to. I wanted the peace and serenity that Welling and the others had. Maybe I could get it. Maybe if I pretended to be sure, eventually *pretending* would melt into *being*. Maybe.

"So you don't miss anything about your old life?" I asked.

"Nothing," he said. "I wouldn't give up standing here, being me, for all the money and blow and blow jobs in the world."

I smiled weakly.

"Don't worry," he reassured me with a grin. "You'll have the avocation. I know you will. You need to give yourself permission. Leave your toxicant life behind. Don't worry about what has happened in the past or what might happen in the future. Everything is only *now*."

I felt myself sink back into darkness. I could never forget what happened. I could never forget Anton.

"Ruby." Welling's voice was serious, his brows drawn together in concern. "I was a terrible person before. I was greedy and selfish. I treated people like they were nothing. Especially women. When I think of how I treated the girls I dated back then . . ." He shook his head. "But I left that behind. I'm not that person anymore. So whatever it is that you're afraid of — you don't have to be that person either. It's your choice."

"I'm afraid." My voice was barely more than a whisper. "I'm afraid that I won't be able to be who I want to be."

Welling put his arm around me and gave me a friendly squeeze. "That's where the technic comes in," he said. "You don't have to do it alone. There are steps. Pathways. And all the other members are there with you, supporting you, cheering you on. It's not just the diet stuff, you know. Feeling healthy is a big part of it, but once you move beyond that to the next stage, everything changes. Your IQ skyrockets and you can perform mental feats that surpass even what supercomputers can do. You are free of disease — diseases of the body *and* of the mind. No more anxiety or depression or addiction. Your memory, eyesight, and hearing are flawless. Your mood is always joyful. It's . . . well, it's sublime."

Even though it sounded ludicrous, a part of me wanted to believe him. "Are you saying you're all those things?"

Welling's expression was tinged with longing. "Not yet," he said. "But I will be. I'm getting closer every day."

I wanted that peace, that clarity.

"Here," I said, reaching out for the bottle of water. "Let me help. I want to."

5

"So it's a cult," said Minah, stirring another spoonful of sugar into her coffee.

"No," I replied. "It's not a cult. Don't be so dramatic."

I knew I shouldn't have told her. But I hadn't been to school for days, and I wanted to tell her about Fox. I wanted to tell everyone about Fox. He filled my every waking thought, and it was impossible to exist in the world without a little bit of him spilling out of me. I couldn't talk to Mom or Auntie Cath about him, so Minah it was. I'd asked her to meet me in the café I'd first taken Fox to. I'd started to order my usual latté, but then I stopped myself. I didn't need all that sugar and dairy and caffeine clouding my thoughts. I ordered a seltzer water instead.

"So what is it then?"

"It's a different way of living. It's nurturing the body. Did you know that we are capable of so much more? But people clog their bodies with cholesterol and artificial preservatives so everything swells up and slows down. Stan calls normal people *toxicants*."

Minah raised her eyebrows. "Sounds like a cult to me."

I sighed. "What do you even mean by *cult*? Is every gathering of like-minded people a cult? Is your art class a cult?"

"No," said Minah. "A cult is something that indoctrinates you into a restrictive ideology by suppressing your sense of freedom and cutting you off from your friends and family."

I opened my mouth to disagree with her but then realized I didn't know anything about Maggie's family, or Lib's, or Welling's. I knew Fox's father was back at the Institute, but did that even count? I decided to change tactics.

"People used to think Christianity was a dangerous cult."

Minah looked at me as if I was insane. "Christianity *is* a dangerous cult," she said. "It's *the* most dangerous cult. Have you met my parents?"

I rolled my eyes, exasperated. Minah obviously wasn't going to change her mind. She was stuck in her own rigid way of thinking. I'd seen this happen before. She was stubborn and never admitted she might be wrong. She saw compromise as a weakness, not a strength. I sipped my seltzer water, feeling as clear and sharp as the bubbles that were surging through it.

"Is there yoga?" asked Minah. "Cults always start with yoga."

"No," I said. "There's no yoga. And yoga isn't a cult, anyway."

"Maybe not," said Minah, "but there's something about all that deep breathing and stretching that makes people's minds more susceptible to bullshit. It's a gateway drug. There was a group called the Great White Brotherhood that was all about yoga, and you *know* that anything called the Great White Brotherhood is going to be a bad scene. And Aum Shinrikyo? The cult responsible for the Tokyo Subway gassing in the nineties? That started as an elite university yoga club. And have you ever talked to someone who does that weird hot yoga? They are drinking some kind of Kool-Aid for *sure*."

"I know you're trying to look out for me," I said. "But believe me when I tell you that I'm OK. I'm in control. In fact, I feel more in control than I have in ages. I'm eating healthier and I feel *lighter* and *clearer*. I think I'm becoming a better communicator. A better person."

Minah shook her head in disbelief. "Who even *are* you? What do they put in those water bottles?"

I laughed. "Just water," I said, then wondered if that was true.

Minah's resolute scowl faltered a little. "There'll be weird sex stuff," she said darkly. "There's always weird sex stuff."

She was joking now, and I knew I'd won her over a little. "I promise I won't do any weird sex stuff," I said with mock seriousness.

"And it's never *good* weird sex stuff," Minah went on, ignoring me. "It's always creepy old dudes trying to control women's bodies. Or worse." She made a face.

"You know me," I said. "You know I'd never get involved in anything that messed up. You have to trust me."

Minah ripped open a sugar packet and poured white granules onto the linoleum table, drawing it into swirls with a finger. "Look, Ruby, I know we don't talk about it much. About what happened and everything. I figured you didn't want to, that you needed space. But I am seriously worried about you. Since you started seeing this Fox guy, you've totally changed. You're *glowing*. You're all shiny-eyed and hopeful and —"

"Isn't that a good thing? Aren't you glad I'm happy?"

Minah tore open another packet of sugar, frowning. "Ruby, Anton *died*. And joining some cult *or whatever you want to call it*," — she held up a hand to cut off my protest — "it's not going to bring him back."

I felt the black tide rise around me at the mention of Anton. But I didn't let myself sink into it. I didn't want to drown anymore.

"I know," I said. "I think it's time I moved on."

Minah poured out a third packet of sugar and carefully pressed her fingernail into each of the swirls she'd made, forming spikes and thorns. I raised my glass of seltzer water to my lips but didn't allow any into my mouth. The bubbles popped against my lips, hard and bright.

Eventually Minah nodded. "Just be careful, OK? It may seem benign now, all peace and love and harmony. But that's how brainwashing begins. It starts with meditation and yoga, but before you know it, you're drinking juice laced with arsenic in order to ascend to a higher plane."

"I promise I'll be careful," I said. "And . . . you could always come with me. Come to the Red House and meet everyone."

Minah made a face. "No way am I coming to your cult headquarters," she said with a grimace. "Even if there *is* no weird sex stuff, I don't want any of these mystic crystal revelations you've been OD-ing on. I have *art* to make."

I laughed. "Suit yourself."

"But I want to meet him."

Fox? She wanted to meet Fox? I felt an initial stab of doubt. Fox was so open and happy, and Minah was dark and closed. Would they understand each other? But Fox could charm anyone, I was sure of it.

"Bring him to the Wasteland," said Minah. "We'll be there all afternoon."

I tried to imagine Fox sitting on a milk crate surrounded by garbage, listening to Minah talk about her latest art project. It was like trying to imagine a wild bird at a heavy metal concert.

But I was certain that once Minah got to know Fox, she'd come to love him as much as I did.

I found Fox in our usual spot in the park by the pond and settled myself beside him on the grass. It was one of those crisp early spring days where everything felt full of possibility. The bare branches of the trees around the pond had broken out into a delicate green fuzz, and some were swelling with pink blossoms. The irises and daffodils were beginning to unfurl into splashes of yellow and purple. Birds twittered everywhere, as though the whole world was waking up.

Fox was watching a duck lead a cohort of fuzzy ducklings across the muddy bank and into the pond. One tiny one kept falling over, and the mother duck kept having to stop the parade and nudge it back to its feet.

"If people did not love one another," said Fox, his voice low and dreamy, "I really don't see what use there would be in having any spring."

Was Fox saying he loved me? I reached out and took his hand. "That's beautiful."

"It's from *Les Miserables*," he told me. He pronounced it without the French accent: *Less Mizzer-ubbles*.

"The movie?"

"The book. There's a movie?"

I nodded. "Of the musical, though. Not the book."

"There's a musical?"

I laughed. "How can you not know there's a musical of *Les Mis*?"

Fox shrugged, and a wistful expression passed over his face. "There are lots of things I don't know."

"But you've read the book," I said. "They say the book is always better than the movie."

"Do they?"

A thought occurred to me. "Fox, have you . . . have you ever seen a movie?"

Fox shook his head. "Sometimes I can see a television through the window of a shop, when I'm handing out the water bottles. Daddy says television poisons the mind." His expression grew distant, and a faint smile stole over his face. "But when I read *Les Miserables*, I imagine the story playing out in my head. That's like a movie, isn't it?"

"Sort of," I agreed.

"It must be sad, when the pictures in the movie don't match the pictures in your head."

"It is," I said. "Some people get very upset."

Fox nodded. "Then I'm glad I haven't seen the movie, because there's no way it could be as good as the book. The book is the most wonderful thing. I've read it hundreds of times."

I didn't think he was exaggerating. "Did your dad teach you to read?"

"It was Lib," Fox replied. "She read me stories when I was very small, and once I could read she brought me books of my own. *Paddington Bear. The BFG. Love That Dog.* I couldn't get enough. But Daddy took them all away when I became a Monkey."

I frowned. "A monkey? You mean you were naughty, and he took your books away as a punishment?"

Fox looked away, his forehead creasing in a frown. "Books are wonderful, but . . . there are so many different worlds. If you read too many books, you get confused about which is the real world. You have . . . doubts. It's dangerous."

"Did your dad tell you that?" I asked. "That books are dangerous?"

Fox didn't reply. His face was etched with sadness, and I wondered what he was grieving for. His lost books and the worlds they contained? Or was it something else?

"But you have *Les Miserables*, right?" I asked. "Your dad didn't take that one away?"

"Val gave it to me years ago," said Fox. "He knew I missed my books. It was very difficult to understand at first — so many words I didn't know. But I kept trying, and after a while I realized how beautiful it is. Don't tell anyone I have it. I wouldn't want to get Val in trouble."

I pictured Val's vast frame, his pale, scarred face. Maggie had said that he was dangerous, an ex-criminal. But that didn't sound like the kind of man who would secretly find a book for a sad little boy.

"Once I read *Les Miserables* upside down," Fox said. "To see if it would be different."

"Was it?"

He tilted his head to one side. "Yes," he said. "It felt . . . more delicate. As if every word were placed so carefully, and a strong gust of wind could blow them all off the page."

The mother duck successfully got her ducklings into the pond and began a triumphant victory lap. I let the sunlight soak into my face. It warmed me all the way through, even the dark, secret places that I'd thought would never be warm again. Fox's hand was solid and real in mine. I felt as though I had finally woken up after sleepwalking for months.

"Which books have you read?"

Fox was always full of questions. He was intensely curious about the world and everything in it. He wanted to know every last detail about my life. He asked about school, about my teachers and the subjects and the desks we sat at and what school bells sounded like. He asked about my childhood birthday parties, made me describe each one and got frustrated when I couldn't remember what kind of cake I'd had or what gifts I'd received. He asked me about camping trips, about beaches and the feeling of sand between my toes. Every question filled a little gap in my knowledge about him. I realized he'd never been in a school. Never been to a birthday party. Never been to the beach. He talked often about how great his childhood had been, how wonderful his father was. But his hunger for knowledge of everyday life told a different story.

I told Fox about my favorite childhood books. About trips to the library and reading stories to Anton.

"Don't you think it's weird?" I asked him. "That your dad took your books away?"

Fox's shoulders hunched in a shrug. "I think lots of things are weird," he said. "I think it's weird that our bodies are born knowing how to breathe and they don't forget to keep our hearts beating. I think it's weird when people cross the street instead of taking my water bottles."

He seemed oddly defensive, so I didn't push it. We watched the ducks.

"What do you want?" asked Fox, after we'd been silent for a long while.

"What do you mean?"

"Out of life."

I closed my eyes and let the sun turn the insides of my eyelids golden. "I want . . . I want my family back. I want my mom to get better. I want Dad to come home."

Fox stroked my hand with his thumb. "That's what you want for other people," he said gently. "What do you want for *you*?"

I opened my eyes and was surprised all over again to see how much color there was in the world. The blue of the sky reflected in the pond. The green of the grass and the fresher green of the new growth on the trees. The pale pink blossom. The vibrant yellows and purples of the flowers. Had the world always contained so much color? Had I just not noticed? Had I forgotten how to see it?

"I want to feel whole again," I said. "I've lost so many pieces of myself. Anton. Dad. Mom. Sometimes I think I'm only flesh and bone, without anything real inside, you know? Just fragments, like the pieces of a broken china plate that don't get swept up and thrown out with the others."

Fox leaned sideways into my shoulder, and the warmth of him spread through me, even more than the warmth of the sun had.

"What about you?" I asked. "What do you want out of life?"

Fox didn't reply for a long time. It was clear he was struggling with something, his brows drawn together and his jaw set. Finally he sighed, and it was as if he was letting a heavy weight drop.

"I know what I'm supposed to say," he said at last. "But I can't lie to you, Ruby. What do I want? I want to never forget how beautiful the world is and how lucky I am to be a part of it. I want to feel everything, see everything, experience every sensation that this world offers. I want to help people to see how extraordinary we all are."

I wondered why that had been so difficult for him to say. "My friends want to meet you," I told him. "Do you think that would be OK?"

Fox's expression cleared, and he grinned at me. "Really? I'd *love* to meet your friends. Can we go now?"

"Are you sure?"

He grabbed my hand and pulled me to my feet. "I want to know everything about you. And friends are a piece of you. If you want to put your china plate back together, we have to find all the pieces."

★ ★ ★

The Wasteland was an empty parking lot behind a long-abandoned bar. Minah liked it because she said it reminded her of the permanence of concrete in stark contrast to the entropy of humanity. Harrison had dubbed it the Wasteland after the T.S. Eliot poem, because it was full of disillusionment and despair. I decided not to share any of this with Fox.

"So," I said to him as we made our way down the hill toward the sketchy end of town. "You might not like this place very much. Or these people."

"I like everyone," said Fox. "And everywhere."

"We might be challenging that today. This place is pretty ugly. It's kind of the point."

"Ugly places often have beautiful secrets."

It was true that if anyone could find any beauty in the Wasteland, it was Fox. The bar had never been a nice one — it was the kind that had slot machines and a smoking cage out back. I doubted it had ever been the kind of bar where interesting people met after work and sipped craft beers and munched hand-cut fries. It seemed scented with desperation. When it finally shut the doors for the last time and boarded up the windows, the parking lot became a dumping ground. It wasn't near anything else, so there were never any cars. Just junk and my friends.

I tried to see them through Fox's eyes as we approached, and I started to feel a little uneasy. They were sitting on an abandoned couch, surrounded by empty soda cans and rusted shopping carts. Minah was carelessly smeared in paint as usual. Ali was in his trademark skinny jeans and baggy flannel shirt, a cigarette hanging from his bottom lip. Harrison wore a thrift-store cardigan over an ironically cheerful Peppa Pig T-shirt, and Flick was all in black, her nose and eyebrow glinting with silver studs, teal slashes on her fingernails.

I took Fox's hand as we approached, as much for myself as for him. It had been a long time since I'd been to the Wasteland.

"Hey," said Minah, looking up. "You must be Fox."

Fox ran his free hand through his hair, pushing it back from his eyes, and for the first time I realized he might be nervous too. He smiled at Minah.

Minah turned to me. "I thought I'd exaggerated that face in my mind," she said. "But he really does look like an angel, doesn't he?"

I introduced Minah and then the others. I left Ali until last. Seeing him brought back the taste of cigarette smoke, the false laughter of flirtation, the chilling pit opening up inside me as I answered the phone and listened to my mother's shaking voice. I couldn't even recognize the girl who had flirted with him. Who was she? Why was she taken in by his skinny jeans, his heavy-lidded eyes, his lazy grip on a cigarette? My voice faltered as I said his name, and Fox squeezed my hand and greeted Ali as politely as he had the others.

Ali didn't look at me. We'd pretty much ignored each other since Anton died. I saw Flick glance from Ali's face to mine, her expression tight.

"I'm so pleased to meet you all," said Fox. "If Ruby's friends

64

are anywhere near as wonderful as she is, you must be pretty special."

There was an awkward pause as we took our seats on a pair of milk crates. "So," I said, feeling jumpy and exposed. "What were you guys talking about?"

Flick grinned, white teeth flashing under black-red lips, and gestured to an ancient cassette deck, the kind rappers carried around on their shoulders in the eighties. "Listen," she said, and reached over to press play.

Music warbled out, muddy and twisted. The tape was so old and mangled that it was barely comprehensible, but I dimly recognized it as a croony eighties pop song that Mom used to listen to, in the days when Mom still listened to music.

"Isn't it amazing?" Flick said, closing her eyes and swaying to the dull, slow hiss of it.

Fox leaned forward, fascinated. "It's beautiful," he said, and I wondered if he'd ever heard recorded music before.

Flick nodded. "So warped," she said. "Like, you're listening to something decay and die. Every time I play it, it gets worse, more distorted. I love it."

"Who is singing?" asked Fox. "What's his name?"

"Who cares?" Flick shrugged. "That's not the point. It's the act of death, the process of atrophy. The original source material is irrelevant."

A flash of irritation passed over Fox's features. "But he was a person," he said. "A person with a name and an actuality. A person who felt something, who turned his feelings into a song. Isn't that worth caring about?"

Flick and Minah exchanged a look that spoke volumes. "Sure," said Flick. "I guess, if you're into that."

Flick definitely wasn't into that. Was I? I wasn't sure

anymore. I'd been split in two. Half of me was embarrassed by Fox's naïveté and childlike wonder. It was too much, too earnest, too open. The other half was embarrassed by my friends, their dark pretensions and obsession with death.

Minah glanced at me, eyebrows arching. "What do you think, Ruby?"

"Um," I said. "It's . . . very interesting."

"Isn't it." Minah gazed at me for a moment too long, and I could guess what she was thinking. About Fox. About cults.

Flick's lip curled, and she turned to Fox. "Did you know that Ruby's a musician? She plays piano and writes her own pieces. She doesn't like this sort of music, though. What do you call it, Ruby? Tooth-rotting schmaltz, I think is how you described it. Shallow. Empty. Worthless."

Fox looked at me, confused. I wasn't sure how to respond.

"I remember Ruby once saying that she'd rather stick forks in both her eyes than listen to a love song," Flick continued, watching Fox like a predator stalking her prey. "I remember she once said that there was no such thing as love. Just something invented by greeting-card companies to civilize a primitive surge of hormonal activity."

I glared at Flick. But what could I say? I couldn't deny it — I *had* said those things. And if I told her I'd changed my mind about love . . . she'd eat me alive.

Flick leaned back, satisfied for now.

Ali tapped cigarette ash into an empty beer can, and Fox watched curiously.

"What does it feel like?" Fox asked.

Ali's face wrinkled in contempt, as though Fox had said something unbelievably stupid. "What?"

"Smoking. What does it feel like?"

Ali shrugged and offered Fox the cigarette. "Try it."

Fox laughed. "Oh no," he said. "I can't do that. I'd probably die."

He was smiling, but I knew he was totally serious. Fox didn't exaggerate. Ali took another deep inhale. Fox shook his head, bemused and fascinated.

"So, Fox," said Flick, ready for more blood. "What's your deal?"

"My deal?"

"Yeah. You're in a cult, right? A bunch of kale-eating hippies? Do you dance naked under the moon? Commit ritual sacrifices? Worship alien lizard-gods?"

Fox chuckled. "You're funny, Flick. I see why Ruby likes you. To answer your questions, I've never done any of those things — except eat kale, I suppose. Although dancing naked under the moon might be quite an experience."

Ali snorted and stubbed out his cigarette. Flick's eyes flashed with triumph, and I realized that she liked him. She'd always liked him. Her barbs and jibes at me, when I'd been flirting with Ali, and Ali had flirted back. With a wave of sadness, I realized that even if Anton hadn't died, our little friend group would have imploded anyway. I hadn't seen it before, but now . . . now everything was clear.

I didn't belong with these people. Not anymore.

Ali lit another cigarette and narrowed his eyes at Fox. "So, dude," he said. "You and Ruby . . . what's up with that?"

Fox met Ali's gaze with a cool expression. For a moment they just stared at each other, and it felt like something primal was happening. Some unspoken battle.

"Ruby is amazing," Fox said at last, his voice calm. "I've never met anyone like her. She's very wise."

"Wise?"

"Yes. She's full of knowledge. And kindness. And love."

Minah had pulled out her phone and was pretending not to listen, her face a mask of disapproval.

"Have you filled her up with your love, then?" said Ali.

Flick giggled nastily.

Fox's coolness didn't waver. "I'm trying to."

"Fill her right up?" said Ali. "Right up to the brim? Until she's *overflowing* with your . . . love?"

Harrison choked back laughter. Ali had a cruel, sarcastic look on his face. I knew I should speak up. Defend Fox. Protect him. Take him away from my vulture friends. But I was frozen. The sun had disappeared behind looming clouds, and here in the Wasteland it didn't feel as if spring would ever come. Here, it was always winter. Always cold. Always dark. I felt the black tide rise around me, thick and choking.

Fox pursed his lips, and I realized that he understood Ali's crude subtext. He almost looked like he felt sorry for Ali.

"Isn't that what we're all trying to do?" he asked. "Fill each other up with love? What's the point of feeling love if we can't share it with others?"

I didn't think I could be strong like Fox. I couldn't be brave and vulnerable and try to see the good in everyone. That wasn't who I was.

"So, Fox," said Ali, leaning forward. "How many people would you say you've filled up with your love?"

"Ali, cut it out," said Minah. "He's not worth it."

Minah. Thank goodness for Minah. Minah, who was braver and stronger than me.

Fox turned to her, the furrows on his brow deeper than ever. "Minah, everyone is worth it. Every human being on this planet is worth *everything*. Worth whole oceans. Worth galaxies."

Minah rolled her eyes, then looked back at her phone. "Sure, whatever."

Fox tilted his head to one side. "Don't you think you're worth it, Minah?" he asked gently. "Don't you think you're worth a whole galaxy of stars?"

Minah's detached expression faltered for a moment. She slipped her phone into the back pocket of her jeans, one eyebrow raised. "You know, Fox, you're very pretty. I'll give you that. But you sure do talk a lot of bullshit."

I expected him to flinch, but Fox just gazed at her thoughtfully. "Sometimes I think I'd like to be normal," he said. "To go to school. To have a birthday. To live in a normal house with a normal family. But then I meet people like you, and I realize that Daddy is right. You have everything right at your fingertips. And you're wasting it all. You're not even really alive."

"*Daddy?*" Flick's eyebrows disappeared beneath her bangs.

Fox ignored her and turned to me. "Let's get out of here," he said.

I stumbled to my feet.

"Nice meeting you, Fox," Flick called after us, her voice dripping with scorn. "Come back soon."

"Are you OK?" I asked as we walked away.

Fox looked at me, pity in his eyes. "How do you do it?" he said, shaking his head slightly.

"Do what?"

"Be like that. Every day."

"Be like what?"

"Like them. Shutting your heart away and letting bitterness and emptiness rule. Pretending that decay is to be celebrated and ignoring everything that really matters. Don't you feel yourself disintegrating when you're around them? Feel as if you're getting sucked into their swamp of narcissism and hatred?"

My skin prickled defensively, but Fox was right. They *were* shallow and bitter. *I* was shallow and bitter.

Fox took my hand. "You're worth it too, you know," he said quietly. "Worth a million galaxies."

I wasn't.

"Don't you feel it? Like there's more to be? Like you're on the edge of something astonishing? Something so vast and beautiful that every cell in your body is aching to be a part of it?"

I'd felt that way before Anton. Not anymore. I plunged into blackness, wrapping myself up in it, but I couldn't block Fox out. His words penetrated the dark tide like beams of golden light. I could feel his living warmth against my palm.

"I've seen the other side, Ruby. I know what's out there. It's . . . it's everything. It's joy. It's peace. Don't you want to feel peace?"

Peace.

"Ruby." Every time Fox said my name, a little piece of the darkness evaporated, rising like wisps and whisking away into nothingness. I wanted to believe him. I wanted to be healed. I wanted to be healthy and pure and full of peace and joy and wonder.

But I couldn't.

"Ruby."

Could I?

Fox leaned forward and brushed his lips against mine, and I was undone.

6

"I have to go back to the Institute," Fox told me as we wandered through the park the next morning.

My stomach felt suddenly hollow. Was it because he'd met my friends? Had he realized the kind of person I really was? That he'd been wrong about me? I felt sick with a sudden wave of self-loathing.

"Come with me," he said.

I stared at him.

"Come with me to the Institute. I just found you, Ruby. I don't want to lose you already. I . . . ." He frowned, his eyes intense. "I don't know what this is, between you and me. But I know that it's important. You feel it, don't you?"

I did feel it. I felt it so much I thought I would break apart. "Sure," I said at last. "I'll come visit you. Is it far?"

Fox looked away, his frown deepening. "It doesn't work that way," he said quietly. "The Institute is . . . things are different there. You can't visit. You have to commit."

"You want me to *move* there?"

He nodded. I could see tears in his eyes.

"Fox, I can't. I can't *run away*. My mom . . . she needs me. She has no one else."

Auntie Cath didn't count. She wasn't going to stay forever, and when she left it'd just be me and Mom again. Alone in our cold, empty house.

"I need you too," said Fox. "And you need me. I can't let you sink down into the darkness again."

I swallowed, my grip already faltering. The black tide was chokingly close. I didn't want to go back there. But I couldn't leave.

"So stay," I said. "Don't go back. Stay with me."

"I'm not allowed."

"Says who?" I demanded. "Your father? You can't let him tell you what to do forever. Just walk away. We could . . ." I trailed off. What was I suggesting? That Fox and I live together? I took his hand. "Don't you want to see the world?" I asked gently.

I could see longing on Fox's face, but it was quickly replaced with something else. It looked like fear.

"I can't," he said. "I have to go back. The monkeys need me."

Monkeys? "Where is it?" I asked. "How far?"

"I don't know. We go in a van, but only Lib and Stan know the way."

"And there are others who live there . . . like you?"

Fox nodded. "There are twenty-two members of the Institute," he said. "Eight men and fourteen women. Plus some monkeys."

Fox kept mentioning monkeys. Was it possible the Institute was some kind of research center?

"Do you want to go back?" I asked.

"Of course I do," said Fox, but I didn't believe him.

For a moment I imagined going with him. Really belonging somewhere, not just visiting. Being with Fox every day. After all, if I didn't like it I could always leave, and maybe after a little while I could convince Fox to leave with me.

The blackness reached for me, suffocating, familiar. "I can't," I said. "I just can't."

Fox's face crumpled. I couldn't stand to see him looking so sad. If Fox was sad, nobody else in the world could feel happiness. The sun wouldn't shine, and the birds would refuse to sing.

"Then this is goodbye."

My chest filled with despair. "Already?"

A tear rolled down Fox's cheek. "I don't want to leave you."

"Then don't."

"I don't have a choice."

He kissed me on the cheek and reached out to cup my chin in his hands. I drank him in — his cascade of sandy hair that fell into stormy eyes. His pale skin and rosy lips. I wasn't sure if I could live without him.

And then he was gone.

★ ★ ★

I didn't know where to go. To school? I hadn't been for almost two weeks. I'd been deleting Helena's voicemail messages from Mom's phone. I knew I got a certain amount of leeway on attendance due to being a broken shell of a human, but two weeks was stretching it. There would be questions and meetings and consequences, and I couldn't face that. I couldn't go home to Mom's ashen emptiness and Auntie Cath's fake cheer and false nails. I couldn't go to the Red House, because Fox was leaving.

I couldn't go to the Wasteland, because I hated my friends.

So I stayed in the park. I wandered around the perimeter. I stood by the pond and looked for the ducks, but they were nowhere to be seen. Everything was chilled and gray, with low, threatening clouds releasing the occasional drizzle of rain. My fingers went numb. I kept walking, around and around. Joggers passed me without a second glance. A homeless man dug through a trash can, and I envied his fingerless gloves and beanie. A crow perched on a park bench, watching me with a beady black eye.

I walked and walked and tried not to think about what would happen tomorrow, and the next day. The dark tide rose around me once more, and I welcomed its suffocating blankness.

★ ★ ★

Minah texted after she finished school, asking if we could talk. She met me by the duck pond, her face dark with concern, her mouth twisted as though she was struggling to get the words out.

"I get it, OK?" she said. "The guy is super-hot. But he's . . . he's not all there. He's like a little kid."

Fox wasn't like a little kid. He was innocent, yes. Undamaged by cynicism and bitterness. But he was also wise. He understood more about the world than I ever would. He understood people. He understood *me*. And the physical intensity when we were together . . . Fox was *definitely* not a little kid.

"You don't know him."

"I don't have to know him," said Minah. "I know *you*. And this isn't you."

"Maybe it is me," I said. "Maybe this is who I've been all along, but I needed Fox to show me."

Minah shook her head. "What is it about these people? Why are they so great?"

I thought about it. About the Red House. The long dinners full of debate and laughter. The closeness. The trust. The honesty. The clear-headedness I had experienced over the past few weeks. The loss of it was sharp, like a knife slicing through my lungs, filling them with cold, suffocating fluid.

"I don't know," I said at last. "They helped me to see things differently. Myself. My life. For a moment I felt like maybe there was a possibility for happiness after all."

Minah raised her eyebrows. "Happiness?"

I shrugged. "After what happened . . . I didn't think it was ever going to be an option."

And maybe now it wasn't.

Minah bit her bottom lip and looked away for a moment, as if deciding whether or not to say something. Then she turned back to me, her brow wrinkled in frustration.

"I don't understand you at all, Ruby. You called yourself an artist. We used to talk for hours about where creativity comes from. About humans' extraordinary ability to channel grief and anger and oppression and turn it into something *more*, something outside of themselves. And then it happens to you — you experience tragedy, the big death and everything. And you just opt out. You don't face your grief. You don't turn it into something beautiful. You don't put it on a canvas or shape it in clay or turn it into a song. You become a robot. You don't *feel* anything. You pretend everything's OK, and we pretend along with you because . . . I don't know why. Because we're kind of scared of you. And then you meet some granola-munching hippies and all of a sudden you're signing up for their twelve-step bullshit?"

I stared at her. "What are you trying to say?"

"I think you're running away."

"And why shouldn't I? What is there left to stick around for? My brother is dead. My dad is in jail. My mom is a ghost. What reason is there not to run away?"

I saw Minah flinch. She knew I wasn't sticking around for her. "Problems don't go away because you want them to," she said. "You have to face them. Turn them into words and art and music. Work through it."

I blinked. "You think my brother's death was an *opportunity*. You think I should be grateful that he died, because now I get to be a real live tortured artist."

"That isn't what I meant."

I stared at the pond, feeling fat drops splash on my cheeks, not sure if they were tears or rain. It was getting late, and the light was leeching away from everything. I turned to Minah.

"I think it is, actually. You think because you can make a sculpture out of dead animals, it means you understand death. Well, you don't. You don't understand anything. You talk all the time about art and pain and creativity, but you don't feel anything either. You think emotions are for the weak. You'd rather turn rotten fruit into art than accept the fact that *you're* rotten on the inside. You're just as blank and empty as I am. The only difference is, I'm trying to change."

Minah's jaw trembled. "Whatever," she said between gritted teeth. "Throw your life away. Shave your head and call yourself Daffodil Moonblood. If you think that's your path to freedom, who am I to stand in your way?"

She stood up and walked away toward the street. She didn't look back.

★ ★ ★

Auntie Cath ordered pizza that night and opened a bottle of wine to celebrate how well we were all doing. The house stank of cheese and garlic — a smell that had once been appealing to me, but now made my stomach turn. Auntie Cath hadn't even ordered one with any vegetables. It was all meat and cheese and flour, melded together into an oozing hideous mess.

I got myself a carrot and a handful of almonds from the kitchen.

"You should have seen your mom today at the hairdresser, Ruby," said Auntie Cath. She licked grease from her fingers, and I looked away, repulsed. "She was amazing. Calm and poised and confident."

I glanced at Mom, who was nibbling her pizza slice. She *did* look different, and it wasn't just her newly cut and colored hair. Her cheeks were pink again, and although she still didn't talk much, she followed the conversation with her eyes and responded to direct questions with soft, short statements.

"You know what would make you feel better?" said Auntie Cath to Mom, pouring more wine into her glass. "Acrylics. You should come with me tomorrow so we can get our nails done. I've found a great girl down at the mall. She does French manicures and Vinylux. It'll be a real pick-me-up for you. Just what you need."

I shuddered, thinking of how my eyes watered whenever I walked past a nail salon. How could anyone surround themselves with chemicals like that?

"You should come too, Rubes," said Auntie Cath.

I stretched my lips into a smile. "I think I'm busy."

"Plans with your friends?"

I pictured Minah and the others sitting on their hoard of junk at the Wasteland, and an aching bitterness rose inside me. Was that all I had left? I thought about the Red House. What were they doing right now? Probably sitting around the communal table, eating real food and talking about real things. There would be warmth and laughter. I imagined Welling and Stan getting into a debate about states of being. Fox would be there too, smiling and listening and adding his own insightful thoughts to the conversation. Or had he left already? The ache intensified.

Fox. Would I really not be able to see him anymore? Maybe he'd come back to the Red House to visit occasionally.

But I knew that even if this was true, "occasionally" wasn't enough for me. I *needed* Fox. I needed him like air and water. He was the only thing stopping me from falling back into darkness.

Auntie Cath reached for another slice of pizza. Her chin glistened with grease and her flamingo-pink fingernails were clogged with tomato sauce. She cackled at something on the television.

I glanced at Mom. She ate mechanically, nodded in response to Auntie Cath, and answered her questions. But even though she seemed to be getting better, I could see she wasn't really there. She was just pretending.

I remembered what Fox had said. *You have to want it.* Mom didn't want to get better. There was nothing I could do or say to drag her out of her empty, blank little world, and I was scared that if I stayed any longer, she'd drag me down into it as well.

Auntie Cath gave me a hug before she went to bed, enveloping me in her powdery smell. Her arms felt soft and flabby around me, and I flinched. I didn't ever want to be like her.

"You know, Ruby," said Auntie Cath, trying to look meaningfully into my eyes, "you are the author of your own story. Your life is a book, and you are the one who gets to decide when to turn the page."

It was her usual garbage, quoted directly from whatever self-help book she was currently reading. But her words didn't slide past my ears and evaporate the way they normally did. She was right. I was the one who got to decide how my story was going to go.

"This pain you're feeling — it will pass. You're growing up so quickly. Soon you'll be going off to college. You'll meet someone. You'll fall in love and have children of your own. A career. A beautiful life. And this will be a distant memory."

I could see it. I could see myself on that path. College. My own family. Supermarkets and nail salons and new cars and summer vacations. I'd never forget Anton. And I'd never forget Fox. Never forget the possibilities he showed me, the glimpse of a bigger world. And I knew in that instant that if I didn't go with him, I would regret it every single day, for the rest of my inconsequential little life.

"I know what you need," said Auntie Cath.

So did I.

"You need chocolate. Tomorrow I'll take you to this place I found where the hot chocolate is so thick you can stand your spoon up in it."

I grimaced at her. I definitely wouldn't be going anywhere with Auntie Cath tomorrow, let alone to a place where I could coat my insides with sugar and fat and chemicals.

I went to my room and waited, lying fully clothed on my bed, until I was sure everyone was asleep. Then I left a carefully composed note on the coffee table and slipped out the front door into the night.

7

Lib opened the door in a white cotton nightgown, gazing at my backpack without comment.

"I'm so sorry to wake you," I said. "Um. Is Fox around?"

Lib hesitated, and for a moment I feared she was going to turn me away. Then she stood back and opened the door wide. "You'd better come in."

She ushered me into the kitchen and poured me a glass of water.

"I want to go to the Institute," I told her. "I — I can't stay at home anymore."

"Fox left this afternoon," Lib said. "With Welling and Stan."

"Am I too late?"

"Val, Maggie, and I are leaving tomorrow. I can take you with us, if that's what you want."

I nodded.

"Are you sure?" Lib's expression was troubled, as if she were searching for something in me that she wasn't sure she wanted to find.

"I'm sure."

She led me up to Fox's room, telling me we'd be leaving first thing in the morning. I put my backpack on the floor and crawled into the bed, kicking off my shoes. The sheets still smelled of him. I buried my head in the pillow and breathed deeply, imagining Fox lying right here beside me, his fingers curling into mine, my head resting on his shoulder. We could have that now. Once I got to the Institute, Fox and I could be together.

★ ★ ★

Lib shook me awake just after seven, and I followed her downstairs into the kitchen, where I found Val and Maggie sitting at the counter eating bowls of what looked like quinoa. Val didn't look up. Maggie grinned at me and saluted me with her spoon.

"I hear you're going to be a sublimate," she said. "Congratulations."

I slid onto a stool next to hers. "Thanks. What's a sublimate?"

"Like a new recruit. A new team member."

"Are you hungry, Ruby?" Lib asked.

I shook my head. My stomach was fizzing with nerves, and I wasn't sure I could keep anything down. Lib nodded and bustled out of the kitchen, leaving me alone with Val and Maggie.

"What's it like?" I asked Maggie. "The Institute?"

Maggie chewed thoughtfully on her quinoa. "It's . . . different," she said at last. "It's not like here. It can be a bit of a shock to the system. I know it wasn't what I'd been expecting."

"When did you first go there?"

"About four months ago. I'd been here at the Red House for

maybe a month before that. Then Lib said she thought I was ready to meet everyone, and she took me to the Institute as a sublimate. I . . . I didn't like it at first, to be honest. But you get used to it."

She swallowed her last mouthful of quinoa and stood up to wash her bowl in the sink. When her back was turned, Val raised his head and looked directly at me. It was the first time he'd made eye contact with me. He shook his head slowly and deliberately.

It felt like a warning.

Maggie turned away from the sink, and Val's gaze sank back down to his quinoa.

"Sometimes I have doubts," Maggie said. "But . . . I guess at the end of the day, I have more doubts about the world out here than I do about the world in there. You know? So there has to be some truth in it all."

I stared at Val for a moment, waiting to see if he'd do anything else. My phone buzzed in my pocket, and I pulled it out. There was a text from Auntie Cath. I switched the phone off without reading the message, put it back in my pocket, and turned to Maggie. "Truth in what?"

Maggie smiled. "You'll understand when you meet him."

"Him?"

The smile grew wider. "Zosimon."

★ ★ ★

A white van was parked in front of the Red House.

Maggie, Val, and I climbed in while Lib locked up the house.

Val's hands were cupped, holding the cicada husks he'd collected.

"You don't have a bag," I said to Maggie.

"Nothing to put in it," she said with a shrug.

"Nothing? What about underwear and books and a phone? Or did you leave that stuff behind when you came here?"

"I don't really have any stuff," Maggie said. "None of us do."

I wrapped my arms around my backpack, balanced on my knees. I hadn't packed much — a change of clothes and some extra underwear and socks. A couple of books that I thought Fox would enjoy. My phone charger. A small toiletries bag with a toothbrush, deodorant, a box of tampons, and a strip of condoms. I couldn't imagine not having anything at all.

Maggie glanced out the van's window to the Red House. Lib was still inside, checking the locks on the windows. With a furtive glance down the street as well, Maggie leaned forward and pulled up the hem of her shirt, revealing a secret pocket sewn into the seam. Inside the pocket was a gold necklace with a little jade pendant — a milky green disk engraved with whorls and waves.

"It was my grandmother's." Maggie tucked the pendant away and straightened her shirt. "I didn't want to give it up when I arrived. I . . . I wanted to have something that was just mine, you know? Something that nobody could take away from me."

I nodded. I hadn't brought anything sentimental with me because I didn't have anything. The reason I was going to the Institute was because the one thing I wanted was already there.

I heard the front door to the Red House close and turned to see Lib making her way down the front path toward us.

"Don't tell anyone, OK?" said Maggie urgently. "We're not supposed to have jewelry or anything."

"Of course," I said. "I won't say a word."

Lib hauled open the van's sliding door and glanced in at us. "Ready?"

We nodded.

"I'm sorry," said Lib, holding up three strips of dark cloth. "But the Institute's location is top secret. I'll have to blindfold you."

I almost laughed at her. Blindfold? What was this, a James Bond movie? I glanced at Maggie and Val, but they had both already taken strips and were tying them over their eyes as if this were a totally normal occurrence. So I shrugged and leaned my head forward so that Lib could blindfold me.

"Here we go," I heard Maggie say, as the van sputtered into life and I felt it accelerate. "Down the rabbit-hole."

The van rumbled along, turning corners so often that after a while I began to feel carsick. But it was soothing, the darkness, the vibration of the engine, the musty smell of old vinyl. We were stop-starting regularly, so we couldn't be going far — either that or Lib was avoiding the freeway. I didn't hear much other traffic noise, so I also guessed she was taking the back streets. It was all so clandestine — these guys really took themselves seriously.

Maggie was silent beside me, as were Val and Lib. After a while I slipped into a half-doze, and time spooled out around me so I couldn't tell how long I'd been in the van. My stomach growled, and I regretted skipping breakfast. On the other hand, breakfast probably wouldn't have helped the woozy motion sickness.

Suddenly the van slowed, and I started out of my nauseous reverie.

There was the sound of squealing metal — a gate opening? The van rumbled and pulled forward slowly. The metal squealed again, and the van stopped.

"We're here," said Lib.

Maggie elbowed me in the ribs. "You're going to hear some crazy stuff over the next few days," she said, her voice low. "Some of it is pretty extreme. Just . . . go with it. It's easier than making a fuss. I find it helps to look at it all as a kind of metaphor for life, you know? It's like the Bible. All the woo-woo is there to help us to understand some of those ideas."

"Right," I said, feeling suddenly nervous.

"Don't worry," said Maggie. "Nobody's going to force you to do anything you don't want to. You don't have to believe in any of it. You don't have to stay if you don't want to. You are totally in control. These are good people. They'll look after you."

My eyes were flooded with brightness as someone pulled off the blindfold. I squinted and blinked, and the whiteness slowly faded to something more manageable.

It wasn't what I'd expected.

I'd thought we'd be somewhere . . . remote. In the middle of nowhere. A secret country home. The kind of commune I'd seen on TV, with a farmhouse and barns and chickens and orchards heavy with fruit.

But as far as I could tell we were still in the suburbs. The van was parked in a concrete parking lot, surrounded by high gray walls. Most of the parking lot had been dug up to make a large vegetable plot, and a few people were on their hands and knees, digging and planting. They looked up as Lib cut the engine and yanked on the emergency brake.

"Welcome to the Institute of the Boundless Sublime," she said.

I wasn't sure if it was the name, or the gray chill of the day, but a shiver ran over me.

I climbed down from the van and stood on the hard-packed earth, studded with broken concrete rubble. Looking up, I could see long strings of power lines, and the tops of other, similar warehouses on the other side of the wall. Traffic rumbled outside. Wherever we were, it wasn't remote.

A large dark warehouse rose to the left of the vegetable plot, a monstrosity of corrugated iron and crisscrossed steel girders. To the right were three squat brick buildings painted a bleak gunmetal gray. Small, high, barred windows of whitish opaque glass stared out from the gray bricks like milky eyes. Several were broken, and the whole place looked as though it had been abandoned for many years. It seemed a million miles from the cozy simplicity of the Red House, or the rustic nature-loving communes of my imagination. But at least the garden was impressive — neat rows of cabbages and broccoli and chard. Young tomato plants were being staked, and broad beans sprouted fat pods and crimson flowers. Vertical herb gardens lined the thick concrete walls, sprouting coriander, parsley, and other things I didn't recognize.

"I've really gotta pee," Maggie declared, and dashed off toward one of the buildings. Val lumbered off after her, his hands still cupping the cicada husks.

Lib explained that it had once been a food distribution warehouse, before they had moved in.

"Why live in a warehouse?" I asked, thinking of the comfortable elegance of the Red House.

Lib shrugged. "We don't ask those kinds of questions."

"How long has it — the Institute of the . . . what did you call it?"

"The Institute of the Boundless Sublime."

"How long has it been here?" I asked.

"Long enough."

Lib clearly wasn't interested in answering my questions. I

remembered how open and encouraging she had been when I'd first gone to the Red House. What had changed? She seemed different here, after only a few moments. More subdued and less friendly. Perhaps she was tired from the drive.

I persisted. "How often do new people join?"

"We get many visitors at the Red House," she said. "Only a select few are invited here to the Institute."

"And how many stay, once they come?"

"It depends," Lib said. "Some people become a part of our family. Others decide the Institute isn't for them. Nobody is forced to stay, or forced to leave." She pointed at the building closest to the vegetable plot. "A Block is our communal area — where the kitchen is, as well as the mess hall. The Inner Sanctum is in there too. B Block is living quarters. Everyone has their own room. We encourage solitude at night. The mind needs time to recharge, with no distractions from other bodies."

Thank goodness. I'd been terrified of having to sleep in a dorm room with a bunch of strangers. And it meant that Minah had obviously been wrong about there being weird sex stuff going on.

"What about the other building?" I asked, pointing.

The third building was tucked away in a corner of the property, behind a second parking lot that was still completely paved over. A tangle of weedy plants choked the edges of it, as well as broken bricks and bits of concrete and office furniture that had been dumped there. Little sunlight reached that part of the complex, so the building looked mildewed and somehow sinister.

Lib's eyes flickered over to the dark building, and a frown creased her forehead. "C Block," she said shortly. "We pack and store the water bottles in there. Also the laboratory is there, but it's out of bounds, as is the Monkey House at the rear of the building."

I opened my mouth to ask what on Earth a Monkey House was, but Lib continued. "Over there is the courtyard where we gather every morning before breakfast. After dinner we meet in the warehouse for Family Time."

I looked at the people working in the garden. Nobody had come over to greet us. I didn't recognize any of them. There was no sign of Fox. Gray rain started to drizzle from the sky. I shivered. This didn't feel right.

A door in one of the buildings opened, and Stan came bouncing over to us.

"Ruby!" he said, enfolding me in a big hug. "Kiddo, it is so great to see you here. I can't wait to finish the discussion we were having the other day about moral relativism."

I felt myself relax a little. The Institute looked grim, but who cared what it looked like? It was the people inside I'd come to see.

Stan reached out and took my backpack. "You won't be needing this."

"But all my stuff is in there," I said.

"It's just stuff," Stan said, his white hair swinging as he shrugged. "It ties you to the world. Holds you down. To be truly free, you gotta let it all go."

"What will I wear?"

"We'll provide you with everything you need," said Lib. "Don't worry, if you decide to leave, all your belongings will be returned to you. Do you have a cell phone?"

I felt my shoulders tense and considered lying. "Yes."

Stan held out his hand. "Give it up," he said. "Those things give you cancer."

"But my mom . . ."

"Kiddo," said Stan. "Let it go. Trust in the process. Be open to all the possibilities of life. Don't let the rest of the world make your choices for you."

I pulled my phone from my pocket and hesitated. "I can get it back if I need it? If there's an emergency?"

"Of course," said Lib. "Whenever you want. All you have to do is ask."

I handed it to Stan, who held it at arm's length as if it were emitting some kind of deathly radiation. I took a deep breath. I could get it back if I needed it. I'd wait until tomorrow morning and then ask for it back. So I could check that Mom was OK.

Stan slid the phone into the front pocket of my backpack, and his face split open in a wide grin. "That was really hard, huh?" he asked, his whole body bouncing in an understanding nod. "Well done."

★ ★ ★

Lib showed me my room. Like the others, it was one of the old offices, small and cramped with only the dim light from a single high window to see by. It was simple, like Fox's room back at the Red House, with a single bed and a small bedside table.

I mustered up my courage to ask the question that had been on my lips since we'd arrived. "Can I see Fox?"

Lib shook her head. "Sorry. The rules of the Institute state that sublimates must be solitary until you've been elutriated."

"Elutriated?"

"It's a decontamination process," Lib explained. "You've been in contact with too many outside toxins."

I pictured scenes from a film I'd seen, where naked people were sprayed down with high-pressure hoses.

"We live cleanly," said Lib. "I know that everything looks a bit gray and dull when you first arrive, but soon you'll realize how pure everything is here. You'll see the joy in it. The beauty. But in order to keep things pure, we have to make sure no outside toxins get in. The elutriation process isn't invasive or unpleasant. You'll fast in solitude for the rest of today and tonight, here in your room. Then tomorrow, before breakfast, you will receive an elutriation draft."

"I have to drink something?" I prickled with suspicion, remembering what Minah had said about juice and arsenic.

Lib nodded. "It's water with a little added sulfur. It's what we all drink here. Don't worry, it's perfectly healthy."

"OK." I felt small and dirty, like a child embarrassed after wetting my pants.

Lib seemed to notice, because her expression softened momentarily. "It's going to be fine," she said. "Don't worry if it seems a bit weird at first. Remember that you chose to come here. And you made the right choice. Trust us."

I nodded. I would. I'd trust them. For now.

Lib closed the door behind her as she left, and I stayed sitting on the bed, waiting. I had no idea what time it was, but it couldn't have been later than midday. I felt hollow and empty. I hadn't eaten since my handful of almonds and carrot sticks the night before. I hadn't had any water either. That explained the dizziness.

Automatically, my hand went to my jeans pocket to pull out my phone, but it wasn't there. I felt a sudden surge of panic, as if I'd been set adrift on the ocean with no flares, no drinking water, no navigational tools. What if there was an emergency at home? What if something happened to Mom?

I couldn't text Minah. I couldn't check my email. I hadn't

used social media for months, but I was suddenly lost without it.

More than anything, I wasn't sure what I was going to *do*.

Hours stretched before me. No food. No water. No people. No phone. I didn't even have a book to read.

I waited.

I picked at my nails.

I counted the seconds as they passed. I counted in 3/4, then 4/4, then 6/8, then 5/4.

I hummed the *cavatina* from Beethoven's 130.

I explored every inch of my tiny office room. I took the blankets off the bed and looked under the mattress. Everything was clean, sparse, spartan. There was a paler square on the gray wall over the bed where a picture frame had once hung. A crack running across the ceiling. A brown stain on the faded carpet near the door.

I stared up at the tiny high window. The glass was frosted with mesh woven through it, so I couldn't see anything but the slowly changing light as the day wore on.

Was it a test? Was I supposed to do something? Find something? Solve a puzzle? Discover some secret? Was I supposed to have an epiphany?

I heard a light step in the corridor, and my door swung open to reveal a little girl with a shaved head, wearing a plain white tunic that fell to her knees. She held a bundle of clothes.

"Hi," I said. Was her head shaved because of an outbreak of lice? Or was she sick?

"Hello," she said, her tone oddly formal. "These are for you."

She held out the clothes, and I took them. I guessed she was about eight years old.

"Thank you," I said. "I'm Ruby. What's your name?"

The girl looked puzzled.

"You can tell me," I said. "It's OK."

"I'm a monkey," she said.

"You're a monkey? Or your name is Monkey?"

The girl shrugged and nodded. Perhaps it was a nickname. Although she didn't seem very cheeky or monkey-like to me.

"Do you live here, Monkey?" I asked. "With your parents?"

"I'm not supposed to talk to you," the girl said, her expression grave. "You're still a toxicant. You must change into clean clothes before you can become a sublimate."

She backed out of the door, her head held high and stiff, pulling the door closed as she did so.

The clothes were the same as all the other Institute members wore — a light-colored linen shirt and dark gray pants. There was also a cotton nightgown, along with a white crop top, white underwear, some socks, and a pair of sensible shoes. I wondered how they knew what size I was.

Either way, I was still wearing the jeans and T-shirt I'd left home in last night, and they were starting to smell, so I stripped and changed into the clean clothes, wishing I could take a shower as well. I folded my old things carefully on the end of my bed and waited.

And waited.

Had the girl locked the door behind her, or had she left it open?

Did the door even have a lock?

I got up and tried the handle. No lock.

I sat back down on the bed and stared at the door.

Maybe it *was* a test. Maybe I was supposed to go out. Maybe this was some kind of hazing ritual, a joke.

I stood up again and opened the door, poking my head out into the hallway. There was nobody in sight.

"Hello?" I called, my voice wavering in the silence.

Footsteps approached, and Lib turned into the hall. "Ruby?" she asked, frowning a little when she saw me standing in the doorway. "Is everything OK?"

It wasn't a test. I really was supposed to stay in my room.

I felt weirdly guilty and upset to have let Lib down.

"Um," I said. "I — I need to go to the bathroom."

Lib nodded briskly. "Follow me."

She showed me to a small office-style bathroom, complete with chipped sinks and empty soap dispensers, and waited outside a cubicle while I peed. There were bare patches on the walls above the sinks where mirrors had once been, and the locks on the cubicle doors had been removed. Coming out to wash my hands, I longed to cup them under the tap and have a big drink of water. But Lib hadn't said I could drink anything. She'd told me I'd have to fast. And I wanted to prove that I could. So I followed her meekly back down the hallway to my room.

It was getting dark. The light bulb in my room was broken, so the room grew murkier and murkier until I could only make out the dim outlines of things. The air grew cold and still, and I climbed under the blanket to keep warm. It smelled musty, and the single bed sagged in the middle.

Although I'd been eating much less junk since I'd begun hanging out at the Red House, I was still used to having a full stomach. I'd moved past the point of hunger hours ago, and now all I felt was a hollow, sick emptiness. But my thirst was still strong. My lungs rasped like dry corn husks. I licked my cracked lips.

I hoped Mom was OK. She had Auntie Cath to make sure she had enough to eat, and that the bills got paid. Auntie Cath would stop her from smoking and make her shower and put clothes on. I couldn't do that. Mom was better off without me. Everyone said that Anton and I looked alike — dark curls and big eyes — *like a marsupial with a perm*, Minah always said. I was living proof that he was gone — a bookmark keeping place on an empty page. Better for Mom to forget all about us — me, Anton, and Dad. Poor Dad.

It had been on the news, the accident. There had been callers on talk radio. Mom wouldn't listen to a word of it, but I couldn't help myself. I couldn't stop listening to those sharp, ugly voices telling the world that my father was a monster. That he deserved the death penalty. That he'd end up in hell. They painted him as a drunk, careless, and abusive, and Anton and I as victims of his neglect.

Dad was none of those things. He wasn't a monster. He drank a lot, yes. Too much. But he was always a happy drunk. I'd resented it nonetheless, as a kid. There was nothing more embarrassing than waking up to hear your father slurring his way through some U2 song at three in the morning. But he never got angry or sad or violent. Dad was . . . human. He worked hard so Anton and I could have a better life than him. He wanted us to go to college, get good jobs. He wanted me to join an orchestra, travel the world with ribbons of music floating behind me. He loved us. He loved Mom.

But now he was in some minimum-security facility on the edge of the city. Who knew when I'd see him again? What would happen when he got out? I couldn't imagine him coming home. I couldn't imagine waking up every morning and seeing his face. I couldn't see how he could live with us, surrounded by constant reminders of what he'd done. What we'd both done.

I heard strains of singing and laughter coming from what I assumed was the warehouse. It sounded joyful, and I wanted more than anything to be there, surrounded by the warmth and love and thoughtfulness of my friends. Stan would be there, telling some hilarious story about his hippie days. Welling would be eloquent and sophisticated. Maggie would be arguing with everyone, full of fire and opinion. Lib would preside over everything like the stern but loving matriarch she was. And Fox would be there, full of gentleness and love and serious thoughts — thoughts big enough to encompass the whole planet. Whole galaxies. I imagined myself there with them. With Fox. His hand in mine. The warmth of his body pressed against my side. His mouth curled in the smile that he only smiled to me. His eyes full of me, just as mine would be full of him.

But I wasn't there.

I was alone in the cold, damp darkness, torn between memories of what I had lost and dreams of what I had yet to find.

8

I woke confused and disorientated in the dark. A cold hand was gripping my shoulder, shaking me. For a moment I thought it was Anton, back from the dead to . . . what? To warn me?

"Ruby." It was Lib.

I sat up, struggling to shake off sleep and doubt. "Is something wrong?"

"Time to get up."

"But it's the middle of the night."

Lib whisked back the blanket and hauled me up. "It's morning. We begin our day at dawn, and he wants to see you first."

"He?" I asked. "You mean Zosimon?"

Lib pushed me toward the door. My eyes were starting to adjust to the dim early morning light.

"You'll want to wash your face and hands before you see him for the elutriation."

Maybe Lib was taking me to a shrine or meditation room.

Maybe Zosimon was a ceremonial title, like the Dalai Lama or the Pope. Lib led me down the gray corridor to the same bathroom I'd visited before. A fluorescent light plinked on overhead, and I squinted.

"Are there showers?" I asked.

Lib shook her head. "Just these bathrooms."

I shivered. "Hot water?"

"Hot water dries and damages the skin," said Lib. "Cold is better for you."

I imagined trying to bathe here in the bathroom, standing on icy tiles. This commune lifestyle was definitely not for me.

Lib handed me a threadbare towel, and stepped out into the corridor while I used the toilet. When I went to the sink to wash my hands and splash cold water on my face, I noticed there was a child in one of the other cubicles, crouched on top of the toilet seat. I blinked. Was it the same little girl I saw yesterday? She certainly had the same big eyes and shaved head, and she was wearing the same shapeless white tunic. But she looked . . . younger now. Or had I been mistaken before?

"Hello," I said, wiping my face with the towel.

The girl's eyes flickered to the door, where she knew Lib was waiting.

"Are you Monkey?" I asked, keeping my voice low.

The little girl nodded. So it was the same one. Maybe it was the light that made her look different.

"Right," I said. "We met yesterday."

The girl frowned and shook her head.

"Ruby?" Lib called from outside.

The little girl lifted a finger to her lips and gave me an impish grin.

"Coming," I said, and stepped out into the hall.

"Quickly," said Lib, leading me out and down a different hallway. "You mustn't keep him waiting."

★ ★ ★

A cardboard sign was pinned to the door. INNER SANCTUM. Lib knocked respectfully, paused for a moment, pushed the door open, and stood back to usher me in. I took a step forward, and the door clicked closed behind me.

The room was totally different to the utilitarian grayness that was all I'd seen so far. The walls and floor were painted white, and candles lined the walls. The scent of jasmine hung in the air, and the floor was scattered with large cushions. A pale wooden desk sat against the wall farthest from the door, dotted with more candles. It reminded me of the Red House — calm and serene. Just walking into the room made me relax.

On the largest cushion, in the center of the room, sat a man.

He certainly didn't look like anything special. He appeared to be in his sixties or seventies. He had gray hair with a neatly trimmed beard and large wire-framed glasses. He wore a loose white shirt and white cotton pants. Around his neck hung a silver chain with a single polished stone, red streaked with white.

"Ruby," he said, rising to his feet and shaking my hand with a smile. "I've heard much about you."

His voice was low and calm. His smile was reflected in his bright blue eyes. His hand against mine was warm and dry.

"Please sit down."

He sank gracefully onto his cushion, and I hunkered down in front of him.

"Sublimates always have many questions. Please, feel free to ask them. There are no secrets in this family."

I hesitated, suddenly shy. I glanced at his fingernails. They were perfectly smooth and shiny, the kind of nails Auntie Cath would kill for. I wondered if he maintained them himself or whether he got regular manicures.

"Let me ask you a question first, Ruby. Do you believe in Jesus Christ?"

Was this a test? "No," I said, after a moment. "Or at least, I think there was a historical person called Jesus. But I don't believe he was the son of God or could walk on water or any of that."

"Do you think that's what Christians believe? That Jesus could perform miracles?"

I thought about Minah's parents, who went to church every Sunday in their best clothes and prayed for their daughter's soul. "Some of them do. But I guess others see it as more of a metaphor. I don't really know."

"Clearly you *do* know, Ruby. You've hit the nail right on the head." Zosimon looked pleased, and I felt irrationally proud that he was impressed by me. Why? I hadn't even said anything clever.

"Was Jesus really the son of God? Was he just a carpenter's son with some big ideas? Was he a manipulative rabble-rouser? It doesn't really matter, in the end. People will believe what they need to believe. It's what they *do* with that belief that is important. Do the things you believe shut down your world? Make it smaller and darker and uglier? Or does your belief open everything up, flooding the whole universe with light and love and consciousness?"

Zosimon lifted the red stone that hung around his neck and toyed with it, running his fingers over its smooth surface. "The world is aphotic, Ruby. I know you feel it. Everything is growing dark. We stand on the edge of a precipice, and once we go over, we can never come back."

I remembered Fox telling me about his fears of contaminated sludge and hideous mutants. If this guy Zosimon had all the answers, then why was he hiding in a warehouse instead of being out there, changing the world?

"So what's the solution?" I asked. "How do we fix it?"

I waited, but Zosimon didn't answer. His eyes seemed unfocused, as if he were staring at something that I couldn't see. I wondered if he'd forgotten I was there.

Finally he took a breath and looked up at me. "You know," he said. "I heard a story once, about a young man residing in Athens around 400 BC. He was put on trial, accused of heresy. You might have heard of him. His name was Socrates."

Zosimon smiled, as if he was remembering something fondly. "Socrates was a great man. An intellectual giant. He could have ruled the world, if only he hadn't had such a hot temper. He told his jurors that they were weak, obsessed with their careers instead of their actuality — their souls. He told them that he had been singled out for greatness, that he had eclipsed the base potential of humans, and ascended to something higher. Something more pure."

"What happened? In the trial?"

"They killed him. Made him drink hemlock." Zosimon's face crinkled in sadness, and he leaned forward. "He said he'd rather die than admit he was wrong. He was arrogant, and it was his undoing. People don't like to be told they are wrong. That what they believe is false. Arrogance is weakness, and it must be overcome. This is why I won't ever tell you what to believe, Ruby. If you wish, I can share with you the things I have learned. But you are not forced to believe any of it. You are strong, I can see that. Trust in yourself. Trust your own avocation, your own judgment. Believe what you *know* to be true. Not what people tell you."

This didn't feel like brainwashing. Or, if it did, it was brainwashing in a literal sense. Cleansing. Getting rid of all the bullshit and guilt and fairy tales and magical healing amber beads. Cult leaders were supposed to be crazy. Zosimon didn't seem crazy to me.

"You're probably thinking I'm crazy."

I started, and he chuckled. "Maybe I am. I'm probably not in the best position to judge. But you know what, Ruby? I don't feel crazy. I feel like I'm really onto something. Something big."

"What is it?" I asked.

Zosimon regarded me thoughtfully. "I don't think you're ready for that avocation yet," he said, and something inside me twisted. Did he sense my doubt? Or did he just not think I was good enough? "But you will be soon. I can tell that you're special. Will you believe what I tell you?" He shrugged. "That's your choice. Nobody has any right to tell you what to believe. I have no desire to head up an army of mindless slaves, obedient to my every command. We are a family here. A family of free thinkers who share a common goal. If the things we believe aren't true for you, then they aren't true. This is entirely your choice. Your will. Your truth."

"Does it work?" I asked. "Your . . . program or whatever you call it?"

"In my experience," said Zosimon, his eyes never leaving mine for a microsecond, "my technic works one hundred percent of the time when properly observed and carried out by truly committed individuals."

I was fuzzy-headed with competing thoughts. Zosimon didn't seem to be trying to pressure me into anything. Wasn't cult indoctrination supposed to be all violent brainwashing? Fear and sexual abuse and moral absolutes?

"Can I ask about the water bottles?"

"You can ask anything you like," said Zosimon. "What would you like to know about the water bottles?"

"Is it . . ." It seemed almost stupid to ask. "Is it just water?"

Zosimon lifted one shoulder in a half-shrug. "Water," he said. "With the smallest trace of sulfur."

"Why sulfur? Is it dangerous?"

"Of course not. Sulfur is a cardinal element. It elutriates, drawing moisture and dampness from the corners of the mind, liberating a person's actuality."

Now it was starting to sound more like the amber healing beads nonsense. I felt oddly disappointed. "Why do you hand them out?" I asked.

"People get thirsty."

That was what Lib had said too. And Welling. "But that isn't really a reason," I said. "You don't include any information on the label, so you can't be doing it to raise awareness of an issue or to encourage new people to join you. So why?"

A slow, crafty smile spread over Zosimon's face. "You are a clever one, Ruby. You're right, there is another reason my children hand out free water. But I'm afraid I can't tell you what it is. Not yet. Instead, why don't you ask me the other question. The one you *really* want to know the answer to."

What other question? I frowned, confused.

Zosimon nodded knowingly. "Is this a cult? That's what you want to know, right?"

I hadn't expected this. Perhaps he was bringing it up in order to deny it. Maybe that was part of the brainwashing process?

Zosimon tipped his head to the side and considered me. "Do you know what the botanical definition of a weed is, Ruby?"

"No."

"There isn't one. A weed is simply a word we use for a plant that is unwelcome. Is the Institute of the Boundless Sublime a cult? I don't know. Personally I do not think so, for the simple reason that we do not promote religious belief. My technic is rooted in science, empirically proven over many thousands of years. However, my technic is also radical, and many people fear what they don't understand. So, like the harmless weeds, many would see us as unwelcome, unwanted. These people might call the Institute a cult. But I don't really care what those people think. I care what *you* think. That's the beauty of life inside these walls. You get to make your own avocation."

I nodded, but I hadn't gotten the reassurance I wanted.

"You're unsure," said Zosimon, his voice gentle. "That's perfectly natural. If you were one hundred percent convinced at this point, I'd be worried about you. All we ask of sublimates is that you be open to the possibility that life can be . . . something more than your previous experience."

"I didn't know I'd have to give up my phone," I said. "I thought I'd be able to contact my family."

Zosimon's face grew very serious, and he leaned forward again. "Ruby, I will *never* prohibit you from contacting your family," he said. "Family is the most important thing in the world. I only ask that, in order for my technic to work, you allow yourself to truly focus. To leave behind the things that tether you to your sadness, that weigh down your actuality and pollute your mind. Let yourself be *you*. And let us lift you up. Let us be your family too."

"But I can still contact my mother?"

"Of course. Perhaps we could arrange a scheduled time for you to call her. That way you can use your other time here to truly *be here*, with no distractions. Does that sound OK?"

I nodded hesitantly.

"We are your family now," Zosimon explained. "We're all equals. I'm not here to tell you what to do or how to think. I can help you, if you'll let me. But only if it's what you want. If at any moment you don't want to be here, you are free to leave. Do you understand?"

I nodded.

"And do you still want to be a sublimate?"

I hesitated. What harm could it do to stay for a few days? I could be with Fox. And if it got really weird, I could always leave.

"Yes," I said at last.

Zosimon's face broke into a grin. "I knew you were special the very first moment you walked in here. I can tell, you know. Ruby, you're going to be extraordinary."

I felt an odd warmth at his words. The black tide was growing stagnant. Did I still need to hide down there in the darkness? Maybe it was time to come up into the light. This man — this bizarre, enigmatic stranger — he believed in me. He thought I was special. That I could be extraordinary.

Fox thought so too. I could see it when he looked at me, drinking in the depths of my gaze. Fox was strong and powerful and good. If Fox believed in me and Zosimon believed in me . . . then maybe I could too. Maybe I could forgive myself.

"You carry a great sadness with you," said Zosimon. "It pulls you down into darkness."

The black tide. He knew. He could see it.

"Tell me."

So I did. The words spilled out of me like grains of rice being poured from a sack, and with each grain I felt lighter and more able to move. I told him about Anton and Dad and the funeral. I told him about Mom crumbling into gray ash. I told him about Auntie Cath's fingernails and the paint smears on Minah's jeans.

I told him about how Fox found me in the darkness and brought me back into the light.

But I didn't tell him everything about Fox. About how he made my shriveled cold heart pump and swell again. About how he was all I saw, all I thought of. About how the thought of him made me writhe in my bed at night, damp with longing.

"Tell me, Ruby. In your heart of hearts, what is it that you want?"

I remembered Fox asking me the same question. I wanted Anton to be alive. I wanted my dad to not be in jail. I wanted my mother to be a functioning human being. I wanted to wake up and learn that the last six months had been a dream. I wanted to see Fox. No, I wanted more than that. I wanted to crawl inside Fox and wrap myself up in him.

I shifted my position a little. "I want to know that my brother's death wasn't for nothing."

A wave of sadness passed over Zosimon's face, and he looked down at his folded hands. "Then I'm afraid I can't help you," he said. "Anton's death *was* for nothing. It was senseless and meaningless. I can't tell you that he's at peace now. I can't tell you he's in a better place. He isn't. He's just dead. There's no after. No peace. He was a beautiful, shining little life, and now he is extinguished."

I wanted to put my hands over my ears, to block Zosimon's words out. But I didn't, because I knew he was right. He wasn't offering journals or amber beads or self-help books. He wasn't asking me to channel my grief into art, or spouting nonsense about *healing* and *inner peace*. He was speaking the simple truth, and hearing it was exhilarating, like plunging headfirst into an ice-cold ocean wave.

Zosimon reached out for my hands, grasping them with a

soft, firm touch. He angled his head to catch my gaze, and I found myself unable to look away.

"Your brother died because your father has a disease," he said, his voice calm and quiet. "You did nothing wrong. Any sense of guilt that you may have is false and has been implanted in you by your parents who don't want to take any of that responsibility on themselves. You are a child. They are your parents. It was *their* responsibility to care for Anton, not yours. Your father is a toxicant, poisoned with alcohol. He is bound to it, body and mind. It binds him, just as it binds so many millions of toxicants on this planet. He is weak, and he doesn't deserve to be your daddy."

I remembered taking a drag from Ali's cigarette. "I'm weak too," I whispered.

Zosimon smiled gently and shook his head. "If you were weak, you wouldn't be here. You tower above them, Ruby. You are perfect."

I knew he was trying to win me over, but a part of me wanted to believe him.

I heard a jangling noise outside the room, like someone was walking up and down the halls ringing a bell.

Zosimon stood up and walked to the desk, where there was a metal pitcher and a glass tumbler. With ceremonial slowness, he filled the tumbler with water from the pitcher, and returned to me, holding the tumbler in both hands.

"This elutriation is a rebirth. A clean slate. It will cleanse your actuality of the past. It will burn away the aphotic darkness that binds you, and remake you, a fresh sublimate. But it is only the start of the sublimation technic. You must elutriate your mind and your body, and it is a long road. It will not be easy. But I promise you, if you trust me, you will triumph. You will be strong, powerful, boundless. You will be sublime."

He handed me the tumbler, and I lifted it to my lips. The water was warm and tasted sour and eggy. I screwed up my nose and had a momentary flash of panic, remembering stories of drugs and poison. What had I done?

"Don't worry," said Zosimon. "It's just purified rainwater with a little sulfur."

I wondered if he could read minds. I finished the water and handed the glass to Zosimon, who smiled and put it back on his desk.

"All that remains is to find your name and introduce you to your new brothers and sisters."

"But I already have a name."

Zosimon sank back into his cushions and nodded gently, his face full of sympathy. "You do have a name," he said. "A name forced upon you. A name that chokes you and shackles you to the conventions of toxicant society. Who is Ruby, anyway? Do you like her?"

I thought about it. I saw myself huddled on a milk crate in the Wasteland, coughing cigarette smoke and trying to impress Ali, while my phone vibrated in my bag. "No."

"Me neither," said Zosimon, with a dismissive shrug.

I felt stung. Hadn't he told me a few minutes ago that I was special? That I could be extraordinary?

"Ruby isn't who you *are*," said Zosimon, leaning forward, his face suddenly intense. "Deep inside. Haven't you always felt that? Like you were playing a part? Hiding your true actuality away, because you were scared of what people might think?"

I thought everyone felt like that. I thought it was part of being human.

"Set her free," said Zosimon, lowering his voice so I had to lean forward to hear him. "Let that girl out of her cage. Leave plain old Ruby behind, and let your true self shine."

I swallowed and nodded. What was the worst that could happen? I'd stay for a day or two, realize that it wasn't for me, and go home. But wasn't there a chance that Zosimon was right? If I really had been hiding my true self — my extraordinary self — away . . . didn't I want to get to know her? That extraordinary girl?

"Ruby?" Zosimon was watching me carefully.

I squared my shoulders. "There is no Ruby," I told him. "Not anymore."

He smiled and rocked back and forth in a full-body nod. "Come outside," he said. "It's Daddy's Hour."

The concrete courtyard was washed blue in early morning light. Everything still felt damp and silent, although beyond the walls of the Institute I could hear the rumble of traffic and the squealing of garage doors opening and machinery creaking into life. There were twenty or so people waiting for us, sitting cross-legged on the cold, hard ground. They had their eyes closed as if they were meditating. I saw a fall of sandy hair and, with a thrill, realized it was Fox. Zosimon nudged me forward and indicated that I should sit at the front, between Stan and a woman I didn't know. I hesitated, wanting to join Fox, but Zosimon was still gesturing to the ground in front of him, so I sank down, wincing as I felt the achingly cold concrete through my thin linen pants. Stan lifted his head, peeped at me, and gave me a friendly nudge. It was weird to see him so still — at the Red House he had always been in motion, bouncing up and down on the soles of his feet.

At the front of the group was a raised platform — once a large garden planter, now covered over with wooden boards and decorated with red and purple cushions. Zosimon stepped onto the platform and settled down, also cross-legged, on one of the cushions. I shifted uncomfortably, the chill seeping into my bones.

Zosimon took a deep breath, and, without opening their eyes, everyone started to sway back and forth. Left to right. I closed my eyes and swayed too, opening them a crack every now and then to check that I was still doing the right thing.

I felt my breathing slow, and after a while I didn't notice how cold and hard the ground was or the sick aching hunger in my belly or the dryness in my mouth. I just breathed and swayed and felt oddly calmed.

After a few minutes of this, Zosimon began to speak, his words washing over us like warm waves lapping at a sandy shore.

"You are a higher being.
You are not bound by your mortality.
You can meditate for as long as you choose.
You feel no pain or irritation.
You are immune to bacteria.
You are unaffected by curses and unlucky numbers.
Your avocations are strong and without doubt.
You are never bitten by mosquitos.
You can juggle seven balls at once.
You feel no sexual desire.
Your actuality is dry and pure.
You are immune to brainwashing and hypnosis.
You are better off without the things you have lost
and left behind."

An image of Anton swam into my mind. He was maybe two years old, chubby and full of smiles. He'd found my hidden stash of Easter eggs and eaten them all. When I'd discovered him, he was smeared in chocolate with the most delighted grin on his little face. It was impossible to be mad at him. My calmness evaporated. How could I be better off without him?

I opened my eyes the tiniest crack to watch Zosimon as he swayed and spoke. His expression was calm, almost blank. I wondered if he recited these same words every day. If they ever changed. I wondered if he really believed it.

"Awaken, my children," he said at last. "So I can tell you of my dream."

There was a rustle as everyone opened their eyes and adjusted their positions so they could see Zosimon, who lay his hands on his crossed knees and looked out at us with eerie calm. I resisted the temptation to turn around and look for Fox, glancing instead at Stan, who was looking straight ahead at Zosimon, waiting.

"I dreamed of a white alabaster temple, with a giant snake guarding the door. I took my knife and cut the snake's skin from his flesh, and his flesh from his bones, and separated each bone from the other. Then I took the pieces and remade the serpent anew, and he granted me entry into the temple." Zosimon paused for effect, looking around at us.

"Inside, a stream of pure water glittered like sunlight. Seated in the stream was a heavy-limbed man made of lead, bound in chains. He rose and bade me to follow him, deep into the heart of the temple. We climbed winding staircases, each with seven hundred steps. At the very summit, we stood over a pit of boiling fire."

Stan swayed and nodded, as if he was imagining the stairs, the pit, the leaden man.

"The man turned and tried to speak to me. But his eyes turned red and filled with blood, which ran down his face in dark rivulets. His body convulsed, and he began to vomit, casting up great chunks of meat and bone and blood, until all his flesh was gone, leaving behind a wizened little creature, white with age. This barely living thing, crying out in agony, clawed at his mortal body, and cast himself into the fiery pit. The flames blazed high and green, then died down to reveal the man's shape, reborn. As he emerged from the flames and stood once more before me, I saw he was no longer a man of lead, nor a man of flesh, but a man of pure gold."

Zosimon frowned and his head sank down onto his chest. His breathing became steady and slow, and I wondered if he had fallen asleep. I stole a look at Stan, but he was still staring at Zosimon, entranced. Was I missing something?

My ankle itched, but I didn't dare move to scratch it. We were all waiting for something. But what?

After several excruciating minutes, Zosimon's chin jerked back up again. For a moment he looked confused, as if he wasn't sure where he was.

"You know . . ." he said, trailing off and nodding vaguely.

I felt my cheeks burning with embarrassment. He *had* fallen asleep! But nobody seemed to notice. Stan was just as mesmerized as before.

"In 1918 I was working as a safety inspector at the Union Pacific Railroad in Omaha." I started — Zosimon's voice had taken on a distinct Midwestern drawl. Again, nobody seemed to react.

"It was my job to sign off every train as fit for service before it could leave the rail yards. Every evening, a bunch of the guys from the yard would go to this little diner off the interstate, and sometimes I'd go with them, although of course I'd never order anything. We'd sit in the third booth from the door, which had a great view of the Missouri River. And one of my buddies would always order the same thing: two cups of black coffee and a Reuben sandwich. A Reuben sandwich, if you don't know, is served hot. It has corned beef, Swiss cheese, and sauerkraut, grilled between slices of rye bread. He claimed it was the greatest sandwich in the whole world and was always trying to get me to try one."

1918? Was this some kind of a joke? With the accent and everything? Nobody was laughing. Maybe it was a kind of parable. A metaphor.

"One day, I was weak. It had been overcast for weeks, so I hadn't been able to recharge from the sun. My buddy offered me a bite of his sandwich, and my resolve crumbled. I took a bite. A single bite. And it almost undid me. I lay awake all night thinking about it — the crunch of the toasted bread, the hot, sour sweetness of the Russian dressing. I was consumed, betrayed by my own body, the body I had striven to keep pure for hundreds of years. The next morning at work I couldn't clear my head. I walked in an aphotic fog, my body vacillating between aching hunger and pounding nausea. Overnight I had become a toxicant. I felt polluted, filthy, heavy, as if the blood in my veins had been replaced with molten lead. I couldn't focus, and I couldn't do my job. I signed off on a new passenger steam engine, which headed to Tennessee. It had a mechanical fault — a simple one that I should have recognized. A few days later, that train collided head-on with another train, killing one hundred and one people and injuring hundreds more. It was my fault. My weakness. That was the only time in the past seven hundred years that I allowed food or drink to pass my lips, and I pay for it every single day. The blood of those victims is on my hands. We must remain pure. We must elutriate ourselves of heaviness. We must all cast out the lead man that tethers our actuality and become beings of pure gold."

I listened, confused. Wasn't gold almost as heavy as lead?

"My children," he said. "Today is an important day. A great day. Today we welcome a new sublimate into our family." Zosimon turned his head toward me and smiled, holding out his hand to me as he got to his feet. "Come," he said. "Join me up here."

"Great job, kiddo," Stan whispered.

I stood up, my joints creaking, my bottom and thighs completely numb. I stumbled up onto the platform, and Zosimon took my hand.

"This young woman . . ." He trailed off, shaking his head with a smile. "I tell you. You're going to love her. She's the real deal. The whole package. She's brave. She's strong. She is young, but she's already overcome so many obstacles. So many challenges. And she's aced it all. I'm so glad she's found us."

The people in the crowd were nodding. I heard someone shout out the word *yes*.

"You know when something happens, and you realize that you had been lacking something? That a little part of your life, a piece of your puzzle had been missing or lost? But then you have an avocation, and everything clicks into place, and whatever you thought contentment was before, now it's entirely redefined. Entirely reshaped. You're more whole than you ever knew you could be. You know that feeling?"

The crowd murmured in agreement.

"Well, that's how I felt when I met her." Zosimon put his arm around my shoulder. "She belongs here. With us."

Even though I didn't really believe him, I felt tears spring to my eyes. It had been a long time since I had belonged anywhere. I saw Lib and Stan and Welling beaming at me. Maggie gave me a covert thumbs-up. Even Val was smiling.

And Fox.

Fox was at the back, his hair in his eyes, his cheeks wet with tears, with the biggest, happiest smile I'd ever seen on his face. It took every scrap of my willpower to not leap off the platform and push through the crowd to him.

Lib stepped up on the platform, slightly behind us. She was holding a silver goblet, which she passed to Zosimon, ducking her head in a kind of bow as she did so. Zosimon drew me gently to him, his body behind mine, his arm reaching around me so he could place his hand over my eyes. He smelled of cinnamon.

"I elutriate the lead in you," he said solemnly. "May your actuality burn bright with fire. May you shine with gold. May you banish poisons and toxins from your mind. May you float free and boundless in your true body. Your sublime body."

I felt the trickle of liquid on my head as Zosimon poured the cup of water over me. It ran in rivulets over my face, splashing into my mouth and drizzling into my collar. It was the same warm, sour, eggy water that I'd drunk in the Sanctum.

"You are a part of this family. You are loved. You are safe. You are extraordinary."

Zosimon withdrew his hand and stepped away from me. I turned to look at him.

"Everyone," he said, his face glowing with pride and pleasure. "I want to introduce you to my daughter — your newest sister. This is Heracleitus. Heracleitus, welcome to the Institute of the Boundless Sublime."

I blinked at the sound of my new name. Heracleitus. It was kind of a mouthful.

The crowd broke into applause, and everyone rose to their feet. People came forward and embraced me, welcoming me to the Institute. People I'd never met before, crying happy tears and telling me that they loved me. I thanked them, confused and oddly touched.

Then they all melted away, because Fox was there, standing before me, his eyes shining. I drank in the sight of him, feeling peace spread throughout my body. This was why I was here. He gathered me into his arms and held me tight. I felt cocooned and safe, and I turned my face into his chest so I could breathe him in. Fox. My Fox.

"Now we can be together," he said. "I'll never let you go."

I felt a lump rise in my throat, and tears started to trickle down my cheeks. He was here. Solid and real and loving me. My hunger and exhaustion and uncertainty melted away. I didn't care that people were probably staring at us. I was never going to let him out of my sight again.

Someone cleared their throat behind us, and Fox's embrace slackened. I turned my head to see Zosimon, smiling indulgently at us.

"How lovely," he said, "to see a reunion between such good friends. I wish we could all show this much affection to our fellow human beings."

Fox pulled away from me. "Thank you, Daddy," he said, bowing his head. "Thank you for bringing Rub— for bringing Heracleitus here."

It was an odd thing to say, I thought. After all, it wasn't Zosimon who had brought me to the Institute. I'd decided to come of my own accord. For Fox. If anything, Zosimon should be thanking Fox for convincing me to come. I also realized with a shock that Zosimon was the Daddy that Fox had been referring to. Zosimon was Fox's father.

"It breaks my heart to do this," said Zosimon with a twist of his mouth. "But I must steal Furicius away. There is something very important he must attend to. A matter of extreme urgency."

Fox hesitated, looking at me, his expression torn.

"Come along now, Furicius," said Zosimon gently. "I have a special task for you, and you alone."

Fox brushed his fingers against mine. "I'll see you soon," he promised.

I nodded, trying to gather as much of his face as I could into my mind, so I could savor it until the next time we were together.

"Enjoy your first day with us, Heracleitus," said Zosimon. "Libavius will show you around after breakfast."

He took Fox gently by the arm and began to lead him away.

"Zosimon," I said, and maybe it was the exhaustion, or the hunger, or the excitement of being reunited with Fox, but his name felt magical on my tongue. He turned around. "Thank you," I told him.

"Please," he said, his stiff face rearranging into a warm smile. "Call me Daddy."

9

I followed everyone into the mess hall for breakfast. It looked as if it had once been an open plan office space — the floor was covered with dark gray carpet squares, and the low ceiling was striped with fluorescent lights. Tables and chairs were arranged in rows. I hung back to see how it all worked, joining a line in front of a server's station where a woman stood in front of a large pot with a ladle. When I reached the front of the line, she slopped something white and gluey into a bowl and handed it to me, along with a glass of cloudy water.

I remembered the lavish vegetable dishes at the Red House and looked around to see if there was anything else to choose from, but it seemed that the slop was all there was.

There didn't seem to be any particular seating arrangement, so I took my bowl and glass to one of the long benches and sat down. A somewhat horsey girl sitting opposite me looked up and smiled. She looked a bit older than me — nineteen, maybe twenty, her long yellow hair pulled into a ponytail.

"Welcome, Heracleitus," she said.

"Thank you," I replied, touched that she'd remembered my new name.

"I'm Pippa — Agrippa," she said. "I know you're going to be happy here. There is nowhere like this in the world. We're so lucky."

I nodded politely — I would have felt more lucky with a fruit salad or a smoothie — and spooned a mouthful of porridge. Looking at it closely, I realized it was quinoa. I put the spoonful into my mouth.

And nearly spat it out again.

"Are you OK?" asked Pippa.

"Salty . . ." I choked, trying to force the mouthful down.

Pippa nodded. "It took me a few days to get used to the sodium too, when I was a sublimate. Soon you won't notice it. Sodium is a cardinal element."

I took another bite of porridge and felt my mouth pucker. It was like eating pure salt. I reached for my water glass, but that was worse. The water was warm and tasted of rotten eggs, like the glass that Zosimon had made me drink earlier. I gagged and turned my eyes back to Pippa.

"Water is full of poisons," she explained. "Even the rainwater that we drink. It has to be purified with sulfur. Sulfur is a cardinal element too."

"What's a cardinal element?"

Pippa scrunched up her nose. "Daddy will explain everything when you're ready. Just trust him. Daddy knows best."

Daddy? Was Zosimon Pippa's father as well? Fox had never mentioned having any siblings. I searched her face, looking for a familial resemblance, but found none.

I left my breakfast untouched, hoping there'd be something

more palatable at lunch. Pippa shook her head sympathetically and touched me gently on the arm.

"Don't worry," she said. "It'll all make sense soon." She scraped her bowl clean and beamed at me.

Everyone here was a lunatic. I was pretty sure I wouldn't last more than a day.

After breakfast we lined up again at a different table where Welling seemed to be handing out pills.

Pills? Were we being drugged?

Maybe this *was* one of those cults where everyone was given LSD and told that aliens were waiting for them on another planet.

When I got to the front of the line, Welling nodded at me. "Hey, Ruby," he said, and then corrected himself with a smile. "Heracleitus."

"What are the pills for?" I asked.

"Don't worry," said Welling, his eyes meeting mine, his expression frank. "We're not drugging you. These are your vitamin supplements. They'll speed up the elutriation process. You don't have to take them if you don't want to."

He passed me a small handful of colored capsules and a glass of the warm eggy water.

"Vitamins?" I asked.

"It's the standard dose for sublimates. Once you've been elutriated, we can tailor your supplements to your particular needs."

"I've been eating at the Red House for two weeks," I said. "And haven't had any meat or dairy at all."

"That's wonderful, you've been doing a great job. But dietary changes are only the beginning. You have been drinking water filled with chemicals, eating vegetables grown in tainted soil.

Here, everything is pure. It'll take your body a while to get used to it. You have too much mercury and lead running in your veins — I can see it in the color of your skin, the limpness of your hair. You need iron and sodium to purge those toxic elements. Magnesium to keep your will strong. Zinc to help you see the truth."

I looked at the capsules. It sounded like nonsense to me, but what harm could it do? Surely it was no worse than taking a multivitamin.

I tossed them back with a mouthful of warm eggy water. "See?" said Welling. "You already fit right in."

The mess hall cleared quickly as everyone took their supplements and headed out to do . . . whatever it was they did all day. I helped Lib pack up the supplement bottles while she explained how the daily routine worked at the Institute.

"We wake at dawn," she said. "A bell rings to get everyone up, but you'll soon start to wake when it gets light. Make your way directly to the bathroom — the quicker you are, the shorter the wait will be. Wash your face, under your arms, and between your legs. Cold water only, of course. Once a week we fill a bath to wash properly. No soap, no shampoo, no deodorant. The unpleasant odors and smells that come from a toxicant body aren't natural. They're your body purging yourself of toxins, and after you've been here for a while, you will be elutriated and won't smell anymore."

That made sense. If you weren't putting anything unpleasant into your body, nothing unpleasant would leak out.

"What about toothpaste?" I asked. "Toothbrushes?"

Lib shook her head. "Unnecessary for the diet we eat."

She led me into the concrete courtyard that we'd sat in earlier. A group of identical children were strolling past. There were about eight of them, all young — the oldest was maybe twelve, and the youngest seemed to be around four. They were all chattering and giggling happily. Some were holding hands. They seemed a totally ordinary bunch of kids, except for the fact that they were all dressed in the same white outfit and their hair was shaved down to stubble. I looked closer and realized that they weren't all girls, either. Some were definitely boys, and some I couldn't tell. Had I seen just one girl in the bathroom and in the hallway outside my room? Or had it been two different children?

"Who are they?" I asked Lib.

"The Monkeys."

"The who?"

One of the children said something that caused the others to shriek with laughter. Then they all scampered around a corner, disappearing from view. Lib frowned and didn't answer my question.

"After you've washed up, you come here for Daddy's Hour. Daddy will lead us in meditation, then speak to us on the topic of his choosing, as you saw this morning. Then breakfast."

Lib called him *Daddy* too, and she was too old to be his daughter. Maybe that was just what everyone called him. It was . . . creepy. I decided to save that question for later.

"Is breakfast always so salty?"

Lib nodded. "Sodium is a cardinal element."

There was that phrase again. *Cardinal element.*

"I wasn't expecting the food rules to be so . . . strict," I said. "The food at the Red House was so delicious."

"Breakfast is a simple meal — quinoa or buckwheat. But don't panic — lunch and dinner is just like at the Red House. There's plenty of variety."

I nodded obediently.

"There are six work teams," Lib explained. "You'll start off in Domestic. You prep and serve the meals, and do the laundry and cleaning."

That sounded boring. "What are the other teams?"

"Cultivation works the earth, growing the vegetables we eat. Reconstruction maintains and develops our buildings — clearing out the old offices for more living space and breaking up the concrete in the parking lot to make more garden beds."

"What team are you on?"

"I'm in Sanctify, the only permanent team. The others rotate. We work with Daddy, creating the work teams and the daily schedule, as well as bottling and packing the water we hand out on the streets. And of course we look after Daddy, making sure he is comfortable and has everything he needs."

"That's only four teams," I said. "What are the other two?"

"Outreach," said Lib. "They stay in the Red House and hand out the water bottles. And Procurement, which is currently on hiatus."

"What about Fox?" I asked. "Which team is Fox in?"

Lib paused for a moment, then turned away from me. "Come on," she said. "I'll take you to the kitchen."

★ ★ ★

The kitchen was tiny. It had obviously been the break room for the old food distribution company — the kind of place that just had a fridge, a sink, and a coffee machine. The coffee machine was long gone, but an ancient fridge still hummed and ticked in the corner. A set of shelves that had probably once held teabags and grimy mugs were now lined with baskets full of fresh produce from the garden and big tubs filled with various nuts, grains, and beans.

A woman stood at the counter, chopping heads of cauliflower into small florets. Her head barely reached my shoulder, and she was as thin and delicate as a bird. She had brown skin and a mass of glossy black hair wound into an enormous bun — it looked like it might reach the ground if it were loose.

"Newton," said Lib. "This is Heracleitus. The new sublimate."

The woman cast an appraising eye over me. Despite her diminutive stature, I found myself shrinking under her gaze. She was obviously a woman you wouldn't want to mess with.

"You can finish the cauliflower," she said, speaking with a trace of Indian accent. She nodded toward a knife block on the counter.

"I'll leave you to it," said Lib.

I selected a knife and began to chop, trying to get my cauliflower florets the same size and shape as Newton's. She moved over to the opposite countertop and began scooping cups of dried lentils out of one of the plastic tubs and placing them in a large bowl to soak, sprinkling them with several handfuls of salt.

"Um," I said. "I have a friend here. Fox. Do you know where he is?"

Newton's stern face took on an unexpected softness. "You know Fox?"

I nodded eagerly. "He's why I'm here. I'd really like to see him."

"Fox is deeply loved here," said Newton. "He is very special."

"I know he is."

I saw Newton's eyes narrow slightly as she considered me. Was she trying to warn me about something? Or was she just protective of Fox?

"It'd only take a minute," I said. "I can come right back and finish the cauliflower."

"I'm sorry," said Newton, her expression tinged with what looked like pity. "I'm afraid Fox is busy today."

I turned back to my cauliflower, disappointed. Busy doing what? I glanced over at Newton and attempted to make conversation.

"What are we making?" I asked.

Newton was silent for a moment before answering. "Lunch."

I left it at that. Clearly she wasn't interested in making conversation.

After the cauliflower, I cut up several bunches of kale, then a ton of zucchini. Bored, I looked at all the shelves and surfaces and realized there was no oven, no stovetop, no microwave.

"Don't you ever cook anything?" I asked.

"Never," said Newton. "Cooking realigns the molecular structure of food. Nitrates become nitrosamines, which are carcinogenic."

"But . . . everyone cooks food. If cooked food was bad for you, we'd know."

Newton snorted. "That's what they said about cigarettes." She put down her measuring cup and turned to me. "We have many rules here for food. Each one is based in pure science — chemical truths."

"So what are they?" I asked. "The rules?"

"First and foremost, nothing grown beneath the ground. The earth is aphotic, full of lead and other poisons, and all root vegetables are contaminated. The Cultivation team ensures that none of our produce touches the earth. Vegetables that produce fruit low to the ground, such as zucchini, melons, and pumpkin, are placed on flour sacks to protect them from the soil."

I opened my mouth to point out that all plants had roots in the soil, and wouldn't any so-called contamination affect them, no matter how far the actual vegetables were from the surface? But then I thought better of it.

"OK," I said. "What else?"

Newton ticked things off her fingers. "No roasting, grilling, boiling, or frying," she said. "No nightshades — that's tomato, eggplant, pepper, potato. And no grains, except for quinoa, chia, millet, and buckwheat. Dairy, meat, sugar, and gluten are poisons."

"What about alcohol?" I asked, curious.

Newton shuddered. "Fermented foods and beverages are rotten. They corrupt your body from the inside. Food should cleanse and purify the body, not torture it."

"Explain the salt thing," I said. "People keep telling me it's a cardinal element. What does that mean?"

"Sodium is the most necessary element," said Newton. "Daddy will explain it all to you in time."

"But what does cardinal element mean?" I asked. "My whole life I've been told to cut down on salt."

Newton's lip curled in a sneer. "Nonsense. Misinformation. It's all part of the conspiracy."

Uh-oh. "The conspiracy?"

"They want to keep you a toxicant," said Newton. "Sluggish, docile. They don't want people to reach their full potential. So they deny you the basic ingredients you need to survive. And worse, they trick you into believing that what you're doing is healthy."

"They? Who are they?"

Newton's eyes shifted from side to side, as if she were checking the room for spies. "Daddy will explain that too."

And she wouldn't say any more on the matter. She set me to chopping a huge bunch of parsley. I chopped and chopped, piling the vegetables and herbs in enormous bowls where Newton transformed them into a feast. She made almond meal and chard falafel, dressed the cauliflower florets with a pumpkin seed and coriander pesto, stuffed cabbage leaves with chestnuts and zucchini, and threw together a snow pea, apple, and walnut salad.

I soaked millet for dinner, then set to work scrubbing the kitchen floor.

It was hard work. Really hard. Harder than I'd ever worked before. I was dizzy with hunger, and I wished I'd eaten more of my quinoa porridge.

"What time is lunch?" I asked.

Newton looked up from the countertop. "Daddy says that time is a human construct designed to trick our bodies into aging."

"Um," I said. "OK. When is lunch?"

"When the bell rings."

"When will that be?"

Newton shrugged. "When you hear it."

I tried to turn back to what I was doing, but I had too many questions.

"Why is the water so disgusting?" I asked.

"It's not disgusting," said Newton with a disapproving shake of her head. "It's elutriating. Pure."

"It doesn't look pure."

Newton sighed. "Tap water is full of poisons. Aluminum

sulfate, chlorine, ammonia, fluoride. Why do you think they add all those chemicals to your water?"

I shrugged. "Fluoride is for our teeth. I guess the other stuff is . . . I don't know. To keep bacteria out or something?"

Newton raised her eyebrows. *"Or something,"* she repeated. "You've never really thought about it, have you? Why is that? It's not because you're not smart — you're definitely intelligent, otherwise you wouldn't be here. No, those chemicals drug you. They keep your brain in a haze of dopey contentment so you won't ask any dangerous questions."

"More conspiracies?" I asked.

Newton looked at me with grudging respect. "You learn fast."

It sounded crazy, but she was right. I'd never wondered what went in our water before. I'd always assumed that water was . . . empty. That it was all the other stuff we had to worry about. Sugar and salt and artificial sweeteners and pollution and pesticides.

"So why the egginess?" I asked. "And why so warm?"

"We only drink rainwater," said Newton. "To avoid the toxins. Heating the water to precisely 98.6 degrees elutriates it of airborne toxins."

"But Lib said warm water was dangerous."

"On the skin, yes. But cold water is equally dangerous to the inner body."

That logic sounded dubious to me. "And the egginess?"

"Sulfur is added to the water once it's heated," said Newton. She showed me where the canister of powdered sulfur was kept, and the silver spoon used to measure it out. "Sulfur is a cardinal element."

There was that phrase again.

"So . . . what's in the water bottles that you hand out?" I asked. "It isn't the sulfurous water, is it?"

"Of course not. But it contains a minute amount of sulfur that cannot be discerned."

"Why do you hand them out?"

Newton shrugged. "People get thirsty," she said.

After an eternity, a bell rang for lunch, and Newton and I handed our huge bowls of salad and platters of vegetables over to the members of Domestic who were in charge of serving meals. Then I lined up with my plate like everyone else. I looked around for Fox but couldn't see him. Perhaps he was still helping Zosimon. I sat down next to Val and a bunch of people I hadn't met, who all smiled kindly and murmured greetings. Val nodded to me in recognition, and I suddenly remembered the weird moment from the previous morning at the Red House, when he'd shaken his head at me. But hunger took over before I could think about it, and I dug into my meal.

Unlike breakfast, lunch was more like the meals I'd had at the Red House, tasty and filling and fresh. Conversation buzzed, and I let it wash over me, too shy to join in. Beside me, I noticed Val slipping snow peas into his pocket. Maybe he didn't like them.

I didn't see the children again and decided they must eat meals separately. I made a mental note to ask Fox about them later on, when we got an opportunity to talk.

From what I could tell, Zosimon didn't attend any of our meals — I guessed he wanted to maintain his air of mystery.

After lunch, Maggie came up to talk to me in the courtyard. "Heracleitus, huh?" she said, slinging a casual arm over my shoulder. "I like it."

"Does everyone get a new name when they join?"

Maggie nodded. "But we shorten them to make it easier. You'll probably be known as Hera."

"So Maggie isn't your real name?"

"It's Magnus," she said.

"Magnus is the name that Zosimon gave you?"

She nodded again.

"So what's your real name?"

"I've had lots of names over the years," Maggie said. "If you mean the name I was born with, it's Jiao. Jiao Wei Qin. But I left that behind a long time ago."

"What are the long versions of everyone else's names?"

"Lib is Libavius. Val is . . . Valentius, I think. Stan is Stanihurst. Fox is Furicius. We're all named after alchemists."

"Alchemists?" I raised my eyebrows. "Like, turning lead into gold? The Philosopher's Stone? Isn't that all a little Harry Potter?"

Maggie chuckled. "You should talk to Fox about Harry Potter. I tried to tell him the story, but I couldn't remember what all the characters were called. He was totally into it, though."

I smiled. Fox *would* like Harry Potter.

"Just —" Maggie paused and gave me a funny look. "Keep it quiet, OK? You and Fox. I know you guys are close, but it's probably better if you don't broadcast it to the world."

"Why?"

Maggie looked uncomfortable. "It's just how things are here."

I felt a prickle of uneasiness. "But what do you mean —"

She cut me off. "The alchemy stuff — it's metaphorical, right? The lead refers to the prison of the body, and gold is pure actuality. Or something. I don't know. I always zone out when Zosimon talks about it."

"The prison of the body?"

Maggie chuckled. "I know what you're thinking, but don't worry. When he talks about casting out the lead inside you, he doesn't mean casting off your body in a literal sense. This isn't a suicide cult. It's more about learning to control your body, instead of letting your body control you. Ridding the body of addictions and toxins. That sort of thing."

"OK," I said. That didn't sound so bad. "So the Reuben sandwich thing was just a story? A metaphor?"

Maggie pursed her lips and tilted her head from side to side in a *maybe* gesture. "You'll get used to all the rhetoric," she said. "Some of Zosimon's lectures are pretty hilarious, but I figure, hey, let the old dude tell us his mildly racist stories about Arabian snake-charmers or Native American medicine men or whatever."

"Magnus." It was Lib, standing behind us with a stern look on her face.

I wondered how long she'd been listening.

A flash of something crossed Maggie's face — fear? anger? — but was quickly replaced with her usual casual breeziness. "Hey, Lib."

"Daddy would like to see you in private."

Maggie nodded, and gave me a casual wave over her shoulder as she strolled off. I turned to Lib.

"Have you seen Fox?" I asked.

Lib hesitated, then took my elbow and drew me gently away from the open courtyard, under the shade of the warehouse. "So," she said, pursing her lips. "We should talk about some of the rules here."

More rules?

Lib looked genuinely uncomfortable. "Relationships — romantic relationships — are discouraged."

I felt the blood rush to my cheeks. "Oh," I said. "Um. Can I ask why?"

"Sexual . . . urges are another way that we are trapped by our flesh bodies," Lib explained. "Like hunger or illness or addiction. To free our actuality, we must deny the body those urges."

This sounded . . . wrong. We were supposed to not feel? Not fall in love? How could anyone think those things were bad?

"Don't worry," said Lib hurriedly, seeing my expression. "We don't discourage love. The Institute is all about love. But it's real love, untainted by the urging of the flesh. It's pure. It's like nothing you've ever felt before."

"Have you felt that?" I asked. "The pure love?"

Lib closed her eyes for a moment. "I have glimpsed it," she said with a slightly sad smile. "I have brushed it with my fingers, and it makes me all the more determined."

I tried to dampen my disappointment. No relationships. No Fox. My fantasies of us curling up next to each other every night evaporated. I was tempted to turn and head out the gates that very moment, to go back to my house and my ashen mother and school and my friends . . .

But then there'd be no Fox at all. At least here I could still see him every day. Talk to him. It was true that I *wanted* Fox in a way that Lib definitely wouldn't consider to be "pure," but that wasn't the only thing I wanted. More than anything, I wanted to be close to him. And maybe he'd agree to leave with me.

"OK," I said. "No relationships. But if Fox and I are just friends . . . could we be placed in the same work unit?"

Lib frowned. "Work units aren't for socializing," she said. "They're for work."

"Oh, we'd still work hard. Harder, I promise. It's just . . .

Fox is my friend. I came here to be with him, and I've barely seen him."

Lib's gaze turned cold, and I felt myself shiver. She was different here. Smaller, somehow? Shrunken? "I just organize the roster," she said. "Any changes must be approved by Daddy." She said it with a kind of finality — as if for her, these words ended the conversation. But I wasn't going to back down that easily.

"Great!" I said chirpily. "I'll go ask him."

Lib looked shocked. "You — you can't ask him. Daddy doesn't have time for your inconsequential concerns. His mind is pure, focused on larger goals."

"It'll only take a minute."

"Daddy doesn't have a *minute*." She snapped the words out, and I knew I hadn't been imagining it. She *was* different here. She was on edge, almost as if she were afraid.

"What don't I have a minute for?"

Lib's face drained of color and she spun around. Zosimon was standing in the doorway to the kitchen, immaculate in his white linen and smiling indulgently. Lib opened her mouth but couldn't seem to find the right words.

"Daddy . . ." she stammered.

"I was feeling a little hungry," said Zosimon, winking at me. "Thought I'd pop outside for some fresh air and sunshine before my session with Magnus."

I frowned, confused. If Zosimon was hungry, why didn't he go to the kitchen? I glanced at Lib, who looked . . . strange. Frightened. Awestruck. Infatuated.

"Is everything OK?" Zosimon turned to me. "Heracleitus? Are you settling in well?"

"Yes, thank you," I said. "Actually, I wanted to ask a favor."

Zosimon raised his eyebrows, but he was still smiling. He stepped out of the doorway and raised his face to the sun.

"Go on," he said, his eyes closed.

Lib appeared to be holding her breath.

"Could I possibly join the work team that Fox is on? We'd really like to be together."

A flicker of . . . something . . . passed over Zosimon's face. Disappointment? He opened his eyes and looked at Lib with a slightly quirked brow, but Lib's face was like stone. Zosimon closed his eyes again, nodding benevolently.

"Of course," he said. "Libavius should have put you two in the same unit to start with. You and Furicius have a special bond, I can see that."

Lib's expression didn't falter.

"Thank you," I said. "I promise we'll work hard."

"I know you will. Libavius, can you make sure Furicius and Heracleitus are placed in the same work team at the beginning of the next rotation?"

Lib opened her mouth as if to say something, then pursed her lips into a single whitish line and snapped her head in a nod. My spirits sank a little. The start of the next rotation? Why couldn't we be together right away?

"Don't worry," said Zosimon. "This rotation is almost over."

I nodded. How long could it be? A few days? The end of the week? I could definitely stick it out until then.

Daddy lowered his head and opened his eyes, looking right at me. "Heracleitus," he said. "It was brave to ask me that favor. There are lots of people here who wouldn't be brave enough to do that."

Was it? Lib looked furious.

Daddy nodded. "Brave," he murmured. "Heracleitus is brave. I like that." He turned his head back up to the sun, taking deep breaths.

Lib grabbed me by the elbow and hauled me inside.

"You have some nerve," she hissed. "You're lucky Daddy didn't reduce you to a pile of atoms."

"Really?" I said. "It didn't seem like a big deal. He didn't mind."

Lib shook her head and hissed air through her teeth. "You'll learn respect. I hope it won't be too late for you."

I wasn't able to ask her what she meant by that, because Daddy came in. He patted his stomach and grinned at us both. "I'm about to burst," he said. "Couldn't eat another thing."

Lib led me back to Newton, and I got to work scrubbing all the lunch dishes. Then I mopped the floors again and wiped down the tables and countertops before being sent into a storage room to help Newton measure out the supplements for the evening meal.

The Institute was really into supplements. Everyone took a basic dose of Vitamins A, C, and D (but never B, E, or K), sodium, choline, magnesium, potassium, chromium, copper, iron, and sulfur. We were then prescribed specific supplements depending on our moods or energy levels. I wasn't sure how the members of the Sanctify team determined who needed what — did they ask people about their moods, or just observe them? Either way, they were written up on a long list that was posted inside the kitchen for whoever was measuring them out. There seemed to be hundreds of possible supplements, but glancing at the list, I noticed iodine being prescribed to counteract doubt and confusion, vanadium for exhaustion, selenium for sadness and melancholy, manganese for anger or bitterness, and silicone or zinc for anxiety. Newton told me Daddy made all the supplements in his laboratory, but I didn't believe her. They looked exactly like the vitamin pills in our cupboard at home.

Two women I hadn't met before came in to help Newton get dinner ready — broccoli stalk "pasta" with green beans and sage, buckwheat and endive tabbouleh, and a snow pea and arugula salad with hazelnuts. They were friendly and warm, telling me ludicrous stories about Zosimon's adventures as a botanist in the Amazon jungle. It was crazy stuff and obviously made-up, but hugely entertaining. At dusk, the bell sounded, and everyone came inside for dinner. The children didn't come in — I wondered where they ate their meals. Maybe they left the Institute every day to go to school.

After dinner, I helped the rest of the Domestic team clean up and soak the quinoa for the following morning's breakfast. Then I followed them into the old warehouse for what I was told was Family Time.

Fox came up to me, his face full of smiles.

"Where have you been all day?" I asked. "You weren't at lunch or dinner."

"Sorry," said Fox. "There was all this stuff I had to do. Because of being at the Red House for so long."

He didn't hug me or take my hand. I wondered if Lib had talked to him too. It didn't matter. I was so happy to see him. He showed me to a pair of crates he'd found for us to sit on, as proud as if they were silk cushions. We sat down side by side, close enough that I could feel the warmth of him beside me.

Family Time was what I'd overheard the previous night, when I was quarantined in my room. Someone had lit candles and kerosene lamps so the warehouse glowed with a warm, golden light. Everyone was smiling and chatting and relaxed, and it was easy to forget about the dietary restrictions and the weird philosophies. Zosimon came in and chatted with us — nothing like the formal lecture we'd had that morning. It was more conversational. People asked him questions, and he told us silly stories about his supposed "past" — about ancient Rome and the frozen Arctic north and the Galapagos Islands.

It was a kind of running joke in the Institute — that Zosimon had lived for thousands of years and had all these adventures.

"Sometimes," he said to the enraptured crowd, "I really don't know my own strength. I remember once when I was working as a code-breaker during World War II, I reached for the telegram machine too eagerly and crushed the whole thing to dust. It was rather embarrassing."

Everyone cackled with laughter, and I laughed too. It felt easy, bubbling up inside me. Fox looked over at me, his eyes crinkled with pleasure.

Stan had a guitar, and we all sang together, old campfire songs and ballads that everyone knew, our voices twining together and rising up to the dusty warehouse rafters. After a while, the gathering broke into smaller groups. Fox and I sat with Pippa, Newton, and Val. Newton, who had been so stern all day in the kitchen, seemed like a totally different person. Her dark hair was unbraided, and fell in long, loose waves down to her waist. She spoke in soft tones, telling me about her life before the Institute, getting married too young in order to escape her strict parents. When she and her husband failed to get pregnant, Newton had sunk into a deep depression. Her marriage had fallen apart, and she'd ended up aimless and drifting, looking for answers. She'd found those answers at the Institute.

"Now you," said Fox to Pippa. "Tell Ruby your story."

This was nothing like being at the Wasteland with Fox. In

comparison to the people at the Institute, my friends seemed like sea urchins, cold and thorny — sharp spines of insecurity and jealousy preventing them from ever connecting with each other. Here, even voiceless Val seemed to be a part of the group. People acknowledged him when they spoke, smiling and making eye contact, and he nodded as he listened to their stories.

"I'm afraid my story isn't a very interesting one," said Pippa, shooting me a sheepish smile.

"Don't sell yourself short," said Fox with a frown. "It's interesting because it's *your* story."

Pippa smiled fondly at Fox. "Fine," she said. "I'm a poor little rich girl. I had everything I ever wanted growing up. I was one of those kids who asked Santa for a pony and then actually got one. Senior year, I was on track to get into all the top colleges. And I had this perfect boyfriend, Aidan." Her expression tightened a little. "The day before exams started, we were at a party and I saw Aidan in one of the bedrooms with . . . with a guy. I didn't want to deal with what that meant, so I just went home and got up the next day and went to school and did the best I could. But after my last class, Aidan was there, waiting for me when I came out. I thought we'd talk about it. He'd tell me he was gay, we'd both cry a little, you know. But instead he got down on one knee and pulled out an engagement ring. I . . . I didn't get it. I asked him how he could do that . . . ask me that, after what I'd seen. He admitted that yes, he did like guys. But that didn't have to stop us from having this perfect life together. It made me so sad to think he couldn't have the life he wanted with another guy."

"Why couldn't he?" I asked. "I mean, he could have married a guy, had kids and a career."

Fox nodded, and I knew he'd asked Pippa the same question. Pippa sighed. "His family is religious," she said. "They wouldn't be OK with it. It made me realize how much of a facade it all was — rich people living these lives that looked so perfect but inside were rotten to the core. So I didn't go to college. I didn't want to be a part of that world anymore. I met Welling, handing out water bottles, and we started talking." She glanced over at Welling and smiled. "He really got it, you know? He'd lived that privileged life too. He knew how fake it all was. So he brought me here. That was about a year ago."

The conversation wandered to other topics, and I marveled at how open and understanding everyone was. There was no judgment of past mistakes. No malice or selfishness or greed. Just love and understanding and acceptance. People talked about the future, about hopes and dreams for the world. For the first time in months I missed my piano, missed coaxing music from stiff white and black keys with fleet fingers.

I felt like these people were a kind of life raft, holding me up above the black tide, carrying me toward dry land. My muscles were tired from working all day, but in a fuzzy, pleasant sort of way — the weariness of honest labor, instead of the exhaustion of a restless mind.

When Family Time was over, Fox walked me to my room, his fingers brushing mine as we said good night. His touch was thrilling — all the more so knowing it was forbidden. We stared at each other for as long as we dared, our eyes doing all the things that our fingers couldn't. Then Fox drifted down the hall to his own room, and I was on my own.

I climbed onto my bed and pulled the damp-smelling blanket up around my chin. I was exhausted, but I couldn't sleep. The warm, clear feeling I'd had at Family Time slowly leached out of me until I was left alone and empty.

"Ruby!" said Anton's voice, and I sat up in bed, glancing

around wildly at the darkness. My heart pounded, and my jaw clenched. I wanted to push it away — the memories, the sadness. Bite down until everything went white. I thought of Zosimon that morning, breathing and swaying, and me, breathing and swaying along with him. And I didn't bite down. I took a deep breath and imagined Fox's face. His eyes. His smile. The touch of his hand.

And I let it come.

Anton, waking me up at five o'clock on Christmas morning. Anton, laughing so hard at one of my terrible jokes that he could barely breathe. Anton, scowling because Mom wouldn't let him stay up to watch the Olympic diving. Anton, crying after another kid had pushed him at school. Anton, forcing Mom and Dad to sit and watch him shout nonsense songs while I accompanied him on the piano.

Eventually, the memories stopped coming, and I sunk into sleep.

★ ★ ★

The days slipped by. I worked hard in the kitchen with Newton. I ate my over-salted food. I listened to Zosimon's lectures with a skeptical ear. I drank the eggy water. I sat with Fox at meals and Family Time, occasionally letting my hand brush his. Everyone was vague as to when the current rotation would end, but I felt a kind of patient peace about it all. It would come. And then Fox and I could spend every day together. I had so much to tell him, to ask him, but I wanted to wait until we had some privacy.

Each night I lay awake in bed, reliving every moment, every conversation that Anton and I had ever had. I'd been afraid I'd lost him completely, but he was still there, vivid and solid in my memory. I let him laugh into the silence of my room. I fought with him over who got to sit in the front seat of the car. I gave him a hug when we heard Mom and Dad fighting and told him that everything would be OK.

Then, with the sound of his voice still ringing in the darkness, I would relive the day he died. Flirting with Ali. The bitter sting of cigarette smoke in my lungs. The missed calls on my phone. Eventually listening to my messages, hearing my mother's voice turn from irritated to angry to hysterical. Arriving at the hospital only to be told I was too late. Feeling like an actor in a medical drama — not sure if I should cry or scream or faint. Sitting with Mom in the special room they put aside for people like us and feeling suddenly, overwhelmingly ravenous, but not knowing how to ask Mom for money for the vending machine. Realizing after hours that Dad wasn't there, and asking Mom where he was.

I went over the funeral again and again. It was just us — a small, gray, numb affair. We didn't want a big fuss. Dad was allowed to come, but he stood off to the side and didn't look at us. Tears ran down his cheeks, and occasionally I heard a broken, choked sob. Mom and I were silent. Cold, blank. Empty. Anything else hurt too much.

Other memories came too. The details of Dad's trial and sentencing. A reporter coming to our door to ask for a comment. A social worker helping me navigate a website that let Mom get welfare payments.

But mostly I just saw *him*. I imagined the accident. The smile on his face when he saw Dad's car. A slight frown or widening of the eyes when the wheels skidded on the gravel.

The *thunk* of his little body hitting the hood. The silence left behind after his heart stopped beating.

I lay awake in the darkness night after night, seeing it all over and over again. But it wasn't like before. It wasn't painful. It was sad and intense, but it felt *right*. Methodical. Like rinsing a wound until it ran clear.

After two weeks at the Institute, I fell asleep minutes after climbing into bed and slept for a solid eight hours for the first time in months. When I woke the next morning I felt as though I was finally whole again.

10

"And so there I was, being chased out of the Imperial Harem by fifty albino eunuchs while the poor Ottoman Sultan was howling for the Grand Vizier. Little did he know that the Vizier had run off with the Queen Mother with all the gold they'd embezzled together."

Everyone laughed heartily. Zosimon's laugh was the loudest — tears sprung to his eyes.

"That was a long day," he said, and got to his feet. "This has been a long day too. You've all worked hard and have earned a restful night." He turned his head. "Pippa, please join me in the Sanctum."

I saw Pippa's cheeks turn pink and her eyes widen.

Lib's face flashed with . . . jealousy? But the expression was quickly replaced with a smile that showed too many teeth. "Well done," she whispered.

Zosimon exited the warehouse with Pippa following as everyone murmured, "Good night, Daddy." I wondered why he'd asked Pippa to go with him. Surely it wasn't to share his bed. Zosimon was old enough to be Pippa's grandfather.

We stayed there for a while longer, chatting and singing, until people started to drift off to bed. As we stood up, Fox brushed deliberately against me.

"I need to see you," he whispered. "Please."

I smiled at him and said good night, hoping he would read a different message in my eyes.

He did. I waited in my room for half an hour, shivering in my nightgown under the thin blanket. Then there was a soft tap at my door, and Fox was there. We threw our arms around each other and stood there for a moment, holding on tightly. I felt him breathing, his heartbeat against my chest. It calmed my doubts, my worries.

Eventually we broke apart, and Fox sat on the bed, his knees drawn up to his chest.

"We have to be quiet," he said, his voice whisper soft. "But I needed to see you. I miss you."

I grabbed his hands. "I miss you too. But we're going to spend more time together. I asked Zosimon, and he said we can be on the same team at the next rotation."

I imagined long summer afternoons, Fox and me, working side by side in the garden. We'd work the soil with our hands, coaxing sustenance from the bare earth. We'd talk for hours, the sun warm on our backs and in our hearts. Everything would be perfect. Then I realized I'd never seen Fox working in the garden.

"Wait," I said. "What team are you on?"

Fox was staring at me, his eyes wide. "You asked Daddy?"

"He said it was fine."

"Are you sure? What exactly did he say?"

I shrugged. "He said he could see we were important to each

other and that we should have been on the same team from the beginning. It was no big deal."

Fox's expression said that it *was* a big deal.

"Everyone seems scared of Zosimon," I said. "I don't understand why. He seems nice."

Fox blinked, confused. "Not *scared*," he said. "It's about respect. Daddy is . . . special."

"How so?"

"He is sublime." Fox's face was very serious. "He has lived for thousands of years. He doesn't eat or drink. He only needs sunlight to sustain him."

"But you don't really *believe* that," I said. "It's . . . a metaphor. A parable."

Fox shook his head. "No, it's true. It's all true."

I felt a little sick. Did Fox really believe it? Was he that naïve?

"But he's not your real father," I said.

"He's the only father I've ever had."

That wasn't an answer. "What about Pippa?" I asked. "Why did Zosimon ask her to join him in the Sanctum tonight?"

"I don't know," said Fox, looking uncomfortable. "I — I asked Lib once. She told me it was a secret, and I didn't have clearance to know."

"So it's happened before? He asks people to join him at night?"

"Yes."

"Is it always women?"

"I know what you're thinking," Fox said. "But Daddy wouldn't do that. He doesn't feel that way. He doesn't feel the . . . pull of bodies."

Fox's voice had grown husky, and he looked away, his cheeks

pink. His words hung in the air, and I knew we were both feeling the same thing. The same pull.

What made him so sure? Fox had so many questions about the outside world, how did he not have any about life inside the Institute? I had seen the doubt on his face when I'd asked him if he'd really wanted to come back here. What wasn't he telling me? Or was it something he wasn't telling himself?

"I brought this," said Fox, clearing his throat and showing me a battered paperback copy of *Les Miserables*. It had been read so many times it looked as though a strong breeze would cause it to crumble to dust. Fox handled it as if it were a precious relic.

I flipped through it, feeling the thinness of the paper under my fingers. Familiar names rose from the pages, and snatches of music echoed in my ears as I remembered going to see the musical with my parents when I was little, when Anton was still a baby.

A photograph slipped from the pages and fell to the floor. Fox made a grab for it, but I was closer and picked it up first.

It was an old black and white photo, creased and faded on soft, thin paper. A woman held a baby. She had long dark hair pulled back into a low ponytail. She was kissing the baby's temple, and her expression seemed sad, her eyes downcast.

I turned the photo over to check for a name or date and saw a few lines written in an awkward script with pale gray pencil.

plane crash
starvation
gamma radiation pulse
contaminated water supply
nuclear fallout
suffocated by pollution

"Give it back." Fox's face was white, his lips clamped into a thin line.

"Who are they?" I asked.

Fox met my eyes. His gaze was cool and blank. "I don't have a mother," he said. "Only Daddy. Daddy rescued me from darkness." It was as if he was reciting something.

I looked back down at the photo. "You . . . you think this is your mother?"

It was too old. But . . . people at the Institute did dress very simply. Maybe it was Fox's mother.

"Fox, did your mother die?"

Fox hesitated, then nodded.

"How?"

A shrug. "I don't know."

I looked at the words on the back of the photo. Guesses? Hypotheses? It seemed . . . bleak and hysterical. No ordinary death for Fox's mother. Nothing as banal as a car accident on the street by a soccer field.

I looked at the baby and thought I recognized something — the softness of the mouth, the intensity of the eyes.

"This is you?"

Fox tucked his hair behind his ears and bobbed his head in a nod.

"Do you remember her?"

"Sometimes I think I do," he said. "Other times I think it's just wishing."

"What's the first thing you remember?" I asked.

"Daddy."

So Fox had been here since he was a baby? What about his father? Grandparents? Aunts and uncles? There had to be someone who had cared about him.

"What about the other children?" I asked.

"Who?"

"The children. You know. The terrifying identical children."

"Oh," said Fox, his brow clearing as he cheered up a bit. "The Monkeys."

"Pretty sure they're human children."

"We call them the Monkeys," said Fox. "It's short for *Homunculi*, but also because they play and chatter a lot, like real monkeys."

"They don't have names?"

Fox shook his head. "Not until they're older. Daddy says you don't become a whole person until a spark lands on you. It happens when you're about thirteen, I think. That was when I became a person, anyway."

"You were a Monkey?"

"Of course."

"Where do they all come from?"

"C Block. The building at the back, by the wall, behind Daddy's laboratory."

So that was why Lib called it the Monkey House.

"But where do they *originally* come from?" I asked. "Where are their parents?"

"We have no parents. We didn't exist before Daddy. Daddy made us into people."

"That makes no sense," I said, frustrated. "What about when you were little? You told me Lib used to bring you books."

"I'm the oldest, so it was different for me. I grew up at the Red House — we didn't move here to the Institute until I was . . ." He paused and shrugged. "Maybe seven? That's when the other children started to come too. It was nice to have other kids to play with, but other things changed. That was when we became Monkeys."

"So you just . . . stopped being a person?"

Fox shook his head, frustrated that I wasn't getting it. "People are like plants. You have to look after them when they're little sprouts, but they don't mean anything yet. The Monkeys are like that. When they get their spark, their actuality, then Daddy will give them a name and they'll officially join the Institute."

"You didn't have a *name* until you were thirteen?"

Fox shook his head.

"Fox, that's *terrible*." I wanted to grab his hand and walk right out the door that instant. Forget the clean living and simplicity of daily life. Forget Family Time. This wasn't a family.

"It sounds much worse than it is," Fox said. "But being a Monkey is the best way to grow up. The Monkeys play and make up stories and sing and dance all day. That's why they have most of their meals in the Monkey House, because the grown-ups are supposed to be quiet when they're eating, but the Monkeys don't have to be. They can laugh and talk and play as much as they want. Everyone is so nice to you when you're a Monkey. Because you're special. The Monkeys are the future. We are Daddy's children, so everybody loves us."

I remembered them all filing into the mess hall for breakfast. "Did you look like that too? With the shaved head and tunic?"

Fox nodded. "The Monkeys are blank. They don't have any characteristics yet. Once they become real people and Daddy gives them a name, then they get to grow their hair and wear different clothes."

I thought about Anton, jumping on his bed. Building a castle out of Legos. Crying when he accidentally crushed a ladybug under his shoe. Anton hadn't been blank. He had been a real person. I imagined Fox as a child, with his shaved head and his tunic, being told that he wasn't a real person. I imagined his face the day Zosimon had taken his books away. Had he cried? A sudden resentment flared in my chest. That was no way to grow up. Perhaps the only way Fox could deal with his constricted childhood was to treat it as idyllic. I remembered the little girl crouching on the closed toilet lid, grinning with her finger to her lips.

"Right," I said, half to myself. "No characteristics."

"It's getting late," said Fox. "I should go."

"Can't you stay?"

Fox sighed. "I wish I could. But I'll get in trouble if they find me here."

Who did he mean by *they*?

"Should I read to you for a little while?" Fox asked. "To help you fall asleep?"

I smiled. "It's too dark. You won't be able to see the page."

"I don't really need it," said Fox. "I know it all by heart."

By heart.

I knew Fox by heart. Fox *was* my heart. I could save all my questions for another day.

I snuggled down onto my thin foam mattress, drawing the scratchy blanket up around my chin. I closed my eyes and let Fox's husky words wash over me.

"There is one spectacle grander than the sea, that is the sky. There is one spectacle grander than the sky, that is the interior of the soul."

★ ★ ★

It was easy to fall into a routine. Getting up early for Daddy's Hour, then working with Newton in the kitchen all day until dinner and Family Time, and then a clandestine meeting with Fox in my room. At first, I lived solely for those stolen moments in the dark, Fox reciting snippets from *Les Miserables*. Sometimes I'd tell him stories — fairy tales and fables that he'd never heard before. He especially liked the one about the twelve dancing princesses. Often we'd hold hands, but we didn't let things go any farther than that. I wanted to, and I could tell that Fox did too. But we were committed to Zosimon's process and didn't want to derail it.

After a while I found myself enjoying the work too. I felt clearheaded and sharp. Although I still didn't believe any of Zosimon's wild stories, I found myself listening more closely, learning to extract essential truths from his words. Did it really matter, after all, if he claimed to have been a slave in ancient Egypt? Or a courtier in Renaissance Florence? Or a salt merchant during the time of the Byzantine Empire? Zosimon was wise. He knew the best way to communicate ideas was through story, and he was a great storyteller. I felt safe around him, as though I was being looked after. Whatever his background, there was no doubting his love for us all. When I felt his eyes on me, I sat up straighter, angled my head attentively, so he'd know that I was listening. That I understood him.

★ ★ ★

On my twentieth day at the Institute, I saw Maggie shuffling through the courtyard, her head bowed. I hadn't seen her for weeks — not since Zosimon had summoned her just after I'd arrived at the Institute. I'd assumed she'd gone back to the Red House. I called out her name, but she didn't respond. I chased after her and touched her on the shoulder.

She spun around in shock, lifting her hands to shield her face, and I noticed that her left eye was swollen and bruised.

She shrank from my gaze. I was reminded of my mother, folding into nothing on the couch, just a gray shroud and a smoldering stick of ash.

"Maggie?" I asked. "Are you OK?"

She seemed thinner, smaller, her limbs hanging loose and awkward, like a broken doll's. She nodded slowly and smiled. "Hello, Heracleitus," she said. Her speech was a little slurred, as if she hadn't spoken for weeks.

"What happened to you?" I asked. "Where have you been?"

I thought I saw her wince slightly. "I've been studying," she said. "Working closely with Daddy."

I'd never heard her call him that before. "What happened to your eye?"

Maggie looked down at the dirt beneath her shoes. "I did it to myself," she said. "The work we've been doing . . . it's difficult. Challenging. The body is aphotic. It wants things. The body fights back. The body wants to be bound to the earth. But we must elutriate."

She shuddered with her whole body, as if something were trying to crawl up her spine and she was trying to shake it off. I stared at her. She was . . . like a different person. What had happened?

"What exactly have you been doing with Zosimon?" I asked.

"Hera." It was Lib, standing in the doorway to the kitchen, a frown creasing her face. "Daddy wants to see you."

"OK." I looked back at Maggie, but she was shuffling away, shoulders hunched.

I vowed to ask Zosimon about her and set off to the Sanctum. As I headed into the main building, a flash of white caught my eye. I turned and saw one of the Monkeys, squatting in the dirt in a concealed corner. Was it the one I'd seen that first day, perched on the toilet lid? It was so hard to tell. The Monkey looked up at me, and I noticed that it clutched a fistful of bright green snow peas. It stuck its tongue out at me and scampered off toward the back of C Block, all knees and elbows.

★ ★ ★

In the Sanctum, Zosimon sat cross-legged on his cushion, his head bowed as if in deep contemplation. I hesitated on the threshold.

"Come in, my dear Heracleitus. Sit down."

I stepped into the room, closing the door behind me, and sank onto the floor opposite him. I didn't take a cushion for myself. It didn't seem right, and I was getting used to sitting on hard floors. Zosimon looked up and smiled at me, his twinkling, knowing smile that made me feel as though he could see right into my soul.

"We haven't spoken properly since your very first day here," said Zosimon. "Libavius tells me that you're settling in nicely, but I wanted to check for myself. How are you?"

"Good," I told him. "Very good."

"I'm so pleased. Is there anything bothering you? Anything you'd like to know? I'm sure you have many questions."

I thought about asking him again about working with Fox. About when the next rotation would start. But it seemed too trivial to be bothering Zosimon with. I'd ask Lib later on. I hesitated, another question forming in my mind.

"What happened to Maggie? She has a black eye."

Zosimon's face grew serious. "Magnus is a troubled girl," he said. "Or at least she was when she came to us. One of the most polluted toxicants I've ever seen. Her elutriation is very painful and difficult. I'm helping her the best I can." Zosimon leaned back and laced his fingers together. "You know, Magnus reminds me of another young woman I once knew, a long time ago. This woman was a trained assassin, highly skilled. But death clouded her mind, and her body succumbed to the lure of the opium poppy."

Assassins? Opium? "What happened to her?" I asked, playing along.

Zosimon's face was washed with sadness. "She gave in to the body. I couldn't help her."

"Can you help Maggie?"

"I will do everything in my power. But ultimately, only she can decide which path to take." Zosimon sighed. "I am no prophet or messiah. I haven't been visited by angels or struck with a gift of prophecy. I am just a man like any other. The things I have achieved, I have achieved through my own will, my own strength. My technic is difficult, but it doesn't require supernatural gifts. It isn't beyond your grasp or Maggie's grasp or the grasp of any human being."

"But you're a . . ." I struggled for the right word.

"Guru? An oracle? No. I am a scientist. I am an expert in the field of microbiological chemistry and atomic phenomena. Nothing more." Zosimon nodded his head slightly, his eyes not leaving mine. We were sharing a secret, but I still wasn't sure what the secret was.

"I'm sure you're missing your family." Zosimon rose, opened a desk drawer, and presented me with my phone laid flat on the palm of his hand.

I took it from him and switched it on, suddenly overcome with the need to communicate with the outside world. Had Minah been texting me? Had Mom left voicemails? What was going on in the world, on Facebook, in the news?

The raw need for data and communication was shocking. I

felt like an addict who had started to detox but had then fallen hard off the wagon.

"It binds you to your toxicant life," murmured Zosimon. "Its hold on you is strong. But you are stronger."

I took a deep breath and closed my eyes for a moment, steadying myself. He was right. I could control this. It was all in my mind, after all.

"Can I call my mother?" I asked. "That's all."

"Of course you can," said Zosimon. "You don't need to ask my permission."

My fingers moved over the screen, and I held the phone up to my ear.

"Ruby?" Mom's voice was unexpectedly loud, laced with panic and fear.

"Hi, Mom," I said.

"Ruby! Where are you? Are you safe?"

"I'm fine, Mom. I'm safe."

"I've been so worried," she said, and I could tell she was crying. "I've been to the police, but nobody knows anything. . . ."

"It's OK," I said. "I'm . . ." I realized I didn't even know where I was. I couldn't tell her even if I wanted to.

"Ruby, please. Come home. Just come home."

"I will," I said. "I promise. But not yet. I love you." I hung up before I could hear more.

"Well done, Heracleitus," said Zosimon. "I know that was difficult for you. But you're doing the right thing. Already, see how much you've changed. How easily you communicate. How open and honest you are."

I realized he was right. When had I last told my mom I loved her? Not since I was a little kid. Despite all my cynicism, I had to admit that Zosimon really *was* helping me. Once you got past all the alchemy nonsense, the core elements of his methods — his *technic* — were sound.

"Did your mother say she had been speaking to the police?"

I nodded. "But they couldn't do much because I left a note."

"What did the note say? Did you tell her about us?"

I shook my head. "Just that I was going to stay with some friends."

I wondered if he was worried that the police would come looking for me. But he shouldn't worry. We weren't doing anything illegal.

Zosimon sighed. "People fear what they do not understand," he said. "I pity your mother. I hope she finds the peace she seeks. The next time you speak to her, you must dissuade her from continuing to pursue you through the police. They will fill her mind with lies and fear. I have many enemies, Heracleitus. Enemies in high places. They will seek to undo me."

"I understand." Although I didn't, really.

Zosimon swept the phone off the desk with one hand and dropped it into the drawer. Then he laced his fingers together and leaned forward, gazing at me with sharp intensity.

"Heracleitus. Darkness is coming, faster than I predicted. Soon we will have to act. It's time you learned the truth."

My skin rippled into a shiver. Was this more rhetoric? More alchemy and metaphor? Or was I really about to discover the secrets of the Institute?

Zosimon leaned back and brought his steepled fingers to his lips, as if contemplating where to begin.

"Humans are extraordinary creatures," he said at last. "We've conquered worlds — conquered the stars themselves. But we are capable of so much more. The human race has been duped by a small but powerful few. They are toxicants, mindless drones, slaves to corporations and money. Their bodies and minds are dulled, warped, contaminated. By alcohol. By sugar. By the endless parade of artificial preservatives and chemicals found in processed foods, in the water, in the poisons prescribed by the charlatans who call themselves doctors. It binds them. You must feel it, Heracleitus. You're eating real food now, for the first time in your life. Can't you *feel* the difference?"

I could feel it. It felt amazing. I wasn't sure I believed in any giant government conspiracies, but I could absolutely believe that most people weren't operating at their full potential. I'd seen it first hand — my mother wasting away on a diet of microwave dinners and cigarette smoke.

"Through these drugs — these poisons — the powerful few have turned humanity into a toxicant army, obedient and ravenous. There will come a time when this army will rise up and turn on itself, and all of humanity will be destroyed." It was a powerful idea. But I didn't believe him. How could I?

"Heracleitus," said Zosimon, and I looked up at him, even though it still didn't feel like my name. "The human body is a delicate instrument — after elutriation, it must be perfectly attuned, each chemical element in perfect balance. Once this alchemical harmony is achieved, the human body starts to ring like a bell, awakening your actuality. Your boundless self. Your sublime body."

"Does everyone here have a sublime body?" I asked.

Zosimon shook his head. "That is what everyone here strives toward," he said. "Some are very close. Very close indeed. But there is only one who has a true sublime body."

"Who?"

Zosimon gestured down at his own entirely unremarkable body. His glasses flashed in the candlelight. "Me."

"Is that why you tell stories set hundreds and thousands of years ago? You're talking metaphorically about your . . . sublime body?"

"Something like that." Daddy smiled wryly. "It seems such a simple thing, right? Believe me, it takes most people a lot longer to grasp the concept. You're one of the clever ones."

I thought it over. I already knew that the human body was made up of chemical elements, and that if they were unbalanced, you'd get sick. It made sense that if you managed to perfectly balance the elements, you'd be healthier. Health*iest*. Your perfect self. It probably would make you live longer. For the first time I wondered how old Zosimon really was.

"You have a question," Zosimon said gently. "Please, ask it. I want you to be honest. It's perfectly normal to have doubts."

I hesitated, not wanting to admit that I didn't believe him. "Why are you doing this?" I finally asked. "What's in it for you?"

He was going to tell me that he wanted to help people. That it was all altruism. And I wasn't going to fall for that.

"There aren't many people who would be brave enough to ask me that, Heracleitus. But I knew you were brave. And you may find that the answer shocks you. Not everyone here knows the truth — the real truth. People are only told when I deem them ready."

Curiosity burned within me. I straightened my back and raised my chin. I was ready. Or at least, I wanted him to think I was ready.

"Some people have been living here for years, and still they haven't had this avocation," said Daddy. "You've been here for three weeks. What makes you think you can handle it?"

"I can," I said, giving him my most confident look. "I know I can."

Zosimon's mouth spread into a broad smile. "Yes," he said. "I can *feel* it. You are remarkable."

Despite myself, I felt a swelling of pride.

"The ringing of a sublime body is echoed in the sublime bodies around it," Zosimon said, choosing his words carefully. "If enough bodies are ringing together, then something happens. A kind of spark. The Scintilla, it's known as. This spark will set us all alight, releasing us from the ties that bind us to the earth. We will become more than human — endowed with physical prowess, enhanced mental capabilities, and eternal vigor."

Reality came crashing back down again, and I had to struggle to keep myself from rolling my eyes. "You mean like . . . superheroes?"

Zosimon chuckled. "I suppose that's one way of putting it. Look, Heracleitus. I know how this sounds. I've presented this avocation hundreds of times before, to hundreds of different people. And it doesn't get any less ridiculous to my ears. There are many who don't believe it — who cannot avocate. Many of them change their minds eventually and come into the light. Some cannot grasp the hugeness of this at all, and they leave us. There have been an unfortunate few for whom this knowledge has been disastrous — it has overwhelmed their minds and driven them mad. But there are a very small number — a mere handful — who grasp the avocation instantly. No hesitation, no questions. Because deep inside, they know, right down into their very core, that I am telling the truth." Zosimon took off his glasses and passed a hand over his forehead. "I'd hoped you would be one of those very few, Heracleitus. But . . . perhaps I was mistaken." His face fell, disappointed, and I felt stung.

"You weren't," I said hastily, trying to put as much intensity and truthfulness into the words as I could. "You weren't mistaken."

Zosimon stared at me, his expression unreadable. Could he tell I was lying?

"Good," he said at last. "I knew I was right about you."

I didn't believe it. Of course I didn't. Conspiracy theories, superhumans — none of it was true. But Zosimon thought that I was extraordinary. And I didn't want to prove him wrong.

★ ★ ★

That evening, I found myself sitting across from Pippa at dinner. I leaned forward to speak quietly. "So . . . what happened last week?" I asked. "In the Sanctum? You seemed surprised to be chosen."

Pippa looked down at her bowl, a faint blush staining her cheeks. "I'm not really supposed to say," she said. "You have to have clearance."

Her eyes darted up to mine, and I could see she wanted to talk about it. "I promise I won't tell anyone," I said.

Pippa glanced around to make sure no one was listening. "The Sanctum is where women receive Daddy's actuality."

I stared at her.

"Women are incomplete," explained Pippa. "In order for us to become sublime, we must receive the actuality of a man."

"The actuality of a . . ." I shuddered, remembering how sure Fox had been. "I thought we were supposed to be resisting the urges of the body."

Pippa shook her head and smiled. "Receiving Daddy's actuality isn't about *desire*," she said. "It's not a carnal act. Daddy's actuality is boundless."

"Oh," I said, relieved. I'd been mistaken. Maybe it was some kind of ceremony. "Sorry, I thought you meant something else."

"Receiving from Daddy may *mirror* the carnal act, in the same way that the food we eat here is a mirror of the food consumed by the toxicants. But they are as different as night and day. One is pure and elutriating, and the other is corrupt and tainted."

I looked down at my salted quinoa. The little white tails on the grains looked suddenly suggestive. I put down my spoon, horrified.

"I'd heard stories," said Pippa. "We're not supposed to talk about it, but you know how it is. I thought some of it must be made up. Some of the things that happen in there. But it's all true, Hera. The golden light. The sound of bells. The floating. Every last word."

I remembered Zosimon's chanted affirmations. *You feel no sexual desire.* If he felt no sexual desire, then why was he taking girls back to his room? My skin crawled with revulsion, imagining him putting those perfectly manicured hands on Pippa. How was she OK with that? How were the other members of the Institute OK with that? What did Maggie think? Had he tried to make *her* go to the Sanctum? Had she tried to resist him? Was that where she got her black eye?

Pippa reached over to touch my hand. "As soon as you turn eighteen you'll be able to receive Daddy's actuality too. You'll see."

I forced my mouth into a smile, vowing to start talking to Fox about leaving as soon as I could.

11

"You do not feel the cold.
You are ambidextrous.
You can lift weights heavier than your own body.
You can grasp a new avocation in an instant.
You do not require food or drink to survive.
You are loved by your true family.
You love your Daddy."

I struggled to keep my composure at those last words, unable to erase the mental image of Zosimon with Pippa.

"No."

I started at the sound of a voice that wasn't Zosimon's. I opened my eyes and turned around, noticing that the others sitting cross-legged around me were doing the same.

It was Maggie. She had a wild look about her, more alive than I'd seen her for days. She held a knife, and was making her way shakily but deliberately to the raised platform where

Zosimon was seated. He rose to his feet, seemingly unperturbed.

"Magnus," he said mildly. "What's this all about?"

"Stop," said Maggie, taking relentless steps forward, her knuckles white around the knife's hilt. I recognized it as being one of the kitchen knives we used to cut up vegetables. I remembered that Newton had sharpened them only a few days previously.

"Stop talking," Maggie was saying, her voice high and on the verge of hysteria. "Stop your lies. Your poison. You sit up here like a god, but it's all lies. All of it."

Zosimon smiled a concerned, sympathetic smile. But he didn't speak.

"I know who you are." Maggie's teeth were clenched, her eyes wet. "I know what you did."

Still Zosimon didn't speak. Maggie stepped up onto the platform and raised the knife to point it at his throat. Val moved toward her, but Zosimon gave an almost imperceptible shake of his head.

"Go ahead," said Zosimon, his voice calm. "Cut me. Make me bleed. Kill me, if you think it will help you. I'd happily give my life for you."

He reached out and placed his palm over the blade of the knife, curling his fingers around it. Maggie trembled. Zosimon's hand flexed, squeezing the blade, and I felt my stomach turn over as I saw blood dripping from his fist.

"Magnus," he said gently. "My dear Magnus. There is no such thing as pain. It's a trick of the body. Don't let your pain trap your actuality. Cast your pain away. Embrace love."

They stood there for a moment, frozen still, while we all watched with pounding hearts and held breath. Then a shudder went through Maggie, and her hand slipped from the knife's hilt.

She collapsed, her body shaking with silent sobs.

A look passed between Zosimon and Lib, and a nod. Lib stepped forward.

"Come on, then," she said, taking Maggie's arm and helping her to her feet. "Let's get you cleaned up."

As they shuffled off toward the main building, I tried to piece together what had happened. I felt shaken, and not just because of the knife and the blood.

Maggie had been my ally — the only other person at the Institute who didn't seem completely under Zosimon's thrall. The only one who seemed to have doubts. Had the Institute somehow broken her, snapped some vital part that caused everything else to fall apart? Had something happened in Zosimon's Inner Sanctum? I remembered her outburst at the Red House and how quickly she'd snapped out of it. Had she been unhinged all along?

Zosimon, too, had shaken me. He had shown no fear in the face of death. Not so much as a flinch. It had been unnerving, but strangely compelling. I was starting to see what it was about him that attracted people.

Zosimon turned to the rest of us with a rueful smile. "Well, that was rather dramatic. I think we'd better cut Daddy's Hour short today, don't you? Head on into breakfast."

Daddy went inside, and we all rose to our feet. I immediately went to Fox's side. His face was white, and instinctively I reached out and gripped his hand.

"Fox." It was Welling. "Are you OK?"

Fox hesitated, then nodded. "Do you think she'll be OK, Welling?"

Welling's eyes flicked down to our joined hands. "I hope so."

Fox slid his hand out of my grasp. "I'd better go," he said, his voice small. But as he walked away, he looked over his shoulder at me and mouthed the word *tonight*.

Nobody else mentioned Maggie's outburst. Nobody moved to pick up the knife or clean up the blood, but when I walked through the courtyard after lunch, there was no sign that any of it had ever happened. I resolved to seek Maggie out that evening and ask her what was going on. What had she been working on with Zosimon? Where had she disappeared to for nearly three weeks? Something felt off, and I was convinced I wasn't seeing the whole picture.

We were told at dinner that evening that Maggie had decided to leave the Institute and return to her old life. I looked down at my salad and eggy water, the uneasy feeling growing stronger. I had to talk to Fox, convince him to leave with me. Maybe after what had happened with Maggie he'd be more amenable.

★ ★ ★

"I knew she was struggling," he told me that night in my room. I was curled on my bed — he was sitting on the floor, one elbow propped on his knee. "But I never imagined she would try to hurt anyone. It's awful. I really liked her."

"Me too."

"We used to talk a lot," Fox said. "She told me all about her adventures. Places she'd been. People she'd met. I can't believe she's really gone."

"How often do people leave?"

Fox squirmed uncomfortably. "We're not really supposed to talk about it," he said. "Daddy is so sad when people leave. He feels like it's his fault, that he failed them."

"But people do leave, right?"

"Not often. Sometimes people stop taking their supplements, stop following the technic. They get sick and the brain becomes aphotic. Daddy tries to help them, but sometimes it's too late."

"Is that what happened with Maggie? She stopped taking her supplements?"

"I guess so. I know Daddy had been working very closely with her. She always had doubts — from the very beginning. That's why she went back to the Red House with us. Daddy thought she needed a break from the Institute. That it was too much, too soon. I guess he was right."

I opened my mouth to tell him about my own doubts — about where Maggie had gotten her black eye, about what Pippa had told me happened in the Sanctum. But I didn't know where to begin. It was becoming clear to me that Fox didn't see certain things in the Institute, that there were certain questions he knew not to ask. I didn't think it was deliberate. It was the only life he knew, and to question it meant potentially destroying the very fabric of his existence.

"What's your first memory?" I asked him instead.

"Daddy," said Fox immediately.

"You don't remember anything before the Institute? Where you lived? Your parents?"

"There was no time before the Institute," said Fox. "I've always been here. First I was a Monkey, and now I'm me."

"You know that's not true," I said. "You've talked about the Red House. About Lib reading you stories. Before the thing with the Monkeys."

"That doesn't matter," Fox said. "None of that is important."

"What about the photo?" I asked. "The one of you and your mother."

"She isn't my mother," said Fox automatically. "I don't have a mother."

"Then why do you carry it around?"

He paused, the lines in his forehead growing deeper. "I don't know," he whispered at last. "I — I found it. Tucked inside the pages of *Les Miserables*. And as soon as I saw her . . . I knew her."

"So you assumed she was your mother?"

Fox let his breath whoosh out of his chest. "Yes," he said, his voice barely more than a whisper. "She is. I know she is. I feel it."

He slipped a hand into his pocket and pulled the photo out, gazing at it, his face full of sadness.

"Sometimes I imagine that I was a normal kid," he said softly. "With her. That I grew up in a house. That she baked cakes and bread. There was a garden full of flowers. We had a dog named Barker. I'd play in the yard, climbing trees and finding birds' nests. Barker and I would run through forests. I'd throw sticks for him. At night, my mother would tuck me into bed and sing to me until I fell asleep."

My heart was breaking for Fox. He had seemed so full of joy when I met him. So at peace with his life. But now I could see that was just a mask he wore. Behind it, Fox was longing for more. Longing for what could have been.

"What do you think happened to her?" I asked, turning the photo to see the penciled words scratched on the back.

"I don't know," said Fox. "I . . . can't think about it. Let's talk about something else."

I pressed him. "Have you tried asking someone? Lib, or even Zosimon?"

Fox shook his head. "How can I? They've always told me I don't have a mother."

"But everyone has a mother."

Fox folded the photo up and tucked it back between the pages of *Les Miserables*. "Not me."

I remembered the wild, broken look in Maggie's eyes. What if that happened to Fox?

"When does the next work rotation start?" I asked. "It's been forever since I asked. I want us to be together."

Fox coughed out a sharp laugh devoid of humor. "That's never going to happen."

"Why? Why can't we be on the same work team?"

He bit his lip and hesitated for a moment. "Because I'm not on a work team."

I stared at him.

"I work with the Monkeys," Fox said. "I look after them in the Monkey House. Make sure they are clean and safe and have enough to eat. It's what I've always done."

"But Lib said . . . *Zosimon* said . . ."

"They said it to make you stop asking. They want to keep us apart."

"But why didn't *you* say anything?"

Fox's face was miserable. "He told me not to."

I didn't understand the control Zosimon had over everyone in the Institute. He was compelling, yes. But how did he inspire so much fear and awe?

"It doesn't have to be like this," I told him. "You don't have to stay here. You can leave. You can have the house and the yard and the dog. And me. We could leave together. We could make that home together."

Fox looked away. "No," he said, his voice thick with emotion. "That can never happen."

"Of course it can," I said. "I'll look after you. We'll look after each other. I promise."

A flash of anger passed over his face. "You don't understand. If I walk out that gate, I'll vanish. In a puff of smoke. It will be like I never existed. You won't be able to look after me, because there won't be any me to look after."

His voice was still low so that no one would hear, but his cheeks were flushed, and tears stood out in his eyes. I reached out a hand to him, and he flinched away. He clenched a fist and slammed it onto the concrete floor, making me flinch in shock. Fox's face collapsed into misery and rage.

"Without this — without him — who am I? I'm nothing. I don't exist. You can go back to your old life. This is all I have. *All I am.*" Fox thumped his chest with each word, his face blotched red and white. His words came out as silent screams.

I sat frozen, unable to respond. His raw pain frightened me, reminded me of the intense sadness I thought I'd left behind. And I finally realized what it was that drew me to Fox. It wasn't his dreamy optimism or his innocence. It was that he was broken, like me. *That* was our connection. We recognized each other on a deep, painful level. And I knew in that moment that we could make each other whole.

Through the curtain of his sandy hair, Fox noticed my expression, and his shoulders slumped.

"I'm sorry," he said, his voice normal again. He pushed his hair back from his brow. "I should never have brought you here. I should never have talked to you."

His words took me aback. "Don't say that," I said. "You *saved* me. Without you, I'd be nothing."

Fox turned solemn eyes up to my face. "Without me, you'd be free."

"I *am* free," I said. "I'm here because I *choose* to be. Because of you. Because I choose you."

Fox's eyes wandered away from my face, settling on the stained carpet. "They all say that," he said, his voice hoarse and small. "They all believe it. Until they don't, and by then it's too late."

"What do you mean?"

"Maggie chose to come here," he said.

"Yes," I told him. "And she chose to leave."

"Did she?" His words hung in the air, and the uneasy feeling from earlier returned, making hairs stand up on the back of my neck. I didn't know what Fox was implying. I wasn't sure I wanted to know.

So let's leave, I wanted to say. I wanted to grab his hand and sprint out of the building, down the gravelly driveway and through the gate, away into the night. But I didn't want to upset him again.

"Shhh," I said, gently reaching out to brush his hair back from his forehead. I used the corner of my sleeve to wipe away his tears and then, hesitantly, leaned down from my bed and kissed him on the mouth.

I was crossing a forbidden line. I knew that. But this wasn't about the urges of the body. This was different. This was one friend comforting another.

Except it wasn't. It wasn't, and I knew it. But I kissed Fox anyway.

And he kissed me back. Slowly at first. Slow, gentle kisses that melted away his tears and my doubts.

It was a kiss. Just one kiss. Then we'd stop.

We didn't stop.

Fox scrambled up onto his hands and knees and climbed on the bed beside me, his hands reaching out to take mine. He leaned forward and we kissed again, a deeper kiss that made my whole body pulse with desire.

I knew that if I fell much farther, I wouldn't be able to stop.

I pulled away, and it was like pulling an industrial-strength magnet from a steel bar. My whole body thrummed, and my heart was racing.

"Fox," I murmured. "We're not supposed to . . ."

He drew back from me, his eyes wide, pupils large and black and still glistening with tears. "Do you want to stop?" he asked. "If you want to, we will stop. But I don't want to. Do you want to stop?"

I took in his disheveled hair, flopping over his forehead. His wild eyes and kiss-stained lips. In my fantasies, I'd always been the one pushing Fox toward sex. Teaching him about pleasure and desire. But this Fox wasn't the Fox from my fantasies. This Fox knew what he wanted, and it only made me want him more.

"No," I said. "I don't want to stop."

Fox slid his hands into my hair and cupped my face, leaning his forehead against mine, his breath panting sweet and heavy. I pulled him closer, sliding my hands up under his shirt to feel his chest, his ribs, his spine. My mouth sought his out again, and we tangled together, hot and aching.

"Ruby," Fox whispered against my lips. "Ruby."

It had been days since I'd heard my real name. It felt like coming home.

"How can anything that feels like this be wrong?" murmured Fox. "Don't you *feel* it?"

His lips were at the base of my throat, his fingers unbuttoning my nightgown. I'd spent weeks listening to Zosimon's lectures about denying the body and tried to follow his instructions, tried to control my urges and needs. It felt good to let that go. To touch and taste again. To *want*.

"Yes," I replied. "Yes."

He peeled away my nightgown as I pushed his shirt from

his shoulders. His skin against mine was overwhelming, simultaneously calming and searing hot.

We shed the rest of our clothes and lay pressed against each other, skin on skin. We explored each other with gently brushing fingers and lips that grew hungry and fevered as we rose on a wave of incandescent need. It wasn't holy or pure. It was messy and awkward and sweet and *real*. My questions and fears and doubts all fell silent. This was right.

★ ★ ★

I'm not sure how long it took me to realize that we weren't alone. But when I did realize it, I pulled away. My lips felt swollen and every atom of my body ached and buzzed for Fox. But it was all drowned in self-conscious confusion when I saw Zosimon standing in the doorway, illuminated by the fluorescent light of the hallway. As my eyes adjusted to the harsh whiteness of it all, I saw his expression. It was a curious mix of disappointment, disgust, and rage.

Fox and I sprang apart and fumbled for our clothes. I felt my cheeks flare red. I glanced at Fox, expecting to see my own embarrassment mirrored on his face. But I saw something else entirely. I saw terror.

"Daddy," whimpered Fox, hunching over like he was trying to make himself smaller. "Daddy. I'm so sorry. Please, Daddy. Please forgive me. Please. Please."

Zosimon turned his back on us. "Follow me."

12

Zosimon led us down the hall past a series of dingy storage rooms. I'd never been there before — Lib had told me that the area was off limits, that the rooms were dangerously dilapidated. He led us down another hallway and pushed open a heavy metal door. The stench of mustiness enveloped me, and I glimpsed a dark, empty room, not much bigger than a cupboard.

"Get in," Zosimon said to Fox, his voice expressionless. "Wait for me there."

"Look," I said. "I get that we broke the rules. We're sorry, OK?"

Zosimon ignored me. Fox, still hunched over and small, slunk into the room. He didn't look at me.

Zosimon pushed the door shut with a deep, booming clang, and led me farther down the corridor. The fluorescent lights plinked on and off overhead. Everything smelled of damp and dust. We reached another door and another room, identical to the one that Fox had entered. Zosimon ushered me inside, flicking on another fluorescent light, and shut the door behind us.

"Please," I said. "Let me explain."

Zosimon drew back his hand and struck me across the face, hard. I recoiled in shock. His expression remained calm.

"I'm so sorry it's come to this," he said, his voice almost pleasant. "You have so much promise. I really hope we can work this out."

I stared at him, speechless, my hand pressed to my cheek.

"Your behavior is unacceptable," Zosimon went on. "I realize you're still adjusting to life here with us. But you must understand that the rules have to be followed. If I made an exception for you, then I'd have to make it for everyone, and our peaceful little family would crumble."

"Fine," I said. "Let us go. Me and Fox. You'll never hear from us again."

He hit me again. One of my teeth sliced into my cheek, and I tasted blood.

Zosimon shook his head. "You don't want that," he said. "You see, you're still a toxicant. That's why you behave in this way. Your body is still bound to the earth, choked with toxins. I don't want that for you. I care about you too much."

He kicked my shins, knocking me to the ground. My wrist took my body weight and twisted painfully.

Zosimon bent over me, pulling a roll of thick tape from his pocket. He tore off a strip and pressed it roughly over my mouth. I tried to cry out, but my nose was running blood and mucus, and I could barely breathe.

"You must think of your brothers and sisters," said Zosimon. "Do you want them to suffer too? Your words poison the air. You will contaminate the others, and I'm afraid I just can't have that. You. Must. Be. Elutriated."

He kicked me with each word, again and again. With every kick he told me I was dirty. That I was polluted. Toxic. That he was disgusted by me. I felt my bones bend and my flesh tear. But Zosimon's expression remained mild, as if we were having an ordinary conversation. I closed my eyes and whimpered under the tape, hoping that if I submitted it would be over soon. I remembered the crazed look in Maggie's eyes and her trembling words.

I know who you are. I know what you did.

Eventually I realized that he had stopped, the light had been turned off, and I was alone in the small damp room. Dimly, I heard a voice. I tensed. Was Zosimon coming back?

Then there was a scream, a scream that unmistakably came from Fox.

I tried to get up so I could pound my fists on the door and demand that Zosimon beat *me* instead. But my broken body refused to move. I lay there and listened to Fox, my mouth straining against the tape in my own silent howl.

Then there was silence.

There were no windows in the little room, so I had no idea how much time had passed. My stomach started to cramp from hunger, and my full bladder ached. I groped around the room on hands and knees until I found a metal bucket to urinate in. Then I shuffled to my feet, my limbs aching and tender, and tore the tape from my mouth, ripping off a layer of skin that left my lips raw and stinging. I banged on the door and yelled at the top of my lungs. I used every swear word I could think of — hurled insults and slurs against Zosimon and Lib and everyone else in the Institute of the Boundless Sublime. I told them I'd contact the police, that they'd all go to jail. I screamed until my throat was raw.

Nobody came.

I couldn't see my body in the darkness, but I could feel the swelling and imagine the bruising. My wrist was definitely sprained, and I knew I had a black eye and a split lip. Breathing brought on a jagged, rasping pain in my chest, which I thought could be a cracked rib.

I was stuck there. Nobody from the Institute was going to come and help me. And nobody else knew where I was. Had Mom stopped looking for me?

A great, shuddering fear clawed its way into my throat as I realized there was a very real possibility I could die there, in that tiny musty room.

What had I done?

It all seemed so clear, in the dank, dark basement. The Institute wasn't the answer to the meaning of life. The Institute was a cult. Zosimon was the typical charismatic leader — compelling, mysterious, appealing. And totally full of shit.

He wasn't thousands of years old. He didn't subsist on sunlight and oxygen.

There was no such thing as sublimation or the Scintilla. Everyone up there, slaving away — they were all brainwashed. Deluded. Wasting their lives for a charlatan.

For a moment, I'd almost believed it. Zosimon had offered me a way out, a light at the end of my tunnel of grief. He'd offered me peace. Purpose. A reason to keep fighting.

And he'd offered me Fox.

Zosimon had dangled Fox in front of me like a ball of yarn in front of a kitten. He'd tempted me into his lair and slammed the door behind me. But why? Had it been some kind of a test?

If so, it was clear that I had failed.

Sometimes, if I closed my eyes and held my breath, I could hear sounds from beyond the room. The hum of activity as the world went on, totally oblivious to what was going on inside the walls of the Institute. Birds flew overhead. I heard cars swooping by and the rhythmic beeping of a truck reversing. Sometimes I'd hear a snatch of music from a car radio or the faint sound of someone talking on a cell phone. How could people just walk by? Drive their cars down the street? Didn't they know? Had nobody ever wondered what went on behind the high concrete walls?

There was no light in the room, but I had some idea what time it was by the sounds from outside. When I heard the strains of song and laughter, I knew it was evening, and Family Time was taking place without me. Without us. Had anyone noticed that Fox and I were missing? Did anyone care? Surely they'd be worried for Fox even if they didn't care about me.

When the noise of Family Time died down, I curled up on the floor against the wall and tried to sleep, my bruised body slipping gratefully into unconsciousness.

Nobody came for me the next day, or the day after that. I found a leaking pipe running down the wall that dripped water. I licked it eagerly, desperate to quench my thirst. It tasted like rust. On the third day, I started to sing. I beat rhythms out on the walls with the palms of my hands and sang everything I could think of — the National Anthem, Top 40 hits, nursery rhymes. My fingers flitted over the damp walls, pressing invisible keys, playing and playing until my fingertips bled. I played Rachmaninov's *Prelude in G minor* and Mendelssohn's *Rondo Capriccioso in E major*. I pounded the walls with Prokofiev's *Suggestion Diabolique* and thundered away at

Lecuona's *Gitanerias*. I played Tori Amos and Metallica and Lorde and Taylor Swift.

I filled the room with music so I didn't have to listen to the silence.

But eventually the silence smothered my music, wrapping its fingers around my throat and forcing my songs back down into my chest. I curled up on the floor and listened. Listened for the sound of Fox nearby. Of Zosimon coming to release me. Of anyone. Of humanity still existing.

I thought about Maggie, her fist gripping the hilt of the knife. Was this where she had disappeared to? No wonder she'd gone crazy. But they let her out eventually.

Hadn't they? Fox had said something, back in my room. Something that suggested that Maggie hadn't chosen to leave the Institute after all.

Had they brought her back here after the incident with the knife? Was this where dissenters were sent, to starve and shiver and rot, while outside vegetables were planted, floors were scrubbed, and meals were doused with salt?

The darkness descended. This time it wasn't the familiar black tide, the numb darkness that I could wrap myself up in. This was a giant, gaping, empty darkness. It was terrifying, and all I could do was scream into it as it screamed back at me. The world turned inside out, until I couldn't hear the sounds from outside any longer. No more birds or rumbling of trucks or clanking of machinery. No singing and laughter from Family Time. It had all gone. Something inside me broke, and I sat surrounded by pieces of myself, with no idea of how to put them back together again.

I felt my body slowly breaking down, betraying me as it leached toxins and pollution. It was disgusting. The swelling and bruising went away, and my ribs stopped aching. But everything else got worse. I could feel the contamination spreading through me, and I regretted every processed snack I'd ever eaten. Every fizzy soda. I regretted the cigarette I'd smoked with Ali in the Wasteland, fingers of poison wrapping around my veins and squeezing away everything that mattered.

It was all my fault. Like some kind of plague, everything I touched withered and died. Anton was dead because of me. Dad was in jail because of me. Mom was a gray husk of a person because of me.

And Fox.

What had happened to Fox?

Was he still in the room down the hall? I hadn't heard him since that first night. Since he'd screamed.

Daddy must have taken him away. Moved him to another room.

Or Fox was dead.

I had seduced him. Me. Fox had been pure and beautiful. Before I met him, he'd probably never thought about sex. To him, love was something clear and wonderful, like sunlight or fresh air. But I had dragged him down to my level. I'd taught him about the longing of the flesh. I'd spread my plague to him, my dirtiness. My contamination. And just like everything else, it had poisoned Fox. Made him shrink and warp and crumble. I'd pressed my filthy body against his, and I'd destroyed him.

Just like I'd destroyed Anton. For the second time, I'd let my own lust rule, while the people I loved died.

With trembling hands, I groped around on the floor for the piece of tape, and pressed it back over my mouth. I didn't deserve to be heard. I was nothing. This was where I belonged, lurking like a blind earthworm in the damp, empty darkness.

My body was repellent to me, a skin sack full of putrid flesh, slowly liquefying and decaying. I imagined that I was filling with maggots, and scratched feverishly as I felt them crawl and wriggle under my skin. I felt like I needed to urinate constantly, but whenever I crawled over to the bucket in the corner and squatted over it, nothing came out, and a burning sensation spread through my abdomen. I whimpered.

My heartbeat pattered faster and faster, rising in my throat, on my breath. My muscles ached, and it became difficult for me to drag myself from my sleeping corner to the corner where my waste bucket sat.

I felt no hunger. I was no longer woken in the middle of the night by growling pangs. No longer choked as a bilious tide rose in the back of my throat. I was hollowing out, like my flesh was slowly being eaten away leaving nothing but papery skin and bone.

I forgot where I was. I forgot who I was. I forgot about my mother and father and Anton. I forgot about Fox.

I slipped

out

of the world

and into

nothingness

★ ★ ★

I don't know how many days passed before the door finally opened. It could have been as few as six or as many as sixty. But it did open, and a huge figure filled the doorway, silhouetted in blinding fluorescent light.

It was Val. I was surprised he was still alive. I was surprised anyone was still alive in the world.

He stepped into the room, and light spilled in after him. I cowered away from it. Val raised a finger to his lips, urging me to stay silent. He emptied a bowl onto the floor. Bits of peel and bruised vegetable bounced around me. Some of them were furred with mold. Val bent over and removed the tape from my mouth, and I felt more skin come away with it. I said nothing. I didn't want to hurt him with my words. I wasn't sure I even knew how to make words anymore.

I groped toward the food with cracked, peeling fingers and raised a wrinkled carrot to my mouth. My tongue felt enormous. I tried to bite down on the carrot, and I felt one of my teeth wobble dangerously, as if it were no longer anchored to my jaw. I gnawed at the carrot with my back molars. The roughness of it cut my mouth. I tried to swallow, but I'd forgotten how. I gagged and spluttered. Val waited silently while I choked down the scraps. There wasn't much. Not more than a handful. The food felt alien and strange, sliding down my throat, coating my shiny, pink insides.

Val leaned over to replace the tape over my mouth. I tried to show him with my eyes how grateful I was, how much I appreciated his kindness. He didn't look at me as he left, and I welcomed the return of the darkness as the door closed behind him.

I was invisible. An empty shell.

I curled back into my corner and slipped into a dreamless sleep.

★ ★ ★

Val came regularly after that. I didn't know how often. Every day? Each time he brought a bowl full of kitchen scraps.

Sometimes he brought a handful of supplements and a glass of sulfurous water. The pills were difficult to swallow, and I retched as I tried to choke them down, spilling water all over myself.

I knew better than to talk to him.

I knew what I was. What I deserved.

When he came in I crawled to the back of the room and hunched down on the floor to show him respect. I didn't try to meet his eyes. To touch him. I scraped myself against the floor and waited until he'd gone before I gobbled up the few meager offerings he left behind.

Perhaps this was how my life would be now. Perhaps I would live here forever, in this tiny room.

There were worse ways to live.

★ ★ ★

Finally, Zosimon came to me. He crouched down beside me, unperturbed by my filth. He pressed a cool cloth to my forehead, raised a glass to my lips.

"Shhh," he said. "Everything's going to be all right. I promise. I won't let anything bad happen to you."

He brought in a tub of water and carefully sponged me. He dressed me in clean, dry clothes, and fed me juice, wiping my mouth to catch any spills. He spoke to me in soft tones. He forgave me for letting my body take over. For what I'd done to Anton and Fox.

Under his gentle care, I was finally elutriated. For days, he nursed me back to life, whispering secrets about the future, about the Scintilla. About how when I became sublime, he and I would float right up into the sky, boundless and golden and shining from within. I drank in his words, my eyes never leaving his face. He was everything.

"It's time for you to rejoin us," he said at last. "We need you, Heracleitus. Darkness is coming, and we need you."

I nodded, my eyes swimming with tears of gratitude. "Thank you, Daddy."

13

Daddy led me from the tiny room down the hallway and out into the courtyard. The light was blinding. It pierced my skull like a white-hot knife sliding in through my ocular cavity. I'd forgotten the world was so big. So open. I was afraid the sky might swallow me up. Daddy took my hand, as if he could sense my fear.

"It's OK," he murmured. "Daddy's here."

His dry hand engulfed mine, and I felt his strength flow into me. He took me to the Inner Sanctum and sat me down on one of the large soft cushions. He passed me a smooth object, and I stared at it for a moment before recognizing it as my phone. The hunger I'd felt for it had gone, the addiction broken. Now I regarded it with a mix of disgust and confusion. How had this simple, flat device had so much power over me? How had I let it enslave me? Let it fill me with poison and toxicant lies?

"Speak to your mother," said Daddy. "She will be eager to hear from you."

I switched the phone on, and my fingers moved over the

screen robotically, my body remembering what my mind didn't. I lifted the phone to my ear. I could feel radio waves and electricity seeping in through my skin, making my pulse slow and my teeth ache. I longed to be rid of it.

"Ruby? Is that you?"

I didn't know how to answer. I wasn't Ruby. I was Heracleitus.

"Ruby, I miss you. But . . . maybe you're doing the right thing. Maybe you need to be there right now."

I barely recognized her voice. I'd forgotten what it felt like to have a mother. Why did I need a mother, anyway? I had Daddy. I looked up at him, and his blue eyes crinkled at the edges as he smiled, encouraging and strong. Calmness radiated from him, and I let it wash over me, erasing my fears and doubts. I breathed deeply and could smell turned earth and green leaves.

"I understand," said the woman on the other end of the phone. "I — I trust you. I trust that you'll come home when you're ready."

Home. The word niggled at me, worming its way in through Daddy's barrier of calm. I ended the call, unsettled. Daddy reached over and grasped both my hands in his. I noticed that he had dirt under his usually perfect fingernails.

Darkness is coming.

"Well done, Heracleitus," Daddy said, his voice low and intense with emotion. "You truly are extraordinary."

Was I?

"Do you remember when you first spoke to your mother?" he said. "When you had recently arrived at the Institute? She was nearly hysterical with worry over you, and there was nothing you could say to make it better. But this time, you used my technic. All the powers you have gained as you approach sublimation. And your mother responded. She was calm, trusting. You told her the truth and immediately she accepted your avocation."

I couldn't even remember speaking. But I must have. Daddy was right. I was growing powerful. I was becoming sublime. Daddy was proud of me.

★ ★ ★

We went back into the courtyard, and I was struck by the beauty of the Institute. It had seemed so drab when I'd first arrived. So stark. But now I saw it for what it truly was. The concrete block walls of A Block and B Block stood strong and true, and the soaring timbers of the warehouse made it look like a cathedral. Everything was beautiful. Everything had meaning.

I looked over at the vegetable garden and saw broken stalks and mounded earth. I frowned. It didn't seem like the right time of year for such a big harvest. The vertical herb gardens were bare, and some of their support beams had fallen down.

Darkness is coming.

Daddy placed his palm on my back and steered me toward the space where the rest of my family was gathered, waiting. I felt a surge of love to see them all again. Lib, her face stern. Stan, bouncing on the balls of his feet and nodding as he listened to something Welling was saying. Newton, her long black hair coiled in a braid. Pippa, blinking sleepily in the morning light. Implacable Val, who had brought food when I needed it most. Other friends I had come to know over my weeks in the Institute, each one wise and beautiful and precious in his or her own way.

And Fox.

I glimpsed him and turned my eyes to the ground as emotions flooded through me. Relief. Longing. Shame.

I had to be good. Daddy's hand was still on my back, and I focused on that, on the strength that flowed from him into me. I had to win back his trust.

The morning sun struggled over the wall of the Institute and washed me in warm light. I closed my eyes and felt my face turn up to it, felt the sunlight soak into my skin. I was being bathed in living actuality. It filled my body with a satisfaction that no meal had ever done. I understood, now, how Daddy did it. How he lived on air and sunlight. It was better than anything I'd ever tasted. It was transformational.

Opening my eyes, I saw Fox again, only a few feet away from me. He looked thinner, his cheekbones more angular, his lips a little less full. But his eyes were the same, and their yearning was as painful to me as Daddy's boot had been, sinking into the soft flesh of my belly. My skin flushed with heat, and the fulfillment I'd felt from the sunlight began to fade as an aching, gnawing hunger clawed its way into my chest. I bit down hard on my lower lip, and my mouth flooded with the metallic tang of blood. The pain gave me the strength I needed to tear my gaze away.

I looked over my shoulder at Daddy. Daddy, who had saved me. I had to be strong for him.

He dropped his hand from my back. "You have found wisdom, Heracleitus," he murmured. "I am so proud of you. Your courage, your determination . . ." He shook his head admiringly. "You truly are my daughter."

I felt myself swell with pride, and the hot flush faded from my skin.

"I'm so glad you have returned to us," said Daddy. "I will need you by my side for the coming war."

War?

"They're coming, you know. They've been waiting for centuries. Millennia. But now they come."

I swallowed down my questions. I'd get answers soon enough. "Yes, Daddy."

Nobody commented on my return, but several people smiled and nodded, and their unspoken support warmed me to my core. I looked at Lib, but she narrowed her mouth into a flat disapproving line. I wondered if she knew what I'd done. With Fox. No wonder she was disgusted with me. With my weakness. But I'd changed, and I'd prove it to her. I'd prove it to them all.

Daddy looked different too. His white shirt was dirty. His hair, usually neatly braided, hung loose and wild around his shoulders in steely tangles. His glasses were smudged and sat slightly askew on the bridge of his nose. It made him seem almost elemental, as if the sheer raw power of him couldn't be contained by his frail meat body. My breath caught in my throat, and I was filled with awe.

"They are coming," he said again, raising his voice so everyone could hear.

We waited for him to continue. I felt a chill spread through me — a heavy feeling of dread.

"The Quintus Septum."

The words were meaningless to me, but the foreboding in Daddy's eyes was enough. A low murmur passed through the group.

I could still feel Fox's eyes on me. My skin prickled, but I kept my own gaze on Daddy. I had to let Fox go. There had been a time when the mere thought of his name would thrill me to my core, flooding my body in waves of longing and anticipation. No longer.

I understood now why Daddy had punished us. Why what we'd done was wrong. My heart had been so full of Fox that I had no space for the sublime. Fox was a distraction of the flesh, dragging my actuality down into leaden toxicant mortality.

I had to learn to resist my flesh — its pull, its mechanical urges. Locked away in the tiny room, I had begun to push the lead from my body, down through my feet into the earth where it belonged. Now my mind was becoming sharp, and I was learning control. I was elutriated. Clear, hollow, pure.

"Some of you will have heard of the assault on the Institute that occurred last night."

I felt a prickle along my spine. Assault?

"The walls of the Institute were breached, and two agents from the Quintus Septum broke in. They destroyed our crops before heading to C Block. It was at this point that I was alerted to their presence and drove them off. But it is my firm avocation that their true target was the Monkey House. They sought to steal our children. To poison them and torture them in order to reveal our secrets."

I pictured the innocent Monkeys. Scampering all over the Institute, laughing and playing. Their lives had been so simple and carefree. Who would want to end that?

"The Quintus Septum have declared war on us," said Daddy. "We knew this was coming."

I felt fear ripple through my brothers and sisters, but I steeled myself against it. Fear was a weakness. I felt only certainty. Daddy would save us. Under his guidance, we would fight this new enemy, and we would triumph. "From now on, the Monkey

House is on lockdown. The Monkeys must stay inside where they will be safe. They can only come out if they are silent and supervised by an adult. They are too valuable. Too precious."

I was struck once more by the intensity of Daddy's presence. I could *see* his actuality flowing through us all, connecting us in a network of glittering, throbbing power. A thread of it was flowing into me, filling me with an exultation so profound that I nearly floated free from the aphotic soil beneath my feet.

"The Quintus Septum are our ancient enemies," said Daddy. "Soldiers bound by lead and Earth. For millennia they have hunted us, searching to destroy us and take the secrets of the Scintilla. They want to unlock it and use it, not as a tool for purity and ascension, but as a weapon. We must not let them succeed."

The Scintilla. Daddy had whispered its secrets to me as I'd recovered. Once enough of us became sublime, our clear, hollow, shining bodies would begin to ring like bells. This would activate the Scintilla, which would unlock the true powers of sublimation. The way Daddy described it, it was a key that took the form of a glowing red gem.

"Once the Scintilla is activated, we will become gods. We will cast off our mortal flesh and fly boundless and free. We will have unimaginable strength and skill and intellectual capacity. Then we can rise up and defeat the filthy Quintus Septum. But until that day we must act with caution. We must learn to move unseen. To live with one ear to the ground. I will train you in the arts of stealth and cunning, technics that I have mastered over the centuries from the greatest masters to ever walk on this planet. You will move like shadows, swift and silent. You will gain even more mastery and control over your bodies. We must redouble our efforts to become sublime, to call forth the Scintilla."

My skin tingled with a savage joy. The Scintilla.

I could imagine it now — glowing red with a pure fire. A fire that would spread through me, burning away the blood and the flesh and the lead and dirt, leaving me shining and pure.

Daddy spread his arms wide. "The Scintilla will come and light the way for us. The Institute of the Boundless Sublime will rise above all. The Quintus Septum will be vanquished, along with all their toxicant meat-followers. We shall rule over all, gods of light and science. You, my children, will gain powers beyond your wildest imaginings. And I will be everyone's Daddy."

14

Things swung into action. Due to the assault on the vegetable garden, our food was heavily rationed. We had to subsist on a few handfuls of soaked grains or beans each day. This wasn't an issue for me — I'd gotten used to subsisting entirely on sulfurous water and the occasional food scrap, so even a spoonful of salted quinoa felt like a feast. We rarely saw the Monkeys anymore — they only left C Block for a few minutes each day, under escort, and we weren't allowed to go anywhere near the building without Daddy's express permission.

I threw myself into the preparations so I wouldn't have to think about Fox. I felt him watch me wherever I went. A few times he tried to catch me alone, but I managed to slip away. I didn't want to face him. I didn't know if I was strong enough.

During Daddy's Hour, we learned more about the Quintus Septum. They were a sinister group of sorcerers, Daddy said, representing the five most powerful institutions in the world — politics, religion, science, business, and celebrity. The president was a member. So was the pope, along with Oprah, Madonna, Jay-Z, and a bunch of other famous people.

"They control *everything*," hissed Daddy, and I felt a chill pass through me.

Daddy explained to us that we would need to be prepared for when the Quintus Septum came after us. We would be trained in new technics, to be fit and alert and sneaky. We might need to infiltrate enemy bases, and Daddy wanted us to be sure we were ready. We abandoned our usual work units in favor of survival technics, doing hundreds of push-ups and sit-ups or commando crawling through obstacle courses that Stan and Val assembled on the bare earth where the garden had once been. We learned how to coax fire from dry twigs and to use mud and leaves to camouflage ourselves from sight.

It was exciting. My days melted into scenes from a movie training montage. What we were doing felt *important*. I imagined sneaking into hidden compounds, stealing secret weapons and plans from right under the enemy's nose. I imagined returning to the Institute a hero, handing a locked briefcase over into Daddy's hands to thunderous applause. Daddy would smile at me. He wouldn't say anything. He wouldn't need to. The look of approval and love in his eyes was all I needed.

Fox seemed to understand too. He stopped trying to talk to me. But he still watched. I felt his eyes on me constantly, and despite my best efforts, I couldn't ignore him. But that just made me determined to train harder.

I shed the aphotic weakness I'd developed in my cell and felt my body grow hard and strong with exercise and work. I could easily subsist on only a few mouthfuls a day. My mind was clear, and my body was transforming. It was working. I was becoming sublime.

★ ★ ★

One morning, Daddy called Fox, Pippa, Welling, and me into the drafty old warehouse, where he'd set up a table and chairs in the corner.

"Welling and I have been working on a top-secret technic," Daddy explained. "It is dangerous and complex, but we have selected you three to join us, due to your proven tenacity and intelligence."

Daddy laced his fingers behind his back and raised his eyes to the ceiling thoughtfully. "The universe is composed of elements," he said. "The Quintus Septum would have you believe that this planet's elements are all discovered. That they can be contained in a table and are constricted by rigid categories like atomic weight and protons and isotopes. This, of course, is all a ruse, designed to prevent us from avocation."

"I have a question," said Fox.

Daddy frowned at him. "Later, Furicius. In my lifelong search for the Scintilla, I have made many discoveries. I have uncovered many secrets. Secrets that have been buried deep for many thousands of years. But these secrets often uncover yet more mysteries. One of those mysteries is the secret of aether."

Fox shifted uncomfortably, and I saw him glance out of the warehouse's large open door. From where we were sitting, we could see the top of the building on the other side of the Institute's walls. A fluorescent light came on in one of the offices.

"We talk about being boundless, about becoming sublime," Daddy went on. "Well, aether is the ultimate in boundlessness. It is what is formed when all the chemical elements are perfectly balanced — or *sublimated*. It is perfect lightness and harmony. It will help us reach our goal. It will help us summon the Scintilla."

Fox still wasn't paying attention. But I was. I sat up straighter in my chair and pushed thoughts of Fox from my mind.

"This technic can be very dangerous. If handled incorrectly, these elements can transform into unstable radioisotopes. One single gram of such a substance could be as deadly as a nuclear bomb."

Fox looked back at Daddy. I could sense his restlessness, the flood of questions that threatened to pour out of him, like water from a burst dam. But he stayed silent.

"This kind of experiment requires practice. I have been working with chemistry for many centuries, but you are all novices. This is why I have instructed Welling to drill you in the basic sublimation technic first, before I expose you to any of the harmful chemicals I keep in my laboratory."

Daddy produced a cloth bag and drew from it a handful of wooden tokens, spreading them out onto the table between us. Each one had a blackened symbol on it, as if they had been branded with something burning hot. Some of the symbols were recognizable letters: He, O, F, Li, Be. Other symbols were unfamiliar — arcane squiggles, all curves and angles.

Daddy pointed at the letters. "Does anyone recognize these?"

"Are they . . . elements?" asked Pippa. "From the periodic table?"

Daddy beamed at her, and I felt a stab of jealousy. I suddenly wished I'd paid more attention in science class. Then Daddy might be smiling at *me* now.

"You are one hundred percent correct, Agrippa. These are first elements of the periodic table." Daddy lined them up one by one and pointed. "Helium, lithium, beryllium, boron, carbon, nitrogen, oxygen, and fluorine. The astute among you," — here he glanced at Pippa and twitched the corner of his mouth in a smile — "will have noticed that the very first element, hydrogen, is missing. This is because hydrogen, having only one proton, cannot bring about sublimation in other elements. It is a non-reactive element, and therefore it does not concern us. It is the number of protons that determine an element's atomic number. Helium is the second element because it has two protons. Lithium has three. Beryllium has four, and so on. This is simplistic stuff that some of you will remember from childhood. And your toxicant schoolteachers were correct, for those first few elements. After that, things get a little more complex. This technic works with those first elements, excluding hydrogen, as well as the Sovereign Four."

"The Sovereign Four?" asked Pippa. "I don't remember that from school."

Daddy chuckled. "For good reason, Agrippa. The Sovereign Four are the hidden elements. The ones that people don't want you to know about. Ask a chemist out there, and they will tell you that these elements don't exist, that they're compounds of other things. But that's just what the Quintus Septum wants you to think."

He pointed to each of the curly symbols. "Calx. Galena. Nix alba. Bismuth. These are the Sovereign Four. They are considered to be special because unlike other elements, they share the same number of protons: ten."

Pippa was frowning, her lips moving silently as if she were reciting something in her head. "Neon!" she said at last. "Isn't neon the tenth element? Doesn't that mean it has ten protons?"

Daddy glanced at Welling, and they both laughed. "I'm sure that's what the toxicants told you," said Daddy, rolling his eyes.

Pippa blushed.

"What's that one?" asked Fox, pointing to the last tile, which had a small black dot in the center.

"I'm glad you asked, Furicius," Daddy said with a nod. "This one is quicksilver, or mercury, and it is the most dangerous of all the elements. Its atomic number is unstable, and can change. Sometimes it disguises itself as hydrogen, with only one proton. Sometimes it has eleven. You must be extremely careful when working with it, making sure that you are certain which atomic number it has at that precise moment."

I saw Pippa open her mouth to ask a question, a frown crinkling her forehead. But she shut her mouth again and said nothing.

Daddy looked down at the wooden tokens and then back at us. "Welling will be teaching you an ancient technic for balancing these elements — what we refer to as the process of *sublimation* — in order to produce aether." He nodded to Welling. "I'll leave them in your most capable hands."

"OK," said Welling, after Daddy had left. "So the sublimation technic is very simple, and it involves keeping mental tally. When you see the elements helium, lithium, beryllium, boron, and calcium, you add one to your count."

"You mean carbon," said Pippa. "Not calcium."

"Carbon. My apologies," said Welling, flashing Pippa a quick smile. "So then for nitrogen, oxygen, and fluorine, you do nothing. For the Royal Four plus mercury, you subtract one from your tally."

"The Sovereign Four," said Fox.

"What?"

"You said the Royal Four. Aren't they called the Sovereign Four?"

Welling looked irritated. "Yeah, the Sovereign Four. What difference does it make?"

"How did you learn so much about chemistry?" asked Fox. "You said you worked with money before you came here. Not elements."

"I have studied with Daddy," said Welling smoothly. "We've been working together on this for quite some time. I've had many avocations about the process."

"But I thought —"

"Enough questions, Fox," said Welling, his voice firm.

Fox stared at him for a moment, and I got the feeling that there was a kind of unspoken battle going on. A test. Eventually, Fox looked away and slouched down in his chair.

Welling swept the tiles back into the bag and shook it to mix them around. Then he pulled out one tile at a time, laying them on the table and instructing us to keep count. There were around a hundred tiles in total, and it was difficult to remember which element was which.

"What number do you have?" asked Welling as he put down the last tile.

"Two," said Fox.

"Negative one," said Pippa.

"Zero," I said.

Welling flicked me an approving glance. "We will train like this for an hour every morning after breakfast, before you resume your assigned duties or training. Now let's try again."

He swept the tokens back into the bag.

★ ★ ★

Sometimes Daddy would select people for individual training missions. I was selected for Operation Hush-Hush. In order to learn the technic of covert infiltration, Daddy instructed me to sneak into nearby houses in the dead of night. I was to quietly break in and achieve some arbitrary goal — moving furniture or turning books spine-in on their shelves — before leaving the house with no other evidence that I'd been there. I spent a week training beforehand, learning to walk silently and stick to the shadows. Daddy taught me how to behave if I was caught — I was to pretend to be sleepwalking, and "wake up" all embarrassed and flustered.

"But you won't be caught, Heracleitus," Daddy said, turning the key in the lock that opened the ancient garage door that separated the Institute from the rest of the world. "You are extraordinary."

I stepped out into the night. It was the first time I'd been outside the Institute since I'd arrived. How long had it been? Weeks? Months? I had no idea anymore. I couldn't recognize the toxicant girl who had arrived here in the minivan, full of doubt and grief and tainted flesh. I'd thought I knew everything. But I'd been a puppet, a slave to my meat body, drugged and docile, an implement for the Quintus Septum to use like the lowliest of pawns.

I gazed up and down the dark street. It was like stepping into Narnia or Platform 9¾, except the other way. Going from the magical world back to the mundane everydayness of the real world. I'd been blindfolded when we'd first arrived, so I had no idea where we were. From the outside, the Institute was just a gray concrete wall, with a large metal garage door in the center like a gaping mouth. On one side there was a similar industrial facility — the sign on the front read SINGH & SMITH FOOD DISTRIBUTION.

The rest of the street was the same. On the corner there was a shabby apartment building with tattered curtains and broken windows, and a parking lot full of banged-up old cars and stolen shopping carts. I wondered how many toxicants lived in there. I imagined them cramped and miserable in their hovels, decaying from the inside, sleepwalking through life like zombies. Did they know how close they were to salvation? How all the avocations they didn't know to look for were right under their noses? There was trash in the storm drains and the smell of engine grease and gasoline in the air.

It felt a million miles from the tranquility of the Institute, even though I'd only walked to the end of the block. No wonder Daddy didn't want us to go out. The real world was awful.

"Need some company?"

I flinched and whirled around. Fox was walking beside me, half a pace behind. He smiled at my shocked expression.

"What are you doing here?" I asked. "Daddy didn't choose you for this mission."

He shrugged. "I wanted to talk to you. Somewhere you couldn't avoid me."

His casual dismissal of Daddy chilled me. Didn't he understand the danger he was in? What he was risking?

"How did you get out?" I asked.

"Same way as you," said Fox.

"But Daddy . . ."

"Daddy went back to the Sanctum. Come on."

He set off, and I followed him, a feeling of unease creeping over me. I'd barely spoken to Fox since Daddy had caught us, but I could tell he'd changed. Something was different, and it wasn't good.

I'd expected the world outside the Institute to be somehow altered. For there to be an obvious military presence, signifying the Quintus Septum's rise to power. But everything seemed totally ordinary. The warehouses and factories on the street were dark and silent. Television screens flickered in the occasional shabby apartment window, but otherwise all the toxicants seemed to be asleep. Streetlights burned orange overhead. Movement tickled the corners of my vision, and I looked up, expecting drones or cruise missiles, but it was just a flock of bats gliding silently into the night.

"It's beautiful out here," said Fox. "The sky is so much bigger."

We headed up the hill. I felt alert, alive. The real world was dark and dangerous, but I could handle myself. The night air was cool on my cheeks and lips, and I felt my body following every direction I gave it. I was in charge of my body. It didn't rule me.

"Wait!" Fox was bending down, picking something up from the sidewalk.

It was a quarter, dull and grimy. Fox peered at it, frowning.

"Leave it," I told him. "It's filthy."

Fox weighed the coin in his hand. "Why is it here?"

"Somebody dropped it."

"Won't they miss it?"

"It's only twenty-five cents. It's nothing."

Fox turned the coin over, read the words inscribed on it. "It can't be nothing," he said. "What can you buy with twenty-five cents?"

"You can't buy anything with twenty-five cents."

"Then why does it exist?"

I didn't have time to explain it to him. "Because humans are idiots."

"You're a human too."

I wasn't. Not like them, anyway. I was becoming something *more*. Something better.

"How many of these would I need?" Fox asked. "To buy something?"

"Fox, *leave* it," I snapped, wheeling around on him. "Money is aphotic. It weighs us down. You *know* that. You've heard Welling talk about it. You've heard Daddy."

Fox didn't flinch at my harsh tone. He pushed his hair back from his forehead and gazed at me, his expression untroubled.

"But Daddy uses money," he said. "So does Welling. They use it to buy our food and our supplements and the water bottles. There's other stuff too. Stuff they don't want you to know about."

"They do it because they have to," I said. "It's part of our mission. Once we are sublime, we won't —"

"Don't you want to know where it comes from?" Fox interrupted. "The money?"

I had, once. "No."

Fox ignored me. "Mostly new sublimates," he said. "When people join, sometimes they bring money. When Pippa arrived, she brought a lot of money. Daddy was really pleased. That was when he started doing the water bottles."

I walked faster, trying to leave Fox and his voice behind me.

"I know money can be bad," said Fox. "It can make the world very ugly. But surely it can also make the world beautiful. Money can help sick people get better. It can take you to new places. You can buy *books* with money."

I stopped. "Please," I said, trying to keep my voice calm. "Please stop. Please get rid of it."

He nodded, his eyes not leaving mine for a second. I heard a tinkle as the coin hit the pavement.

Fox followed silently as I walked a few blocks to a newish housing subdivision where the streets curved into each other like a barrel of plastic monkeys, each one featuring identical houses. It was all so fake, so totally devoid of anything real or true. I felt trembling and weak — a feeling that intensified with every step I took away from the Institute and Daddy. It was because of Fox and his questions and his doubt, but it wasn't just that. It was as if the chemicals in the air were leaching my strength from me, infecting my pores with powerful toxins.

But I would resist. I could control my body. I was strong.

I chose my house carefully, checking for signs of an alarm system or a dog.

"Wait out here," I said to Fox.

"OK," he replied, not even bothering to lower his voice.

I glared at him and stepped onto the concrete path that led up to the house. Another step. And another.

Suddenly I was spotlighted in blazing whiteness. I stopped dead, my heart pounding, waiting for voices or an alarm. My eyes searched for Fox, but all I could see was bright white bordered by darkness. I let my face go slack and my expression blank, ready to play the part of a confused sleepwalker. I waited. The light clicked off. I shuffled forward once again. The light clicked back on. A security light. I'd forgotten they existed. I squinted, locating the light, and smoothly moved out of its range. It clicked off again, and I waited, crouching by the smooth plaster wall of the house, listening for any signs of disturbance from within. Nothing. All I could hear was my own breath, panting in rhythm with my pounding heart.

I gingerly tried the front doorknob, then slipped around the side of the house and tugged at the sliding door. It gave way, and I slid it open silently. It felt like an incredible stroke of luck, but Daddy would say there was no such thing as luck. Perhaps I had been able to sense the unlocked door all along. Perhaps my instincts had led me to this house, this door. I stepped into the house and slid the door closed behind me.

My feet sank into unexpectedly soft carpet, and for a moment I felt unsteady, so used to the comforting solidity of concrete and earth. The house was warm and smelled artificial and sweet — a sickly smell that I guessed was from a plug-in air freshener. I tried to take shallow breaths so as not to draw the scent too far into my lungs. Who knew what effect it would have on my mind?

My mission from Daddy was to unplug all the appliances in the kitchen. I crossed the living room floor in the half-light cast by the standby lights on the television and DVD player. I went into the kitchen area and unplugged the coffee maker, the toaster, the microwave, and the panini press, then turned to head back into the living room. But something stopped me. I reached out and pulled open the pantry door.

Shelf after shelf of neatly stacked and packaged foods. Tall boxes of pasta and bulging bags of rice. Cans of tomatoes and beans and corn and peaches. I saw brands and logos that I'd forgotten. Old El Paso taco shells. Cheez-Its. Ramen instant noodles. Teddy Grahams. Heinz Baked Beans.

"You should eat something."

I bit down hard on my lip to stop myself from crying out. "Fox!" I hissed. "You were supposed to stay outside."

Fox shrugged and pushed past me to peer into the cupboard. "What *is* all this?" he asked. He picked up a bottle of ketchup and squeezed a small blob onto the tip of his finger, licking it experimentally. His eyebrows shot up. He replaced it and reached for a jar of peanut butter.

"What are you doing?" I whispered, trying to elbow him away from the pantry. We hadn't been this physically close since that night in my room, but I couldn't let him distract me. There was too much to lose.

"What's this?" Fox asked, holding up a bottle. "It's called Magic Shell. Is it really magic?"

"Put it down," I said. "Please."

Fox was slipping away. What we'd done together . . . it had changed him somehow. Daddy was right. It had been wrong. I knew that, but I hadn't realized how serious it was. What would happen if Fox continued down this path, poisoning his body? Who knew what effect it would have on his mind?

I knew that if I didn't do something, I might lose Fox forever.

"Come on," I told him. "Let's go."

Fox's finger was in his mouth, and his eyes were wide. "It *is* magic."

"Fox," I said, pulling at his sleeve. "Please. Do this for me."

He looked up and met my eyes, and I didn't understand what I saw there. Longing. But something else. Something angry and untethered. "OK, Ruby."

I flinched. "Don't call me that."

"OK," Fox repeated. "I'll do whatever you want. I promise. If you'll do one thing for me."

He held out the bottle of Magic Shell.

"Taste this first. Then I'll come back with you. I'll do what Daddy says. I'll be good."

I stared at the plastic bottle. The thought of tasting it filled me with disgust. I couldn't believe I'd ever put that sort of thing into my body. That I'd begged for it at the supermarket. That it used to be a treat or a reward. I remembered Easter eggs and Christmas cookies and pancakes slathered with butter and maple syrup, and I didn't know the girl who had eaten them.

It couldn't have been me. How could I have polluted myself? Desecrated my own body with such mindless indulgence?

"I can't," I said at last.

Fox held the bottle out for a moment longer. Then his shoulders slumped, and he turned to place the plastic bottle back on the pantry shelf.

"OK," he murmured, and slipped away into the darkness. I heard the soft scrape of the sliding door open, then close.

I stood there for a moment more, staring at the Magic Shell. Then I carefully closed the pantry door and left the kitchen. I had to get back. Back to Daddy. My hand reached out to push the sliding door open. But something made me pause. A memory, rising unbidden from depths I thought I had buried.

A Saturday morning at home, back when everything had been normal. Back when my parents loved each other, and my little brother was a living, breathing human being, not just charred bone and ash. He'd woken me up at dawn, and we'd crept into the kitchen to make breakfast in bed for Mom and Dad. Waffles with ice cream and strawberries and a chocolaty coat of Magic Shell and a pot of coffee. We'd put daffodils from the garden in a vase and arranged it all on a tray. Then we'd carried it proudly into their room and climbed onto the bed. Dad had the coffee, and Mom had the strawberries, and Anton and I demolished the waffles and ice cream. We'd talked about silly things — about how far it was to the moon and whether dogs could remember their dreams. When breakfast was over, we'd snuggled in under the comforter and made shapes from the cracks in the ceiling, telling stories about them until we drifted into a sticky, contented morning slumber, warm and safe and loved.

I let my hand fall and turned and padded silently down the hallway, past the bathroom and laundry to the master bedroom.

The door was ajar, and the slightest touch from my hand was enough for it to swing gently open. I stepped inside.

She was curled up in a ball, as if she were trying to shield herself from something. He was spread out on his back, his mouth hanging open, a thin white crust forming at the corners of his lips. The debris of their lives littered their bedside tables — half-drunk glasses of water, dog-eared novels, smartphones plugged in to charge.

I thought about their bodies, rotting from the inside, grunting and squelching away, engines devoted only to breaking down fats and acids, living compost heaps. No wonder they never really saw what was right in front of them. No wonder they slept through their lives. What else could they do?

The longer I watched them, the less real they seemed. They were shells, empty meat cases, like the butchered carcasses of pigs hanging up at the market. Were they even breathing? What if they'd died in their sleep? What if every toxicant out here had suddenly dropped dead, and only me and Daddy and the rest of our family were left in the whole world?

Would that really be so bad?

He twitched and snorted, and I stepped backward into the hallway, making my way to the sliding door and slipping out into the night. Fox wasn't out there waiting for me, and I returned to the Institute alone.

15

As I crossed the courtyard the next day, I heard the garage door at the front of the Institute groan, signaling the return of the latest Outreach team from the Red House. Daddy had announced that there would be no Outreach program for a while after this, because the risk of being captured by the Quintus Septum was too great.

I paused to watch the white van rumble in. Three Institute members climbed out, then two strangers, dressed in ordinary street clothes, blinking in the light and holding their blindfolds.

They were older than me — maybe late thirties or early forties. They were holding hands and looking around nervously. I remembered my first glimpse of the Institute — how bleak it had seemed. I hadn't noticed the green things growing in the garden. I hadn't heard the laughter of the Monkeys. Hadn't felt the love radiating from Daddy's Sanctum. I hadn't understood anything.

The man took a few steps forward, eager to see it all, learn our secrets. His partner seemed less sure, holding back a little, but allowing him to pull her along. I wondered whether many couples had joined the Institute over the years. It would be hard to sever yourself from those yearnings of the flesh when your partner was there with you. How could you become boundless with someone tethering you to the earth like a lead balloon?

I headed back inside, but paused in the doorway to the mess hall. Lib and Fox were standing in the entrance to the kitchen, their voices raised in anger.

"If Daddy is sublime," Fox was saying, "why does he wear glasses? Shouldn't he have perfect eyesight?"

"You need to stop this," said Lib. "Stop the questions. Stop the attitude. It won't do you any good."

"You can't tell me what to do," said Fox. "I'm not a Monkey anymore. I'm a whole person. I want to make choices."

Lib's mouth was pinched pale with anger and worry. "Perhaps you'd like me to fetch Daddy. *He* can tell you what to do."

They stared at each other for a moment — Lib furious, Fox stubborn and glowering. But finally Fox looked away. His shoulders hunched over defensively.

"Fine," he said, and slunk away.

★ ★ ★

Fox was clearly fascinated by the new sublimates. He sat next to them in the courtyard the next morning as we waited for Daddy's Hour to start, bombarding them with questions. He asked them where they were from, how old they were. Were they married? Did they have children? Any pets? The sublimates answered, charmed by Fox as everyone always was.

"Why didn't you have children?" Fox asked.

"It seemed irresponsible," the man said. "Overpopulation,

global warming. We didn't want to contribute to that."

Fox frowned, considering this. "I get it," he said. "But if there are no new children, then who's going to fix the world?"

I glanced sharply at him.

"Fox!" Pippa hissed. "What are you *talking* about? You know it's Daddy who will save us."

The sublimates looked from Pippa to Fox. For a moment I thought Fox was going to respond, but he ignored Pippa and turned back to the newcomers.

"Have you been to the ocean?" he asked.

The woman laughed. "Of course," she said. "It's only half an hour away from here." She looked up at the high walls of the Institute and frowned. "I think."

Fox shook his head, smiling in disbelief. It didn't seem possible to me either, even though I knew it was true. At the Institute, everything seemed worlds away.

I mechanically spooned salted quinoa into my mouth, making sure I only ate half my allocated ration. That was all I needed. Soon, I wouldn't need any more fuel. I'd be like Daddy, surviving on air and sunlight.

When Daddy arrived, he introduced the sublimates to us as Ashmole (her) and Tausend (him), and by lunchtime they were known as Ash and Toser. Against my will, I remembered Fox telling me about how new sublimates usually came with money. But perhaps he had been mistaken. After all, I hadn't brought any money with me to the Institute, and Daddy had never mentioned it.

Daddy gathered us together in the afternoon for a special meeting.

"I've been in my laboratory," he told us. "Working around the clock on a new technic."

I thought of our element drills with Welling and Daddy's quest to find the secret of aether.

Daddy held up a small glass beaker filled with a clear liquid.

"It looks like water, doesn't it?" Daddy said. "Harmless. Pure. But it isn't. This is a deadly cocktail of aconite, mercury, lead, and cyanide. One drop of it mixed with our drinking water could kill everyone here in a matter of seconds."

I felt a stab of fear at the suggestion, realizing how vulnerable our bodies were. How permeable. This was why we had to work so hard. This was why we had to become sublime. To save us from these useless bodies that could be felled with a single drop of clear liquid.

"Valentius is going to drink it all," said Daddy. "Every last drop."

I looked around at the others. Lib's face was utterly expressionless, as was Welling's. I swallowed down my panic. Daddy knew what he was doing. I trusted him.

I glanced at the new sublimates. Ash had gone white, her eyes wide with concern. But Toser's eyes burned with a fierce intensity, almost as if he wanted Val to drink it, to die.

I looked at Fox. His cheeks were pink and his eyes were wild, as if he was fighting to stay composed.

Daddy held out the flask to Val, who took it.

"No!" Fox burst out, leaping forward with his arms outstretched.

Welling and Stan caught him. Fox struggled against them. "Don't make him do it!" Fox yelled. "He is a person, with dreams of his own. Don't make him die."

Val drank the liquid in the flask without hesitating for a moment.

Daddy smiled and patted Val kindly on the arm. "Thank you,

Valentius," he said. "You may sit down now."

Val handed the flask back to Daddy and sat down.

"You must understand," said Daddy, "that everything I do, I do to protect you. Sometimes my technic may seem cruel. Sometimes you may not be able to avocate my intent. But you must trust me. I will not let you come to harm. You are my children, and I would give my life for you in a heartbeat if I thought it would keep you safe."

I glanced over at Val. He seemed completely fine.

It had been a test. Daddy had been testing us. To see if we trusted him. Had he done this sort of thing before? Lib and Welling didn't seem surprised, but everyone else looked shaken. Had Val known? Had Daddy let him in on the secret beforehand? Or was he really that loyal?

"There is a plan," said Daddy. "A plan to defeat the Quintus Septum and all their toxicant meat-followers. A plan that will elevate us all to the sublime, to cast off everything that binds us to this muddy rock. I cannot tell you what it is yet. But you must trust me. Daddy's going to make everything OK."

I believed him. What choice did I have?

Daddy turned his gaze to Fox, who was still being held by Welling and Stan, his eyes bright with tears. "Furicius," he said, his face solemn. "I'm disappointed in you."

He opened his mouth as if to say more but then evidently thought better of it, shaking his head as he walked away, disappearing inside.

Welling and Stan released Fox, who shook them off with a resentful glare and stalked off to B Block.

Lib's eyes turned to me, and I saw hatred festering there.

This is because of you, her look said. *You did this to him. You ruined him.*

And I knew she was right.

Everyone headed off to their allocated work, but I stayed outside, heading to the site of the destroyed garden. Trellises, pots, and other implements had been organized to make a kind of obstacle course that we trained on whenever we had a spare moment. I didn't want to be around the others. Around Fox.

I threw myself into the course. I sprinted and climbed and wriggled until my body ached and my clothes were soaked in sweat. Daddy said dampness was weakness. That to be sublime, we had to shed every last drop of moisture. That our actuality must be dry in order to call forth the Scintilla.

"I need to talk to you."

It was Fox. I ignored him and ran the course again. My lungs burned for air, and I felt dizzy and nauseated. But I didn't stop. I was in control.

I thought he'd go away. But he didn't. He just waited. I ran the course again.

And again.

Eventually my legs gave way beneath me, and I collapsed, gasping for breath. I felt the lead in the soil seeping into my hands and knees and ordered my body to stand.

My stomach heaved, but I swallowed hard. I was in control. I was strong.

Cool hands touched my shoulders and helped me to my feet.

"I need to talk to you," Fox said again.

I yanked my elbow from his grasp and composed myself. "Furicius," I said, my breath still strained.

"Don't call me that." Fox pushed his hair away from his face and frowned.

"Furicius," I said again. I had to be cool. Formal. I couldn't let him see how he made me churn inside.

"You can't avoid me forever," he said. "I know you too well."

It was true. Fox knew me better than anyone. But I had changed. I was strong now. I was in control. I started to walk away.

"I'm worried about the Monkeys," Fox said.

I hesitated, then turned. "What do you mean?"

"They're hungry. And scared. They're only allowed outside once a day to exercise, and they have to be totally silent. Daddy tells them stories that frighten them. They have nightmares, and they don't play and laugh. They're getting . . . quiet."

"Daddy's only doing it to keep them safe," I told Fox. "The Quintus Septum *broke in*. They went for the Monkeys."

"Did they?" asked Fox, giving me a serious look. "Did anyone else see them? Is there any evidence?"

I scoffed. "Do you think Daddy would lie about it? Who do you think destroyed our garden, then?"

An image flashed into my mind of Daddy, leading me out of my imprisonment, telling us about the attack. His hair had been wild, his usually pristine white clothes smudged. Dirt under his fingernails.

"He would never do that," I said firmly.

Fox's head snapped up, and he looked at something behind me, his eyes narrowing slightly.

"Heracleitus." It was Daddy, crossing the courtyard toward Fox and me. "Heracleitus, I wish to speak with you." He glanced at Fox and nodded, expecting Fox to obediently slink away so we could speak in private.

But Fox just nodded back. His jaw was set stubbornly, his eyes fierce. After a moment's pause, Daddy turned back to me.

"Heracleitus, I wish to speak to you about your role in the upcoming Boundless Family plan. I have a series of tasks that must be handled delicately, and you're the only one I trust enough to carry them out as I intend."

I felt myself warm a little under his praise. "Yes, Daddy."

Daddy's eyes flicked back to Fox. "But perhaps this is not the time for talking strategy," he said. "In any case, I must return to my laboratory. I have an important experiment I must conduct."

He turned as if to walk away, then turned back, holding up a finger, as if something had just occurred to him. "You know, Heracleitus," he said to me with a smile, "soon you'll be old enough to join me in the Inner Sanctum in the evenings."

I heard a sharp hiss of breath from Fox and felt him tense beside me. I thought of the women following Daddy after Family Time most nights. When I first learned about it, I thought it was just sex. But now I knew Daddy better, and avocated the path to sublimation. I needed to receive his actuality in order to become whole. I'd never be boundless without it. Was I ready for that? To give myself over to Daddy? The other women spoke of it as something magical. They said they glowed from within, that they flew around the Sanctum and could project their actuality right up into the stars.

"Yes, Daddy," I said.

Daddy reached out and patted me on the cheek. "Good girl." Then he turned to Fox. "Was there something you wanted to say, Furicius?" he asked, his voice mild.

Out of the corner of my eye, I saw Fox's hands clench and unclench. "No," he said at last. "Not yet."

Daddy's eyes narrowed slightly, but his smile didn't waver. "Very well. Good morning."

Once he was out of sight, Fox wheeled around on me. "You can't," he said.

"It's none of your business."

"You can't let him do it. I couldn't bear it. Don't let him force you into it."

"The only person who is trying to force anything is you, Fox," I said, forgetting to be cool and calm. "If I go to the Inner Sanctum with Daddy, it will be because I choose to. You don't get a say in it. You don't have a claim over me."

"Maybe not," said Fox. "But you have a claim over me. I *need* you."

"You don't. It's your doubt. You've let your body take over. You can't think anymore."

Fox barked out a hoarse laugh. "Thinking is all I can do! I can't stop thinking. I can't turn it off. Ever since we . . . It changed me. And it changed you too."

Hot blood raced through my veins, and I willed it to slow and grow cool.

"No, it didn't," I said. "It meant nothing."

"You can pretend all you like, but I know you remember. What we did. How it felt."

"It was wrong."

"Why? Because Daddy says so? Why is it wrong when we do it, but he's allowed to do it to whoever he likes?"

"That's different." I could hear the doubt in my own voice, and I hated it.

"It wasn't wrong. You know it wasn't. It was . . ." Fox's Adam's apple bobbed as he swallowed. "I didn't know I could feel like that."

I felt tears spring to my eyes, and I cursed my body for betraying me once more. "I'm so sorry," I said. "I did this. I pushed you."

"Don't be stupid. I wanted it. I wanted it from the very beginning. From the first day we met."

I couldn't help myself. "Why?"

Fox's eyes softened. "Because you saw me. You saw me and I saw you and you made the world bright and strange and I wanted to see more of it."

I felt my body come to life, independent of my mind. My skin remembered the aching sweetness of Fox, the hot flush of desire. I bit the inside of my cheek and drove my fingernails into my palms, trying to regain control.

"You woke me up, Ruby. And now I have so many questions. I want to know who my mother was. I want to know how I came here. I want to know why we hand out water bottles on the street. I want to know what it feels like to stand with my feet in the ocean. I want to know how the world works. And I want *you*."

"What we did was wrong," I told him.

"It wasn't! *This* is wrong. All of this."

Fox was my weakness. I didn't need Daddy to tell me. He was the one thing preventing me from becoming sublime. He was what shackled me to the earth, what pulled my actuality down into the cage that was my body. I knew I had to let him go.

"Let's leave," said Fox, hushed and urgent. "Tonight. You and me. We'll walk out the gate and never come back. We'll go somewhere. Anywhere. To the ocean. Across the ocean. As far away as we can. We'll find a house with a yard full of flowers and get a dog called Barker."

I stared at him. "Fox," I said. "No. You're . . . you're not thinking right. You've lost your way. But you can get it back. You need to be elutriated. You have to trust Daddy."

"*No.*" Fox's voice broke. "I'm done with him."

"But the plan . . . the Quintus Septum."

Fox tossed his head to the side, as if to cast my words away. "I can't anymore."

"What about the Monkeys?"

His expression faltered, and he hesitated. "I can't help them here," he said at last. "I can't protect them anymore. Maybe if we leave, we can . . ." He floundered, searching for the right words. "Ruby, please —"

I flinched. "That isn't my name."

"Ruby. Ruby. *Ruby*."

He moved closer to me, and I was drowning in him, his scent, his breath, the heat of his skin. He slid his hands up to my shoulders and bent forward to kiss me.

It took all my strength and resolve to pull away.

"I can't," I said. "*We* can't. You know we can't. We have to trust in the plan. We have to trust Daddy."

I fled. I couldn't trust myself around him. I had to get my body back under control. I went to the bathroom and splashed cold water on my face, taking deep breaths and muttering to myself.

"Boundless body. Boundless mind. Boundless body. Boundless mind."

I knew what I had to do. It had worked before. I needed to be elutriated. I'd deprive my body of what it was demanding. I'd fast. No food or Fox for a few days. Then I'd be OK again. I'd be in control. Maybe then I could talk some sense into him, before it was too late.

I trained harder. I worked harder. I ran and climbed and crawled. I ignored the gnawing hunger in my belly and the dizziness that overcame me each time I stood up after Daddy's Hour. When stomach cramps woke me in the middle of the night, I rolled out of bed and did push-ups or jumping jacks until I was close to passing out.

I stopped visiting the mess hall for meals. I asked to be

excused from Family Time, preferring to train by myself. I made sure to arrive slightly late to Welling's sublimation drills, so there would be no opportunity for Fox and me to talk.

I didn't let myself think about Fox. I didn't let myself think.

Even though the weather was still warm, I was cold all the time, no matter how hard I trained. The autumn wind whipped me right to the bone as I hurried to the warehouse where Welling drilled me, Pippa, and Fox. It had been two weeks since my encounter with Fox, and I felt like I had finally purged myself of him. I'd gone the whole previous day without noticing him, without feeling his eyes on me. The morning sublimation drill would be my test, to see if I was truly elutriated.

Pippa and Welling were in their usual seats, waiting for me. But Stan sat in Fox's place. Fox was nowhere to be seen. Daddy stood at the head of the table, his glasses glinting.

"Where's Fox?" I asked. I saw Daddy's eyes narrow, and I knew he was disappointed I'd asked.

"You won't see him again," Daddy told me. "Never. He's gone."

For a moment, I forgot how to breathe. I sank into my chair, hoping that no one would notice. Fox was gone? He had left? Without me? Maybe it wasn't true. Maybe it was one of Daddy's tests. Surely he wouldn't abandon the Monkeys?

But I knew it was true. Fox had been slipping away from us ever since that night we'd shared together. I had tried to hold onto him, to draw him back in. But I had failed.

A part of me wondered if I should have gone with him. Maybe he needed some time out in the real world. Some time to realize how lucky he was to have all this. To have Daddy. Maybe I could have persuaded him to return.

"He was poisoning our family," Daddy continued. "I

discovered his deceit and confronted him, and now he has slunk back to his masters like the dog he is."

"Yes, Daddy."

Could it be possible that Fox had crossed over, become an agent for the Quintus Septum? Was that why he'd been asking so many questions?

It made an awful kind of sense. How long had it been going on? He must have been recruited when he was at the Red House — it would have been his only opportunity for outside contact. And it explained his behavior, why the sublimation technic wasn't working for him. Daddy said that none of it would work if the person wasn't fully committed, body and mind. That was how the Quintus Septum had managed to infiltrate us. That was why they'd targeted the Monkey House, because it was the area Fox had access to.

Everything we'd shared had been a lie. Fox had never loved me. Not the way I thought he had. But despite my shock and grief, I was eager to believe Daddy, because it let me off the hook. If Fox was a secret agent, it meant that his slide into rebelliousness wasn't my fault. He was already aphotic before then. And Daddy knew. That's why he'd isolated me. To elutriate me from Fox's poison and prevent me from infecting anyone else. He'd tried to save Fox too. Of course he had. Daddy loved Fox as much as I did. I could see the pain in his eyes even now. I took a deep, shaking breath and pushed thoughts of Fox from my mind. There were more important things.

"The Quintus Septum have taken over the government," Daddy said gravely. "It is only a matter of time before they come for us."

Images flashed through my mind. The front door of my old house being beaten down and masked soldiers storming in, hauling Mom up from the couch and taking her away. Minah and my friends being handcuffed in front of the milk crates at the Wasteland and bundled into an unmarked van. Dad locked away deep in solitary confinement with no one to hear his cries.

"Sublimation is our only goal, and we cannot let the Quintus Septum stand in the way of that." Daddy paused, looking around at us. "I had hoped you would have more time for training, but we cannot wait any longer. Welling, the mission status is now active. It's time to take the technic into the field. Lib is waiting in the A Block storage room with your supplies. Stan, ready the bus for an immediate departure."

We stood, ready to file out of the warehouse. Stan bounced nervously on his heels. My thoughts of Fox were crowded out with new questions — what supplies would we need? Where were we going in the bus? But I knew better than to ask them. Daddy had chosen me for a mission, and I would do everything I could to make him proud.

"You must be alert," Daddy warned us. "They will try to trick you. It will look as if everything is normal. The Quintus Septum are like oily snakes — they will slither around you, whispering comforting lies. They will move unseen, behind curtains and under floorboards. They will hypnotize you with sugar and flashing lights and the gleam of coin. But you must resist, children. You must stay strong."

I squared my shoulders and raised my chin. I would stay strong. I'd do it for Daddy.

As I crossed the courtyard to A Block, I glanced up at the windows of the offices next door and saw the glow of computer screens. What lies were those toxicants being fed? What twisted truths? Did they really think they were safe? Did they think their leaders protected them? Did they have any idea of what was to come?

I shook my head. They were all fools.

"Here," said Lib, handing us each a pile of neatly folded clothing.

I blinked as I accepted my bundle. It wasn't the usual muted linens. I'd been given a black dress — the kind of neat, conservative-but-revealing thing that female lawyers on TV wore. Lib also passed me a pair of black high heels and a little bag containing makeup and jewelry — a simple silver necklace, a bracelet, and a diamond ring.

I stared at them, uncomprehending.

"Get changed," said Lib.

The dress felt strange against my skin, tight and itchy, even though it was a size too large. The high heels felt ridiculous, and I marveled again at how completely the human race had been duped. They didn't need to have tyrannical overlords controlling them — toxicants were happy to torture themselves, strapping on painful shoes and clothes, pumping their bodies full of aphotic poisons.

I didn't have a brush, but I pulled my fingers through my hair and didn't feel anything as handfuls of it came out. I watched the strands drift to the floor and wondered what kind of supplement I should be taking to counteract hair loss. Not that it mattered. Hair was just a part of the body. When I became sublime, I could grow as much hair as I wanted, in any color.

There were no mirrors in the Institute, but I did my best with the makeup anyway — a little foundation and eyeliner, a brush of mascara, a smear of lipstick. The powdery smell of it was overwhelming, and I felt it seeping into my skin, toxic and suffocating. It would take weeks of work to elutriate myself of it, but I did it uncomplainingly. It was for Daddy.

I slid the diamond ring onto my finger. It was beautiful. Hard, indestructible, and full of light. I felt like with each passing day I was becoming more like that diamond. Soon I would glitter and shine like that. Soon I would be indestructible.

I went outside and joined the others. Welling wore a suit, his tie casually loosened. It was as though he had stepped out of the pages of a magazine, his skin dark brown against the pale pink of his shirt, the pinstripes on his jacket falling from his shoulders in crisp lines. Pippa was in jeans and a sparkly top. In tight clothes, she looked plumper than I'd expected, and I wondered if she'd been sneaking extra food. Stan was dressed in a lurid Hawaiian shirt, shorts, and socks with sandals.

Pippa took my hand and admired the ring.

"Do you think it's real?" she asked, turning my hand from side to side so the diamond caught the light.

I shrugged. "Does it matter? It's just a rock."

Pippa smiled — too brightly. "Yeah," she said. "You're right."

I remembered the story she'd told, about her boyfriend proposing to her. Did she ever wonder what would have happened if she'd taken that ring? Pippa turned and clambered into the van, and I made a mental note to keep an eye on her. She was weak.

We were blindfolded once more, and Stan drove us out of the Institute and into the world. After an hour or so of bumping and swaying, he told us we could remove our blindfolds.

We were in the city.

Everything was different. New shops and billboards. Buildings had been torn down and replaced with steel scaffolding and construction. I couldn't believe how much had changed. How long had I been away?

I kept an eye out for Fox. I couldn't help myself. I wondered where he was, what he was doing. Was he in some kind of Quintus Septum facility? Was he scared? Did he miss us? Miss me?

I saw floods of toxicants clutching greasy bags of processed food, each one isolated from the world with earbuds or headphones. I watched them fill their mouths with poisons and turn their eyes away from each other. How could people be so stupid? They were killing themselves, each one in a prison of solitude that they built for themselves.

Stan shook his head. "Poor suckers," he murmured pityingly, and I knew we were all thinking the same thing.

He drove us to the edge of the city and into a public parking garage. Welling retrieved a dark briefcase from under the passenger seat of the van. Then we continued on foot, winding our way through alleyways and down crowded sidewalks.

"You can't be too careful," said Stan, glancing around. "Stay alert. Make sure we're not being followed."

I could smell doughnuts and cigarettes and car exhaust and perfume. It was overwhelming. Toxicants jostled us, and I stared open-mouthed at them. Couldn't they see how lost they were? Couldn't they tell how much *better* we were? Were our disguises really so good? Why weren't these people humbled before us? Filled with awe?

Stan led us over a footbridge across the river, where boats belched oil into brown sludge and toxicants held hands and pretended to be in love. We followed the riverbank for a while, past restaurants and street performers, until we came to a large building — solid and windowless as a fortress, spreading down the side of the river like a giant hulking beast.

"Um . . . where are we going?" asked Pippa. "What does this

have to do with balancing the elements to make aether?"

"You'll see," said Welling.

He brushed some invisible dirt from his lapels and led us into an enormous lobby with gleaming, shining marble surfaces and glinting with chrome and brass. We waited by a floral arrangement that was twice my height while Welling went up to a curved sweep of marble counter. A line of neatly presented people waited, wearing identical elegant uniforms.

When Welling returned, he carried a small plastic card. He led us over to an elevator, and we got in. The vertical movement made my stomach lurch, and I was relieved when it finally opened onto a long hallway lined with doors.

A hotel. We were in a hotel.

Welling led us to our room — actually a suite of rooms, with a living room and two bedrooms, one for me and Pippa and one for him and Stan.

We gathered in the living room and sat on the floor, ignoring the comfortable-looking sofa and armchairs.

"We're not . . . here to steal something, are we?" asked Pippa, looking around nervously.

"Of course not," I told her, my voice haughty with superiority. "Daddy wouldn't make us steal. Theft is aphotic."

Welling nodded. "Hera is right," he said. "What we're doing is perfectly legal. It's more than legal. It's *right*."

"So . . . what are we going to do?"

"This is a house of lead," said Welling. "The toxicants who come here fill their bodies and minds with heaviness. The more they spend, the worse they feel. The more money this place makes, the more toxicants come here. It feeds on their greed. We are lifting that burden. We are elutriating the toxicants."

Pippa frowned. "But we're not stealing?"

Welling shook his head. "We're *winning*."

Pippa stared at him, realization dawning on her face. "This is a *casino*? What about the aether?"

"We need funds in order to procure supplies. To make the aether." Welling popped open the clips on the briefcase and raised the lid.

"So . . . what was the point of all those drills?" asked Pippa. "All the counting?"

Welling flashed her a bright white smile. "I'm glad you asked," he said.

He brandished a flat, rectangular box. I stared at it, the familiar blue and red patterns seeming like the most incongruous thing in the world.

"Have you ever played blackjack?"

16

Welling slid the cards from the pack and fanned them out on the floor in front of us.

"Each card has a value," he explained. "The number cards are self-explanatory. The picture cards are all worth ten. In a casino, you and whoever else is playing will be dealt cards. The house also gets cards. The goal in blackjack is to get as close to twenty-one as you can. If you go over, you lose. If you are the closest to twenty-one, you win. Simple."

We nodded. I was churning with questions. What were we doing at a casino? Why was Welling teaching us to play blackjack? What possible purpose could it serve? Wouldn't we become contaminated? But I said nothing. Daddy had sent us here. Welling knew what he was doing.

He dealt out cards, and we played eight rounds of blackjack. As we played he explained the rest of the rules and taught us a basic strategy.

Welling won five of them, I won one, and Stan won two.

"What's the trick?" asked Pippa.

"It isn't a trick," said Welling. "It's about focus and precision. Clearing your mind and letting your actuality take over. You'll get the hang of it. The game is easy. The hard part is knowing when and how much to bet."

He reached into the briefcase again and took out a wad of bills secured with a rubber band. My heart started to pound. I realized I hadn't seen money for . . . how long? Months?

We were each passed a thin stack of twenty-dollar bills. I felt them, smooth and real under my fingers. This wasn't play-money. This was the real thing. I realized how powerful money was — how just seeing it and touching it made me feel aphotic. I could feel grease and toxins seeping into my fingertips. I shuddered and put my stack down on the carpet next to me. Pippa was flicking through her bundle. She raised it to her face and inhaled its scent. I felt ill.

"Downstairs we'll be playing with chips," Welling said. "But we can practice with the real thing."

We played another eight rounds. Welling won four, I won two, and Pippa and Stan both won one. I bet conservatively and only lost forty dollars out of the two hundred I'd been given. Pippa bet lavishly and was left with only a single twenty-dollar bill. Stan started off conservative but then panicked at the end and ended up with forty dollars. Welling, however, seemed to know exactly when to bet high. He ended up with over four hundred dollars.

"OK," he said. "Now it's time to apply the sublimation technic."

I blinked. How were the drills we'd done related to this? How could learning how to balance the atomic weight of elements have anything to do with blackjack?

"It's just like with the element chips," said Welling. "When you see a card revealed, you adjust a running mental tally. If the card is between two and six, you add one. If it is between seven and nine, you do nothing. If the card is a ten, you subtract one. Understand?"

It was the same. The counting system was the same. Was . . . was this what we had been learning all along? I'd thought I'd been trained in something magical, something that was going to help me reach sublimation. But in fact I'd just been learning to count cards. I glanced at the others. Welling was looking at his cards. Stan was muttering numbers. Pippa met my eyes with a frown, and I knew she was wondering the same thing. I bit back my disappointment. I wasn't weak like her. I had to trust Daddy. I knew we'd need money for the war — especially since our crops had been destroyed. And what better place to take it from than the darkest house of lead? Welling was right: we were *helping* the toxicants by taking their money, the source of all their greed and heaviness.

Welling shuffled his deck of cards with deft fingers, and I realized why Daddy had chosen him for this mission. He'd probably spent plenty of time gambling in his life before the Institute, when he was a successful stockbroker. Daddy was no fool. He knew how to take our weaknesses and turn them into strengths. How to harness our skills and vices and use them as tools to draw us closer to the sublime.

Welling put down one card at a time. We each counted in our head, just as we had been doing every morning for the past two weeks. The numbers flicked through my head, and I felt them soothe me, order in chaos, silencing my questions and doubts. Numbers were pure, elutriating the oily heaviness of the money.

"Now we will play again," said Welling. "Pippa, Stan, play as normal. Hera — count as we go. Bet high whenever your count reaches three or above."

We played another five rounds. I only won two, but I managed to win more money than I lost.

"Good," he said. "Pippa, your turn."

Numbers swam through my head as we played hand after hand, and Welling explained betting strategies.

We worked on our blackjack game late into the night before Welling finally called a halt, and Pippa and I dragged ourselves into the adjoining bedroom.

An enormous king-size bed took up most of the room, invitingly swathed in crisp white linens. A large window overlooked nearby skyscrapers, and I felt dizzy when I realized how high up we were. I saw Pippa eyeing the plastic-wrapped pillow mints on the bed. I swept them off the covers and marched into the bathroom, depositing them in the trash can so she couldn't be tempted anymore. Who knew what poisons they contained?

I caught a glimpse of myself in the bathroom mirror and felt a stab of fear at the sight of the unrecognizable girl staring back at me. She looked like a skeleton — sallow skin drawn tightly across bone, face gaunt and hollow. I remembered something Daddy had told us.

As you approach sublimation, you will notice signs that your flesh-body is ready to be discarded. Do not be alarmed. Soon you won't need it at all.

Back in the bedroom, Pippa was climbing into the bed, but I shook my head with a frown.

"We want to stay sharp," I told her. "Alert. We sleep on the floor."

Pippa opened her mouth as if to argue with me, but closed

it again, casting a longing glance toward the fluffy comforter and pillows before settling down onto the floor beside me.

I ordered my body to sleep, but the toxins leaking into me through the makeup and synthetic fabric and the pollution of the city had made my body rebellious and sluggish to respond. Beside me, Pippa shifted uncomfortably, rolling from side to side and sighing. I let my breathing slow so she would think I was asleep. I needed to set a good example.

But sleep didn't come.

Pippa was restless all night, getting up to use the bathroom several times. I hoped she wasn't sneaking in there to eat the pillow mints and resolved to hide them somewhere else in the morning. I could hear the *ding* of the elevator out in the hallway, and the low, constant roar of air conditioning. I shuddered at the thought of what it might be pumping into our room.

Morning finally came, and Welling tapped on our door, letting us know it was almost time to head down to the casino floor.

"Are we having breakfast first?" asked Pippa, dark, sleepless pouches under her eyes.

"No," I told her. "You don't need breakfast. Food will slow you down."

I went into the bathroom to get ready. I eyed the shower, imagining the feeling of the hot jets hitting my back and shoulders. I imagined lathering up handfuls of soap and shampoo and breathing in great lungfuls of warm steam.

Hot water was damaging to the skin. Soaps and other chemicals would be absorbed into the body, creating disharmony and sluggishness.

But if we are discarding this body soon anyway, what harm will it do? asked a pesky voice inside my head.

I put the plug into the drain and filled the bathtub up with cold water, using a hand towel to sponge myself clean. This was better than a shower. The elutriation offered by the cold water was a thousand times better than the simple flesh-pleasures of heat and steam.

* * *

As the elevator doors opened, a roar of tinny music, clacking chips, and human voices swept over me. It was completely overwhelming, and for a moment I hesitated. I could go back up to the quietness of the hotel room. Just for a moment. To gather my thoughts. I wasn't ready for this. The lights — all bright, all flashing, all artificial. The swirls of light on slot machines and patterned dresses and the riotous carpet. The smells of alcohol and perfume and plastic. It was too much.

Welling shoved me in the back, pushing me out onto the casino floor. "Keep it together," he muttered between clenched teeth.

We walked past bank after bank of slot machines, each one with its own jaunty, jangling music and flashing lights. Despite the noise, the casino was relatively quiet — it was still morning. A handful of toxicants sat at the slot machines, mostly sagging men with vacant stares and older women clutching purses. They were barely people — just withered husks, mindlessly pressing a button over and over. What was the point of being alive? I longed for the Institute, for the simplicity of my days, for the feeling of belonging, of higher purpose. I was so lucky to have it. These toxicants had nothing. They were passing time before the inevitability of death, being eaten alive by their own internal acids.

Overhead, grand swoops of orange and gold gave the room a dim, intimate glow. Waitresses sailed past us carrying trays of drinks, as if in here mornings didn't exist, and it was always happy hour. Occasionally there was a shout of delight or dismay from a gaming table. It was a prison, hidden away from natural light and air. Toxicants voluntarily filling their bellies with poison, their brains with emptiness, their actuality with lead.

Black-suited security guards were everywhere, and I felt my heart rate increase as their eyes slid over me. Were they really Quintus Septum agents? Would they see past my disguise?

Someone was shouting behind me, calling out a name. I walked on.

"Ruby!" A hand grabbed my elbow, and I spun around.

Ruby.

It was someone I had once known, a million years ago. One of Mom's friends from a book club she'd been part of. Her face was caked in foundation, which sank into her wrinkles, forming powdery beige crevasses. Her lipstick was bleeding into the lines around her mouth, and her teeth were stained yellow from cigarettes and coffee.

Ruby.

The woman peered at me, leaning in. Her perfume was cloyingly sweet and made me long for lungfuls of fresh air. I held my breath so as not to be polluted by her any further. Her eyes drilled into mine, and it was as though she could see right through me. Then she shook her head and released my elbow.

"I'm so sorry," she said. "I thought you were someone else."

She walked away, and Welling came up beside me.

"What did she want?" he hissed.

"Nothing," I told him. "She thought I was someone else."

"Are you sure? She didn't plant anything on you? A tracking device?"

I shook my head. "It was a misunderstanding."

Welling hunched his shoulders uneasily. "Be careful. The Quintus Septum has eyes everywhere. We must be vigilant."

We split up — Pippa, Welling, and I each heading to a different blackjack table. Stan was stationed at a slot machine, positioned where he could see all of us. Once the count at our table got really favorable, we were to signal Stan, who would then pass the signal on to the others. They'd come over to the hot table and we'd all bet high. That way we were increasing our odds of winning.

I found a table over in a dimly lit corner of the casino floor, near the bathroom. A bored croupier sat looking at his phone. I checked to make sure I could see Stan, took a deep breath, and slid onto a stool.

"Bet?" the croupier asked.

I stared at my stack of chips. How much to bet? Five dollars? Ten? A hundred? Welling had given me two hundred dollars in chips — but I'd forgotten how I was supposed to start.

The croupier sighed and rolled his eyes. The sounds of the casino rose around me like a tidal wave of noise — dinging, humming, squealing. Laughter and screams and such an overwhelming press of humanity — flesh and machines all clanging and pinging and overflowing with grease and money and electricity. I felt bile rise in my throat and teetered on my stool. I was going to faint. My ears were ringing and the gaudy carpet was heaving around me in ripples and waves.

I couldn't do it.

I needed quiet and fresh air.

"Are you OK?" asked the croupier. "Do you need a glass of water?"

I did, desperately, but I wasn't going to drink the poison that he called water. Why hadn't I brought a bottle of sulfurous water with me? I shook my head at him and smiled weakly.

I could do this. I was special. I was close to sublime. I was the master of my flesh-body, not a slave to it.

I closed my eyes and breathed deeply. I pictured Daddy's calm, smiling face and felt my racing heart slow.

I was here for him. For Daddy. He believed in me. I had to prove him right. I was special. I was *extraordinary*.

Daddy's face blurred and shifted, and became Fox.

Fox.

Fox was a traitor.

But I couldn't help it. I couldn't banish his face. I still loved him.

I knew it was weak. My feelings for Fox were all tangled up in the cravings of my body, and I couldn't separate out which parts of him I loved with my mind and which parts I loved with my heart and my blood.

My heart ached, but it felt good to *feel*. Anton's face swam into view as well, and Mom's and Dad's. I breathed deeply and felt my muscles relax. The noise and clamor of the casino faded into silence, and I opened my eyes.

"Are you OK?" the croupier asked again.

I smiled at him. "Yes. I'm OK."

I selected a chip from my stack and slid it across the green felt of the table. The croupier dealt me two cards — a Jack and a Queen — and two for himself, face down. With a deft movement he flipped one of his cards over — a nine. I passed my hand over the cards like Welling had taught me, indicating I wanted to stand.

The croupier flipped the other card over — a King. I had won! My twenty dollars was now forty.

I felt a thrill of victory and relaxed. I could do this. I kept ten back and bet with thirty.

My next hand was a six and a Queen — sixteen. Had Welling said to stand on sixteen? Or was it seventeen? I tapped the table and the croupier dealt me another card. A four. He bust out at twenty-four on his own hand, and suddenly my thirty dollars was sixty. I was a natural.

I won the next round too, and the one after that. It seemed to come naturally — keeping the mental tally of the high and low cards felt effortless, and the chips kept sliding across the table to me. I lost a few, but I placed my bets carefully and before long I was slowly, steadily making some serious money. The endless drills Welling had put us through were paying off. Even though I was dealing with cards now instead of elements, the count felt familiar and comforting. I felt myself settle into the rhythm of the technic.

After thirty minutes, I leaned back on my stool and surveyed my little pile of chips. One thousand, six hundred dollars. I had never owned that much money in my life. Not that I really owned it now, but for this brief moment I felt like I did. I was powerful and strong.

I bet with more confidence, taking more risks and betting larger amounts when the card count got high. I kept a meticulous count, waiting for the magic number to appear so I could signal Stan and get the others to come over. Before long I had five thousand dollars in chips and was still going strong.

Daddy had been right. It couldn't be this easy for everyone or else casinos would all be broke. It was *me*. It was my own innate powers of thought and analysis, unlocked and free as I approached sublimation.

My five thousand dollars quickly became ten thousand. "Wow," said the croupier, not so bored now. "You're having a lucky day."

He turned over another card, and my mental tally reached +6. I felt a zing of power course through me. It was time. I glanced over to Stan, then casually lifted a hand and slipped my ponytail from its elastic, letting my hair settle around my shoulders. Stan stood up and moved sideways to the next slot machine.

I slowed my betting, waiting for the others to join me. Welling arrived first, then Pippa. They ignored me other than a polite nod of greeting. As far as anyone was concerned, we were complete strangers. They settled at the table and lay bets. Big bets. Thousands of dollars.

"Um," said the croupier. "Are you sure you don't want to try one of the private rooms?"

"Perhaps in a moment," said Welling. "I'd like to play a couple of hands here first."

The croupier shrugged and looked at me expectantly.

I divided my chips in half, kept five thousand, and slid the rest into the center of the table.

The croupier raised his eyebrows but dealt anyway. He dealt himself a Jack. Welling got low cards — fourteen. He waved his hand, a frown wrinkling his face. My mental tally climbed to +8. Pippa busted out.

It was up to me.

And I had two Queens.

Two Queens. Welling had told me never to split tens — but I *knew* that the cards in the deck were high. If I split, then I would win big. Really big.

The avocation was the most powerful I had ever experienced.

It shook me to my core, and in an instant, I *knew*. My hands didn't tremble as I pushed the remainder of my chips into the center of the table. I was going to win. I was going to win twenty thousand dollars, and I would take it back to the Institute, and Daddy would smile his knowing smile at me and tell me that he always knew I was special.

"Split," I said to the croupier.

"Are you sure?" he asked, looking at me as if I was crazy.

I nodded. I'd never been more sure of anything in my life. The croupier dealt me an eight and a ten. Eighteen and twenty. He had the Jack, but it didn't matter. I was going to win.

"Stand," I told him.

He flipped over his other card. A five, putting him at fifteen. I almost whooped with joy. He'd bust on his next card. It was guaranteed. I felt power course through my veins. I felt like I could rise above the table and fly right out of the casino. I was everything.

The croupier flipped over a six. A six.

I heard Welling suck air in through his teeth.

I stared at the croupier's hand. The Jack. The five. The six. Twenty-one.

"Sorry," he said, pulling out a little rake and whisking away my chips with a practiced flick.

I stared at the bare green felt in front of me. I had lost. But the count had been so high! And then . . . fives and sixes? It didn't make sense. I'd followed all the rules. I'd done everything Welling had told me to. But I'd lost.

I'd lost everything.

Welling and Pippa slid off their chairs and disappeared. Stan had gone too. I was on my own.

"You were trying to count cards, weren't you?" asked the

croupier. "It won't work here. We use eight decks at once and a shuffling machine."

His words washed over me like waves of static. I had lost everything. Everything.

"Bad luck," said the croupier.

I stood up from the table. "There's no such thing as luck," I told him numbly.

★ ★ ★

We gathered in the hotel room, but nobody really knew what to say. We'd started the day with nearly a thousand dollars between us. Now we had nothing. What would we tell Daddy?

"Why didn't it work?" asked Pippa. "What went wrong?"

Welling shook his head but didn't say anything.

"I mean, I thought we had it all worked out," said Pippa. "The counting thing. Did we do it wrong? Did Hera make a mistake?"

I hadn't made a mistake. My count had been perfect. My strategy had been perfect. But we had still lost. I had still lost.

"Because I thought the technic was supposed to be foolproof," Pippa continued, oblivious to our shock and silence. "I mean, Daddy said we'd definitely win, right? Was Daddy wrong?"

I slapped her, my hand snapping out and striking her cheek before my brain could even register what I was doing.

"Daddy wasn't wrong," I hissed at her. "Daddy isn't wrong. *We're* wrong. *We* failed him. *Us.* We weren't good enough. Weren't pure enough."

It was the air, I was certain. The pollution and the air conditioning and the cigarette smoke and alcohol fumes and fluorescent lighting. We'd only been here a day and it had already contaminated us. Seeped into our pores and begun to rot us from the inside.

Pippa had her hand to her cheek where I'd struck her, her eyes wide and filling with tears.

She'd never be sublime.

"Hera," said Welling, his voice weary. "Go to the bathroom. Take a moment to elutriate."

He was telling *me* what to do? I wasn't the one who was blubbering. Pippa was an amateur, a slave to her body's synapses and nerve endings. But I obeyed, slipping into the bathroom and closing the door behind me.

I slid the diamond ring off my finger and set it on the counter beside the sink. I turned the tap on and splashed cold water onto my face. My mascara and eyeliner smudged, and I grabbed a towel and scrubbed it off. I felt a strong and sudden need to see my face, my *real* face. The white towel was soon streaked with beige and black and pink. But I still didn't recognize the girl in the mirror with her sharp cheekbones and sunken eyes. Who was she? Who was I? I thought I was Heracleitus, but Heracleitus wouldn't have failed today. She wouldn't have let Daddy down. She wouldn't have lost her temper with Pippa.

I heard a knock at the door to the suite and Welling's footsteps as he crossed the carpet to open the door.

"Room service?" said a voice.

"No," said Welling. "We didn't order room service."

There was a pause, and I heard the crinkling of a sheet of paper. "I'm so sorry, sir," said the stranger's voice. "I have the wrong floor. My apologies."

The door closed.

I took a few deep breaths and went back into the main room.

"It's them," said Stan with an ominous glance at the door.

"The Quintus Septum. They're here. Watching us. Sabotaging our mission."

I nodded, feeling a frightened chill settle over me, as well as . . . relief. The Quintus Septum had made sure I lost at the blackjack table. It was sabotage. It wasn't because I had failed, all on my own. I hadn't let Daddy down.

"What do we do?" Pippa asked. "Do we try again? Go to a different casino?"

Welling shook his head. "They're onto us. We have to return to the Institute and report to Daddy." He stood up and shrugged on his jacket, picking up the now-empty briefcase. "Come on."

Pippa and Stan stood up too and walked to the hotel room door.

An image flashed into my mind of the diamond ring sitting by the bathroom sink, where I had taken it off to wash my face.

"Just a minute," I said, and ducked into the bathroom.

I picked up the ring and slipped it onto my finger. As I turned to join the others, a glint of gold plastic foil caught my eye.

The pillow mints were still in the trash can. My heart started to thump.

No. Poison.

No.

I saw the croupier turn over the last card.

Sorry, he'd said. Had he been a plant? A minion of the Quintus Septum, sent to make me fail? Had he tricked me into thinking I was winning and slipped in his winning hand at the last minute?

Or had he told me the truth? That the casino had measures in place to stop card counters. Measures that Welling didn't know about.

Was it possible I had lost because that was what happened at a casino? Because despite the strategies and tricks, blackjack was ultimately a game of chance and the odds were always stacked in the house's favor?

I took a step toward the basket, moving as silently as possible in order not to alert the others who were standing a few feet away on the other side of the door.

They'll know. They'll smell it on you.

I bent over and picked up a mint. The plastic foil crackled under my fingers, glinting and reflecting the white bathroom light.

No.

No.

No.

I remembered the woman from the casino. The way she had stared at me like she was searching for someone. I remembered the name she had called.

Ruby.

My name. Ruby.

I remembered Fox saying my name and the way the whole Earth shifted a little when the syllables signifying me spilled from his lips. I remembered the taste of hot coffee and white bread. I remembered spring blossoms and ducks floating on a pond and the white-hot urgency of Fox's skin under my fingers, his hands tangled in my hair.

I tore the wrapper away and stuffed the mint into my mouth.

It was electrifying.

The thin chocolate layer melted away on my tongue, leaving rich darkness and the sharp, sweet shock of mint.

I felt like I could fly.

17

As the van rumbled into the Institute two hours later, I could still taste the chocolate. It fizzed through me like lightning. Daddy had told us that sugar was aphotic, that it would make us sluggish and vacant. But I felt as if I'd woken up. I vibrated with nervous energy. My brain wouldn't switch off. It kept asking questions, always questions.

What happened, back in the casino?
Why did we fail?
Have the Quintus Septum really taken over?
Do they even exist?

Everyone was gathered in the courtyard, waiting for us. Daddy stood on the dais. My heart swelled when I saw him and the proud look on his face. I was washed with calm, and the questions all dissolved into wisps and curls of smoke that drifted away on the breeze.

I was home.

Nobody needed to know what I'd done. It had been a mistake. One mistake. I'd never make it again.

Daddy welcomed us onto the dais beside him, his eyes shining with love. I'd worried that he would be disappointed in us. That we had failed him. But instead we were greeted like heroes.

"My children," he said, embracing each of us with emotional warmth. "You have returned. You are stronger than I ever imagined. You faced the Quintus Septum, and you returned. All of you. No casualties."

The others stood around us, their faces open and admiring. Pippa's forehead was creased in a frown. She opened her mouth to speak, but Welling stepped in front of her, addressing Daddy and the crowd.

"They were everywhere," he said. "And they were onto us from the beginning. They knew we were coming."

Daddy's eyes closed, and he breathed a sigh of deep sadness. "Furicius," he said, and the name stirred something deep within me.

Welling nodded. "His betrayal runs deeper than we realized."

The voice snuck back into my mind. *How would Fox know we were going to the casino? Daddy didn't announce the mission until after Fox left.*

"You are lucky to have made it out alive," said Daddy.

"There were some close calls," said Welling. "One of them hunted us down in our hotel room, dressed as a waiter pretending to bring room service. I managed to confuse him and temporarily drive him away while we made our escape."

I saw Pippa's eyes dart from Welling to Daddy to the open-mouthed admiration of the others. I saw the cogs turn. Then she nodded. "Welling's right," she said.

"One of them confronted Hera," Welling continued. "Right on the casino floor, in front of everyone."

I remembered Mom's friend grabbing my arm and saying that name over and over.

Ruby?

Ruby?

Ruby?

"Hera was something else," said Stan, shaking his head in wonder. "She slipped from their grasp and vanished into the crowd. Just vanished! I've never seen anything like it."

This isn't true, said the voice. *None of it is. You know that woman wasn't a member of the Quintus Septum. She was a woman who your mom used to be in a book club with.*

Daddy reached out and clasped my hands. "The Quintus Septum can't hope to challenge our Heracleitus." I felt myself swimming in the intense blue of his eyes. "You are magnificent," he said, his voice low and just for me. "I knew I was right to send you."

I let Daddy's words pour over me and run through my veins, and once more the chocolate voice was silenced, replaced with strength and certainty.

Daddy squeezed my hands. "Your efforts will not go unrewarded, Heracleitus," he murmured, his voice low. "I have a very special honor planned for you."

He skimmed his eyes over my body in a way he'd never done before. I felt a ripple of unease, and the certainty melted away.

"We must redouble our efforts," said Daddy, raising his voice and turning back to the crowd. "We will not give in to the Quintus Septum's reign of terror. We must help the toxicants to be elutriated. It's time to prepare for the final battle. The endgame."

The endgame. I took a deep breath and pushed away my fear.

Daddy was giving out orders, sending people off on jobs all over the Institute. At last he turned to me.

"Heracleitus," he said. "Libavius is in C Block. Please join her for your task."

I nodded crisply. In all my months at the Institute, I'd never been in the third building — the one where the Monkeys lived. Curiosity prickled inside me, but I kept my face neutral as I headed off.

The Monkeys marched by, escorted by Newton, and I realized it had been days since I'd seen them. They didn't giggle or scamper or chatter the way they had when I'd first arrived. Now they walked in single file, their heads bowed and shoulders hunched. They looked hungry and afraid, blinking as if they weren't used to daylight.

The Monkey at the back looked different from the others. Her cotton shirt hung slightly askew, and her hair had started to grow back in orange corkscrews. I saw something in her fist — something brown and shining. I remembered the cicada husks lined up along Val's bedroom window at the Red House and Val sneaking snow peas from his plate. Then the Monkeys turned the corner and headed to the back of the building, out of my view.

C Block was large and must have been used as a secondary storage site, after the warehouse. Double doors opened out onto what would have once been a loading dock. One of these doors was ajar. I slipped inside. Lib was waiting for me in a large room, in front of a wall of stacked cardboard boxes. She was turned with her head slightly away from me, and I realized she hadn't been there earlier to welcome us home.

As I approached her, I caught a glimpse of the other side of her face and felt my steps falter.

"Your eye," I said. "What happened?"

It was swollen almost shut, yellow and purple bruises blooming halfway across her cheek.

Lib lifted a tentative finger to brush the swelling. "Nothing," she said with a sad smile. "A stupid accident. My own fault. I let myself become aphotic with worry for . . . for you and the others. On your mission. I wasn't paying attention. I let the body take over for a moment, and it lost control."

She's lying, said the voice in my brain. *Someone did that to her.*

I tried to recall the look on Daddy's face when he'd told me I was magnificent. I tried to recapture that feeling of calmness and safety. I shook my head to clear it of the chocolate voice and smiled at Lib. There was nobody here who would have hurt Lib.

Yes, there is. You know who did it. He did it to you too.

"So," I said, my voice a little too loud. "What's the plan?"

The door behind me opened, and Val came in carrying another cardboard box, which he placed neatly by the others. There were hundreds of them, stacked almost to the ceiling. I saw Val glance over at a door on the back wall of the room, and the scar on his forehead twitched into a frown. I followed his gaze.

"What's through there?" I asked Lib. "Is that the Monkey House?"

Lib didn't respond, and Val left the room.

A few of the boxes were open — they were full of water bottles with sealed blue lids but no labels. Other boxes farther back contained empty bottles.

"Who puts the water in?"

Lib's face was as cold as stone. "Welling and I usually prepare and bottle the water. This batch has a different formula —" She broke off suddenly and turned away.

"Different?" I asked. "Different how? There's usually a little bit of sulfur in the water, right? Is there more this time? Is there something else?"

The questions spilled out of me, beyond my control. It was the chocolate. It had weakened me. I remembered what had happened to Fox, the questions that had eventually driven him away. I had to fight it. I had to elutriate.

Lib opened another box to reveal a stack of printed adhesive labels, each one bearing the Institute of the Boundless Sublime symbol and the words

BOUNDLESS BODY
BOUNDLESS MIND

This was Daddy's special task for me? Sticking labels on water bottles? How did this relate to the plan? How were water bottles going to overthrow the Quintus Septum?

I realized I'd never fully figured out what the purpose of the water bottles was. Whenever I'd asked anyone about it, they always responded with the same meaningless words.

People get thirsty.

"Why are there so many?" I asked Lib.

"Daddy wants us to hand out water bottles on Black Friday."

"Why?"

Lib frowned. She didn't like questions.

"Because of the Quintus Septum, of course."

It was Daddy, standing in the doorway, framed with white light from outside.

"My dear Heracleitus," he said. "You have been to the house of lead. You have seen the toxicants imprisoned there. You know how dangerous it is."

I nodded.

"The Quintus Septum use the power of money to control the toxicants. Black Friday is their triumph, their highest feast day. It is when every house becomes a house of lead. If we can encourage the toxicants to keep their minds clear on that dark day, then maybe there is a spark of hope for us."

"Hope?"

"I want the toxicants to turn and run as far away from it all as they can. For them to realize that corruption and evil are everywhere. That they are all tainted. That the only solution is to —" He broke off abruptly and turned his head away. "Forgive me," he murmured. "Sometimes I can't help myself. I get so angry, seeing so many actualities in pain. So much potential enslaved to aphotic, rotting meat bodies. It breaks my heart."

"What were you going to say?" I asked. "What is the only solution?"

Daddy sighed, crestfallen. "I wish I knew, Heracleitus. I wish I could help them all. But even I don't have that kind of power. All I can do is look after my own family and hope that one day we can be strong enough to summon the Scintilla, who will liberate us all from this tyrannical oppression."

He nodded at us slowly and solemnly, then wound his way through the stacks of boxes to the back of the room. He disappeared behind a small wooden door that was partially obscured by boxes, in the corner where the door to the Monkey House was. Lib continued mechanically peeling and sticking labels, her face unreadable. I looked back at the closed door. I imagined a gleaming, state-of-the-art facility, full of stainless steel and curled glass tubes.

"Is that Daddy's laboratory?" I asked.

She looked up at me, and for a moment her face was stricken in deep lines of fear and grief. But then she regained her composure, leaving me wondering if I'd imagined it.

"Enough," she snapped, her voice suddenly harsh. "Stop asking questions and get to work."

I obeyed her, but as I peeled and stuck, I couldn't help my eyes from wandering back to the closed door.

★ ★ ★

Sleep evaded me once more. I could still feel the chocolate, thick and black on my tongue. It had woken something inside me. Something beautiful and electric and wrong. I vowed to increase my dosage of supplements and withhold all other foods until the toxins were elutriated from my system. I would be strong — as hard and clear as the diamond that I'd worn in the casino.

★ ★ ★

After our usual meditation the next morning, Daddy looked over us with a grave expression, blinking with slow, heavy sadness.

"There is an aphotic in our midst," he said. "A festering wound. It spreads poison among us."

His eyes met mine, and I felt a chill pass through me. He knew.

"There is no pain greater than that of a parent betrayed," said Daddy. "A parent — a Daddy — puts his trust in his children. He pours love, strength, compassion, patience into them. He gives them everything he has in the world. They are his reason for existing. His everything. So when one of his children betrays him, it is an act of violence. An act of malice and spite."

He knew about the chocolate. About my weakness. Could he hear the voice in my head, asking questions?

"I sent four of you into the world on a mission of great importance," said Daddy. "I chose you because, of all my children, I trusted you to remain pure. To remain loyal. But one of you has been overtaken by shadow. You have brought lead into our home. You threaten our very existence."

I felt my traitorous body start to shake with fear.

I knew I should confess. Throw myself at his feet and beg for mercy. Plead with him to let me stay — to lock me up and punish me again, for as long as it took.

"Agrippa."

It took me a moment to register what Daddy had said. Then I turned and looked at Pippa. Her face was white, tears streaming down her cheeks.

I'm sorry. She mouthed the words, but no sound came out.

It wasn't me.

I wasn't the traitor.

Pippa was the traitor. Not me. Not Fox. Pippa?

"Join me," said Daddy.

Hesitantly, Pippa took a step forward, then another. Her whole body was shaking with fear and silent sobs.

Daddy held out his hand, palm up. Pippa dug in the pocket of her shirt and pulled out a small item, which she placed on Daddy's palm.

The ring. The diamond ring I'd worn in the casino. She'd stolen it.

Daddy held it up to the light, where it twinkled in the early morning sun.

"It's beautiful, isn't it?" he said to Pippa, his voice gentle.

She nodded and gulped.

"Put it on," Daddy urged, handing it back.

Pippa seemed to shrink into herself, looking even more terrified.

"Go on," said Daddy. "I want to see it sparkle on your finger."

Pippa's body curved into a frightened question mark, but she took the ring back, shaking, and slipped it onto her finger.

Daddy took her hand and held it aloft.

"Beautiful," he murmured. "It suits you. I can see why you are drawn to it."

Pippa took a deep breath and seemed to relax a little. Daddy didn't seem angry at all.

Apparently Pippa didn't know him as well as I did.

"Heracleitus," said Daddy, not looking at me.

I rose to my feet and stepped forward.

"Do you think that Agrippa's ring is beautiful?" he asked.

"No," I said, my voice clear.

"No?" Daddy's eyebrows arched in mock surprise, but he didn't look away from Pippa. "And why is that?"

I knew what he wanted me to say, so I said it. "It is an anchor. It shackles her to the earth, dragging her down into the mud."

Daddy nodded. "Do you feel it, Agrippa?"

Pippa's face had gone white again. Slowly, she nodded.

"The weight of it? Do you feel it chaining you to the earth? Pulling you down, further and further into the muck and the ooze? Do you feel how aphotic it is? How your actuality is drowning in it?"

Pippa fumbled at her fingers, trying to tug the ring off. But her hands were shaking, and the ring stuck behind her knuckle.

"Do you see?" said Daddy. "Have you had the avocation?

Your own body is betraying you. The body *wants* things. In order to be sublime, you must learn to elutriate. To master your urges. But you have given in. Your body rules you now."

Pippa tugged harder.

"How do you get your body back under control? How do you teach it that *you* are in charge — your mind. Your actuality. Heracleitus?"

I closed my eyes for a moment and felt Daddy's boot sink into my stomach. I tasted blood in my mouth.

"You punish the body," I said.

Daddy turned his head away from Pippa and locked eyes with me.

"Yes," he whispered, his voice almost inaudible. "Yes."

Daddy held out a hand, and Val passed him a pair of bolt cutters — sharp blades with red rubber handles. My stomach dropped, and I struggled to keep my expression calm.

Daddy can't know. Do anything he says — just make sure he doesn't find out that you have doubts.

He was trying to scare Pippa. Surely he wouldn't really do it. *Would he?*

Wait. Stay calm.

Pippa whirled around, her eyes searching out Lib. "Tell him," she pleaded, her voice high with hysteria.

Lib swallowed, then stepped forward and murmured something to Daddy. His expression softened, and for a moment I thought he was going to let Pippa go, but then his eyes flicked over to me, then back to Pippa.

He sighed. "I'm afraid you don't get any special treatment, my dear." He held out the bolt cutters to me. "Teach Agrippa's body the avocation, Heracleitus."

It was another test. Like Val and the beaker of poison. He'd stop me before I actually did it. I felt the hair on my arms stand on end as thoughts rushed through me. I had to be careful. Very careful. Daddy was testing me. This wasn't about poor Pippa at all — it was about me. How I responded was very important. I kept my face neutral as I took the bolt cutters.

He wanted me to prove myself. Prove that I was still loyal.

That I was still his.

Was I?

All I knew was that if he saw me flinch — if he saw any doubt in my mind — he'd cast me aside. Or worse.

He wouldn't actually make me do it, though.

Daddy reached out and grabbed Pippa's hand by the wrist. He folded all her fingers over into a fist, except for the one with the ring.

I slipped the bolt cutters over Pippa's finger and gripped the red handles. Pippa began to weep, her voice cracking hysterically as she begged me to stop, begged Daddy for mercy.

I paused, waiting for Daddy to tell me to stop. Daddy's eyes bore into mine, cold and hard as steel.

He said nothing, and I realized with a flash of horror that he wasn't going to stop me.

There are so many things I would change, if I could. So many choices I made that I regret. This one haunts me the most. I dream about it regularly, waking each time soaked in sweat and guilt. Because I knew better. The chocolate had woken me up, and I was beginning to see clearly. I wasn't brainwashed — a mindless zombie with no free will. I was afraid. Afraid of being punished. Afraid Daddy would see my weakness, my doubt, and hurt me again.

So I did it.

Pippa screamed. I felt the resistance of her skin give way as the blades sliced through her flesh, then met bone. I squeezed harder and felt the bone crunch and give way. Blood splashed onto the front of Daddy's white shirt, and he released her hand as the piece of finger fell, bouncing on the concrete and rolling away. Pippa's scream was swallowed up by a low moan, and she crumpled to the ground, unconscious, blood pouring from the place where her finger had once been.

Daddy's mouth spread slowly into a smile, his eyes never leaving mine for a moment.

"Good girl," he murmured.

The bolt cutters slipped from my fingers, and I felt a wash of relief. Daddy still loved me. He still trusted me.

"Look after Agrippa," Daddy said to Lib. "I need her healthy." Then he turned and went back inside.

My relief was overpowered by nausea, and I doubled over, retching. I tasted the forbidden chocolate and the acidic tang of bile, but there was nothing in my stomach to throw up, so after a moment of sweating and coughing, I stood up.

Lib was bent over Pippa, wrapping her hand in a tea towel. There was blood everywhere, blossoming red sticky wet. Lib signaled to Val, and he bent and lifted Pippa as though she weighed nothing at all. Then he followed Lib into B Block.

One by one, the others dispersed. Nobody would look me in the eye. They wouldn't even walk near me, taking a wide berth around Daddy's stage in order to avoid passing right by me. I saw Ash whispering anxiously to Toser, and they briefly clasped hands.

That was forbidden. They didn't belong to each other anymore. They belonged to Daddy.

We all belonged to Daddy.

I went into the bathroom and wiped the blood off my shoes.

My shirt was splashed with dark red. I wondered if it would wash out, or whether I'd be stained forever.

Horrified, I looked down at my shaking hands and remembered the crunching feeling of bone between steel blades. I had done that.

I felt sick with guilt and fear.

What else would he make me do? And what had he made others do? Had they all carried out his orders as willingly as I had? What happened to the ones who dissented?

I thought about Maggie and Fox. I'd let myself believe that Daddy had allowed them to leave. But what if I was wrong? If Daddy could order the severing of a finger, could he do more? Could he order an execution?

I tried to tell myself that it was necessary. That Daddy knew best. That what I'd done would help Pippa, help her survive the fight against the Quintus Septum.

The chocolate voice was deafening.

There is no Quintus Septum.

I needed to know the truth. I needed evidence that the Quintus Septum existed — that the danger was real. It was the only way I'd be able to justify what I'd done.

I was sure the answers were in Daddy's laboratory. I couldn't enter through the storage space I'd been in with Lib, as it was in plain sight of the rest of the Institute. Someone would see me and ask why I was there. I'd have to enter through the Monkey House.

★ ★ ★

I didn't go to breakfast. Instead I slipped around the narrow side of C Block, clambering over milk crates, weeds, and broken bottles.

It reminded me of the Wasteland. Minah would like it here. She'd probably try to draw it, except she'd turn the abandoned shopping cart into some kind of monster. I remembered taking Fox to the Wasteland and how curious he'd been.

Ugly places often have beautiful secrets.

It must have reminded him of home. Of growing up in the Monkey House. Of working there, looking after the Monkeys.

I pushed through a particularly weedy patch and came out into the open. I was at the back of the building. There was a heavy wooden door into the Monkey House, and a neat, well-maintained path that led around the other side, back to the courtyard. That was the path the Monkeys used. I reached out and put my hand on the door handle and tried to turn it.

Nothing. The door was locked. I rattled the handle a few times, but it didn't budge. I let my hand drop to my side, and like magic, the door swung open, revealing three stubble-headed Monkeys, their faces solemn.

Up close, I could see that they looked different from one another. The youngest one had ruddy cheeks and was missing two front teeth. I wasn't sure if it was a boy or a girl, though. The middle one I suspected was a boy, painfully thin and pale, with hollow cheeks and an angular jaw. The tallest one had darker skin and brown eyes and was definitely a girl. Her eyes narrowed suspiciously as she took me in.

"You can't be here," she said, her voice cold.

"It's OK," I said, surprising myself by how easily the lie came. "Daddy said I could come."

The Monkeys exchanged glances. "No," said the tall one. "He didn't. You're lying."

My skin prickled with unease. They were so different. When I'd first arrived at the Institute, the Monkeys had been plump and happy. Seeing them scampering around, absorbed in play, had been one of the things that had endeared me to the Institute, made be believe that it was a good place. But now they were skinny and pale and wide-eyed with fear. Fox had been right to worry about them.

"Let me in," I said.

They closed ranks in front of me, blocking my way through. "Go and tell Daddy," said the tall Monkey to the thin one.

"Tell him there's a snake."

The thin, pale Monkey nodded and scampered past me down the path. I didn't worry too much about him — I knew Daddy wasn't to be disturbed.

The tall Monkey pushed the door shut, making the corrugated iron of the warehouse tremble and clang.

I stepped back and searched the facade for another door or a window — there had to be a way in.

"You won't find anything," said a voice behind me, and I spun around, my heart pounding.

It was a Monkey, the one who had been hiding in the bathroom on my very first day. Who ate Val's snow peas and took his cicada husks. I recognized her freckles. She looked older now — thinner, with dark circles under her eyes. Where had she come from? She must have been hiding in the bushes the whole time.

"If you want to get into Daddy's laboratory, you have to go in either through the front door or through the Monkey House. But both doors are locked all the time. Daddy has one key. But there's another."

"Where?" I asked. "Where's the other key?"

"Up in a cupboard. In there." She jerked her head toward the closed door.

"Can you get it for me?" I asked. "The key?"

The Monkey shook her head, and I noticed bruises on her wrists, as if she'd been tied up.

Anger and frustration boiled up inside me.

"I have to get in there," I told her. "I can help you."

"You can't get in there," she said. "Someone will see. But . . ." She trailed off.

"But what?"

The Monkey looked around, as if to check that no one was watching us. "Sometimes Daddy comes to the Monkey House after dinner and tells us a bedtime story."

I shook my head. "So?"

The Monkey rolled her eyes, as if she thought me unspeakably stupid. "So he doesn't go to the Sanctum," she said.

★ ★ ★

I waited. But Daddy came to Family Time every evening. Since the Quintus Septum had risen to power, Family Time had changed. We didn't sing or laugh. Daddy didn't tell us funny stories. Instead, we talked quietly about the coming war. Daddy told us more about the Quintus Septum, about the horrors that they would bring, and made frequent reference to his grand plan to defeat them, although he didn't reveal any details. We retired early, as soon as Daddy had chosen a companion and headed to the Sanctum.

There was plenty of chatter about what happened in the Sanctum. The Institute women seemed immensely proud to be chosen and were eager to tell of the supernatural experiences they had when receiving Daddy's actuality — being surrounded by light, floating up to the ceiling, hearing the ringing of a thousand bells. I'd been told that Daddy's choice of companion depended on the balance inside each woman. We were incomplete without the actuality of a man, but some needed more balancing than others. It had taken weeks for Pippa's actuality to be balanced. Currently he was working with a woman called Cibinensis — Cibby — who had large, doe-like eyes and a stammer. He never chose Lib or Newton. They had been at the Institute for years, and their actualities had reached equilibrium long ago. Lib's face always darkened when Daddy chose a new woman, and I wondered if she got jealous.

★ ★ ★

One night, he stood up and looked around, his eyes skating over Cibby and assessing the other women present. For a moment his gaze locked with mine, and I felt exposed, as if he was assessing my naked body, prying into my mind, my secrets, my doubts.

He was going to choose me.

Excuses piled into my mind. I had a headache. I had my period. I wasn't eighteen yet. But Daddy would know I was trying to stall. I hadn't had a period for months. I'd assumed it was because I was becoming sublime, because I was learning to control my body. Now I wished it back.

I tried to tell myself that it was an honor, that I needed it in order to be sublime, but I couldn't believe it. The idea of having sex with Daddy filled me with revulsion, and no number of stories about glowing light and magical bells would change that. And it was happening. Daddy was going to choose me, and there was nothing I could do to stop him.

But his eyes flicked away.

"Ashmole," he said, his voice light. "Would you please join me in the Sanctum."

I felt a flood of relief as I saw the blood drain from Ash's face. She glanced at Toser, who looked stricken.

"Is . . ." Ash swallowed. "Is it compulsory?"

Daddy's smile took on a blandness, and I knew he was angry. "Not at all," he said mildly. "I would never dream of forcing you to do anything against your will."

Ash looked relieved, but Toser's face was still drawn with concern. He knew that it wasn't that simple.

"As I have explained before," said Daddy, "my technic works one hundred percent of the time, when followed correctly. If you do not wish to follow the technic, you are free to leave."

"It is a great honor to receive Daddy's actuality," Cibby murmured to Ash. "It will help you reach sublimation."

Toser nodded to Ash. "Go on."

Ash's eyes filled with tears, and she stood up, trembling.

Daddy smiled. "You won't regret it," he said. "I promise."

★ ★ ★

Daddy chose Ash the next night as well. This time, Ash didn't cry or tremble. Instead she wore a kind of robotic blankness, following Daddy to the Sanctum with her head bowed, her eyes never meeting Toser's. She didn't look elutriated or balanced. I didn't know what it was that Daddy had done to her, but I knew I didn't want him to do it to me.

Looking back, I realize now that I'd already made up my mind. I knew that receiving Daddy's actuality wouldn't make me sublime — that nothing would. But I wasn't ready to face what that meant. I needed something. A sign. Evidence to confirm my doubts.

Before I headed to bed, I made my way over to Pippa. We hadn't spoken since the incident with the ring, and she was subdued and pale.

She looked at me as I sat down beside her, then lowered her head to look at the ground. Her hand was wrapped in thick white bandages.

"Heracleitus," she murmured.

"Pippa," I said. "I wanted to see how you are. And make sure there are no hard feelings between us."

Pippa's head jerked from side to side in an emphatic shake, and she reached out and took my hands in hers. The gauze of her bandage felt rough against my skin.

"Never, Heracleitus," she said, her voice low and intense. "I must thank you. You . . . saved me. I was in danger of falling into darkness. But you showed me the light."

I remembered the crunching of bone beneath my fingers and pulled my hands away.

"I'm glad you're doing well."

"I am," she said. "Thanks to you."

"Thanks to Daddy," I reminded her, my voice a little stern.

"Of course," said Pippa. "Daddy is *everything*." Her voice throbbed with emotion.

"Yes," I agreed, hoping she wouldn't notice the faint note of doubt in my own voice.

* * *

On the following night, Daddy didn't join us for Family Time. Someone mentioned he was with the Monkeys.

I excused myself, murmuring about needing to use the bathroom, and slipped out of the warehouse into the night.

There was no one around — everyone was talking quietly in the warehouse. I entered A Block and padded down the corridor until I came to Daddy's Inner Sanctum. My heart pounded, and I stood outside the door for several agonizing minutes, straining my ears for the faintest noise.

Nothing.

I opened the door.

The room was unchanged. White walls and floor. Soft white cushions and the flickering candles. I slipped inside and closed the door behind me with a soft click. It was like Operation Hush-Hush again but a thousand times more dangerous. It was easy to thwart the docile, aphotic toxicants, but Daddy was another story altogether. He was sharp. He was sublime. And I knew what happened when you disappointed him.

At the back of the room was the old wooden desk with two drawers. I swallowed. I had no idea what I was looking for. But I still had to know. I opened the left-hand drawer, wincing at the squeak of wood on wood.

For a moment I stood there, unsure of what I was looking at. It looked like . . . treasure. A glittering hoard of gold and bright jewels. Then I realized it wasn't treasure. It was chocolate. The drawer was full to bursting with fun-size chocolate bars, shining in their foiled plastic wrapping. I reached out and brushed my hand through them. Some of the wrappers were empty.

Why did Daddy keep a drawer full of chocolate?

There were other little packets too — individual servings of salt and pepper and moistened napkins, all bearing the logos of fast food restaurants.

A realization began to creep over me.

I slid the drawer closed and tugged at the one beside it. Something clunked inside as the drawer slid open. A half-empty bottle of bourbon, rolling around and knocking against the sides of the drawer, and a battered paperback book.

I felt like my heart was stopping. With shaking hands, I reached in and picked up the book. It was Fox's copy of *Les Miserables*. Why would Daddy have Fox's book? I thumbed through the pages, and something fell out. I bent down and retrieved it. It was the photo of Fox and his mother.

There was no way Fox would have left it behind. No way. Even if he had left without saying goodbye. Even if he'd abandoned the Monkeys. Even if he was a traitor. He wouldn't have left this. So why did Daddy have it now?

Because he didn't leave, said the voice in my head. But Daddy said he left.

Daddy lied.

Daddy doesn't lie.

He lied about food. He says he hasn't eaten for thousands of years, but really he eats chocolate and fast food.

But if Fox didn't leave, where was he?

Dead. Fox is dead. Daddy killed him.

There were other things in the drawer too. A small plush giraffe. A credit card belonging to someone called Glen Ardeer. A wedding ring. A necklace with a jade pendant.

Who had these things belonged to? And where were those people now?

My phone was there too. I picked it up, surprised by how cold and heavy it felt. It called to me, promising answers to all my questions, and almost against my will, my fingers groped for the power button.

But there was no response on the screen. The battery was

dead, and I had no way to charge it. I put it back in the drawer and picked up the jade pendant.

A memory rose before me. Maggie in the van on the way to the Institute, showing me the secret pocket in her shirt. The flash of green and gold. It had been her grandmother's, Maggie had said. The one thing she'd never part with. The one thing she wouldn't give up for the Institute.

I remembered Maggie's unhinged expression as she brandished the knife at Daddy. He'd said that she'd decided to leave. But what if she hadn't?

What if she was dead too?

My knees buckled beneath me, and I gripped the corner of the desk. I'd gone looking for answers, but all I'd found were more questions.

I put everything back except for the photo of Fox and his mother, which I slipped into the waistband of my pants. Then I pushed the drawer shut and slipped back out into the night. The cool air hit my face, and I felt like I was finally starting to see things clearly after months of living in a fog.

I didn't have any answers, but I knew one thing. It was time for me to leave the Institute.

18

You are free to leave. That was what Daddy had always said, but now I knew it wasn't true. There was no way Daddy was going to let me walk out the front gate of the Institute and return to the real world. Not after everything I'd seen.

I had to plan. I had to be careful.

And I had to make sure nobody suspected anything.

So I played the game. I worked with Lib in the warehouse, sticking labels on bottle after bottle of water. I spoke seriously of the Quintus Septum at Family Time. And I sat at Daddy's feet each morning during Daddy's Hour and stared up at him with wholehearted sincerity.

It wasn't difficult. Daddy's stories were as arresting as always. His words as profound. The stillness and peace I'd always found during Daddy's chanting was still within my reach.

I went about my duties. I ate my meager few mouthfuls of salted quinoa. I took my daily supplements.

Every evening at Family Time, I feared Daddy would ask me to join him in the Sanctum. I wasn't eighteen yet, but would Daddy really care about a few months? I knew that sooner or later, he would choose me, and I wouldn't be able to turn him down.

Each night I would lie awake, trying to figure out how to get away. How to give myself enough time to escape.

How would I do it? I could wait for a new mission to come up — chances were there wouldn't be another casino mission, but perhaps there'd be something else. Another round of Hush-Hush that I could volunteer for. Then I could leave, slip away into the darkness to never return.

But as the days passed, it became clear that Daddy wasn't letting anyone in or out. The danger was too great, he said. The Quintus Septum was moving quickly, taking over every facet of society. They had infiltrated government, the military, the media. Nowhere was safe from their surveillance, except for behind the walls of the Institute.

I had to find another way. I had to get over the wall.

I made mental maps of drainpipes and gutters and other structures I could scramble on. I realized I'd have to find a way onto the warehouse roof first. There was a point at the back corner that was only a few feet from the wall separating it from the building next door. I was pretty sure I could jump the distance, although if I slipped and fell, I'd be lucky to get away with a few broken bones. Once over the wall, I could run down the street to the apartments on the corner, knocking on doors until someone answered, and get them to call my mom or the police.

But it was so risky. Nobody was allowed out of their rooms after Family Time. Lib and Welling patrolled the hallways for hours each night to make sure everyone was safe in bed. If they caught me, I'd be hauled before Daddy immediately. And then he'd know. He'd know I'd betrayed him. That I'd given in to doubt. That I'd failed.

I told myself that I needed more time to plan.

I couldn't let anyone guess that I had doubts. I had to become more devout. I cut my already tiny meals in half and spent every spare moment I had training myself.

I let the days slip by.

I would leave, I told myself. I just had to wait for the right time.

Two weeks after I'd broken into the Inner Sanctum, I still had no plan. I felt weak with indecision, as if my body anticipated leaving the Institute and was already starting to betray me.

Could I really leave?

Had I been mistaken about what I'd seen in Daddy's desk? Maybe there was an explanation. Maybe Maggie and Fox had given Daddy their treasures.

And what was I going to do once I'd escaped? Where was I going to go? I had no idea what I'd find at home. Was I going to go back to school? Go back to hanging out at the Wasteland with Minah and the others, like nothing had happened?

I couldn't imagine that. I couldn't imagine going back to the person I'd once been. She didn't exist anymore. She'd been erased, extinguished during my long days incarcerated in the tiny, locked room.

★ ★ ★

"Heracleitus."

Daddy's eyes were upon me, his smile light, his voice casual.

But his words were like the clanging of a gong in the pit of my belly.

I'd put it off too long. Daddy had chosen me.

My mind screamed out in resistance, but my body obeyed, rising steadily to my feet. I ducked my head and smiled with the shy, happy modesty I knew Daddy would approve of. I saw relief flash over Ash's face.

I followed Daddy across the courtyard. Val followed a few steps behind.

"Go and elutriate your body, Heracleitus, and change into your nightgown," Daddy said. "Then meet me in the Sanctum."

I nodded, numb.

Daddy went inside, and I walked around the side of B Block to the bathroom, where I splashed cold water on my hands and face. Val waited outside, a mountain of implacable silence.

Wake up, Heracleitus. Think of something. Do something.

I made my way back to my little room, Val shuffling behind me. He waited in the corridor again, and I wondered if many women tried to run at this point.

I changed into my nightgown. My body was shaking, and I couldn't control it. Each time I closed my eyes I pictured Daddy's perfectly manicured fingernails. Imagined his hands on me. His eyes. His mouth.

My room felt suddenly tiny, like the walls were closing in on me.

I couldn't do it. I had to leave. But Val was outside.

I remembered him drinking from Daddy's flask. He hadn't hesitated. Not for a second. How could I escape now? Val would pick me up like a rag doll and take me to Daddy.

Wouldn't he?

Val had brought me food when I was imprisoned. I'd assumed

that Daddy had told him to, but the more I thought about it, I realized that Val had acted of his own accord. He had given Fox his copy of *Les Misérables*. I remembered the Monkey crunching snow peas in a shadowy corner. It was the same Monkey that I saw around, hiding. The one with the cicada husk in her hand. The one who had told me when I could get into the Sanctum without Daddy noticing.

I yanked open the door to my room.

"Who is she?" I asked Val. "Is she family? Your daughter?"

Val stared at me, his scarred face expressionless. He shook his head faintly.

"You save your food for her," I said. "She . . . she means something to you. She's special."

Val said nothing.

"You know what he's going to do to me, right? When I go in there?"

Val inclined his head in the slightest nod.

"He'll do it to her," I said. "Maybe not soon. But one day, when she's older. Will you stand outside her bedroom door? Will you deliver her to him?"

I saw the scars on Val's skin shift as his jaw clenched.

"Let me go," I said. "And I promise I'll help her. I'll get her out of here. Find her a real family. Just let me go, and wait a few minutes before you tell Daddy. OK?"

Val's eyes met mine, and I saw guilt and pain. We stared at each other for a long moment, then Val's gaze dropped down to the floor. His head bobbed in a nod, and he turned and lumbered off down the corridor.

I took a deep breath and headed the other way, out of B Block and into the night.

It was overcast, light from nearby streetlights reflecting off the clouds and casting a dim brown light on the buildings of the Institute. I shivered through my thin cotton nightgown and wished I'd had the sense to put my shoes on. I kept to the shadows, but there was no one around. Everyone was still in the warehouse for Family Time.

I had no plan. After all those weeks of thinking about leaving, I still had no plan. My idea of scaling the warehouse and jumping across to the wall was ridiculous. I'd slip and kill myself. There had to be another way. I found myself heading to the garage door that led out to the road. Maybe someone had left it open. It was worth checking.

A rumbling sounded nearby, and a wash of light swept over the wall from outside. I froze, terrified. Had we been infiltrated by the Quintus Septum? Were we under attack?

But I didn't believe in the Quintus Septum. Not anymore. Did I?

I looked around carefully, scouring every dark corner and shadow. There was nothing. No movement. No evidence of an invasion. Nothing.

The light dimmed, and the rumble faded. It had just been a car driving past. I let out the breath I didn't realize I'd been holding and took another few steps forward. The garage door was closed, but maybe there was a button or chain.

I reached out and brushed my fingers against the brick wall that separated me from freedom. I was so close. I looked up for the box that controlled the garage door, and my heart sank as I remembered Daddy opening it for my Hush-Hush mission. He'd used a key.

I heard voices as people started to drift away from the warehouse, heading to bed. Panic rose in my throat. I didn't have much time. Soon, Daddy would realize that I wasn't coming. Maybe Val had already told him. Maybe it was too late.

I reached down and tugged at the bottom of the garage door, but it didn't budge.

"We'll be very sad to see you go."

I spun around.

Daddy was there, in the middle of the parking lot, watching me silently, the faint light glinting off his glasses. I felt my blood run cold.

Where had he come from? Why hadn't I heard him? How long had he been there, watching me? My heart hammered.

Was I really going to defy him? I could give in, go back, forget about all my doubts. Forget everything I'd seen. I'd be safe here. Nothing had to change.

But everything had already changed. I couldn't go back.

"I'm leaving," I told him. I was surprised at how confident I sounded. "You can try to stop me, but —"

Daddy took a step forward. I felt my muscles tense, ready to run. He didn't look angry. His brow was wrinkled in concern, but his face was gentle. He raised his hands, as if in surrender. In his left hand there was a bunch of keys. He took another step forward and reached up, inserting a key into the garage door lock and turning it.

The door groaned and clanked as it slowly ascended.

"I'm not going to stop you, Heracleitus," Daddy said. "Nobody is forcing you to be here. If you want to leave, you should leave."

Was this a trick? More mind games? I hesitated. Beyond the gate, the road was dark and deserted.

"I'd be lying if I said my feelings weren't hurt," said Daddy with a shrug. "But you should do what is right for you. You're an extraordinary creature, Heracleitus, and I wouldn't dream of interfering with your chosen path. I'm sure you'll achieve great things."

"Thank you," I said automatically, my mind whirling. Was it really going to be this easy?

I took a step forward, and another, waiting for Daddy to reveal his trump card. Surely he had something up his sleeve? Some last trick? But as I crossed the threshold, Daddy turned the key back the other way, and the garage door began to come down. He watched me as it descended between us, his face as calm and expressionless as if I were heading out to shop for bread and milk.

"Good luck, Heracleitus," he said, barely raising his voice over the noise of the garage door. "Please give your mother my very best regards."

The gate hit the concrete with a loud boom. I heard Daddy's shoes crunching on the gravel as he made his way back into A Block, and for a moment I wondered if I'd made a terrible mistake, if being locked out was worse than being locked in. Which was the real prison, anyway?

Ahead of me, burning orange street lamps lit the road to the corner, then the world faded to nothing, swallowed up in the dark of the night. I felt frozen by fear. What was waiting for me down that road? Home? My family? Or was it the Quintus Septum? Would I be taken and tortured for the Institute's secrets?

I began to walk down the road, stepping quietly between pools of orange cast by the streetlights. I listened for footsteps behind me, convinced that Daddy would send someone to follow me. But there was nothing.

Why hadn't he sent someone? Why hadn't he tried to make me stay? Daddy loved me. He thought I was special. So how could he let me leave?

Because you're not special. You're nothing. You let him down.
You betrayed Daddy. He doesn't love you anymore.

Why did I care so much? I knew he was a charlatan. I'd seen proof. I knew he was crazy, or dangerous — probably both. So why did his rejection hurt so much?

I'd planned this for so long, thought about it day after day for weeks. I never imagined it would be like this. With every step I felt my body growing heavier, more leaden. Was I walking toward freedom or away from it?

I reached the end of the street and started to turn left, toward the housing development, the way I had gone for Operation Hush-Hush. But I stopped. There was nothing for me there. Just sleeping bodies and well-stocked pantries. I needed to find my way home, if such a place even still existed. I turned right, into the unknown.

There was a chill in the air, and I shivered in my cotton nightgown. My bare feet were soon aching and stinging. I'd thought I was tough, after all my training. But I wasn't sure how far I'd make it before I gave up.

Eventually I came to a well-lit intersection with traffic lights and shops. It was on an incline, and before me I could see the lights of the city and the long snake of a highway. I blinked. I knew this place. I'd been here before. Somehow, I'd never quite been able to imagine the Institute as existing in the world, just another building in my city. It had always felt remote, separate. But I knew this place. It wasn't that far from school, from my house. The long, nauseous, blindfolded journey in the van had been a ruse — meandering around backstreets to create the illusion of distance. I could walk home from here. It'd take less than an hour.

I crossed the street and headed down the hill toward home.

I heard the rumble of an engine, and white light washed over the sidewalk as a car pulled up alongside me. I froze. It was him. Daddy. Daddy had come to get me. I felt a giddy mix of terror and relief. At least I wasn't on my own anymore. At least I wouldn't have to make the hard choices. Daddy would do what was right, even if that meant killing me. I closed my eyes and waited.

"Excuse me, miss? Is everything OK?"

I opened my eyes. It wasn't Daddy. It wasn't the Institute's white van. It was a police car, the window rolled down and a man leaning out, his brow etched with concern.

I looked down at myself and suddenly realized how odd I must look — a skinny girl in a white nightgown, out on the streets at night. No bag, no shoes, no friends.

"Miss?"

Everything felt unreal, like I was watching myself on a screen. How did you talk to people who weren't your family? How did you address a police officer?

What if he's a spy? What if he's from the Quintus Septum?

"Miss? What's your name?"

Heracleitus.

Heracleitus.

My name is Heracleitus.

"Miss?"

The passenger door opened and another officer got out, a woman. My mouth filled with saliva, and my body started to shake.

"Miss, I need to know who you are in order to help you. Who are you?"

She came around to the sidewalk and put a hand on my shoulder, and I felt tears ooze from my eyes. "I don't know," I whispered.

I was standing on a cliff. Behind me stood Daddy, Lib, Stan, Welling, Pippa, and the rest of my Institute family. And Fox, looking as dreamy-eyed and beautiful as the day I'd first seen him. Before me was endless blackness, stretching down into an unknowable abyss. I might shatter at the bottom, a heap of dust and dry bones. I might fall forever.

Fox stretched out his hand, reaching for me. I wanted to turn back, to fall into his arms and smell his Fox-smell and forget everything.

But Fox was gone, maybe dead, and I couldn't forget. I couldn't go back.

You can let it keep pulling you down into the darkness. Or you can fly.

My only choice was to jump. It was the only way I'd ever know the truth.

"Ruby," I told the police officer. "My name's Ruby Jane Galbraith, and I'm trying to get home."

★ ★ ★

Life accelerated, and I seemed to jolt from moment to moment. Sitting in the back of the police car, not knowing how to form the right words. Wondering if I could trust them. If I could tell them about Fox and Maggie and the Monkeys. Getting out of the car to find myself not at home but at a hospital.

Mom arriving. Hugging her and recognizing the scent of her lavender hand cream.

A doctor taking blood and urine samples and asking a million questions. What had my diet been like? Had I been taking drugs? Drinking alcohol? When had I last menstruated? I mumbled numb answers. *Simple. No. No. I don't remember.*

She asked me if I'd been taking any medication, and I recited my list of supplements, relieved to have easy answers at hand. *Vitamins A, B, and D. Magnesium. Iron. Sodium. Zinc. Selenium. Picric acid. Silver nitrate. Phosphorus. Calcium sulfide. Copper. Antimony tartrate. Sulfur.*

The doctor looked up at me, her brows raised. She glanced over at Mom and the police officer and then back at me.

"Where exactly have you been living?"

The panic rose in my throat again.

"She isn't ready to talk," Mom said. "She needs to go home."

She squeezed my hand, and I felt grateful tears spring to my eyes.

The doctor made a note on her clipboard. "You've put a lot of strain on your body. You're drastically underweight, and I think you're suffering from vitamin poisoning."

"Poisoning?" asked Mom, her voice tight with anxiety.

"Iron toxicity can give you some serious gastrointestinal problems, as well as fatigue and joint pain," said the doctor. "The selenium you've been taking is causing your hair loss and can also cause mild nerve damage. But it's the Vitamin A I'm really worried about. It can cause dizziness and mental changes, as well as permanent damage to your bladder and kidneys. You can suffer from cracked skin, increased sensitivity to light, an erratic heart rate, and muscle weakness. Some of the other things you've been taking aren't approved supplements — they're ingredients often found in homeopathic remedies, but I don't know what effects they'll have on your body if you've been taking them in high concentrations. We'll have to wait until your blood and urine samples come back from pathology."

I felt my head nod as my mind struggled to catch up. Daddy had known. He'd told us all those things were signs that we were approaching sublime. He said it was the body preparing to release, to succumb to the light within. But all along we'd been poisoning ourselves. Vague and dizzy and sick. Weak. Just the way he wanted us.

The doctor told me I would probably feel pretty terrible over the next few days, as my body detoxed from all the vitamins. In the meantime, I was to drink plenty of water, get lots of rest, and eat a balanced, healthy diet, high in fats in order to regain the weight I'd lost.

I nodded like a robot, wondering exactly what a balanced, healthy diet looked like.

I had to see a psychiatrist next. I tried to say what he wanted to hear, but I couldn't quite bring myself to tell the whole truth. I wasn't ready to betray them yet. To betray Daddy. I kept things purposefully vague, and eventually Mom insisted on taking me home, promising to bring me back for a follow-up once I'd had some sleep. The psychiatrist resisted, urging me to spend a few days in the hospital while they ran more tests. But Mom won.

I pretended to fall asleep in the car so I wouldn't have to make small talk. The house was clean and neat, with no trace of cigarette smoke in the air. Mom looked alert and concerned. Like a mom was supposed to. I mumbled a *good night* and climbed into my bed, feeling like it was so soft I'd get swallowed up in it and suffocate. Mom came to check on me several times through the night. Each time I pretended to be asleep. The rest of the time I just lay there in the dark, waiting for dawn.

I'd spent eight months at the Institute of the Boundless Sublime, and it had taken me less than four hours to get home.

19

I got up when I could hear Mom moving around the kitchen.

I opened my closet and looked at the neatly hanging and folded clothes, and I felt a rising tide of panic. It was too much. Too many choices. I closed the doors and stayed in my Institute nightgown. My feet were still sore, white, and scabbed over from walking the roads barefoot in the cold.

The kitchen was bright and clean and alien. Mom sat at the counter with her hands wrapped around a mug of hot water with lemon. She was trying to look relaxed, but I could feel the tension radiating off her in waves. Her knuckles were white around the mug. She took in my appearance again. My filthy nightgown. I expected to see happiness in her eyes. And maybe hurt. But I didn't expect fear.

She was afraid of me. "Did you sleep OK?"

I nodded, even though it was a lie.

"Good." Mom looked down at her mug, searching for something to say. "Can I make you some breakfast? Something healthy, like the doctor said. Some oatmeal? Fruit salad?"

The thought of eating anything made my stomach churn with nausea. I shook my head.

"OK."

I felt sorry for her. She was trying.

"Thank you," I said, feeling awkward. "For the offer. Breakfast. But I'm not hungry."

I saw her eyes pass over me again. My angular bones. She didn't understand what it was like. The clarity of hunger. The feeling of control, when you stop being a slave to your body. When you become the master. I remembered mornings sitting here at the breakfast bar with Anton, both of us mindlessly shoveling cereal into our mouths, our eyes glued to screens, our brains shut down. I didn't want to go back to that. I didn't think I could.

"So," said Mom, after another agonizing silence. "What do you want to do today?"

It was a question I had no idea how to answer. What did I want to do? I wanted to go back. I wanted schedules and orders and to be assigned a working group. I wanted to be told what to do.

I wanted to burn the Institute to the ground.

I shook my head and shrugged.

Mom attempted a smile, lines of concern knit tight between her brows. "Just take it slow, OK?" she said. "Everything's going to be fine."

She was different. Everything was different. The house was clean and airy and light. Auntie Cath was long gone, but Mom was busy and organized and full of purpose. There was no sign of the despair, the trembling ash that I had left. Something had happened. Something had changed.

You. You left. You left, and she got better. You should leave again. You don't belong here.

Panic clawed through my chest and up into my throat, choking me. I had to escape. I couldn't stay there, being slowly torn to pieces by Mom's sad eyes.

"May I go to the bathroom?" I asked.

Mom frowned. "You — you don't need to ask my permission."

Of course I didn't. I was home. I could do whatever I liked.

It was terrifying.

I went into the bathroom and used the toilet, rubbing the soft toilet paper between my fingers and wondering what they put in it to make it so soft, so white. I washed my hands and splashed cold water on my face. A living corpse stared at me from the mirror — yellowing skin stretched over sunken cheeks. I looked away, sickened. No wonder Mom was afraid of me. I turned on the cold-water faucet in the shower and put my hand under the spray. Slipping out of my nightgown, I caught a glimpse of bony shoulder blades and cage-like ribs in the mirror. Taking a deep breath, I reached for the hot-water faucet. Steam filled the bathroom, warm and inviting. I watched the water splash against the glass shower door, drops running into each other and down to the tiled floor. I stepped in.

It was indescribable. The heat and pressure of hot water on my back, on my scalp, on my face. I cried with heaving, sobbing breaths, tears mingling with the warm water. I'd spent so long trying to be strong. Trying to be sublime. Denying myself food, comfort, warmth. But I didn't have to do that anymore.

I was free.

I lathered myself in body wash, the sickly sweet scent of it as overwhelming as the foaming slipperiness of it on my skin. I washed my hair, handfuls of it falling out as it came loose under my fingers, and watched it swirl down the drain. The warmth of the water on my skin and the steam in my lungs filled me with something new, something I dimly recognized as hope.

After my shower, I pulled on fleecy athletic pants and a baggy T-shirt. Everything hung loose on my bony frame — I could see that I looked ridiculous. I dug in my closet for a sheer red scarf and draped it over the mirror.

I went into the kitchen and let Mom put a mug of herbal tea and a bowl of oatmeal in front of me.

"I know you said you weren't hungry," she said. "But I used soy milk. And the blueberries are organic."

She looked so proud, I couldn't bear to refuse. My mouth and stomach tried to rebel, to tell me that I was doing something wrong. But I chewed and swallowed, drinking half the tea and a few good spoonfuls of the oatmeal. I felt full and warm and sleepy.

I could do this.

I wasn't going back to the Institute. To Daddy. I was here, in the world.

I was going to survive.

"I'm really sorry," I said to Mom. "That I left."

Mom shook her head and smiled. "We don't need to talk about that now."

An hour later, I felt a twisting pain in my stomach and only just made it to the toilet in time, crouching over the bowl and heaving up what little I had eaten, along with foul strings of bile.

I spent the rest of the day in my room, Googling obsessively, reading testimonies from people who had escaped from cults and had gone on to rebuild their lives. I told myself I was looking for coping strategies, ways to ease my transition back into the real world. But I was lying to myself. Those stories were like a drug to me. I picked over them like a vulture, gobbling up scandals and lawsuits and breakdowns.

I read dozens of stories of people who grew up like Fox, not knowing anything about the outside world. I read about them slowly coming around, the veil lifting from their eyes. I read about them escaping and starting new lives. I remembered Fox asking me to leave with him. I saw the despair in his eyes, and the burning flash of hope. Why had I said no? What right did I have to keep Fox imprisoned? I wasn't like the people I'd read about online. I wasn't born in the Institute. I should have known better. I chose to go to the Institute. I chose to stay.

I found nothing about the Quintus Septum. Anywhere. Not a single hit. Not a whisper on any conspiracy websites or anything. It didn't exist.

Or is that what they want you to think?

I closed my eyes and breathed deeply. Daddy had made them up. He'd taken a couple of impressive-sounding Latin words and used them to create some kind of fictitious villain to unite us. To create fear. To draw us closer together, closer to him. To make us more obedient.

Maybe. Or maybe the Quintus Septum are that good. So clever that they can hide their tracks. So secret that not even the Internet has heard a whisper of them.

I couldn't shut out his voice. I just had to keep telling myself it was fiction, to focus on what was real. But I'd forgotten how to tell the difference.

I kept thinking of the promise I'd made to Val, that I'd help the Monkey, that I'd find her a real family. I hadn't mentioned the Monkeys to the police, or to the psychiatrist, even though I knew I should have. Perhaps it was because I knew that if I did, it would be the end of the Institute. And even though logically I knew that would be a good thing, I just couldn't bring myself to do it yet. But I would. Soon.

I tried to find mention of the other Institute members online, but I didn't know anyone's real name. It was Daddy's stroke of genius — he separated us so completely from our lives, our families, our names. I couldn't reach out to other ex-members. I couldn't find people's families. Once I was out, I was out forever. I was totally alone.

Or was I?

I remembered an early conversation with Maggie, just after I'd arrived at the Institute as a new sublimate. I'd asked Maggie what her real name was, and she'd told me.

Jiao. Jiao Wei Qin.

I reached for the keyboard with trembling fingers.

It was surprisingly easy to find her. I found newspaper articles about her being missing, and a website her parents had set up with her photo and contact details should anyone come across her. There was an email address.

I felt a sudden wave of nausea at the thought of reaching out to them, and I snapped the lid closed on my laptop. Maybe later. Maybe another day. One step at a time.

I ate a few bites of broccoli at dinner and managed to keep it down this time. Then I retreated to the safety and silence of my room. Mom hadn't mentioned returning to the hospital like she'd promised the doctors we would, and I didn't want to say anything that would remind her.

I waited until I was sure she was asleep, then I crept downstairs into the kitchen, moving silently as if I was on a Hush-Hush mission. Mom was obviously trying to stock the fridge with things I'd eat — soy milk and vegetables and hummus. I pushed it all aside and dug deep, finding individually-wrapped cheese slices and plastic bottles of juice. I opened jars of mustard, jam, and relish, sniffing the contents. I dipped a finger into each jar, so it made just the lightest brush of contact with the contents. I lifted the finger to my lips, letting a minuscule amount of food spread onto my tongue.

It felt wrong. Forbidden. Dangerous. I stood there for hours, locked in a cycle of temptation and resistance.

When thin daylight eventually started to bleed in through the cracks in the blinds, I slunk back to my room and climbed into bed, pulling the covers up over my head.

I slept fitfully until noon, managing to successfully avoid Mom and the questions I was sure she wanted to ask. I chewed on a few carrots and celery sticks for lunch, coating them with an almost invisible layer of hummus. Mom finally coaxed me out for dinner, proudly showing me the healthy stir-fry she'd prepared. I stretched my lips in a smile and sat opposite her, cutting my food into smaller and smaller pieces, pushing it around on my plate, and placing the occasional morsel in my mouth, making sure the metal of the fork didn't touch my lips. The rest I pushed around into different piles or hid in my napkin. I told Mom I'd had a big lunch. That I'd eat it later. I'd told myself that tomorrow would be different. Tomorrow I'd eat it all.

★ ★ ★

Minah came to see me the next day.

She stood in the doorway to my room for a moment, and I could tell she was considering turning around and walking right out. I could see her taking in my sunken, yellowed skin and peeling lips. My dead, limp hair. The purple hollows under my eyes. The skin pulled tight over my cracked red knuckles. I felt like a monster.

"Your mom called me," Minah said. "Said you were back."

We made awkward small talk. Minah told me about her latest art project — something involving dismembered plastic dolls in apothecary jars — and updated me on school gossip. I nodded and made appropriate noises. It seemed bizarre to me that school was still happening — that every day people got out of bed and went and sat in a classroom, taking notes and learning about dates and numbers and words. Minah's world seemed so . . . small. So insignificant. We'd always talked about big ideas, but now I realized that her life was shallow, only skimming the surface of reality. There was no profundity. No depth. She couldn't see the world for what it truly was.

Like Daddy can.

Like Fox could.

Minah must have noticed the flash of pain that passed over my face as I thought about Fox. She looked down at her hands and picked a flake of paint off her fingernail.

"Um," she said. "So . . . are you OK?"

Of course I wasn't. I was dying inside. Rotting away like the toxicant piece of meat that I was. I'd given up my chance at sublimation. Given up happiness and purpose and strength for weakness and doubt and aphotic water.

"Sure," I said. "I'm OK."

"Your mom went crazy, you know," she said. "When she got your note."

I felt a sickening pang of guilt.

"She came over to my place and grilled me on where you'd been going and what you'd been doing. She . . . she was pretty wild. All skinny and pale, like a ghost. But she was full of fire — desperate to find you. I told her about the guy you'd been seeing — Fox — and how he lived in a commune in that big red house on the hill. She went over there, but the people in the red house said they didn't know you. She knocked on every door in the neighborhood, but nobody knew anything. She called the police, but still nothing. There were announcements about it at school. I put up a Facebook page."

I remembered talking to Mom on the phone the first time. She had been so worried.

"I didn't know," I said at last. "That she was looking for me. I didn't think she would."

"She's your *mom*. Of course she'd look for you."

Minah's face was wrinkled in disbelief and disapproval. Minah. Rebellious, devil-may-care Minah thought that I was a bad daughter. That I didn't care.

Was she right?

"Then she called me again, said you'd been in touch. She said she'd spoken to you twice and that you were OK. She wanted me to take down the Facebook page, because you weren't missing anymore. She seemed so calm. That was a few months ago."

Daddy said I had persuaded her with my enhanced powers of communication. Could that be true? I could barely remember the phone conversation, I'd been so wrapped up in my own guilt and what I'd thought were Daddy's powers of healing. Could he have faked the call? I tried to remember how the voice on the other end had sounded. In my memory, it had sounded like Mom, but could I trust my own recollections?

Minah leaned forward. "What was it like? The cult?"

I shrugged. "I don't know. It was . . ." I spread my hands.

Transformative. Soul-destroying. The greatest thing that had ever happened to me — and the worst.

"Rituals? Drugs? Sex stuff?"

I shook my head. "Nothing like that," I lied.

"So what did you *do* all day?"

"Just . . . stuff. Gardening. Cleaning. Preparing meals."

Getting beaten and locked away for weeks. Playing blackjack. Breaking into people's houses and rearranging their appliances. Uncovering possible evidence of murder.

Minah looked disappointed. "OK. So why did you leave?"

The people in the stories I'd read online had made clean breaks. They realized that they'd been living a lie, and then left. One man described it as like being in a fairground haunted house and seeing the lights come on — once you'd seen the mechanics of it all, it was impossible to be scared again. But it wasn't working that way for me.

I knew what Daddy had done. I knew he was a liar. After seeing the website Maggie's parents had set up, I knew she hadn't left the Institute. Daddy had killed her. Fox too. He was a murderer and a liar, and I knew I should hate him.

But I couldn't get his voice out of my head. I couldn't stop thinking about the Quintus Septum. About the possibilities of sublimation. About the friends I'd left behind. I'd seen the haunted house with the lights on, but I was still terrified.

Minah was watching me, waiting for a response.

I shrugged. "I guess . . . I wanted answers. About things."

"Was it because of him?" asked Minah. "Because of Fox?"

Hearing his name brought a fresh stab of grief. I hesitated. Could I trust Minah? I had to trust someone.

"He — he's dead," I said. Saying it out loud made it real, and I felt something break inside me. "He died. Because of something I did. Something *we* did."

Minah raised her eyebrows but didn't press me.

"I just . . ." I swallowed. "I want to know who he really was."

I pulled the creased photo of baby Fox and his mother from

my desk drawer. "This is him and his mother. I want to find her. Tell her about him."

Minah took the photo and frowned, rubbing the paper between her fingers. "You . . . think this is Fox and his mother?"

I nodded. Minah bit her lip and glanced at me with what looked like . . . pity?

"Ruby, this isn't Fox. Look at it. It's black and white. A film print, not digital." She turned the photo over and read the scribbled pencil words on the back. "This isn't even real photo paper. It's been cut out of a book."

"It's real," I said. "I know it is. I know Fox."

"I'm sorry, but it just isn't." Minah pulled out her phone and pointed it at the photo. I heard the artificial sound of a shutter click. Then she tapped at her phone for a moment.

"I'm pretty sure I know who the photo is of," she said. "I'll show you."

She handed me the phone.

"I don't understand," I said. A line of text jumped out at me from the Google page. *About 5026 results.* "What am I looking at?"

Minah reached over my shoulder and tapped the first result. The photo of Fox and his mother popped into view.

"The woman is Audrey Hepburn," she said. "The baby is her son. It was taken in 1960."

I frowned. "No," I said. "That can't be right."

"I'm really sorry."

I stared at the crumpled photo in my hand. My last link to Fox. Except it wasn't. It wasn't anything. Just a photo cut out of a book. A photo of a stranger. I turned it over and looked at Fox's scrawled words.

plane crash
starvation
gamma radiation pulse
contaminated water supply
nuclear fallout
suffocated by pollution

Were these the things he imagined had happened to his mother? Or were they nightmares about how his life might end? He'd always feared Daddy, even before we were punished. Perhaps a part of him had always known that one day he'd be betrayed by the man he thought was his father, a man who had spun a web of lies so intricate that maybe he even believed them himself.

I'd never know. Fox was now totally lost to me. I didn't even have a picture to remember him by. How long would it be until I forgot his face? His voice? The way he pushed his golden hair away from his eyes?

A chasm of grief opened up underneath me. There was no dark tide to support me or carry me in its wake. The Institute had stripped me of all my coping mechanisms. It'd broken down all my barriers, and now I was alone, falling into the yawning, gaping abyss.

Fox was gone.

"You look like you want to be alone," said Minah, and she awkwardly backed out of my bedroom.

She couldn't get away fast enough.

I sat on my bed for a while, staring into nothing. Then I pulled on some shoes and a coat and went out, not bothering to tell Mom where I was going.

★ ★ ★

Every step was treacherous, as if I was balancing on a high wire and could plummet to my death at any moment.

I walked slowly, like I was in a funeral procession, to the park where Fox and I had spent so many hours.

The blossom and life that we'd watched emerge from the trees had gone. Everything was shriveled and cold, a last few tattered fall leaves clinging to the branches. I shivered even though I was wearing the biggest, puffiest coat I could find in my closet. I was always cold now. I'd been cold since I left the Institute.

The ducks were gone. Empty chip bags and plastic bottles were trodden into the mud around the pond. Everything was cold and empty and ugly.

I remembered lying on the grass here with Fox. I remembered him telling me how beautiful the world was. How in love with it he was. How in love with *me*. I remembered his face, his lips, golden hair flopping into serious eyes.

The world wasn't beautiful anymore. Fox was gone from the world, and without him everything was tarnished, as limp and lifeless as a dishrag.

I turned away from the park to go home, and I saw Stan. He was standing at the edge of the park, handing out water bottles, bouncing on his heels the way he always did.

I remembered seeing Fox the first time. The memory of that first glimpse slammed into me like a wave, and I felt my knees buckle.

His face turned up to the sun. His eyes closed. His lips parted as if he was kissing the sunshine.

Fox was gone. But Stan was still there. My feet dragged me

toward him, and I ached for recognition. Understanding. Family. My family.

"Stan," I said as I drew close.

He looked up and saw me, and his face became a mask of blank politeness.

"I'm sorry," he said. "Do I know you?"

"Of course you know me," I said. I reached out and touched his arm, and he pulled away. "It's me. It's Hera. Heracleitus."

The name felt right in my mouth, like coming home. It'd be so easy to slip back into her. Back into a world with no doubts. No unanswered questions or difficult choices. Back into that certainty of knowing what you were doing was *right*.

Stan smiled the polite, cautious smile of someone placating a crazy person. "I think you must have me confused with someone else."

I stared at him. There was not the faintest flicker of recognition on his face. Nothing. For a moment I doubted myself. My own memory. Maybe it had all been a dream — Daddy, the Institute, everything. Maybe I was crazy.

But I wasn't. I had the scars and bruises to prove it.

Stan's expression was tinged with pity. "I don't know what happened to you, miss," he said, "to make you like this. But I hope you find what you're looking for. Here."

And he handed me a bottle of water.

I took it automatically and stared blankly at the label.

BOUNDLESS BODY
BOUNDLESS MIND

"I have to go," said Stan, shouldering the box of water bottles.

I started to make my own way home. Except . . . it wasn't my home. There was nothing there for me. No Anton. No Dad. Mom had been better off without me. Minah and my other friends were . . . never really my friends to begin with. Not like my family at the Institute had been.

Longing and grief slashed me open, and I was afraid I'd collapse in a mound of oozing flesh right there on the sidewalk. How could I go on without him? Without my family?

My footsteps turned unthinkingly back to the park, and I broke into a run. Past the pond, up the hill. My breath rasped in my chest, raw and wheezing. Only a few days back in the real world, and my body was crumbling. Where was the strength I'd had before? My clarity of vision? I could feel poisons seeping through my pores, spreading fingers of death into my heart, my eyes, my brain. It was already getting harder to think, to reason, to remember.

But I could get it back. All wasn't lost. I could go back to them.

To Daddy.

I tripped on the sidewalk as I came out the other side of the park and went sprawling, my bones vibrating with the impact. A jogger crossed the road to avoid me, looking suspiciously at my stringy hair, my red face, my clothes damp with sweated toxins. I dragged myself upright and headed down the leafy street toward the Red House.

It was time to go home.

20

ELEGANT VICTORIAN BEAUTY
BRIMMING WITH POTENTIAL

The SOLD sticker was bright and angry and mocking. I ignored it, pushing through the iron gate and up the overgrown pathway to the front door. I rang the bell and knocked on the door until my knuckles were red and raw. Then I went around to every window, trying to open it, peering in to see nothing but empty rooms. No furniture. Nothing. The house was as empty and lifeless as I was.

I felt the last threads of myself unravel and drift away on the cold November wind. It was all gone. Everything. I didn't exist anymore.

★ ★ ★

When I got home, Mom didn't ask where I'd been. She just smiled a thin, tight smile, and gently suggested a shopping expedition for new clothes — everything I had hung off my bony frame as if I were no more than a wire coat hanger. I didn't have the energy to refuse her, so I let her drag me around the mall, the bright lights and tinny music hypnotizing me into a trance. I felt eyes upon me — the store clerks, the other shoppers. Everyone was watching me. Did they know? Did they think I was some kind of freak? The cult girl?

Maybe they are spies. The Quintus Septum is everywhere.

I hoped they were. Then I'd know there was some truth in it all. Some point in being alive.

Mom bundled me in and out of changing rooms, and I mechanically put clothes on and took them off again. Each new garment felt like sandpaper, rubbing my skin red and raw. What was the point of clothes? What was the point of anything?

"Ruby," said Mom, as we clambered out of the car at home, weighed down with shopping bags. "I think maybe you should see someone. A counselor. After you left I started talking to someone. It really helped."

I'd seen a counselor before. Helena. She'd given me amber beads and told me that they had magic powers. I told Mom I wasn't ready to talk about it yet, but I'd let her know when I was. The words came automatically, without me having to think about them. Mom crept away and busied herself in the kitchen, leaving me alone.

I felt skittish and delicate, like blown glass that could shatter at any moment. I remembered once writing an essay on some eighteenth-century German poet who attributed emotional characteristics to musical keys. He'd said that if ghosts could speak, their speech would approximate D sharp minor. That was me. A ghost in D sharp minor.

I floated around the house aimlessly, drifting from one room to the other, picking things up and then putting them down again. Mom tried to engage me in conversation, but I could barely manage more than a syllable. I stopped reading Minah's texts. Everything was fake, as though I'd been lured into a TV show and any minute now a curtain would open to reveal the studio audience watching me, laughing and pointing. I couldn't remember how to behave in the real world. I couldn't believe this was it, this was all there was. Before Anton died, everything had been golden.

Then afterward there had been the intensity of grief, the rise of the black tide. In the Institute there had been hope and possibility and fear. But now everything was bland and faded, like flat soda and brittle plastic.

Every night, I had flashbacks to being locked in the dark, cold room at the Institute. The memory came over and over, and it didn't feel like washing a wound clean. It felt like picking at a scab and making it worse. I oozed swollen, sticky memories of pain and hollow, aching hunger.

★ ★ ★

One day, when Mom had gone to see her counselor, I sat down at the piano. I was afraid I'd forgotten how to play. And I was afraid that if I started, if I let my fingers trace their patterns of sorrow and loss on the keys, I wouldn't be able to stop. I was afraid that it would all pour out of me until there was nothing left but skin and hair and fingernails.

I lifted the lid of the piano and stroked the keys with gentle fingertips. I pressed down on one note, and then another. My fingers stretched to make a chord — B flat minor. B flat minor was discontented. Shrouded in darkness and mocking God and the living world as it grew inevitably closer to death.

I played a few bars of Rachmaninov's Piano Sonata No. II, then stopped.

My fingers hadn't forgotten, but my heart had. Music had once filled me with emotion, made me overflow with feelings. But I felt nothing. The notes buzzed in my ears like a swarm of mosquitos — annoying and totally meaningless. I stared at the keys for a few minutes, then let my hands sink down into them wherever they fell, making a discordant drone. Once the noise had faded, I shut the lid of the piano and went back to my bedroom.

★ ★ ★

On the bad nights, when I couldn't shut out thoughts of Fox and Daddy and the endless days I'd spent locked away, I would break. My trips to the kitchen weren't merely observational missions. I dug past the almonds and tofu and apple cider vinegar to find forgotten treasures. I scooped peanut butter from the jar and shoveled it into my mouth. I squeezed mayonnaise into my mouth directly from the bottle, took long slugs of maple syrup. I gnawed chocolate bars and slurped flavored yogurt straight from the container.

Afterward, I'd clean myself up the best I could and climb back into bed, curling up as spasms and cramps wracked my body.

★ ★ ★

Mom didn't say anything about my fridge raids, although she must have noticed. Instead she patiently prepared nutritious meals for me, and then sat across from me at the dinner table and made timid attempts at conversation while I pushed grilled pumpkin and avocado around on my plate and tried not to throw up.

"You'll tell me, won't you, darling?" Mom asked. "If there's anything I can do to help?"

I nodded, my eyes filling with tears.

Mom gave me a supportive little nod and passed me the salt.

Auntie Cath called to check on us. Mom held the phone out to me, and I took it, listening as Auntie Cath prattled on about the weather in Florida and how she was going to try a new pumpkin pie recipe for Thanksgiving. She asked about Mom, and I replied robotically that Mom seemed good.

"I think she's met someone," said Auntie Cath, lowering her voice so it hissed and buzzed in the receiver. "She's keeping it to herself for now, and I respect that, but I'm so pleased for her. She's been through so much."

I put down the phone without saying goodbye. Was it true? Had Mom met someone? Was that where she was going, when she said she was going to her counselor? What about Dad? What about me? We were both locked away, and Mom was shiny-eyed and happy? Mom, who had been so broken and weak?

The doorbell rang, but I made no move to answer it. Whoever it was, I didn't want to speak to them. I didn't want to speak to anyone. Mom came out of the kitchen, wiping her hands on a tea towel and glancing sideways at me.

It was two police officers. One of them was familiar. I realized with a jolt that she was one of the ones who had picked me up the night I'd left the Institute. My heart thumped. Mom showed them in, and they sat on the couch.

"How are you doing, Ruby?"

"OK."

My reply hung in the air. The police officer turned to Mom.

"It's been a week," she said. "We really need to ask Ruby some questions. We're trying to get some more information on this organization she spent time with. We think it has ties with a man called Glen Ardeer and several missing persons cases."

Mom glanced over at me. I didn't say anything. She shook her head. "That's not a name Ruby has mentioned to me."

As if I'd mentioned any names to her.

"This man is wanted for questioning," said the police officer. "We think he might be dangerous. It would really help if Ruby could come down to the station for an official interview."

"I appreciate that," said Mom, her voice firm. "But she isn't ready to talk. She's been through a lot. She needs time."

The police officer nodded. "I understand."

"Maybe in a few days," said Mom. "I can bring her to the station, and you can ask her anything. Just let her finish adjusting back into the real world."

The officers exchanged glances. "OK," said the woman. "We'll see you in a few days."

She gave Mom a card with a number on it, and they left.

"Thank you," I said.

Mom came over and slid onto the couch next to me, her arms wrapping me up in a tight hug.

"I love you so much," she said. "All I want is for you to be safe and happy."

I nodded, aware that I should reciprocate. I should hug her back or cry or something. But I didn't remember how to do any of those things.

"I didn't think it would be this hard," I told her.

Mom gave me a squeeze. "You're doing so well," she said. "You're extraordinary."

★ ★ ★

Mom put on a floral dress to go to her therapy appointment. I wondered again if the counselor was made up, and it was really a date, like Auntie Cath thought. Mom certainly seemed to be excited to be going. Or maybe she was just excited to get some distance from me.

After she left, I trudged back to my room and curled up on the bed with my laptop, my fingers treading well-worn pathways through the Internet.

Zosimon.

Cult.

Daddy.

The Institute of the Boundless Sublime.

Quintus Septum.

Nothing. Not a whisper.

I thought about the Monkeys and felt a stab of guilt. I pictured the police officer's card lying on the table in the hallway. What was the name she had said? The man they were looking for? Another image popped into my mind. The desk drawer in the Inner Sanctum. Maggie's necklace. A wedding ring. A plush giraffe. My phone. And a credit card with a name on it.

My heart began to pound.

I typed *Glen Ardeer* into Google and hit enter.

And there he was. He was younger, but it was unmistakably him. Same silver-rimmed glasses and white hair.

Daddy.

Seeing his face again was like an electric shock. Something inside me exploded, scattering shrapnel throughout my body. Little shards of guilt and shame and longing and hatred. I missed him. I missed Daddy so much. His calm, quiet certainty. His unwavering faith in me.

But that wasn't him. Not all of him, anyway. He was a liar.

He wasn't sublime. He didn't live off of light and air, he lived off of chocolate and whiskey and fast food. He'd lied about Maggie and Fox. He'd been wrong about the casino. And he'd hurt me.

I remembered his face as he beat me. The sick twist of his mouth. The fierce light in his eyes. He had beaten me, and he had *liked* it.

With a shaking hand, I clicked the first link.

Glen Ardeer was notorious. I read the Wikipedia page fifty times, spiraling between disgust and disbelief. He'd been a scientist, working in the nineties on some program to sterilize fruit flies. He'd published a paper proposing a technique for chemically sterilizing humans. It had been pretty controversial — the groups that he'd suggested would benefit from sterilization were what you'd expect from a white supremacist bigot. Lots of comparisons to Nazi eugenics had been made. Ardeer was fired from the university where he worked, and a few months later he was arrested for sending death threats to former colleagues. He did a few months' jail time and disappeared before his parole period was up.

That was it, then. That was Daddy. Not an opium smuggler or a medieval knight or a Civil War veteran. Just some lunatic who wanted to control people.

I saw the ghost of a strange girl, gaunt and hollow, reflected in the glint of the computer screen. I still didn't recognize her.

"OK, then," I told the reflection.

It was time to let go. Let go of Daddy and Fox and the Institute. None of it had been true. It was time to figure out who I was.

When I heard the front door open and Mom moving about in the living room, I went out to greet her, feeling clearheaded for the first time in forever.

"Mom?"

Mom looked up from the kitchen counter where she was making herself a cup of herbal tea.

"I'd like to go and visit Anton," I said.

Mom's expression faltered a little, and she came forward to give me a hug. "Of course, darling."

Anton was the first step.

★ ★ ★

The last few fall leaves were swirling down from the trees that lined the cemetery pathways. Trees and roses were arranged in neat lines, each one with a bronze plaque underneath.

Mom had a bunch of flowers. I'd brought one of the Matchbox cars that Anton had loved so much and his little plastic figurine of Elsa from *Frozen*, which sang "Let it Go" in a tinny little voice if you pressed a button on her back. It seemed appropriate.

A straggly rose was planted by Anton's plaque. Mom told me it was yellow — Anton's favorite color.

"It's just getting established," she said. "It'll be beautiful soon."

I nodded.

Mom talked to the plaque, telling it how happy she was that I had come home. About how she'd watched *Ninja Warrior* on TV and thought of Anton. About how she was making veggie burgers for dinner tonight but wouldn't put any tomato in them because she knew he didn't like it.

I wondered if she expected me to say something. I wasn't sure I could. I couldn't pretend that this dirt and bronze and straggly rosebush were my brother. My brother was gone. He was never coming back.

There was so much lost in the past. What was left to look forward to?

I didn't know.

But I had to find out. I had to keep going.

I set the car and the Elsa doll down beside the plaque. Then I squared my shoulders and turned to Mom. "I think . . . maybe I'd like to go see Dad as well."

Mom looked taken aback, but she nodded. "OK," she said. "I'll talk to our lawyer about how to organize that. But in the meantime . . ." Mom reached out and took my hand. "My counselor runs a therapy group that's meeting tonight. I really think they could help you."

So it was real. There was no secret beau after all. Auntie Cath would be disappointed.

I tried to imagine sitting on a chair in a circle, holding a Styrofoam cup of coffee and talking about my feelings.

Maybe it wouldn't be so bad. Daddy's voice was finally gone from my head, but I knew I was a long way off from being better. I needed help. I nodded.

The smile that broke across Mom's face was like a knife in my gut. Would I ever smile like that?

"I'll call him as soon as we get home," she said. "Let him know that you're coming. He'll be so pleased to finally meet you."

★ ★ ★

Mom was in a dress again, ready to take me to her group. I'd put on some of the new clothes she'd bought me — jeans and a flannel shirt and new underwear. My new bra felt strange — too tight, as if the air in my lungs was slowly being squeezed out of me.

Mom seemed nervous, fiddling with the strap on her watch, and it occurred to me that maybe she *was* seeing someone — someone in this therapy group. Maybe it was even the counselor himself.

We got into the car, and Mom smiled brightly at me as she started the engine.

"It's not far."

It was going to be awkward, whether or not Mom's hypothetical beau was there. They'd all stare at me. Mom said they already knew about me. They knew I was the cult girl. I'd be a curiosity, like a circus freak.

We drove through an intersection that looked familiar. Traffic lights with a view of the city and the illuminated golden snake of the highway. I felt a throbbing in my feet and remembered the numbing pain of walking barefoot away from the Institute.

"Mom?" I asked. "Where exactly is this meeting?"

Mom laughed, and I noticed a brittle edge to it. Her knuckles were white on the steering wheel. "Almost there."

We drove past a shabby apartment building with sheets hanging in the windows instead of curtains and turned down a street of industrial buildings. We pulled in under a garage door that had been left open for us. I felt my veins run cold with dread.

"Mom?" I asked, my voice small and childlike.

"We're running a little late," said Mom, her voice bright, as she parked the car and opened her door. "Hurry up!"

I got out of the car. Everything seemed quiet. I glanced out at the street and considered running. But where would I go?

My hands started trembling.

"Come on," said Mom. "He'll be waiting."

My feet were glued to the ground. "I've changed my mind. Can we just go home?"

"Don't be silly," Mom said. "You're here now. You may as well come in. You don't have to say anything. Just listen."

Her smile was too bright. Her eyes darted nervously to the doorway and then back to me. She reached out and grabbed my hand, tugging me in through the doorway. I let her do it. What choice did I have now?

Mom led me into the mess hall, which was crowded with about twenty adults and a handful of children. They stood with their backs to us. Welling turned around when we entered, and our eyes met. I felt something wrench inside me. It wasn't his fault. It wasn't Welling who had lied, tortured, and probably killed. He didn't know any better. He was as deluded as I had been. I smiled, but his eyes skated right over me, as if he didn't know me. As if I were invisible, a ghost. Then he turned back to face the front. Nobody else noticed us.

It was smaller than I remembered. Dirtier. The chairs and tables had been put away, and despite the stillness and silence of the crowd, I detected a certain nervous energy. I could smell stale urine and sweat and mildew. Was this something new? Or had I just never noticed it? Mom held my hand tightly.

"What have you done?" I muttered. "What's going on?"

"You'll understand soon," she said. "I promise. Daddy will explain everything."

Daddy.

Somehow, he had gotten to Mom. Possibly he'd been getting to her all along. I remembered Minah telling me that Mom had gone to the Red House looking for me. Had it been going on all this time? Had Daddy been slipping out at night, working his magic on my mother, weaving her into his tapestry of lies?

This was what I had wanted. Proof finally that Daddy cared about me. That he would go to extraordinary lengths to keep me close. But the veil had been lifted now. I knew who he was. Glen Ardeer. Daddy was no magician. No savior. He was a liar, and he was dangerous.

As if I'd summoned him with my thoughts, a door opened at the front of the room, and Daddy came in. It had only been a handful of days since I'd last seen him, and yet his presence knocked the breath out of me. He wore a long white robe, and his hair was neatly braided. The wild, elemental Daddy had gone. This Daddy seemed . . . almost holy. He stepped up onto a makeshift stage at the front of the room and raised his arms for silence.

"How could you do this?" I hissed to Mom. "How could you bring me back here?"

Confusion and a flash of doubt passed over her face. "You don't understand," she said, tears in her eyes. "You are *everything*. I have to protect you. For your own good. For the good of us all."

She looked up at Daddy, trust and devotion shining in her expression.

A slow smile spread across Daddy's face, and he beamed down at the crowd.

"This is a great day," he said. "The greatest. What we've worked for has finally arrived. Your hard work, your faith and trust in me will not go unrewarded. It is time. Time for the plan. The Boundless Family."

A ripple of excitement went through the crowd. I felt a corresponding ripple of fear. Whatever the Boundless Family was, it didn't sound good.

"I have spoken to you before of the Scintilla: the key that will unlock the true powers of sublimation and help us shed our mortal flesh-bodies. In ancient prophecy the Scintilla is described as a beautiful gem, full of the fire of life. But prophecy is tricky and easily misunderstood. I have studied this technic for hundreds of years, but I never fully understood it until a few months ago. The Scintilla is here, with us. We have summoned it. It is time for us to rise up against the Quintus Septum and take our places as leaders of this planet."

The crowd broke into rapturous applause and cheers. Beside me, Mom clapped as hard as anyone, tears streaming down her face. What was *happening*?

"The Scintilla," said Daddy, and everyone fell silent. He bowed his head and spoke in low, reverent tones. "A crimson gem, full of life's fire."

Daddy paused, and my feeling of dread intensified. The whole room seemed to throb around me, pulsing with anticipation. Then Daddy raised his head.

His eyes burned a single white line through the crowd, meeting mine, as if he'd known I was there all along. I recoiled from the strength of his gaze.

"A ruby."

My entire body jolted into high alert, humming with fear. Everything inside me was urging me to flee. But I couldn't move. I was pinned to the floor like a helpless creature hypnotized by the swaying head of a snake.

"It's you, Ruby." Daddy's voice was barely louder than a whisper, but I heard every word. "You're the Scintilla."

21

The crowd parted around me, leaving me alone and exposed. On the stage, Daddy dropped to his knees, and one by one, every member of the Institute did too, bowing their heads to me as if I were a king or god. I reached out for Mom, but she was gone, melted into the crowd — another deluded believer cowering before yet another lie.

I tried to protest. I told them it was all bullshit. But it was like screaming into a void.

Daddy rose to his feet and reached out a hand as if to bless me.

"We must be gentle with her," he said. "She is newly born into this body, and her mind is still forming. For the first little while, her actuality will be competing with her host — our lost sister Heracleitus. But soon Heracleitus will subside, and the Scintilla will grow strong and powerful. And under her guidance, we shall all discard our mortal flesh and ascend — true sublime bodies, endowed with everlasting life."

People in the crowd were weeping openly, reaching their hands toward me. At Daddy's command, Val came forward and took me by the arms. I tried to struggle, but I was no match for his large frame. Lib led us both toward B Block, and as we left, I looked up and saw the faintest flicker of a smile play around Daddy's lips.

They took me to the tiny room where I'd been previously incarcerated. It felt even smaller now, even more claustrophobic.

Lib took a breath, as if she was about to say something. But then her eyes flicked over to Val, and her mouth closed back into a thin white line. She nodded briskly at him, and they left, closing and locking the door behind them.

I knew from last time that shouting would do me no good. I didn't want to wear myself out by banging on the door and screaming. This time I was smarter. This time I wasn't going to let him break me. I sat down on the floor with my back against the wall and waited.

Time passed. Hours? I wasn't sure. The door opened, and Pippa stepped into the room, holding a bundle of red fabric, which she placed carefully on the floor before crouching down next to it and leaning her forehead down so it almost touched the damp concrete. I flinched when I saw the bandaged stump where her finger had once been.

"Your holiness," she murmured. "Daddy has instructed me to bring you these robes, which he wishes you to wear as a symbol of his respect for you."

"Pippa," I said, sighing with relief. "You have to help me get out of here."

Pippa stood slowly and looked at me. She seemed different: cowed and small. Even the shape of her was different. She looked soft and swollen. Frail, like a melting candle. Her clothes were too big, hanging loosely from her shoulders. Her eyes were dark hollows, and her hand fluttered nervously in front of her belly.

"It's just me," I said. "I'm not the Scintilla. Daddy's trying to punish me for leaving."

"He said you would be confused. He said it would take a little time."

"I'm sorry," I said. "What I did to you — I can't ever make that right. But you have to listen. You have doubts. I know you do. Listen to them. Listen to your gut. Listen to *me* —"

"Hera, you have to let go. Surrender your body to the actuality of the Scintilla."

Pippa's face was blank and polite, and I knew there was no getting through to her. I let her leave.

And I waited, ignoring the pile of red fabric.

Daddy came in some time later.

"You haven't changed your clothes," he said. "Those toxicant rags you wear are not suitable attire for the savior of all mankind."

He scooped up the bundle of red fabric and offered it to me. I spat on it.

Daddy laid the bundle back down on the floor. "You must surrender. Stop fighting. You have been chosen for greatness."

"I know everything," I said to him. "I know your real name. I know who you are and what you did."

Daddy ignored me. "I'm so sorry," he murmured. "It's all my fault. The pain I put you through."

I turned my face away from him. I didn't want to hear his lies. I knew nothing he said could be trusted.

"I thought I was helping you," Daddy continued. "I thought I knew what was best. I thought you needed to leave Ruby behind and become Heracleitus. I was foolish. Arrogant."

Out of the corner of my eye, I saw Daddy sink slowly to

his knees. He lifted one hand and clasped the red stone he wore around his neck.

"I should have realized. Ruby. *Ruby*. It was a sign. The divine spark. The burning crimson gem. I wasn't listening to you. You tried to tell me who you were from the beginning. That's why you were confused, why you disobeyed me. It was because you were trying to reassert your true actuality."

Daddy placed his palms on the concrete floor.

"I elutriate myself before you, Scintilla," he said. "I am your servant, awaiting instruction."

"Go fuck yourself," I said.

Daddy closed his eyes and bowed his head low. "You're angry with me. I understand."

He withdrew and stood up, backing toward the door.

"I'll have everything readied," he said. "For your ascension. You'll see."

"Let me see her," I said between gritted teeth. "Let me speak to my mother."

The gentle, concerned expression I knew so well arranged itself carefully on Daddy's features. Once I had been fooled by it. No longer.

"The Scintilla has no mother or father," he said. "You are born from elements both cardinal and sovereign. You are the divine spark that heralds a new dawn. But if you are referring to the sublimate who brought forth the meat casing you currently inhabit — you can most certainly have an audience with her."

Daddy bowed low to me again, his eyes flashing up to meet mine with a mocking smile. He left the room but came back a few minutes later with Mom, who had changed into a white Institute shirt. She looked nervous and excited, like a child lining up to meet Santa.

"I'll leave you two alone," said Daddy, and he slipped out, closing the door behind him.

"Mom," I said, stepping forward and grabbing both her hands. "I know how this all seems. But it's all lies. Daddy isn't who he says he is. His name is really Glen Ardeer. He used to be a research scientist, but he got fired for being a lunatic." A thought flickered at the edge of my consciousness, but I brushed it aside. I had to get through to her.

"Do you still have the card of the policewoman who came to our house? Go outside. Get in the car. Go home and call her. Tell her everything. Tell her where I am. You *have* to do this."

Mom tugged a hand free and reached up to brush my cheek. "Thank you for choosing her," she whispered. "Thank you for choosing my daughter as your vessel. I — I lost one child. It was senseless. Pointless. His death was without meaning. But for Ruby — her life now has the ultimate purpose. The ultimate sacrifice."

My toes went cold. "What do you mean, *sacrifice*?"

A tear rolled down Mom's cheek. "When you take full possession of her on Saturday, I will not mourn her. I will know that her actuality, her sublime body, flies free with yours, up into the heavens."

"Saturday? What's going to happen on Saturday?"

Mom smiled. "Hasn't Daddy told you? Saturday is when it all begins. The final technic. When the spark becomes a flame, and we will all be united in elutriation. The Boundless Family."

I did not like the sound of that. Not one bit.

I tried to make her listen, but it was like talking to a brick wall.

"I have to go," she whispered. "Happy Thanksgiving, darling."

Once she was gone, I tried to puzzle it all out. Why had Daddy chosen me to be the Scintilla? Was it because I knew too much? Because I'd guessed what he'd done to Maggie and to Fox? He was wanted by the police.

I suddenly remembered the first time I'd called Mom from the Institute. How she'd mentioned that she'd been to the police. Daddy had been worried. He'd told me to convince Mom to stop talking to them. Was that where all this had started? Was that when he had gone after Mom? To protect himself?

If I was right, he had planned this for a long time. But what now? He couldn't keep me locked up in here forever. And what had Mom meant when she referred to the Boundless Family?

My obsessive Googling had taught me that cults usually didn't end well. Mass suicides. Fatal conflicts with law enforcement. I remembered Daddy making Val drink the vial of liquid that he said was poison. Was that what he was planning? Was that how he would make us sublime? By forcing us to literally cast off our flesh-bodies?

I shuddered.

The door opened again, and Daddy entered, his face flashing with annoyance when he saw the pile of fabric still untouched on the floor.

"You must prepare," he told me. "There is a technic that you will preside over. The others are gathering as we speak."

I laughed at him. "Not a chance."

Daddy's mouth quirked. "You struggle against your actuality," he said. "But you will obey."

"I won't."

Daddy laced his fingers together and smiled his mild, calm smile. "You will do it," he said. "And if you don't, I will kill your mother."

It was no idle threat. He had killed Fox and Maggie and who knew who else.

"Change your clothes," he said. "Val will be along to escort you to the courtyard in ten minutes."

★ ★ ★

A bonfire had been built in the courtyard from bits of lumber and furniture scavenged from around the Institute. Some of the wood was clearly treated, letting off a thick black smoke. The other Institute members were gathered around the fire. On Daddy's stage were three chairs. Daddy sat in the middle one. To his left sat my mother, who stared into the fire as if hypnotized. Val led me to the third chair, to the right of Daddy. A large silver bowl was placed on the corner of the stage near the fire, full of something clear and glistening.

Daddy inclined his head toward me in a mockery of respect. Then he reached out and took Mom's hand, his eyes never leaving mine.

I ground my teeth and sat down. Daddy stood and spread his arms wide, addressing the crowd.

"Did I ever tell you about Heracleitus's namesake, the philosopher and alchemist?" Daddy asked. "He lived in Ephesus about two and a half thousand years ago. I knew him well. I stayed with his family for a time, and we would stroll together in olive groves and play knucklebones with the local youths in the temple of Artemis."

I glanced over at Mom. She was still staring into the fire. "They called him the Weeping Philosopher," Daddy went on, "because he chose not to comfort himself with the usual falsehoods that toxicants tell themselves. He yearned for truth. He believed that there are two kinds of people: those who are asleep and those who are awake. The sleeping people — the toxicants — each inhabit their own individual world of lies and ignorance. But the waking inhabit the one Cosmos, a world not made by gods or men, but by ever-living fire."

The bonfire crackled and spat dramatically, and I saw eyes widen in the crowd.

"Fire, for Heracleitus, was the most fundamental element. He believed that all the other elements — every single speck of the universe — were born of fire. The human soul — the actuality — he told me, is made of fire and water. The water douses the burning purity of the actuality. Temptations of the flesh and other worldly pleasures make the actuality moist. It is only the dry actuality that can ascend to new levels of avocation."

Daddy plunged both hands into the silver bowl on the stage. Then he straightened up and carefully passed his hands through the fire. As he withdrew them and raised them again, I heard sharp intakes of breath from the crowd. Blue flames curled and licked around his fingers. Daddy smiled, not flinching for a second. I remembered him grabbing Maggie's knife, his blood dripping down his wrists. After a moment, he rubbed his hands together, extinguishing the flames. He held his hands up before us, wiggling his fingers to show he wasn't hurt. It was a cheap party trick, but the Institute members appeared spellbound.

"It is fitting that today we honor the memory of the great philosopher and alchemist Heracleitus, as well as our own dear Heracleitus as she transforms into the Scintilla. Heracleitus's dry actuality — her sublime body — has operated as kindling, coaxing the Scintilla to life and letting its fire spread to us all, lifting us up to the Boundless Sublime."

He gestured to me, and I stood up. Daddy had given me my instructions earlier, and I took my position in front of the bonfire, the heat of it making the heavy red robes stick to my skin.

One by one, the other members of the Institute approached me, each one holding a bowl or a plastic tub full of food.

"Now that the Scintilla walks among us, we will all be sublime," Daddy proclaimed. "You no longer need food and drink, as you will no longer hunger or thirst. You will not require sleep. You will not fall ill. All impairments to your hearing and vision will vanish."

The fact that he was saying this while wearing his wire-rimmed glasses didn't seem to trouble any of the enraptured Institute members.

"This is an elutriating technic. It will rid you of every last trace of the aphotic in your actuality. Of lead and water. It will release you from the meat cage of your body and allow you to float free and boundless."

Newton was first in line, holding a large tub of lentils. With shining eyes, she dumped them onto the fire, and stepped forward, bowing her head to me. I dipped a finger into the silver bowl. The stuff inside was gel-like and cold and my senses were assailed with a familiar scent.

"With the application of pure aether," said Daddy, "the Scintilla will draw the last drops of moisture from you, and you will be left sublime."

It wasn't pure aether. I was pretty sure it was hand sanitizer. I drew my finger across her forehead. The cool gel immediately evaporated on her skin. A look of pure joy passed over Newton's face, and I wanted to scream in frustration.

One by one, each member of the Institute came forward and cast food onto the fire, then bowed before me and accepted my blessing. I tried to make eye contact with each person, hoping to see a spark of rebellion, a glimmer of doubt. But nobody would meet my gaze. Their expressions were humbled, awed. They believed it all. They believed Daddy. And why wouldn't they? I had.

I blessed every member of the Institute except for the Monkeys, who were nowhere to be seen. Apparently they didn't get to be sublime. I wondered what they were going to have for dinner, now that all the food was destroyed.

★ ★ ★

I let Val escort me back to my cell. Once we were alone, I spun around and grabbed him by the arm.

"Let me go," I said. "You have to. You did it before."

Val didn't even look at me.

"*Val*. Please. I think he's going to kill me."

Val blinked slowly and turned his eyes down. "You promised." His voice was rumbling deep, and he spoke with a faint lisp.

I let my hand drop. I had. I'd promised. I'd promised to help the Monkeys, but I'd done nothing. I'd made things worse. Now they had no food, and something terrible was coming.

Val pushed me back into the little dark room and closed the door behind me.

Hours passed, and nobody came. I changed out of the stupid red robe, and back into my regular clothes. I went all over the room, searching for some means of escape. I rattled the door handle and tried to break the tiny wire-reinforced window. But there was nothing. I'd be stuck in here until someone came to let me out.

I had to convince them. I still didn't know what Mom had been talking about — the Boundless Family — but it sounded bad. It sounded like I wasn't going to make it out alive. I realized with a searing shock that I really, *really* wanted to be alive. I'd spent over a year walking around in a fog of grief and confusion. The people I loved most had all left me — Anton, my parents, Fox. But I still wanted to be alive. I wanted to breathe fresh air and visit the ducks in the park and tell them about Fox. I wanted to read *Les Miserables* and eat chocolate and play my piano. I wanted to live.

I heard the clunk of a turning bolt in the door, and Lib shuffled in, holding a glass of sulfurous water.

"I thought you might be thirsty," she said, her voice low.

I raised my eyebrows. "Really? I thought none of us ate or drank anymore."

Lib held out the glass, and the surface of the water trembled. I took it and drank, ignoring the wave of nausea and memory that hit when I tasted the eggy sulfur.

I didn't trust her. "Does he know you're here?"

"He's in the Sanctum. With Ash. He won't be out for a while."

I felt my stomach turn over. "You disgust me," I said. "Going along with his bullshit. You know I'm not some magic crystal fairy. You know I'm being held here against my will."

Lib's eyes met mine, and I knew I was right. "My mother," I said. "How long?"

Lib took a breath. "A while," she admitted. "Daddy leaves the Institute sometimes during the day, or after Family Time. He goes to the Red House or to fast food restaurants. He likes cheeseburgers."

I felt a wave of loathing rise in me.

"Your mother first came here when you were at the casino. But she already knew Daddy. He had been going to see her for some time. I think since you and Fox . . ." She trailed off. I'd been right, then. He'd been planning this for months.

He knew I was going to leave. He never trusted me. Not after what happened with Fox.

I handed the glass back to Lib. "Help me get out of here."

Lib hesitated, then ducked her head. "It'll be quiet tomorrow," she murmured, not meeting my gaze. "It's Black Friday. Daddy is sending everyone out to hand out water outside shopping malls. I'll make sure the door is unlocked."

Black Friday was tomorrow. Mom had said the Boundless Family would happen on Saturday. But why did Daddy want everyone out of the Institute? Did he have to prepare something, and he didn't want anyone to see?

Lib's hands were shaking and her eyes kept darting around, as if she was sure we were being spied on.

"You — you have to help him. Help him get out."

"Him? Him who?" Did she mean Daddy?

A small, choking sob escaped Lib's throat. "Fox," she whispered.

I felt blanched white with shock. Fox was dead. Like Anton. Cold and dead and gone. Extinguished.

"Daddy has him locked in his laboratory," said Lib. "In C Block, next to the Monkey House."

My ears buzzed, and my vision blurred for a moment. Had I heard correctly? I grabbed Lib by the arm, digging my fingers into her thin flesh so that she gasped out loud.

"Fox is alive?" My heart was beating so hard and fast it was making my teeth chatter.

She swallowed a few times to try to calm herself. I'd never seen anyone so consumed by terror.

It had been weeks, *weeks*, since I'd seen Fox. Had he been locked up this whole time? I remembered my own incarceration, how easily the pieces of myself had become stripped away. How eagerly I'd grasped onto Daddy when he came to rescue me. How easily my spirit had been broken.

"Lib, why are you telling me this?"

Lib closed her eyes, and pain flashed across her face.

I stared at her, and things started to fall into place. I remembered Pippa standing up and following Daddy to the Sanctum after Family Time. I remembered how plump she looked in her sparkly top at the casino. I remembered her desperate eyes as I squeezed the handles of the bolt cutters and severed her finger. I remembered her fingers fluttering nervously over her belly.

"Fox is yours. Your son."

Lib nodded.

"The Monkeys," I said. "Are they all Daddy's?"

Lib bit her lip. "Not all. Sometimes women come to us with small children, or they're already pregnant. But . . . most of them are his."

Fox's parents weren't dead at all. All that time Fox had spent longing for his mother, she was right there, sitting next to him at breakfast, handing out his supplements.

"All this time," I said. "All this time you let him believe he was an orphan. You watched Daddy hurt him. You let him be locked away in a cell and tortured. . . ."

Tears welled in Lib's eyes.

"How could you do it?"

Lib gave a great shuddering sigh. "When I met Daddy, I was broken. My life had been a string of men who wanted to use my body and cast me aside. But when I met him . . . well, you know how it is."

I did know how it was. I knew how powerful Daddy could be.

"I didn't expect to get pregnant . . . I mean, obviously Daddy and I were . . ." Lib waved a hand. "But it didn't *feel* sexual. It was part of the technic. A ritual. I never imagined it could produce a baby."

She grasped her hands together, knuckles white.

"Things were different back then — it was eighteen years ago. Stan inherited the Red House from an aunt, and we all moved in, like a real family. I gave birth there, surrounded by the others, with Daddy holding my hand. It felt so pure and perfect, bringing an innocent, uncontaminated life into the world."

The faintest smile passed across Lib's face, and I felt my heart break a little for that hopeful, deluded young woman. The smile quickly faded, and her voice shuddered as she continued.

"After he was born, Daddy told me . . ." She paused and took a gulping breath. "He told me that my bond with the baby was just a flesh urge. Like sexual desire. If I gave in to it, I'd be giving in to my body, and I'd never be sublime. Daddy said I had to be separated from the baby. He didn't let me give him a name. He didn't let me breastfeed. He gave the baby to one of the other women to look after. I'd wake up in the middle of the night and listen to him cry, and I'd sob and sob, my breasts leaking milk everywhere. It was proof that Daddy was right. I didn't have control over my body. I resented the baby for taking me over so completely. I stopped trying to see him. I stopped thinking about him. Instead I thought about Daddy. Everything became about Daddy."

I knew how easy it could be. After all, hadn't I given up Fox too? Hadn't I forced myself to forget about him? Believed Daddy's stories of betrayal? Thrown myself completely into the Institute and my quest for sublimation?

"It wasn't long before other children came. The Red House

became too crowded, so Daddy found this place. I don't know how. I . . . know he had money somewhere. When we moved here, he set up the Monkey House. He started talking about how children don't have the spark yet, how they were blank slates. He made us shave their heads and stop referring to them with names or personal pronouns."

I remembered the blank faces of the Monkeys when I'd been trying to find an escape route. I remembered the one Monkey who was always out of place. The one who'd helped me. I wondered who her mother was.

"It makes things easier. That's why he does it. It's easier to let your child go when they don't have a name or a gender or any features to distinguish them from the other children. They have a good life. They have healthy food and fresh air and they play all day. Could I have offered Fox such a life if I'd been on my own? Would he have been as happy?"

"What about when he left the Monkey House?" I asked. "When he joined the rest of you? With a name?"

"I wasn't even supposed to know he was mine," said Lib. "Daddy doesn't let us think that way. The Monkeys are orphans, rescued from the toxicants and made pure. He is their savior. They don't have mothers. So Fox was just . . . Fox. I watched him, yes. More closely than the others. I think deep down I was proud of him. That he was so sensitive. So thoughtful. But I didn't allow myself to *feel* anything. Because if I had, I would have also had to feel the shame. The guilt. Because I gave him up. I abandoned him."

Lib's body shook as she broke into sobs. "I only wanted him to be safe. And I thought he'd be safer here than out in the world. The world had always been so cruel to me. At least if he was here, I knew Daddy would look after him."

"But he didn't," I said. "Daddy didn't look after him."

Lib closed her eyes. "No," she whispered. "He didn't."

"I'm sorry," I said to her. "It was my fault. I . . . he never would have behaved that way if it wasn't for me."

Lib's mouth hardened into a thin line. "You weren't the one who beat him," she said. "Daddy was so angry. I've never seen him like that before. He locked you away and swore that he'd make you pay."

My stomach turned as I thought of my mother with Daddy. *I think she's seeing someone.* That's what Auntie Cath had said. Had Mom done it? *Received* from Daddy? I pushed the thought away in disgust.

"And Fox?" I said.

She shook her head. "I believed Daddy at first — that Fox had been an agent for the Quintus Septum. But you hear things. One of the Monkeys let something slip, and I realized he was still here. Still alive. I begged Daddy to let him out." She winced, and I remembered her black eye. "He told me if I didn't forget about Fox, he'd kill him. So I stopped trying to save him. I let Daddy think I'd forgotten."

Lib took a shuddering breath. "I know what you must think of me. I don't expect you to understand."

But I did understand. Daddy was powerful. The tug of his charisma was so strong it was impossible not to get pulled into his orbit. My rage at Lib dissolved into pity. She was . . . what? Fifty years old? And what did she have to show for her life? Lies, guilt, and loss. I wondered if she would ever escape. If she would ever be able to look Fox in the eye and tell him the truth.

Fox.

Fox was alive, and I had to find him.

22

I waited. I waited as the night grew black, and then the blackness faded away into cold morning. I listened to birds chatter. I heard the rumble of engines. I heard voices from outside, the crunching of feet on gravel.

I heard footsteps approach, and the lock on my door clicked open. Then the footsteps faded away.

I waited as everything grew silent. Then I moved.

The door swung open, and I stepped out into the corridor, listening for the faintest sound.

Nothing.

Outside, the Institute was silent and empty. The warehouse was open, and all the boxes of water bottles were gone.

I crossed the courtyard quickly and skirted around the third building to the Monkeys' entrance. I tried the handle, and to my surprise it turned. I pushed the door open and stepped inside.

At first glance, the room looked like an elementary school classroom. Children sat at low tables, drawing on large sheets of paper with colored pencils. But it wasn't a classroom. The Monkeys were dressed in their usual white tunics, with their pale, stubbly heads. Their faces were calm — blank, even. And every single one of them was drawing the same thing. A man with bright blue eyes, white hair, and glasses. Daddy. I looked around the room. It was papered with drawings of Daddy, stuck clumsily to the wall with masking tape. There were thousands of them.

It was a shrine.

They'd all looked up as I entered. Eight pairs of eyes were trained on me, wide and unblinking, like the countless blue eyes that papered the walls. With their shaved heads and shapeless white tunics, they looked like ghosts.

The tallest Monkey stood up and put her hands on her hips. "You again," she said. "You can't be here."

I remembered the promise I'd made to Val.

"I'm here to help you," I told her. "I'm going to get you guys out of here. I'm calling the police. Someone will come and take you away from here, and everything will be all right."

The Monkeys didn't look at each other or speak. But as one, they put down their pencils, pushed back their chairs, and crawled under the table, crouching low and wrapping their little arms around their heads as if they were expecting a bomb to fall.

I got down on my hands and knees and crawled under the table too.

"Hey," I said, touching one Monkey on the shoulder. "It's OK. I'm sorry if I scared you. I promise I'm here to help. But you have to help me first."

The Monkey didn't respond. It was as if they had been turned to stone. I wasn't even sure if they could hear or see me anymore.

I crawled out from under the table and realized that one of the Monkeys was still sitting at the table. It was the girl I'd seen around the compound. The one who ate Val's snow peas. She was drawing intently.

"Hey," I said gently.

The sound of her pencil scratching on the paper was the only sound in the room.

"I'm looking for Fox," I said. "Do you know what happened to him?"

The girl put down her pencil and reached for a different color.

"Can you hear me?" I asked, trying to keep my voice low and calm and light.

The girl's expression didn't change. I looked down at her drawing and was startled to see it wasn't a picture of Daddy. It was a picture of the beach — yellow sand and blue waves, with colorful beach huts lining the shore. I watched as she added some shells dotted along the shoreline.

At last she looked up. "Are you going to kill us?" she asked, her voice perfectly calm.

I took an involuntary step back and raised my hands. "What? No. I'm not here to hurt you at all. I'm here to *help* you."

"Daddy told us that one day people will try to take us away," the girl said. "And that they will pretend to be nice, but really they are monsters wearing the skins of nice people and that if we go with them they will take off *our* skin and boil our bones into soup."

"I promise I'm not a monster," I said. "You know me. You've seen me here before."

The Monkey nodded. "You're the Scintilla," she said. "Daddy says when you arrive we must be careful, because the end is close. He says if we are careful and hide from the monsters, we'll get to be part of the Boundless Family."

"What is the Boundless Family?" I asked.

The girl narrowed her eyes. "You should know. You're the Scintilla. Unless you are a monster wearing the skin of the Scintilla because you boiled her bones."

I took a deep breath. "You know what? I'm not a monster, but I'm not the Scintilla either. I'm just a person. My name's Ruby. Do you have a name?"

The girl shook her head. "I'm a Monkey."

"OK, Monkey. Do you want to play a game?"

"Daddy says games aren't fun anymore. Daddy says we have to stay hidden. Daddy says we aren't hungry."

I glanced down at the children, crouched and completely still under the table. They were so different from the giggling, scampering Monkeys I'd seen when I'd first arrived at the Institute. What had he done to make them like this?

I looked at the girl's drawing. "That place," I said. "Do you remember it?"

"It's not a real place," she said. "I dreamed it."

"Are you sure? You haven't been there? Even a long time ago?"

The girl gave me a little sideways frown, as if she thought I was crazy.

"It's not a real place," she said again.

I knelt down on the floor beside her. "It is a real place. I've been there."

The girl's eyes widened, then she shook her head.

"It's true," I said. "I've seen that water and those beach huts. Beyond that one there's a jetty that sticks out into the water and a van that sells ice cream. Do you remember?"

The girl's pencil fell from her grasp, and she started to look distressed.

"When I went there, there were lots of people," I said. "Some of them were swimming, and some of them were playing with a beach ball on the sand. There were kids and dogs and grown-ups."

There were no people anywhere in her drawing. Not so much as a seagull.

"I think you should draw yourself on the beach."

The girl's brow creased in a frown, and she stared at me, baffled.

"Go on," I said. "You could be eating an ice cream cone. Or building a sandcastle. Or collecting some beautiful shells. Draw yourself."

"I — I can't," she said, as if I had asked her to walk on the ceiling.

"Of course you can," I said. "You're a good drawer."

"I'm a Monkey. I can't be there. I can't draw . . . me. I don't exist."

I remembered seeing her crouching in the shadow of the warehouse, munching on snow peas.

"You do exist," I said. "You exist because you want things. You want snow peas. You want to visit the beach. You want to escape from here."

The girl looked back down at her drawing. "I can't exist," she whispered. "Daddy will be angry if I do."

"Don't worry about him," I said. "I'm going to take you to a place where he can't hurt you."

The Monkey hesitated, then looked up at me, her eyes wide. "Will Val be there?"

"I don't know," I said. "Maybe. Do you want him to be there?"

"Yes. I like Val. He gives me snow peas."

"Did you know him, before you came here?"

The Monkey shook her head. "When I first became a Monkey, I was very frightened. I didn't understand about Daddy and how he'd saved us from darkness. I tried to run away. Val found me. He was nice, and he told me a story about an ogre who made friends with a princess. He didn't tell Daddy that I'd been bad."

I wondered how the Monkey had come to the Institute. Was her mother or father here too? Or had she been stolen from somewhere?

"Sometimes I draw Val a picture and sneak it to him," said the Monkey. "But he has to hide them, because Daddy doesn't like it when we draw pictures for anyone other than him."

"If you leave here, you can draw pictures for whoever you like. You can draw pictures just for *you*, if you want."

The Monkey bit her lip. "And you won't boil my bones?"

"I won't boil your bones."

"Do you promise?"

"Cross my heart."

The Monkey nodded, as if this were enough. "OK," she said, squaring her little shoulders. "What do we do?"

"First I have to help someone," I said. "Do you know where Fox is?"

"Yes."

I felt a surge of energy course through me. "Can you take me to him?" I asked, trying to keep my voice calm.

The Monkey pushed back her chair and stood up. She walked over to the cupboard, dragging her chair behind her. I followed. The other Monkeys were still crouched under the table, still and silent as porcelain. The Monkey climbed onto her chair and reached for a small metal tin on a high shelf. The tin contained a key ring with two keys. She jumped down from the chair and handed me the keys, pointing to the door at the back of the room.

"Thank you," I said.

"Promise you'll come back for me," said the Monkey.

"I promise," I said, and this time I really meant it.

The door opened out into the large storage space where I had labeled water bottles with Lib. The room was empty now, every last box cleared out.

I remembered asking people about the water bottles in my earliest days as a sublimate. They'd all had the same response.

People get thirsty.

But that hadn't been the real reason. Daddy had told me there was another reason, but that I wasn't ready to know it.

I crossed the room to the door that I knew led to Daddy's laboratory and unlocked it with the second key.

It wasn't the gleaming, spartan facility I was expecting. I'd imagined stainless steel and glass. Glowing refrigeration units and twisting beakers and tubes.

Instead it looked like the kitchen in A Block. A tiny office kitchenette with a sink, an old fridge, some cabinets. The only evidence that it was a scientific laboratory was a small rack of test tubes and a lone Bunsen burner on the countertop. I opened the fridge and saw jam jars labeled with white stickers and messy ink.

hartshorn
diethylstilbestrol
fulminating silver
cyproterone acetate
flowers of antimony

What was Daddy planning? Why the water bottles? Why Black Friday? What was the Boundless Family?

People get thirsty.

I remembered the news article about Glenn Ardeer, his controversial research into sterilization. His trial.

And I heard Daddy's voice, as clear as if he were in the room with me.

The Scintilla will come and light the way for us. The Institute of the Boundless Sublime will rise above all. The Quintus Septum will be vanquished, along with all their pathetic meat-followers. We shall rule over all, gods of light and science. You, my children, will receive riches and power beyond your wildest imaginings.

And I will be everyone's Daddy.

And suddenly I knew what he was going to do.

I had to get to a phone. Call the police and tell them. Why hadn't I talked to the police earlier? When they came to my house? Why had I let Mom ward them off with lies about healing and *not being ready to talk*?

I saw something move beside the fridge and took a step forward, my breath catching in my throat.

23

Fox was in the corner tucked in beside the fridge, crouched over a pile of paper. He was wearing one of the white Monkey tunics, and someone had shaved his head.

"Fox," I said softly as I approached. I noticed that he was shackled to an old pipe that ran along the wall, a bike lock encircling his bare ankle.

He was so thin, skin stretched so tight across his bones.

His face was bruised, and there was a long, blood-crusted slash across his brow. Angry pus wept into his eye.

He'd been here all along. While I'd been playing blackjack and eating pillow mints. While I'd been plotting my escape. While I'd been at home, standing in the shower, watching my hair swirl down the drain.

All along, Fox had been here. Suffering. Slowly slipping away into nothingness. I looked down at the paper. He was drawing Daddy, like the other Monkeys had been. Scattered around him were hundreds of pictures. All the same. All Daddy.

I hoped I wasn't too late.

He looked up at me, his face blank. "Are you here to boil my bones?"

"Fox," I said. "It's me. It's Ruby."

Fox looked around. "Who are you talking to?" he asked. "A fox? I haven't seen a fox."

"I'm talking to you. Your name is Fox."

Fox shook his head. "No," he said. "I'm not a fox. I'm a Monkey."

What had Daddy done to him? "Don't you remember me?"

Fox's mouth curved in a faint smile. "I had a dream about you. I have lots of dreams."

"No," I said. "No, it wasn't a dream. It was real. I'm real."

"Daddy says that good dreams are never real. Only bad ones. Are you a bad dream?"

I had to free him. I had to get him out of here.

I opened drawers and cupboards until I found the pair of bolt cutters I'd used to cut off Pippa's finger. They were still crusted with dark stains. I shuddered, but grabbed them and snapped the bike lock that tethered Fox to the wall.

"Come on," I said. "It's time to go."

Fox looked down at his ankle. It was swollen and bruised where the bike lock had been. "Go? Where are we going?"

I remembered our long talks. Lying on our backs in the park. Holding hands under the table at the Red House. Our secret meetings after Family Time. I thought about the one rebel Monkey, drawing blue waves and yellow sand.

"The ocean," I said. "We're going to the ocean."

A smile spread across Fox's broken face, and it was all I could do to keep from bursting into tears.

"I've always wanted to see the ocean," he said dreamily.

I wrapped his arm over my shoulder and helped him to his feet. He was so light, like a bird. I couldn't quite believe that he was full of blood and bone and organs like me. There didn't seem to be enough of him to be more than a papery shell.

"I think that's enough," said Daddy, from where he was standing in the doorway.

I moved quickly, putting myself between Daddy and Fox.

"Don't come near him," I said. "You've done enough damage."

"Not quite enough, I'm afraid," said Daddy. "I should have taken care of him a long time ago. I hoped he'd come around. See the error of his ways." He sighed and reached behind his back, pulling a gun from the waistband of his pants. "Oh, well."

I stared at it, uncomprehending. A *gun*.

It was black and cold and solid-looking, cradled in Daddy's hand. Had he always had it, this whole time? It didn't seem real. Guns were on television. In movies. Not in real life.

But this, the Institute, Daddy. None of it was real life.

"Monkey," said Daddy, addressing Fox as if he were a puppy in need of training. "Come here."

I heard Fox whimper in fear. I reached behind me and grabbed his hand, squeezing it tight.

"Monkey," said Daddy again, his voice firm.

"It's OK," I said to Fox over my shoulder. "You don't have to do what he says."

Daddy glanced at me, his expression smug. He held out a hand to Fox. "Come along, Monkey. Come to Daddy."

I felt Fox's hand tug away from mine, and my heart broke as he crept out from behind me and shuffled over to Daddy, doubled over at the waist, hunching and scraping with fear and subservience.

Daddy patted him gently on the head, then raised his other hand — the one holding the gun — and struck Fox hard across the face. Fox cried out in pain and sank to the floor, moaning softly like a broken wild animal.

"You see?" said Daddy to me. "They all come back to me in the end. Where else could he go? I'm his Daddy. Just like I'm yours. You'll understand soon."

My mind was whirling, trying desperately to think of a way out. But my eyes kept coming back to the gun. Daddy held it so casually, as if it were something totally insignificant. But I knew he would use it. He'd never let us leave alive.

"Ruby," said Daddy, his eyes burning into mine. "You're confused. You know you are. It's because you're the Scintilla. All this . . . this is your meat body rebelling against the burning actuality, the ruby soul. Give in to it. Let it consume you."

And I realized that I had a spark of power after all. Daddy was just crazy enough to believe in his own lies. Although he had engineered and orchestrated it all, part of him truly thought I was the Scintilla, that I held the key to his immortality. I swallowed. I had to keep him talking until I could figure out how to use my advantage.

"If I'm the Scintilla," I said, "shouldn't you do what I say?"

"Nice try," said Daddy with a knowing smile. "Your toxicant brain is still in control. You must surrender it to the Scintilla."

"When will that happen?"

Daddy's lip curled in a smile. "Tonight. It all happens tonight. At midnight your body will be consumed by the fire of the Scintilla, and your spark will set us all alight. Tomorrow morning we will be born anew, the Boundless Family."

With a noise that was half moan, half howl, Fox suddenly raised himself from the floor and launched himself at Daddy, who staggered back against the countertop, knocking over the rack of test tubes and sending them scattering into glittering shards. The gun flew from Daddy's hand and went skittering across the floor toward the corner where Fox had been chained to the wall. Daddy snarled and grabbed Fox by the neck, squeezing and pushing as Fox clawed and bit and scratched. Finally Daddy managed to wrench him away and heaved him against the refrigerator. Fox fell awkwardly, and I saw his leg twist and give way. I heard a snapping noise, followed by a howl of pain.

"This is getting boring," said Daddy, brushing broken glass off his shirt. "I've had enough of your games. You will go back to your cell, and tomorrow you will burn."

Out of the corner of my eye, I saw Fox reaching out his good leg toward the gun.

"The Boundless Family," I said, trying to draw Daddy's attention. "I figured it out. You plan to sterilize people, right? It's what you wanted to do when you were a scientist. Make a perfect race of people. That's why you're handing out the water bottles. There's something in the water."

Daddy smiled. "I always said you were extraordinary."

It was working. I talked faster. "But how does that play out? Are you going to sterilize the entire human race? You know you can never do that, right? You can't go and hand out seven billion bottles of free water all over the world."

Daddy stretched the fingers of his right hand, as if they had been cramping up holding the gun. "Today is a pilot technic. Plans are in place. I have operatives poised all over the world, awaiting my instructions. Do you think it is just you? Just this pitiful handful of acolytes? No. I have chapters everywhere. The Institute of the Boundless Sublime covers the whole planet, hidden in secret, waiting for my word. People don't only drink water from bottles, you know."

I stared at him. Was there a chance he was telling the truth? Did he really have a massive network of crazed followers waiting for the go-ahead to flood public water supplies with sterilizing drugs? Or was this another of Daddy's ridiculous stories? I couldn't tell anymore.

With a soft, breathy moan, Fox stretched out his unbroken leg to where the gun lay on the floor and kicked it over to me. I bent swiftly and picked it up, pointing it at Daddy.

Daddy chuckled. "Silly girl," he said. "What do you think is going to happen now? Are you going to kill me?"

It felt heavier than I'd expected. A lump of cold, dark metal, frighteningly real.

He was right. I couldn't kill him. I wouldn't. I wasn't like him.

I remembered the burning taste of cigarette smoke as my phone rang and rang in my bag and my little brother took his last breath.

I remembered the feeling of the black tide, its suffocating comfort.

I remembered the crunching of cartilage and bone as I cut off Pippa's finger.

And I realized I could do it.

I wasn't like Daddy, but there was a darkness inside me.

I'd been fighting it for so long. Trying to put it aside. To deny it, escape it. But it was always there, a part of me. I'd thought it was just grief, but it was more than that. It was grief and guilt and rage. Anton's death had let it in, and everything I'd done since then had only fed it. It had seeped into me the way I'd imagined toxins and contamination seeping into my blood and bone. I couldn't be rid of it any more than I could be rid of my own flesh.

I met Daddy's eyes, and I raised the gun. I saw a flicker of fear, but it was quickly replaced by a mocking smile.

"Do it," he said, his voice quiet. "You are the Scintilla. You are here to liberate my sublime body from this flesh case. I welcome it."

Did he really believe that? Or was it all an elaborate bluff, a confidence trick? I had no idea, and I knew that Daddy didn't know either. He'd been playing his games for so long that truth and fantasy had become so muddied, so intertwined that for him it was impossible to separate them.

I'd never held a gun before, but I'd seen enough TV shows to know how to use it. I used my thumb to disable the safety switch.

"Can you do it?" asked Daddy. "Or are you still too closely anchored to your own flesh? Your aphotic mortality cripples your actions, choking your actuality."

I felt my hands tremble.

"You can't, can you?" he said. "You're weak. Just like Magnus was. She couldn't kill me either. She had the knife in her hand, and she couldn't do it. She was a waste of air. A waste of a life. She deserved to die. I did her a favor."

I remembered the jade pendant in the drawer, along with Fox's book and the assortment of other keepsakes. So he *had* killed Maggie. How many others?

The darkness rose up inside me, the old, familiar black tide. But this time it wasn't suffocating; it was powerful. It flowed through my veins, hungry and raw. My hands stopped trembling. I felt completely in control of my body.

I squeezed the trigger.

Click.

Blood rushed into my ears, and my heart began pounding at a million miles an hour. Daddy's mouth hung open in a panicked gape, his hands flung up protectively in front of his face in what looked like an entirely instinctive reaction.

I pulled the trigger again, and again.

Click. Click. Click.

There were no bullets. The gun wasn't loaded. It had all been a bluff. I let it slip from my fingers, and it fell to the floor with a heavy *thunk*. Panic rose in my throat, and I cast my glance around the tiny room, looking for a weapon, an escape route.

Daddy's face twisted. "You fucking little bitch," he said. "After everything I've done for you."

He looked unraveled, with no sign of his benign smile or charismatic twinkle. His eyes were wide, his pupils mere pinpricks. His mouth was contorted into an ugly slash of hatred. I saw him for who he truly was — a sick, twisted old man, choking to death on his own lies.

"I'm going to kill you," he hissed through clenched teeth. "But first, I'm going to make you watch me kill *him*."

He surged toward Fox, reaching out. With his gaze away from mine, I groped behind me until my fingers wrapped around the handle of the bolt cutters on the countertop where I'd left them. I felt my breathing steady as I stepped forward, raised them high above my head, and with every bit of my strength, brought them down on the back of Daddy's skull.

24

Daddy lay on the floor, unmoving. I didn't wait to see if he was OK. I didn't wait to see if he was going to live or die. I grabbed Fox's arm and half-carried, half-dragged him away.

The Monkey was waiting for us outside the laboratory, her eyes wide.

"Did you kill him?" she asked. "Did you kill Daddy?"

"Come on," I said, grabbing her with my spare hand.

The doors at the front of the big storage room were open, and I hauled Fox and the Monkey out into the daylight.

The Institute was deserted. We staggered past the building where I'd been imprisoned. Through the courtyard where I'd cut off Pippa's finger. Past Daddy's Inner Sanctum. The garage door was open, and we stumbled under it and onto the road. Fox faltered and slipped from my grasp, crumpling on the sidewalk. The Monkey looked around with wide eyes, her fingers gripping mine so tightly I thought they might break.

I saw a car turn the corner onto the street, and I let out

an involuntary moan of fear. What if it was someone from the Institute? I glanced down at Fox, who had turned ashen. I couldn't carry him. I had to take the chance.

I held out my arm and flagged down the car.

It wasn't someone from the Institute. It was just a passerby, who looked confused as I stammered an explanation, but willingly called the police when he saw the scrawny, terrified Monkey and Fox, bruised and semi-conscious, on the sidewalk.

A police car arrived within minutes, and this time I didn't hesitate. I blurted out the truth about Daddy, about what had happened to Fox and Maggie. I made them swear they'd get the Monkeys out right away.

An ambulance came for Fox, the Monkey, and me. Someone carried Fox on board and lay him down on a narrow stretcher. The Monkey crouched in the ditch, baring her teeth at anyone who approached.

"Come on," I said. "It's going to be OK."

"What if they boil our bones?"

"They won't," I promised.

The Monkey reached out to me, and I bent and picked her up, shocked at how little she weighed. Her skinny arms wrapped tightly around my neck, and I felt her trembling. We clambered into the ambulance, and the Monkey whimpered as the engine rumbled to life. When had she last been outside the Institute? How many years?

I reached out and held Fox's hand. He was drifting in and out of consciousness. The paramedics worked quickly, slipping an oxygen mask over Fox's head and putting in an IV line, which they hooked up to a saline bag.

"Is he OK?" I asked.

One of the paramedics looked up. "He's pretty banged up,"

he said. "Dehydrated, fluid loss, prolonged pain. His leg is bad, so we're going to give him some ketamine before we splint it."

He inserted a syringe into the base of the saline bag.

With a moan, Fox opened his eyes. I leaned over him and whispered his name. Did I see a glimmer of recognition in his eyes?

"Daddy . . ." he murmured, and his eyes rolled back in his head again.

I swallowed my tears and tried to smile bravely at the Monkey.

★ ★ ★

At the hospital, Fox was whisked away, and the Monkey and I were taken to a room where a doctor came and examined us. Once they were satisfied we weren't in any immediate danger, they brought us sandwiches and soup, and the police came in. I told them the full story, in as much detail as I could. The Monkey didn't speak at all, just demolished sandwich after sandwich.

Then we waited. The Monkey fell asleep, and I fidgeted, hoping every passing footstep was someone arriving with news of Fox, of the Monkeys, of Mom.

I turned the television to the news, but there were only the usual reports from Black Friday — shoppers lining up for bargains and stampeding into shops as doors swung open. What if the police hadn't believed me? What if, all over the country, people were drinking their free water, unaware that they were being chemically sterilized?

Eventually a police officer returned to talk to me. She explained that the police had entered the Institute and removed the Monkeys and the still-unconscious Daddy. I started to panic, but the police officer reassured me he'd been taken to a different hospital and was being kept under police guard. They'd then spread out and rounded up as many Institute members as they could find.

"But the water," I asked. "What about the people who drank the water?"

"It's just water," the police officer reassured me. "We had it tested. It isn't harmful at all."

I didn't believe her. "Test it again."

But the police officer was certain. Later investigations revealed that there was no real evidence of Daddy's grand plan ever existing. No secret hidden chapters of the Institute waiting for Daddy's word to poison the world's water supplies and sterilize the human race. No Quintus Septum. He made it all up. I still don't know if he believed it himself. I think he must have, a little.

Exhaustion took over, and I fell asleep in my armchair, waking up to find a doctor standing over me.

"You can see your friend now."

★ ★ ★

He was propped up in a hospital bed, an IV snaking from his hand, his leg elevated in a fiberglass cast. Purple bruises blossomed on his cheek and forehead, but his eyes were clear.

"Fox," I said, unable to keep the sob out of my voice.

He turned to me. "I ate Jell-O," he said, his voice a little croaky. He pointed to an empty plastic cup and spoon.

"Did you? What flavor?"

He paused and looked uncertain. "Green?"

"Green is a good one," I said. "But wait until you try red."

"I want to try all the colors. Every last one."

"Fox." I was terrified to know the answer, but I had to ask. "Do you know who I am?"

Fox gazed down at the empty Jell-O cup, his brows furrowed. I thought of the dreamy, sad Fox I'd known at the Red House. I thought of the rebellious Fox at the Institute, full of questions and fire. How could I have rejected him? How could I have turned away just when he was beginning to realize who he really was? Looking back, I saw how brave he had been, despite his pain and fear. He had been brave and beautiful and burning to live, to be in the world and experience everything it had to offer. And now . . . was that Fox gone? Replaced with a frightened child?

Was I too late? Had I lost Fox, just like I'd lost Anton?

He looked up. His eyes focused on me, and I saw pain and grief and fear. And relief. And joy. And fire.

"Yeah," he said, the faintest shadow of a smile touching the corner of his mouth. "I see you, Ruby."

EPILOGUE

There's a soft knock on my door. "What are you doing?"

Fox is wearing jeans and a hoodie. It makes him look so different, like a normal teenager. He elbows open my door and shuffles in, carrying his crutches in one hand.

"Making a video," I tell him.

We're living in a group home — a halfway house for teenagers who have lost their way. Fox and I keep to ourselves, trying to figure out who we are now. The cast came off Fox's broken leg a few days ago, but he'll be on crutches for a while. The doctor says he'll probably always walk with a limp.

Fox sinks onto my bed, propping his leg up on a chair. The group home assigned us separate bedrooms, but they don't particularly seem to care that we spend most nights together.

Fox is getting better. Slowly. He's learning how to exist in the real world. Sometimes it's hard to know how to help him. The Institute broke me in just months. Fox was there his entire life. I don't know if he'll ever be whole again — I think he'll always have cracks and missing pieces. We talk about it a lot — Daddy and everything that happened.

I showed him TV for the first time the other day. He really likes nature documentaries. He likes music too, especially *Blackbird* by The Beatles and Allegri's *Miserere*. He listens to them and cries, and I cry with him. It's good to feel again, even when we're sad. When we lie wrapped up in each other, we give ourselves over to sensation and just *feel*, with no guilt or shame or self-consciousness. There's an old piano in the recreation room, and I'm teaching him how to play. Next week we're going to the beach. I can't wait to see his face when he sees the ocean for the first time. I've also promised to show him the movie of *Les Miserables*.

It was Christmas two weeks ago. We had a little tree with colored lights. I taught Fox the words to "Silent Night" and "Winter Wonderland." I turn eighteen in a few days. We've been talking about finding a place together, once the craziness dies down. I want to finish school, go to college. Fox wants to learn to bake and swim and build things from wood and nails. I know that as long as we're together, we'll make it work. Maybe we'll even get a dog and name it Barker.

I lean over and brush his lips with mine. He lets out a soft, contented sigh as our fingers lace together.

"Did you call her today?" Fox asks.

I shake my head.

It's been six weeks, but I still haven't spoken to Mom. She's in the hospital. I've talked to her doctor, who says she is very emotionally fragile. Auntie Cath has visited her, though. She says Mom has good days and bad days. Sometimes she seems almost normal, going for walks on the hospital grounds and chatting with people. Other days she can't get out of bed, can't do anything but stare at the wall. I don't know how she and I are going to deal with what happened, but I hope she gets better. She's suffered enough.

I've talked to Dad on the phone. I understand him better now. After confronting my own darkness back in Daddy's laboratory, I can see how Dad must feel. You can't turn it off. Even though Dad didn't mean to do it. Even though it was an accident. That stain of death is on his hands, and he'll never be able to scrub them clean. I know that now. But I think I can see a way through it — how to live with that darkness and not be swallowed up in it. To rise up through the black tide and stand in the sun, where everything in the world is illuminated — the ugliness alongside the beauty. I hope Dad will find a way through too. It seems a little farfetched to hope that one day we can go back to being a family again, but . . . maybe. This is a start.

"How did your interview go?" I ask Fox. We have regular meetings with our lawyers to prepare us for court.

Fox's lips purse in a tight smile. "The usual."

It doesn't get easier for him, talking about it. In addition to our lawyers, we also meet regularly with psychologists and psychiatrists and social workers. They're good people, and they're helping us, but some days we get sick of talking about our feelings.

"Did you have any of the chocolate pudding at lunch today?" Fox asks. "Do you think Nerida has tried chocolate pudding?"

The Monkeys are in another group home, all together for now, although some of them might go back to their real parents after the legal stuff is sorted out. A team of psychologists is helping them work through everything that happened. Fox and I visited them last week. Their hair is growing, and they all look so different. They have names now that they chose themselves. The one who helped me ran up to us when we arrived and proudly announced that her name was Nerida, which means *sea nymph*. She gave me a picture she'd drawn of herself at the beach, orange corkscrews of hair erupting from her head, an ice cream cone clutched in her hand. Her social worker told us that they aren't sure who her parents are. From what little Nerida remembers, it seems that her mother had known about the Institute and abandoned her daughter at the Red House before vanishing completely. I hope now Nerida has a chance at being a normal kid. I hope we get to stay in touch with her.

Fox reaches out a hand and pulls back the gauzy curtain that hangs over my window. A shaft of sunlight falls over his face, and he closes his eyes and tilts his head back. It was how I first saw him, smiling up into the sun. Fox had seemed so charming then, so innocent and full of wonder. But now that memory is overlaid with another — Daddy standing in the courtyard with his face turned up toward the sun, pretending to be holy and pure when all along he was rotten to the core, full of lies and hate and corruption.

"Did you know that you can make electricity from sunlight?" Fox has discovered the Internet and spends hours soaking up new information, learning all about the world.

"I did know that," I say.

"I guess he was right. Sunlight really is a kind of fuel."

Fox doesn't say *Daddy* or *Zosimon*. Only *he* and *him*. Fox is trying to purge himself of Daddy, but there are so many unconscious things Fox does that remind me of him. Rhythms of speech. Turns of phrase. A certain similarity in profile, in gesture. The same long, delicate fingers. Fox can never truly be free from Daddy, because Daddy is a part of him. Nature *and* nurture.

"Kind of," I agree. "Just not for people."

"No. Not for people."

Daddy is in jail while he awaits his trial. Sometimes I wonder if he's in the same place as Dad, and imagine them running into each other. Dad and Daddy. A bizarre thought.

The media went crazy when the story broke, and we've learned a little more about Daddy — Glen Ardeer. Some ex-members of the Institute have come forward with grizzly tales, and the list of charges against him keeps expanding. Kidnapping. Murder. Conspiracy. Fraud.

We try not to look at all the reports in the newspapers and online, but it's hard to avoid it sometimes. The crazed murderous cult leader planning to sterilize the population with free water is a pretty amazing story, and if I hadn't been wrapped up in it, I know I would have been fascinated too. We get lots of mail — letters of support and some less kind messages. Our social worker screens it all and just lets us see the occasional piece. We're famous. We're the ones who got away. The ones who ended it all.

The trial isn't for months, but we have lawyers and police officers working with us to build the case against Daddy. Because Fox and I witnessed him confessing to killing Maggie, our testimony is vital. My lawyer tells me Val is testifying too — apparently he helped Daddy dispose of Maggie's body. I can't imagine hearing him speak out loud. I hope he gets one of Nerida's pictures.

Tomorrow we're going to see Lib. Fox knows everything now. They've been exchanging letters. She wants to learn how to be his mom, and I think he wants that too. But it'll take a long time. Her lawyer thinks it's likely she'll go to prison, even if she testifies against Daddy. She knew too much, was complicit in too many lies.

We've heard snippets about the others. Pippa was in the hospital for a while, but has now gone home to her family. She's not pressing charges against me, which makes me feel both guilty and relieved. Her baby is due in a few weeks. Ash and Toser have separated. Newton is trying to make things work with her husband. A few are missing, though — Welling, Stan, some others. We think they are still loyal to Daddy, in hiding and awaiting instructions.

"Is the video for them?" Fox asks.

I nod. "Kate says she thinks they're waiting for a message from Daddy or from me. They'll be looking for it."

Kate is my lawyer, and she has promised to help me get the video to the missing Institute members.

"Do you know what you're going to say?"

"Sort of."

I've thought about it a lot. About how easy it was for Daddy to twist words around. About how comforting it was to give in to him, to let him dictate my thoughts and feelings and desires. About how huge and frightening the world is when you have to make every decision for yourself.

Fox looks over at the little camera mounted on a tripod. "Can I help?"

I move over to sit in the chair I've set up. "You can press record."

My name is Ruby Jane Galbraith, and I'm no messiah.

I know you're confused. I'm confused too. You feel like the earth has been ripped out from under you, and you're just falling through space with nothing to hold on to. But that's not true. You can hold on to each other. And hold on to yourselves.

It's a paradox, really. If Daddy was telling you the truth, then I really am the Scintilla, and you should believe every damn word I say. But if I'm not the Scintilla, then Daddy was wrong, and if he was wrong about me, how do you know he wasn't wrong about everything else?

Either way, you lose. We all do.

You want a messiah. Someone who has all the answers. Someone to guide you to freedom. Well, here it is, then. My guidance. My commandments. My first and last testament.

Live.

Go to a store and buy a candy bar. Hand the money to the cashier with a smile. Take your candy somewhere quiet and open the wrapper. Take the tiniest nibble from the corner of the bar. Inhale its aroma. Let it melt on your tongue. Eat the whole thing slowly. Savor every bite.

Spend time outside and feel the wind in your hair. Find your family and tell them you love them. Try new things. Eat strange foods, read books, visit new places. Listen to people, but never stop listening to yourself. Ask questions. Don't be afraid of contradictions — the world is complicated, you are complicated. Find the things that make you happy and do them. Try to make others happy too, but never at the expense of your own well-being.

Live somewhere with a mirror. Look into it every day and learn about the person looking back at you. You will need to look after her, love her, nurture her. She may look fragile and delicate, but inside she is strong, made of flesh and bone and determination.

Daddy wanted us to be boundless. He said that we needed to cast off the things that tethered us to the earth. He was wrong. Without anchors, we just drift away into nothing, like wisps of smoke. Let yourself be bound — to the people you love, to the things that make you *happy, to sensation. If these bonds constrict you, let them go, and find more comfortable ones. The right anchors let you fly free when you wish to but are always there when you return to ground.*

Your body isn't a cage or a prison. It's who you are. Enjoy it. If you want to, you can share it with other people. Feed it. Care for it. Learn its likes and dislikes. Run as fast as you can. Learn to be still.

Forget about him, and forget about me. If you must worship, then worship knowingly. If any person, living or dead, claims to hold all the answers you seek, know he is a charlatan.

Life isn't about self-deprivation or purity or immortality. It's about love and comfort and music and ducks in a pond and eating ice cream on the beach. It's about pain and grief and joy and sex and boredom and chocolate. Life is for living.

So go live.

LILI WILKINSON

Lili Wilkinson is the author of ten young adult novels, including *Pink*, which received the American Library Association Stonewall Award Honor. After studying Creative Arts at the University of Melbourne, Lili established the insideadog.com.au website, the Inky Awards, and the Inkys Creative Reading Prize at the Centre for Youth Literature, State Library of Victoria. She has a PhD in Creative Writing and lives in Melbourne, Australia, with her husband, son, dog, and three chickens.